The Magician

Book I of The Outrider Trilogy

A novel by Kane Kimball-Louks

For Autumn

Tomorrow comes a day too soon

-Flogging Molly

CONTENTS

Chapter One

The Eldritch Flame

"Do you believe in magic? I mean real magic, not the kind you see in decks around Providence. Something that really makes you question what it is you just experienced." Xylen announces from just beyond sight of the crowd. "I see a full bar, and far too many disbelievers amongst you."

He emerges from behind the stage to a sea of patrons. Ranging from the "legal" drinking limit to a possible fit for his own grandmother, all eager to see the show set before them. He saunters out to the edge of the stage to get a better look at the enthralled patronage. His dark red hair swaying back and forth in front of his eyes. A smile as fierce as his hair, beamed toward the audience.

"They call her the magician. For some she takes on the physical representation. Sleight of hand and the uncanny knack to be in two places at once. The latter being a slight over exaggeration. Slight." He chuckles as he places his forefinger and thumb centimeters apart and winks. " For others she is a manifestation of the word. A mystery wrapped tightly inside of an enigma. Enacting feats beyond your wildest dreams. Myself? I prefer something a little less exotic and more grounded. Ladies and gentlemen of Providence. I give to you Annastasia Arlenko."

Nerves. No matter how many times i've been here the jitters never go away.

Annastasia stands beside the curtain, clutching the neck of her violin gently. Her attention is drawn toward Xylen wooing the crowd. Retiring back to the curtain, he beams that identical wide smile in her direction. Their eyes meet briefly, his emerald gaze reflecting her current state back at her.

"Your turn." He says confidently, tapping a hand along his side.

"Hard to compete. You talk me up like i'm something special." Anna says dismissively.

Xylen smirks at her rebuttal. "Try being the one who generally has to follow you. Talk about impossible. Go out there and take what's yours."

Breathing deep, Anna strides to the stage. Her red dress short and cropped elegantly, catching the attention of the first few rows. The color seems to burn outward from its center as if it were on fire.

Approaching the front of the stage Anna stands ridgid before the crowd, poised with confidence. Snapping her fingers a stand appears as if out of thin air, floating beside her. Freeing her hands, Anna places the violin in the free floating stand. Taking this moment Anna collects the loose strands of hair daring to fall out of place and directs them back to their destination. Clapping erupts from the first few rows from the true fans of the night, those who have been here since the first concert. Smiling, Anna curtsies. If Xylen's smile is contagious Anna's is an epidemic. Infectious on sight.

"Welcome to the Eldritch Flame. My cozy little getaway from reality." Anna motions around the room invitingly. "I'm glad to have you all here tonight. This is my last appearance, my final hurrah if you will. Such a turn out, both new faces and long time fans. From the bottom of my heart, thank you for coming and supporting us. Of course you didn't come here to hear me monologue"

Anna scans the Flame. By any estimation they must have exceeded the capacity by at least twenty people. New faces watching, waiting on her. The regulars never change sitting crowded around the bar clung to their stools muttering about how crowded this place is at night. Beyond the bar, a man in his late twenties tends to the mess of drunkards and "hip" crowd corralling them like cattle. His demeanor laid back yet anything but calm. If anyone was to hazard a guess he looks one smart comment from taking them down a peg or two.

"Shall we get started? My first piece I consider one of my favorites. This is The Ship Home."

Anna takes her violin from its personal cage. With a quick lowering motion of her right hand the stage lights dim. Only the spotlight remains. Exactly where it needs to be. The crowd goes silent in anticipation leaving only the trailing voice of the bartender in the distance. Drawing her bow she begins to play softly. Closing her eyes, she begins to dance around the stage. Small circles to a crescendo in the opening piece.

Time halts to a stand still. Forgetting the crowd Anna's mind wanders. With her eyes closed, she sinks into comfortable territory. Nothing matters outside of the rhythm, the correct timing and placement. Her movement echoes her own rhythm, moving in time with the pacing of the song. As she continues on with her set the pace begins to quicken.

The spotlight moves in her shadow as she slinks through. As she flows through the crescendo ambient sounds echo from seemingly everywhere, playing in tune with her song. Adding depth to her violin.

•

Whispered tones are being drown out in the background of the bar. People order rounds for tables across the way to the bartender. He nods approvingly and points toward the stage, gesturing for them to watch the show as they wait. With an understanding nod the patrons turn back to the show, watching the Magician flow across the stage gracefully. Her movements mirroring the emotion implied.

At the other end of the counter Claudette ,the waitress, makes her way to pick up another round of drinks. Leaning against the countertop she shoots the bartender a grin, her light brown hair waving from side to side as she waits for him to finish up the round.

"How much longer for the next round?" She asks discreetly.

"Couple secs love. Just puttin tagether the finishin touches."

Her eyes roam about him, giving him a quick once over. His muscular frame certainly drawing more looks than just hers. He turns back toward her with three glasses of ale balanced between his hands.

"Der we go." He adds, delicately placing drinks onto the tray.

"Thanks Finn" Directing a wink in his direction as she returns to the sea of onlookers.

Smiling, Finn snags a drink of whiskey from the counter as he watches Claudette disappear through the crowd. In one gulp he downs its contents before overturning the cup with a thud onto the bar.

"Hey. Is that my drink?" A male patron disgruntledly asks. His eyes drawn to the empty cup.

"I dunno, is it?" Finn retorts. His accent as thick as his sarcasm.

"I-"

"See. Let me stop ya right there. There ain't no drink for ya here if ya dun learn the rules. Rule one. Never make a scene while the little lady is playin. Rule two. No drink is yours till ya paid up, and believe me we're not even close ta square. Change ya tone, sit down and fuck off."

Insulted, the man rises from his seat. The confusion written along his face tells the tale better than any words. From crossed to irate in less time than it would have taken to pour another drink. He reaches out for the now empty tumbler, grasping it firmly in his right hand.

"Do you know who I am?" He asks. Raising his voice past the threshold of Anna's song.

"If ya have ta ask i'm fairly certain no one here knows nor cares. Ya know what I do care bout? Ya makin quite the ruckus during our farewell. I forgot rule three. If I warn ya once, I won't do it a second time."

The aggravated patron reels back to strike Finn with the emptied glass. Everything stops in that moment. Everything except Annastasia. Her playing continues, almost playing along to the conflict. As momentary as it is.

The crowd's attention slowly begins to pan toward the scene. With one hand Finn has a firm grip on the man's right hand, glass still in his grasp. A look of shock rolls across the patron's face as Finn twists his wrist, loosening the cup from his grip. With his other hand Finn grabs ahold of his neatly pressed shirt collar, pulling him closer to the bar. A soft whimper escapes his target.

"Sorry for the interruption Annie. Da man was about ta go and do somethin real fuckin stupid." Anna's eyes pop open almost as leaving a dream like state. Her attention drawn to the skirmish. Finn smiles cockily in her direction from his position behind the bar. Cocking her head to the side she lets a small sigh. Thoughts flooding through her mind. Not another one. Here we go again. Put him down. It's not nice to pick on the unfortunate.

The cloud of confusion lifts from the patrons face and is soon replaced with fear. Blinking rapidly he is reduced to a stuttering mess.

"I-I-I-I don't want any trouble. J-J-just."He pleads.

"No one never wants trouble but ya don't go knockin on it's fuckin door expectin me not ta answer. Two things gunna happen. I'mma let go o' ya hand, cause I ain't like dat. Hell we might as well play show an' tell."

Finn loosens his grip on the drunks wrist letting him partially free.

Retracting his hand in fear he lets out a confused smile, his mind dancing in a form of victory. Using his momentum Finn tugs hard on the shirt collar driving his opponents head into the countertop with a thunderous slam. For a moment the drunk stands in disbelief as Finn releases his grip fully. The lights go out as the man crumples into a pile on the floor.

"*Shame dat.*" Finn gloats, pride in his smile.

Finn overlooks the audience, each head in the building having turned their attention toward the ruckus caused at the bar. Quizzically he raises an eyebrow, questioning their continued recognition.

"*Alright back to da regularly scheduled program, ya?*" Shooing away their curiosities.

•

Attention returns to the stage only to find it emptied with a wisp of smoke lingering in the air. The thrumming of the music continues overhead as heads turn, quizzically looking to no avail. The atmosphere surrounding the stage transitions through the melody. Morphing from a sincere slow song to a more ominous feeling. A faint humming in the background is quickly followed by war drums. Smoke begins pouring from below the center stage, rising fast to eclipse the lights above. Quickly the room turns a darker shade of blue as the lighting dims, the lingering smoke creeping to every corner of the room.

With a mind of its own the mist seeps down from the ceiling toward the patrons below. The lucky few to feel its caress shiver at it's chilling contact, a sensation of ice running through their veins.

"I hope you're all having as splendid a night as i'm having." Rings out through the speakers. The voice familiar yet distorted. "After Finn's fantastic display I figured I should let cooler minds prevail."

"*I said I was sorry.*" Finn rings out, slumping the unconscious man over his shoulder.

"Do you believe in ghosts? A few inhabit this very bar. Tonight they feel a bit mischievous. Perhaps it's their way of a send off." The voice becomes more distorted, almost robotic. "This song, Sending."

Mist begins to take form around bewildered members of the crowd. Resembling a humanoid shape they begin walking towards the few they came in contact with moments ago. The haze from the smokescreen leaves visibility low.

The drums halt as the apparitions close in on their intended targets, merely inches away. The patrons look wide eyed at the entities, a sense of panic almost kicking in. Cutting the absence of the drums is Anna's violin work. Sharp, quick. Piercing the silence. Annastasia appears through the mist atop the center most table, appearing out of thin air. Trading in her elegant red dress for a casual look, a white tee and jeans. The shirt reads 'i've been told im very sharp' in sprawling letters.

Surveying the change of scenery Anna taps a foot on the table obtaining the apparitions attention. Their formless faces slowly rotating to stare blankly in her direction. Another sharp note turns the fog from a blue to a bright red, outlining their ghostly blue forms. Smiling Anna throws her hair back and begins bounding from one table to another drawing each ghost with her. Giving chase to Anna they begin gliding through the aisles. Her bounds turn to a sprint from one table to the next. As she reaches the stage the song reaches it's crescendo. As her song crests Anna begins to engage the mischievous spirits. Surrounded Anna begins twirling, batting them back with every note. Each one reels back as she comes in contact with its ghost like form. Each note draining their essence, drawing it into her violin. The violin begins to glow a vibrant red as each spirit begins to dissipate. A break in the music draws stunned silence from the crowd. As visibility returns to the Eldritch Flame one essence remains on stage beside the Magician.

It's form begins to contort until it morphs into a perfect copy of Annastasia. Violin poised and ready to play. Picking up where she left off her shadow begins to play, merrily dancing about the stage. Fanning herself Anna laughingly begins to mimic her duplicate, playing in sync with her doppelganger.

"I think i'll let her do all the work from here on out. Let's have a round of applause for my shadow everyone." The audience breaks into an uproar.

Chuckling and clapping for the performance. "Laughing is the best applause. Thank you for coming out. I mean it. You're all my family. I wouldn't have a clue what to do without all of you. Kind of makes my retirement ironic. Either way, ghost me stays but she only does shows on the weekends between 3 and 4 am."

"*Best shows in town happen tween' 3 and 4am.*" Finn says over top of the crowd.

"Thank you peanut gallery."

"Any time love."

"Take this time to top up your beer. Annoy Finn. Be loud and have fun." Anna says sweat beading down from her forehead.

Taking a seat at the foot of the stage Anna dangles her feet over the edge playfully. Weaving through the crowd Claudette approaches Anna, setting down a cup filled with hot tea.

"Thanks Claudette." Anna smiles genuinely.

"Anytime. We both know you needed a drink." Claudette replies, shifting her gaze toward the overwhelming crowd circling the bar like vultures. "You know he didn't mean to-"

"I know. Nothing stops him from being a showboat. It's in his blood." Anna replies. Her smile almost turning devilish. "Something about his 'da' and their 'da' before them and having to keep tradition." Wittily said, sipping from her cup of tea.

Claudette flashes a quick grin. "Keep it up and i'll have to start dating you instead of him. Only thing I love about him is his accent anyway." Claudette whispers into her ear. The cacophony of the Eldritch Flame drowning out their conversation.

"Is dat so?" Anna mimics sarcastically. "I thought you fell in love with him for his shining personality."

"I'd go into detail about the few things I love about him. I'm sure your imagination can fill in the blanks though."

"Oh do go on. I'm quite curious." Anna retorts, her smile shining brightly. "I'm sure it's a short list."

Anna sips from her tea again slowly as they share a silent laugh between them. Claudette begins to fumble with her right hand, rubbing her hand over a small scratch. The scratch mars her elsewise perfect skin. The mark seems fresh, the skin only beginning to grow irritated.

Annastasia raises a concerned eyebrow as her attention is drawn to the bright red scrape

"Before you even ask it was an accident. Some nobody brushed by me. Left me a present." Claudette says quickly.

"Did you see who it was?" A hint of concern peppers Anna's voice.

"No. There were too many people, too much commotion. What are you thinking?" She returns quizzically.

"Nothing." Anna's eye say otherwise as she scans the Eldritch Flame. Taking in the overabundance of patrons. Observing the flood of inebriates, searching for a signal or tick to no avail.

"Liar." Claudette retorts.

"Nothing is an accident. Not in Providence. Not in my bar." She pauses.

Brushing her hair aside Anna gives the crowd a look over once more before turning her attention back to Claudette. Giving her a reassuring smile she grabs Claudette softly by the shoulder. With her other hand the Magician ruffles her hair. Claudette scrunches her nose in disagreement.

"I'm sure you're right though. No need to worry." Anna continues.

"Did you just say I was right?" Breaking the slight tension. "I'm writing this one down."

"Yeah, yeah." Anna says dismissively "Time to get back to work."

"You didn't finish your tea."

"Best to put it back on, no need to let it get cold."

"Never drink cold tea." They both say in unison.

Annastasia rights herself back on the stage. The faint sound of music echoes out as her shadow stops mid ostinato. With a wave of her arm Anna beckons the shadow back to her. Sauntering up she stands inches away from her eerie double, both ready with violin in hand.

Needing no introduction both shadow and magician head into their next duet. Each note flawlessly synchronizing as they begin slowly, softly. Increasing in tempo with every passing second. Gaining the attention of the Eldritch Flame, the room quiets to a dull roar once again. Those waiting for their drinks at the bar divide their attention, enraptured with the show before them.

Her reflection begins to stumble through the cords to keep up as the pace begins to quicken even further. Keeping up the tempo Anna begins to circle the shadowy version of herself as it continues to attempt to keep up with her playing. From the center of its being the apparition begins to change colors. Its smoke grey appearance beginning to burst into flames, a blend of vibrant oranges and reds. From even the furthest corners of the Eldritch Flame you can feel the heat resonating from the stage, the crackling of flames. Annastasia's bow protrudes from the chest of the shadow, culminating the song. The spirit erupts spreading outward toward the crowd turning into a supernova bound to explode. Pieces of the reflection scatter throughout the crowd turning quickly from embers into ash above their heads.

Dumbfounded the crowd stares at the scene on stage, blinking in disbelief. A murmur overtakes the silence, questioning the performance before them. Ash slowly begins to trickle down from the ceiling onto the tables.

"We'll be canceling the reflections of Annastasia show. Sorry for the inconvenience, but now that I have your attention, I would like to direct it back to the stage. We have one final performance for you. Almost every night we've had our share of laughs and our share of heartbreaks in this very bar. I know most of you on a first name basis. I want to end my run here on Providence with something new. I've been working on this one for some time. This song is for my father. Since the day I was born he has been an inspiration to me, in life and in death. He would take me aside, kneel down and tell me. Never hesitate Annastasia. If there is something you want, you take it. Good, bad or indifferent you see it through. Those words see me through and I hope in passing them along to you may shed a new light in your life. I give to you Rekindled."

Tables fill across the Eldritch Flame as patrons being to reclaim their seats. Sloshing drinks and snacks in haste to view the next song. Finn reaches below the bar for a sign, placing it on the bar top. The sign reads Temporarily closed. Pay attention. Eying the regulars Finn motions for them to spin around in their chairs.

"Respect." He says adamantly.

Claudette shills out her few remaining drinks before proceeding behind the bar. Wrapping her hand in Finn's she snuggles up alongside him. A perfect place to watch Anna begins her last song.

Facing away from the crowd Anna wipes away the forming tears in her eyes. She positions herself like royalty, arching her back and releasing a breath of frustration. Putting bow to string she begins her final performance.

Fire erupts from the corners of the stage reaching the ceiling and fanning outward engulfing the area around the stage entirely. Flames roll outward leaving behind a vibrant orange hue.

Annastasia moves about fluidly wisping her way through the pillars of flame. Her blue eyes focused and determined as the song continues.

Mouths agape the crowd stands in awe. Some taken aback by the pillars while others begin reaching out toward the door, their fight or flight instincts taking over. Weaving through the flame Anna keeps the tempo of the song steady yet quick. Navigating the burning stage a confident smile crosses her face.

Abruptly stopping amidst the conflagration Anna begins twirling in the center of the pillars drawing them to her,like a caterpillar in an inferno covered cocoon. From each corner of the ceiling flames burn a path back to its center, to Anna. The music culminates to a break. In silence people watch as the flames converge onto her, wrapping her in their warmth. Slowly the fires dissipate from the center of the stage allowing Anna to emerge from the blaze. Eyes like embers reflect her passion through the blaze itself .Burning away the tee shirt and jeans a dress lay underneath flickering with flames. The violin in her hand transparent, reforged from the flame.

The crowd roars with applause. A few whistle from the back of the crowd as the most begin to stand for their ovation. The patrons seeking asylum from the flames turn back, eyes still caught in panic. Collectively they breath a sigh of relief.

"Today the Magician is reborn. Will you be reborn with me?"

Blinking slowly Anna resumes playing, taking in the cheers of the crowd with stride. Every note perfectly executed. Every step measured.Keeping rhythm to the beat of her heart. The crowd begins to amass around the stage. Their eyes wide with amazement as the skirt of her dress erupts into flames, lengthening its hem. Losing herself to the rhythm Anna begins twirling about. Her skirt flaring out towards the audience, its length extends to the edge of the stage. As the song begins its final crescendo Anna sinks into the flare left behind. Dazzling lights erupt from its epicenter as the song winds down leaving the stage with one less magician.

A cacophony of applause drowns the Eldritch Flame. Those previously sitting stand in ovation, clapping vehemently. Their eyes never leave the stage floor, waiting for an encore. Anticipating on what could possibly follow that breathtaking performance.

Xylen saunters his way back down onto the stage. Smiling never seeming to have faded. Surveying the Flame he cups a hand to his forehead to lessen the spotlight. With confidence he addresses the audience.

"Providence has a few more believers. I see it in your smiles. Truth is you have always believed or you wouldn't have come tonight. Magic, now you know what it is. In essence magic is what we make you feel and see. What you take from tonight is magic. The memories and the moments. Tonight we gave you some magic of your own. Anna's personal gift to each of you."

Xylen raises his arms outward to the crowd in a welcoming fashion. "Ladies and gentlemen. It's been a pleasure to entertain you every night. Each in our own little way. Good night Providence. Let's hear it for the Magician one more time!"

Xylen takes a deep bow with a flourish reciprocating the crowds enthusiasm before retreating offstage. Entering the backstage area Xylen lets loose a loud chuckle, barely audible over the buzzing past the curtain. Noticing Anna, Xylen turns to watch as she peeks from behind the curtain. Approaching the magician, he ruffles her hair. Shooting him a playful glare Anna takes her attention away from the stage.Her smile devilish yet soft.

"Looking at your Annatourage?" Xylen quips.

"Of course." She quickly closes the curtain, giving Xylen her full attention.

"You did wonderful tonight but to paraphrase one customer "She sure does change outfits.". I'm not saying they're right but i'm certainly not disagreeing."

"I knew it! One too many changes." said sarcastically.

"Yeah. One lady even said "Herbert why don't you stare at me the way you stare at her?". Headline worthy for sure. Annastasia and Herbert. Perfect pairing."

Sharing a laugh the two embrace in a hug. Breaking the embrace Anna kisses Xylen on the forehead. In return he gives a cross eyed look, running a hand through his hair.

"Always the bridesmaid, never the bride." Xylen says dismissively.

"Always."

"That's okay. I saw this-"

"Black haired wonder? You kept staring over in the left corner all night. Not like it was obvious."

"I don't know how you do that!"

"It's like i'm a magician or something. Did you get her number?"

"Better."

"Did she get your room number for later?"

"Get out of my mind. Next you'll tell me her name."

"Is...it Deletta?" Anna says sarcastically, putting her hand to her temple.

18

"Ha nope!" He says with glee. "Better luck next time. I'm going to go find mystery girl and avoid telling you her name."

Xylen joyfully bounds back through the curtain, arms open and inviting. Anna begins to mimic his motions, a sly smirk running along her face.

"Hey there! Hopefully you liked the show. We should go before my boss finds out who you really are." She says laughing to herself.

Anna navigates the backstage area heading towards her office. Beyond the curtain silence begins to overtake the room. Its presence calm and comforting. Boxes stacked along the edges of the walls, neat and organized. At the back wall a single door with a sign. OFFICE. Above the door is "Never hesitate. Good, bad or indifferent see it through" written in black paint. Taking one more look around Anna smiles before opening the door to her office. A voice cuts the through the silence like a dagger. Its familiarity sends chills up her spine.

"We need to talk."

CHAPTER TWO

WE NEED TO TALK

The voice echoes in Anna's head as she stands in the doorway to her office. Almost frozen in place. Piercing dark green eyes stare a hole through Anna. Jet black hair swaying as she tilts her head and grins. The woman, clad in a dark leather jacket sits at her desk playing with a handful of crystalline coins resting atop the table. The sound of crystals tumbling breaks the silence in the room as dark haired woman playfully drops the stack repeatedly. Blinking slowly Anna regains her composure. Taking a deep breath she crosses the threshold into her office. Her eyes giving the room a once over, scanning for any inconsistencies as she approaches the desk.

"Tabitha." Anna says cautiously.

"Good evening beautiful." Tabitha replies. "You seem to have seen a ghost."

"Pale, intangible and shouldn't be in my office. Seems correct."

Approaching the desk Anna leans across meeting face to face with Tabitha. A smugness finds its way along Tabitha's face as she stares intently into Anna's eyes. Anna's soft eyes intensify morphing into a glare. For a moment they wage a silent war, a battle of their own egos. Intentionally Tabitha loses control of the tower of blue crystalline coins, sending them tumbling to the ground.

"I've went and toppled your perfect tower." Tabitha coyly remarks.

"Wouldn't be the first time. Certainly not the last."

"Do you remember the last time I looked this deeply into your eyes?"

"It was the day you put a knife in my back. Did you come to reclaim it?"

"Of course not. I would have nothing to steer with. I did come for business. However I wouldn't mind a little pleasure." Tabitha says directiung her attention to the bed at towards the back of the room. "How about we take a tour, catch up first. It has been far too long. I missed you."

Tabitha rises from her chair, her height rivaling the magicians. Straightening out her leather jacket she gingerly walks around the desk, sauntering behind Anna. A hand begins to roam down Annastasia's back. Taking her time Tabitha lingers at her waistline. Statuesque in her composure Anna remains stoic, frozen in her pose. With no sign of disapproval Tabitha continues. Her roaming hands finding their way along the hem of the dress. Biting her lip Anna closes her eyes.

"Enough." Anna says exhaling sharply.

"I haven't even started." Her hands continuing to roam back up the hem.

"I said enough. We were close once, now that truth is eluding."

"Your body says differently."

"This tour is over."

Spinning in place Anna comes face to face with her nightmare once again. Her frustration and anger presiding over her former complacency. Tabitha pulls away, retreating towards the mantle along the left side wall. A cold look replacing her devilish grin. Adorning the mantle is a collection of weapons and artifacts. Each artifact neatly placed on display and marked correspondingly. Running a hand along a rifle stock Tabitha reads the letters engraved into it's stock. 'Archangel'.

Gulping down her pride Anna moves alongside her desk bending down to return the crystal coins to table above. A stack of paperwork and folders lay scattered across her desk. The name on the top most folder reads 'Project Swarm'. Interested Anna prys open the file revealing a list of operatives. Varessa Natios. Varric Natios. Audrey Kemple. Kyle Chase. Tabitha Cosgrove. Returning her attention to the Tabitha, Anna closes the folder opting not to pry into the matter. Tabitha's cold, stern features give way to intrigue as she continues to admire the collection of rare antiquities. Skimming past a few heirlooms Tabitha fixates on an empty spot on the mantle. Running her hand over the bare felt. "The Bloody Handed" etched on the plaque. Taking a moment's pause she glances in the Magician's direction. Catching the beautiful brunette awkwardly spying on her.

"The bloody handed? There is a joke there." Tabitha questions. Her hand roams across the empty space.

"A famous tactician. Deidra was known as a ruthless woman with a nation at her back. Far and wide she was feared and rightfully so. You could go nowhere in her sector without her fleets presence being known. She had a certain spark about her. Interested me. I acquired her axes after aiding her personal war."

"And yet your shrine lay bare." Tabitha snidely remarks.

"She needed them back."

"So it was more of a loan than a present."

"You're stalling."

"Perhaps I am. Maybe i'm just getting reacquainted with my…"

"Past."

"That's a unique way of putting our relationship. Straight to business then."

Tabitha moves unhurried. Tracing a a zigzag pattern along the shelf, eyes flickering with a tinge of unease. Reaching the end of the mantle Tabitha rests her hand on a ring raised up from its display case. 'Arcadia' written elegantly on the inside of the band.

Taking the ring from its home she rolls it around the her finger. The metal cold to the touch. Brushing past Anna on her way towards the desk Tabitha grabs the folder from atop the mess of paperwork. Browsing its contents she stops mid way. Her eyes pour over the page before she rips it from the center holding it outstretched for Anna to see. Names, numbers and redacted text pepper the report.

"Frostscythe killed these people. The numbers are a count of people without identification" Tabitha says almost with remorse.

"Tabitha-" Anna furls her eyebrow. Attempting to soak in all of the information placed before her.

"I'm not finished. They poisoned them all. A neurotoxin that shuts the human body down in record time. It makes ZI-501 look like the common cold. One hundred and fifty dead in the first minute of contact and another three thousand in thirty minutes. It's all in the report."

"As horrible as that is why tell me?" Anna says. Her eyes narrowing.

"To terrify you."

"Goal achieved. How do you know all of this? Most of the information on this file in redacted."

"I did this." Tabitha boasts pridefully.

Taking a step back from her desk Anna looks on at the woman before her. Disbelief plastered across her face. Tabitha advances on the retreating Anna, pinning her against the closest wall. Pressing herself to Anna, Tabitha begins to nuzzle at her neck. The magician tenses at her brash display. Frozen in place as she searches the room for any available option of escape. Coming up empty handed she leans as far back into the wall as possible, attempting to keep Tabitha at a distance.

"You still smell like Cherry Blossoms. Refreshing." Tabitha remarks, enjoying herself. "It was the mission. Tactical reconnaissance they called it. Only one team fit for the job, 'Project Swarm'. We engineered this plague to repel any outside threat to our solar sector. A pathogen that can rip through the immune system systematically. The neurotoxin passed the ground test and shattered projections. Have I told you, you look beautiful tonight?"

Tabitha continues to adventure. Her hands roaming along the sides of the dress once more.

Brushing her head alongside Anna's she works her way downward slowly.

"Your compliments are overshadowed by your thrilling story." Anna says dryly.

Tabitha pauses her advance, looking up to make eye contact with her former partner. Anna pulls her gaze away, avoiding any undue contact with her assailant. Keeping her back pressed to the wall Anna waits for her opening.

"They killed my team Annastasia." Tabitha says continuing on. Not having skipped a beat. "There was one flaw in their plan. I'm immune to the toxin I helped create. Call it a "do it yourself life hack"."

"You infected yourself."

"I did."

"Tabitha-"

"I want you to help me get revenge." Tabitha interrupts. "I want us to get revenge."

Giving herself over Anna wraps her arms around Tabitha, resting them on her upper back. Closing the remaining distance Anna rests her chin upon Tabitha's shoulder giving her a moment of pause before she reciprocates, pressing herself further into Anna's chest.

"You want me to help you?" Anna coos softly into her ear.

"Yes." Tabitha responds without hesitation.

"Just us, like when we were younger?" Her words lingering in Tabitha's ear.

"Yes." Tabitha answers obediently. Her devilish grin creeping back from its hiding place.

A moment passes as the room falls silent again. Tabitha's head lay buried across Anna's chest as the magician playfully twirls her hair, wrapping it in her finger. A wave of comfort rolls across Tabitha's shoulders as her advances are reciprocated. Moving her hands from their resting place along her ex's back Anna runs them along the collar of her jacket. Cupping Tabitha's chin she drags her focus back to eye level.

"And just like when we were younger, I'll tell you the same thing." Anna says. Her soft spoken words becoming harsh. "I will not go down this path for you. I am no killer. I was a thief and now i'm retired."

Tabitha looks quizzically into her eyes briefly before quickly replacing it with anger. Pulling away from Anna, Tabitha keeps her within arms reach. The fury in her eyes matching the intensity in Annastasia's.

 "So quick to refuse me. You truly always have been ignorant to the bigger picture. I won't kill people." Tabitha mocks, her tone changing rapidly. "I came to you because you've always been the one to make a difference. Fuck your scruples. Fuck your principles. I need you now."

"I needed you and you left. No word, just gone." Raw emotion pours out through her words.

"This is-"

"No, you'll let me finish now. If this weapon is as dangerous as you say then so is this Frostscythe corporation. You want me to endanger my family to stop them. A crew of four against a paramilitary organization. That is the definition of a Tabitha idea.   Half cocked and willing to sacrifice anything to get what she wants." Anna's voice trembles. "Of course I see your motivation. You finally had a family of your own and they ripped it away from you. You know how I have felt for seven years. You are still family to me."

"Same propaganda, new year. Save your speeches for the cannon fodder you call fans. You were always wordy. I'm not asking you to endanger your family. They are already in danger. Frostscythe is moving forward with the project and Providence is it's next target. Slowly they will infect this city state and there will be no stopping it."

"How do you know?"

"Because that was my recommendation."

"At face value it seems I have to take you at your word."

"I've never lied to you."

Tabitha parts Anna's hair catching the loose strands and putting them back in place. Relenting, she backs away from the wall. Rubbing her hand along the edge of the ring, Tabitha begins to twirl it around her finger again. Her arrogance returning to form. Annastasia breathes deeply, relishing the small freedom. Pulling herself from the wall Anna straightens her dress out. Watching Tabitha pace back and forth she makes her way towards the bed, sitting down at the foot. Exhaling the magician collapses onto the mattress.

"You really do look stunning."

Tabitha pauses in place, her focus dragged towards the bed. Taking in Anna's slender form another moment of silence passes. Neither party budges, sharing in the collective solace. Through the door muffled yelling is being drown out, a 'last call' given by Finn. His voice carrying through to the backstage.

"Give me tonight to look over the files." Anna sighs.

"You mean that?"

"I never said no before. You just assumed."

"I'll leave the files with you."

"Thanks." Said with sincerity.

Tabitha places the files back onto the stack of paperwork. Running her finger along the band one last time she hesitantly returns it to its display case. Looking back Tabitha watches as Anna runs a hand through her hair, her mind racing with more questions than Tabitha has answers too. Overstaying her welcome she turns toward the door. A chill runs down her spine, a haunting question lingering in her mind.

"Do they know you're alive?" Anna exasperatedly asks.

"I'm not sure."

"Would they follow you?"

" If they knew, i'm sure they want to finish the job."

"There is a bed open upstairs. It's yours for the night Tabitha. Don't frighten our guests."

"I would rather the company of your bed." Tabitha says without pause.

"I would rather retire. We both don't get what we want tonight."

Opening the door, Tabitha looks out into the desolate backstage. Not a soul in sight. The roar of the crowd dulled to a murmur in the late night hour. The ambiance of the bar quieting down. Turning back Tabitha watches Anna sprawl out onto the bed. Catching her words she closes the door, leaving the room in silence.

Lifting herself up from the bed Anna looks at her empty chambers. Closing her eyes as if wincing in pain she lets out another drawn out sigh. I just want to sleep she thinks to herself. Walking to the left corner of the room she begins drawing water for her teapot. Collecting her thoughts she rifles through a drawer mashed with multiple boxes of tea. Pulling a box of passionflower tea from the back corner, setting a bag in the cup. Helps calm nerves! Proven to decrease panic attacks! written on the box. After brewing her tea Anna returns to her desk. The folder staring at her defiantly. Slumping in the seat Anna opens the folder, skimming through the dossiers, mission statements, pictures and reports.

A file highlighted in red stands out among the reports. Pulling the file

Anna pours over its contents. A picture is attached to the back of the paperwork.

In the middle of a deserted town square Tabitha stands beside another female, slightly smaller with a petite frame. The younger woman looks with admiration towards Tabitha as she leans on a propped up sniper rifle, a crooked smile spread wide across her face. Tabitha holds her hand in front of her face in an attempt to shield herself from the photographer. A mess of bodies are strewn about the city streets behind them being carted away by other members of the team.

The document itself is the mission report Tabitha brought up previously. A string of names and numbers. Information on all involved with the mission mostly left with being redacted. Including a handler simply named Mind. The only name the handler goes by is a code name. How strange.

Fighting sleep Anna takes a long sip of tea, flipping through the pages of the folder. Coming across a dossier she matches up the photos. Audrey Kemple. Taking a moment Anna picks apart Audrey's file. No prior military record, nor skills that stand out on paper. A smile peeks from the corners of her mouth as she places a finger on the connection. Handpicked by Tabitha for 'Project Swarm'. Except the picture and dossier Audrey is never mentioned again as if she never existed.

"Why her?" She questions.

Her eyes begin to close as a yawn escapes from deep within. Deciding to close the folder, she chooses to unravel the mystery come morning. Detectiving is hard with no sleep. As Anna closes the dossiers she slumps over in her chair laying her head upon the desk with a heavy thud, forsaking her comfortable bed for instant sleep.

A pounding knock at her door coaxes Anna awake minutes into her slumber. Snapping her head from the desk she begins a quick check of the room. Another knock at her door startles her nerves. Anna moves from behind her desk grabbing her cup of tea as she heads hesitantly toward the door. Damnit Tabitha. Anna's skin crawls as she grabs for the door handle, dreading the thought of a second confrontation in the same night. A voice rings out from behind the door.

"Ya decent Annie?" He says cautiously.

"Of course." Anna says sighing a breath of relief. "Come in Finn."

"Spose i woke ya, yeah?" Finn says entering Anna's office. A drink planted in his hand. He leans up against wall next to the door looking deeply into Anna's eyes. Taking a swig of his own brew he continues. "Me and Dette are goin out for da rest a the night."

"Last night in Providence. I don't blame you." Relaxing her posture she takes a long sip from her tea. "Enjoy it. You guys deserve a good night out after all the work you've been putting in."

"We all put it in. Don't count yaself short Annie. You're da captain that keeps the ship floatin'. Somethin ain't right though. Ya as white as a lily." Finn says, noticing her pallid complexion. "I didn't startle ya did I?"

"Was just about to bed when you knocked. No big deal." Anna says coyly shrugging her shoulders.

"I've snuck up on ya less times than I can count on one hand. Scuse the language but ya feedin me some line of bullshit."

"Well-" Anna begins to say. Grabbing ahold of her left arm nervously.

"See there ya go again. Anytime ya think to start a sentence off splainin', ya be lying ta me. Guilty conscience a yours and all. I can read ya personal problems like a book. You can level wit me Annie."

"It's my own problem Finn."

"Dat's more like it. We have a deal." Said brashly.

"A deal?" Anna asks cocking an eyebrow.

Finn stands himself back upright heading off to the closet in the corner of Anna's office. He opens the closet doors to an overflowing wardrobe. Dresses, jeans and shirts jammed every which way they'll fit. Immediately

Finn begins thumbing through the hangers stopping after every couple. Passing by her desk Anna quickly closes the file, setting in one of the lower desk drawers. Afterwards she plants herself down on the middle of her bed, watching Finn pick out random assortments of clothing. A black shirt, blue skirt, jeans and a pair of boots. A devious smile creeps across his face as he turns to Anna. She returns the smile covering her face with the tea cup, taking another sip.

"'Ere ya go!" Finn exclaims, tossing the clothing towards Anna playfully.

"What's this for?" Anna says laughingly. Batting the clothing away from herself.

"Some color."

"Did you just pick out the most colorful things in my closet?"

"Don't judge my fashionable eye."

"Your fashion sense is taking your shirt off in public."

"And?" Finn quickly responds raising an eyebrow. Chuckling, he continues to pour through Anna's wardrobe.

"You're insufferable. Should I call you king fashion then?"

"Ya best not to make the masses aware to my special bilities. Don't need um' grovelin at ma feet now do I?"

"Oh of course not. God forbid they ask you a fashion question that you stumble around." Anna says sipping from her tea. "Ya. I tink dat'd be great if ya you know, just wore the red ting." Mimicking Finn's accent.

"Oh shut it you. 'Ere go. Another outfit made just for the little princess in bed."

Finn pulls a pair of jeans and grey shirt from her closet. He holds them close to himself modeling them off to Anna. Striking a pose and puckering his lips. A laugh escapes from Anna as she snorts trying to hold back further laughter. The shirt has a simple design of a violin and the words 'Heart of Providence approved'. With one hand he pretends to flip his imaginary long hair to the side while popping his right hip out. Anna gets up from her bed, setting her tea down on her nightstand. She takes the clothes from his waiting hands, tossing them to the bed. Anna grabs ahold of Finn by the side and strikes a pose with him flexing her muscles as if she were Finn, while he imitates her. Suddenly Finn scoops Anna up and throws her back onto the bed. He lets out a hearty laugh as Anna hits the mattress. Rolling over Anna shoots him a false glare.

Grabbing a pillow off of her bed she holds it threateningly above her head. The office door opens again as Claudette slinks into the entry dressed to perfection. A low cut white top and form fitting pair a jeans leaving little to the imagination. In stunned surprise Finn double takes toward the open door giving Anna an opening to strike with the pillow. Winding up she whacks him over the head.

"Did you tell her she's coming with us yet Finn?" Said with a slight snicker.

Claudette watches as Anna lays into him with the pillow. Doing his best to dodge her subsequent attacks Finn pulls away from the bed out of arm's reach.

"I's workin on it. Ya can't just tell her to come with us. Annie and I have dis dynamic."

Anna turns to see Claudette in the silhouette of the door. Her attire even catching the eye of the magician. Tilting her head she beams a smile in Claudette's direction. Rolling out of bed Anna returns to her former posture, straightening her dress out and dropping the pillow back to the bed.

"Where am I going?" Anna questions.

"You're coming with us for a night out. You can't say goodbye to the city you love without spending another night in it." Claudette casually remarks.

"Dat's what I said."

"We're not taking no for an answer."

"Ya. No's no option."

"Who am I to disagree then." Shrugging her shoulders Anna gives in to their demands.

"Exactly." Finn nods. Arching an eyebrow he looks back and forth between the two ladies. "Wait ya what? What kinda sorcery is dis?"

"Woman code." Claudette says laughing. "An unwritten bond. No one woman can go out for the night-"

"While being accompanied by a man named Finn without at least some backup and a witness." Anna finishes Claudette's sentence.

"Is dat how it is? Never heard no complaints fore' tonight. Guess i'll just be takin what's mine and waitin for ya outside den."

Claudette and Anna both raise an eyebrow in anticipation of Finn's reaction. He begins walking toward the door casually. Holding his left arm out he wraps it around Claudette's waist lifting her into the air and hoisting her onto his shoulder. Her face lights up partly with shock as she is hoisted onto his shoulder. Finn continues off toward the door with a prize on his shoulder as Claudette pretends to weakly escape from his grasp. Looking backward towards Anna Claudette catches her chuckling at the two lovers. Whipping the door open Finn strolls on through with Claudette firmly on his back. "Dette make sure ya close da door on da way out ya? It's impolite to leave it swingin open in the wind. See ya outside Annie. Don't make us wait too long kay?" Finn says.

At last glimpse Anna sees Claudette hold her hands up in frustration. Rolling her eyes at the ridiculous request she shuts the door behind her on the way out.

"I wouldn't dream of keeping you both too long." Anna replies as the door closes.

CHAPTER THREE

A NIGHT IN PROVIDENCE

Annastasia opens the door from her office to the cold and empty stage room. The same silence remaining in the room as she enters. Having changed from her dress into some more relaxing street clothes. A tank top reading E equals F flat, a pair of jeans worn tight to her body and white sneakers, discarding Finn's earlier suggestions for something more music chic. Walking out into the barren backstage Anna stops taking a deep breath and closing her eyes. Grinding her foot into the wooden floor below she smiles thinking of pleasant memories.

As Anna proceeds she runs her hand alongside the left wall, feeling every groove and divot etched. Stopping just before the curtain Anna runs her hand along the closest wall. Her fingers running the groove of a heart carved into the stone. She exhales sharply. Forever and a day. Lingering on the heart her mind begins racing with mixed emotions. Finally breaking free from the tether Anna retracts her hand, continuing outward to the stage.

Mugs, half eaten bowls of pretzels and bottles litter the front of the Eldritch Flame. Strewn about in an organized chaos. The now emptied Flame has a serene feel. The chaotic presence felt during a performance all but gone leaving a lingering silence in its place. The countertop decorated in craft bottles with varying remnants. Finn must have been in a hurry. Shame to waste all of that alcohol. Stepping down from the table and dancing her way through the mess of chairs and tables Anna makes way for the entrance. Grabbing the doorknob a chill crawls down Anna's spine. Taking one more look back through the Eldritch Flame Anna catches Tabitha leaning across the upper balcony in the corner of her eye. They share a glance as Tabitha blows Anna a kiss.

"Leaving me here?" Tabitha disturbs the serene silence.

"I would be lying if I said you were invited." She returns quickly.

"Who ever needed an invitation? My guess is Finn doesn't know i'm here. No nonsensical stream of swearing followed by threats."

Anna smiles faintly, a sign of agreement. Hand stuck to the doorknob she waits calmly for Tabitha to continue.

"I thought as much. That neanderthal couldn't hold his composure to save a life. I would say his but we both know he has no regard for his own life. Where are you headed?"

"Out."

"Clearly."

"You don't need to keep track of me. I'm capable."

"Oh i'm aware of your capabilities." Tabitha says. A smirk peeking out from the corners of her mouth. "Wouldn't want to keep the hot head waiting. Have yourself a wonderful night Annastasia."

Tabitha turns from the balcony, fading back into the rear hallway. Anna feels the doorknob twist in her hand. Finn stands with his arms outstretched in front of her as the door swings open. Walking through Finn as though he were a ghost Anna exits the Eldritch Flame into the much larger scope of Providence. The streets hum with electrical current. Warm air wisps past

Anna's face from the exhaust of the passing hover cars passing by just above street level. People navigate through the busy sidewalks brushing past each other in an effort to get nowhere faster. Most too embroiled in their conversation to notice their surroundings. Anna holds her arms out as she walks into the busy city. Staring upward into the dark night sky Anna spins slowly taking in the show of lights and sounds. Breathing deeply she takes in the external stimulus of the bustling streets. One night in Providence is all we ever need. Finn closes the door behind Anna. His eyebrows arched. Perplexment written across his features.

"Thanks for being the gentleman." Admiring her surroundings Anna smiles wide.

"Ya. Not a problem. Ya good there?"

"I'm fine. Sorry it took so long. Had to rearrange my wardrobe. Some fashion guru thumbed through it all."

"Aye he did. I see you're wearin somethin pletely different from his recommendations." Finn gives Anna a once over, scoffing as he turns away.

"Some would say it was an upgrade." Claudette butts in.

"Only upgrade that shirt be havin is I don't get it."

"It's like comparing a porter to stout." Anna comments.

"They da same thing love."

"Exactly."

"OH! I get it now. They da same thing."

As Finn repeats himself Anna lets loose a chuckle, quieted quickly by her hand. I'm just glad he understood the analogy. She look back at the Eldritch Flame. The neon words project from the buildings surface bathing the area below in a beautiful light show. Looking past the Flame Anna peers off into the skyscrapers beyond, losing herself to their towering beauty. At night Providence becomes a beacon of light for the surrounding cityscapes. At the center of the towering structures the Heart of Providence stands tallest among them all piercing the sky with its impressive height. Crafts of all shapes and sizes coming to and from the tower even in the late night.

"Gunna keep gawkin like it's ya first time here?" Finn says grabbing Anna's attention.

"Yes." Anna quickly responds. Her attention elsewhere. "Every night i'm mesmerized by the city I love. I can always find something new to appreciate."

"Well appreciatin' or not. We're runnin' outta drinkin' time."

"Where's the hover at?" Anna looks around quizzically.

"Finn doesn't want to use it." Claudette says rolling her eyes dramatically.

"Member when we used ta have four goddamn wheels on da ground? I hate flyin'."

"Those things are archaic. I've never been in one. Neither has Anna, Finn."

"I ain't dat old."

"But you are old?" Anna retorts laughingly.

"Oh goddamn- Shut it you! I grew up in a small village. No flying hovercraft things ta take our asses up an down da mountain."

"That's mostly because it would just fly you over and around the mountain dear." Claudette says leaning on Finn's shoulder. "Anna we picked a very special place to go tonight. We'll be walking our happy little selves there."

"Let's not hold up the drinking any further. I'm perfectly fine with a walk tonight."

Claudette grabs Finn by the side dragging him along. They take the lead with Anna following slightly behind, giving the lovers their moment. Hovers soar past blowing Anna's hair into her face as they all continue along the sidewalk further into town. The sidewalks become more cramped as the trio closes in on the city center. Groups of inebriants slosh down the walkways making travel like walking through quicksand.

Claudette leans her head onto Finn's shoulder. Exchanging glances Claudette winks at him, sticking her tongue to emphasise her playful mood. A smile lingers as Anna watches the display of affection between the two. Quickening her pace Anna stealthfully approaches the lovers, sticking her head underneath Claudette's arm. Flinching, Claudette gives out a jolt as Anna's head protrudes in between the two.

"What cha love birds saying?"

Finn and Claudette simultaneously burst into laughter. Claudette clasps Anna's head in her arm as Finn starts rustling her hair about. Anna struggles to escape pulling at Claudette's arm. Finn and Dette continue down the street at the same pace dragging Anna along behind them as she plots her escape. Finn's initial outburst of laughter continues as Anna continues her struggle. Claudette loosens her grip and Anna plucks her head from underneath her arm.

"Wouldn't you like to know." Claudette turns to face Anna noting the disheveled look. "I think that style looks good on you. Will be most appealing to the patrons of the fine establishment we're heading off to."

"Thanks Claudette. Couldn't have pulled this off without BOTH of your help." Anna emphasizes

"Anything for a friend." Claudette winks.

Finn and Claudette keep at the same pace leaving Anna to lag behind. Straightening out her hair Anna pulls the last few strands front the front of her face, returning it to its former pristine condition.Whispering sweet nothing again. Don't worry guys i'll catch up. A shadow passes in her peripherals allowing her to only catch a glimpse of something moving in the alleyway beside her. Pausing briefly Anna surveys the corridor.Neat and orderly mostly set up with waste receptacles behind the establishments. Nothing out of the ordinary.

"Are ya comin slowpoke? We're almost there an i'm fuckin parched."

"Yeah, yeah. I saw something. I'm on my way." Anna says jogging to catch them at the corner of the street.

Rounding the corner Finn gestures towards a run down establishment just a small walk further down the street. The building has a neon projection that reads 'Bourbon and a Brawl' in a cold black with white trim hanging just above the door in bold lettering. Actual cars litter the parking lot with no hovers in sight. People huddled in groups out front mark the social setting, most dressed in leathers and low cut outfits. Anna raises her eyebrow questionably toward Finn and Claudette. Their smug smiles reaching their peak as they glance back to towards the violinist.

Finn motions for the girls to follow as he crosses the walkway towards the bar.

"It's been years. This place is still around?" Anna questions looking to Claudette.

"A few new owners over the years, still in the same disrepair. Just don't blink quickly or breathe. You'll be fine." Claudette responds sarcastically.

"Great." Anna says behind gritted teeth.

"Come on ya lilies. Get ya asses movin'. Uncle John ain't waitin much longer."

Claudette grabs ahold of Anna's hand dragging her across the street to rejoin with an impatient Finn. The group approaches the crowded front entrance. Weaving through the social butterflies outside Finn takes point with Claudette bringing up the rear. Few take note of Finn with nods, an unspoken hello.

"The magician!" Blurted out from the back of the crowd, garnering attention from the other patrons and Annastasia.

A bellow of applause erupts as Anna passes by them. With all eyes on her Anna shyly waves to the audience as she passes by. Acknowledging her praise she with a nod and smile. They begin cheer and chant for the popular artist.

As quickly as the clamoring begins it ends abruptly as Finn raises his hands into the air to hush them.

"Alright folks tanks for da applause but da magician isn't ere' tonight. Dis is plain ole Annie. We're lookin ta have some fun for we set sail for new ground, preferably wit sun and sand. Tanks for da understandin'."

"Thank you everyone. Hope you all have a great night." Anna adds.

They continue on through the front entrance into chaos. An overwhelming smell of stale beer emits from the entryway filling their sense as they pass through. The antiqued look of the bar is offset by its utter disarray. Tables strewn about with no rhyme or reason. Drinks lay lazily on every horizontal surface possible. The wood flooring creaks underfoot as the group proceeds to a table in the center of the bar. The singular bartender and waitress working the floor looks overwhelmed. Music blares overhead. Twangy new age guitar work sputtering out from the speakers mostly drown out by the patrons of the establishment. Each person trying to speak over the other groups closest by.

Anna, Finn and Claudette take their seats at the center table. A reserved "sign" made from a scratch piece of paper written in permanent marker sits in the middle of the table. Differing from the surrounding area the table is recently cleaned and presented fairly. As they take their seats the waitress approaches. Looking exhausted she begins her pre programmed greeting.

"Welcome to Bourbon and a Brawl. What kinda fight are you looking to have tonight?" Her voice tired and unimpressed.

"We're lookin ta have a couple a Uncle John's and somethin a little fruity for da misses over there."

"I'll just have a glass of wine." Anna says.

"Alright. Two Uncle John's and a- would you like it red or white?"

"I knew that question was coming. You wouldn't happen to have more than just a basic Merlot or Chardonnay would you?"

"Hun-"

"I'll just have a Uncle John as well." Anna says interrupting the waitress.

"Good call." The waitress responds dryly.

"Dat's da goddamn spirit. We's just here celebratin the night no rush on the drinks ya. I know ya busy an all." Finn says as the waitress takes her leave. "Hopefully you member dis place."

"I do." Anna says. A smile beams across her face. "This is where you first made a fool of yourself in front of me."

"Where you decided I was worth taking along." Claudette says looking to Anna.

"I decided long before that night Claudette. You we're running jobs south of the Providence. Making people's life a living hell. I never heard the end of it." Anna says tracing a circle on the table with her finger.

"That's when you decided hell a life of halfway decency was better than sitting cozy in that tower? Mistake. That was definitely a mistake. Now you're stuck with us." Claudette retorts.

"You were casing the owner of this fine establishment if I do remember correctly." Anna continues. Chuckling at Claudette's previous comment.

"Ya. Dat prick. Ya know he ran a gamblin' scheme down da stairs and off ta da left there ya? He bet against me. Told me ta dive after the third punch-"

"That's right!" Claudette exclaims. "I distinctly remember hearing you scream "fuck dat" as loud as possible. Why were you all even there?"

"Ta fight."

"Of course." Claudette rolls her eyes.

"Doesn't matter anymore. We were working closely with the Leto's at the time. It was the meeting point."

"Secrets don't make friends."

"Neither does snitchin on a job pending transaction."

"They never paid?" Claudette says appalled. "You let them not pay you?"

The waitress breaks up the commotion as she passes by with their round of drinks. Setting them down gingerly tilting the glasses just enough to give Finn a small heart attack. His eyes grow wide in anticipation of the drink. Subconsciously Finn licks his lips as the mug is set in front of him. She looks to the group for a sign of approval. Finn raises his hand and pats her on the shoulder.

"Dat'll do."

"Thank you." The waitress says smiling as she pulls away from the table.

Silence breaks over the table as they each drink. Finn helps himself to the biggest gulps of alcohol while the others sip and enjoy their drinks. Setting the glasses down they share a look around the table. Claudette's hands raise in the air.

"So! They never paid up?" Claudette exclaims.

"No. They didn't pay." Anna replies.

"How did we get paid for the job then?"

"Ya really wanna know love?"

"I paid you all." Anna says briskly. "Even the newcomer to the team. I needed a scout and you fit the role. I wouldn't have tracked you down if your reputation wasn't so highly recommended."

"I'll be damned. That was a lot of cash." Claudette bewilderedly smiles.

"It was."

"Plus I fell in immediate love. Had to make sure ya made da team. Ya welcome for makin' ya look good an all." Finn adds taking another gulp of his "Uncle John".

"Well thank you Anna." Claudette says appreciatively.

"Anytime. You're part of my family. With that comes all the perks."

"Like da next round of booze bein' on her. Best perk round."

Anna snorts at Finn's remark. She looks away towards the back wall quickly covering her face, laughing even harder.

"Did ya just snort Annie? Dette ya better a just heard her."

"It's so cute. Wish we could have recorded it."

As Anna glances away from her friends she notices a man in black clothes at the far table. His long milky hands wrapped around his mug, clung to it. His face sunken into a hood with only the whites of his eyes piercing through the dark background. His eyes dart away as she comes across his presence. The same shiver she felt leaving the Eldritch Flame rolls across her shoulders. Anna shakes off the distraction and returns to the conversation. A wide smile set across her face belaying any bewilderment she may have.

"Did Johnny hit ya hard?"

"What?" Anna responds puzzled, cocking her head.

"Ya stopped talkin you did. Figure the booze hit ya tad bit rough. Nothin like a good Uncle Johnny for ya."

"Sorry someone was more worth my attention then you. You can keep rambling Finn." Anna rebuttals. Her attention returning completely to the conversation.

"Breakin ma heart love. Would refrain from sayin dat again. Be callin ya by ya sistas name instead." Finn says leaning in with a smug look cast upon his face. "Always sayin i'm talkin with no words comin out. Fuck dat."

"I would turn my nose up a bit more if I were her. It would go something like. Do you have to continue Finn? I've tried to pay attention but it just seems the more I focus the less I hear."

"Yea dat sounds like er'. Fuck, ya should imitate her more often. Ya'd be way better at just bout everything."

Finn hangs his head and chuckles. Anna's gaze burns a hole through his chest. He looks back up face a beet red, tears forming in the corners of his eyes. Noticing Anna's angered look Finn points at her, further frustrating Annie. Claudette grins at the dialogue keeping her distance from the actual conversation. She holds her hand up to gain the attention of the waitress while mouthing "another round", making a circling motion towards the bar.

"Did ya know you two had the same angry face?" Finn says coarsely. "Always purse ya lips. Dats fuckin funny. Shame ya don't share her look of utter disappointment."

"It wouldn't suit me very well." Anna responds.

"Ya. We don't need two of her in da world."

Anna again looks toward to the back table. The mug lay half empty upon the table, seat emptied and shoved against the wall. Money lay scattered across the table attached to no bill. Almost left abandoned in a hurry. Anna's eyebrows furl as she looks around the room intending to find the hooded stranger. Their waitress returns with another round of beverages, setting them down individually. Claudette and Finn both give their thanks as she begins to leave.

"Excuse me." Anna says gathering her attention. "Did you see the man in the back corner leave moments ago?"

"Nope." She replies. "Real nice guy. He just kept ordering round after round. Was here for a good couple hours. Did he bother you?"

"No. We shared a moment that's all. Thank you ma'am." Anna says as the waitress walks off to a nearby table.

"A moment wit some random bloke? Did we find ya love after all?"

"I was just waiting for him to serenade me with his staring. It's a lost art form."

"Das who had ya attention. Fuck him and his shitty stare. Ain't more important den our talk."

"At least where we're going people like him won't be following us." Claudette interjects. "Nice beaches."

"Liquor all damn day." Finn says interrupting.

"Longer days. Even better nights and a waitlist to get on planet." Claudette continues

"Sounds like the best vacation ever made. Cept we'll be livin it every fuckin day."

"Best planet in the sector. I want you guys to enjoy it." Anna takes a swig of her beverage.

"What do you mean you want us to enjoy it?" Claudette asks.

"I have-" Anna begins to say.

Screaming from across the bar cuts Anna's speech off. The male patron from the Eldritch Flame stands in the doorway pointing at Finn. Garnering Finn, Claudette and Anna's attention. The disgruntled man moves inside the door allowing a few more people to shuffle in behind him. He cuts across the bar floor making headway towards Finn. The two behind him keeping close. The trio exchange looks and calmly remain at their table. Behind the counter the waitress intently watches on as the group approaches Anna's table, a deer in the headlights look adorning their face. Anna traces another circle in the wooden tabletop calming her mind as she watches the privileged men stride toward them. Claudette sips from her "Uncle John" holding the mug in her left hand, coddling it.

"So Annie are ya tellin me yer not comin to the beaches with us? A bit of a heads up would be nice ya? You could say something like-" Finn says assessing the situation before him. Keeping his cool as they approach.

"Hey asshole, I need to have some words with you." The younger man says. The collar to his shirt still disheveled from their earlier encounter. His forehead bruised and dried blood clung still to his upper lip.

"Ya somethin like dat." Finn says without pause.

"I was going to mention it. I had to find the way to relay it to the two of you." Anna says ignoring the crowd gathering beside Finn.

"Ya could just say ey' i'm tryin ta send ya off."

"I'm talking to you!" the man says visibly becoming frustrated.

"And ya can politely wait ya fuckin turn. I'm talkin with the lasses." Finn says directing his gaze toward Claudette. "Now where was I for I was rudely interrupted? Right, what da fuck Annie."

"I took a job." Anna says nonchalantly shrugging her shoulders. "I couldn't say no."

"You can always say no." Claudette chimes in. "We can help you with that. Who's the job for?"

Running a hands through his hair the young man's frustration grows. He grasps Finn by the shoulder garnering his undivided attention. Finn snaps his head around to make eye contact with the "boy". The patronage at the Bourbon and a Brawl falls silent waiting in anticipation for the coming moments. The other two men both dressed in similar attire to their impatient friend, stand staggered behind him. Angered looks drawn across their faces in an attempt to become more menacing. To their dismay Finn grins like a child on his birthday. Looking up from his seated position Finn questions the men.

"I didn't know ya forehand, now you fuckin got ya hand on me. I'd like to know dat name now. Ya do have one ya?"

"Marcus Price." He says gathering his courage.

"Das a nice name. Ya ma gave it to ya i'm assumin. Forbid da fact she raised a twat in place o' a man. You have your hand on ma shoulder. Kindly remove it for I do it for ya."

Still staring into the eyes of Marcus, Finn internally counts down from ten. Anna and Claudette exchange sideways glances across the table as the thugs attention as well as the rest of the bar is drawn to Finn. Moving the seat back Claudette takes a relaxed position in her chair clutching to her mug even still. Anna continues tracing on the table. Looking up toward the scene placed before her she rolls her eyes and exhales loudly followed by a chuckle. He removes his hand from Finn's shoulder by the count of eight. Finn slowly drags his chair backwards scraping across the wooden flooring leaving grooves in the floorboards. He stands tall in front of the trio before him equaling the height of the two thugs in the back end. He looks past Marcus to them.

"I should know ya names as well boys. Fraid when am done wit ya i'll have to be identifyin ya to da paramedics. Unless ya wanna leave dis where it stand. Run along with those tails tween ya legs. No shame in dat."

"You think you intimidate us? It's three on one." Marcus interjects.

"You're right it's not fair. You need a few more." Claudette says.

"Shut your fucking mouth." He snaps turning his attention to Claudette.

"Here I thought you might have been smart." Anna mutters under her breath, sighing.

Marcus catches a quick motion from the corner of his eye. Attempting to look at the commotion he turns directly into Finn's first punch. It sends him tumbling backwards into his crew. They hold him up gripping him under the arms. Finn wide eyed, stares the two men down. His gaze wild and threatening. Marcus rebounds toward Finn balling a fist. Attempting a strike he comes up short allowing Finn another blow. This one connects with his temple sending Marcus sprawling to the ground in short order. The silent bar begins murmuring as they watch the brawl. Bets being made against the remaining two left.

"Made ya graves. Time to lay in um. Comon biggin time to play." Finn says readying to brawl.

Quickly extending his arm out Finn grabs ahold of a shirt collar. Grasping it with his left arm he begins pummeling the man with vicious rights. Three strikes to a combination of the chest and face, giving his opponent no time to react. Seeing an opening the second thug strikes at the back of Finn's head, a shot of opportunity. Reeling forward slightly from the blow Finn releases his grasp of the collar allowing the deadweight to collapse to the floor. Turning around slowly Finn gives him a once over noticing Claudette having slipped away from her chair. Closing in behind the frightened target, the mug of alcohol still in her hand. His grin returns as he calmly sinks his hands into the pockets of his jeans. Finn walks forward backing the challenger up with each step. The young man readies himself to fight putting his hands up defensively.

"There's one thing ya and ya mates forgot. Never drag a man's woman into ya fight. It's not respectable an if I don't respect ya den it's pretty much ova. Now if ya had been just a bunch a brash twats I could respect that but ya had ta go and bring Dette into dis. Thankfully ya didn't bother Annie. I'd hate ta see what she'd a done in Dette's place." Finn says. His words distracting the man further. "Now what happens next I want ya ta know this is on ya friend Marc."

Finn stops short of the frightened thug removing his hands from his pockets. He motions him forward in a taunting fashion. As they look to square up Claudette walks quietly up behind her target kicking his left knee out, bringing him down to one knee. Swiftly Claudette follows up with the glass mug cracking him across the head. The patrons in the bar make groaning noises in unison as the mug connects with his head their gaze directed at Claudette. Wavering the man goes to the floor clutching his head with both hands. She turns her attention to Finn and smiles.

"I love you." Finn says returning the smile.

"I know." Claudette replies.

Finn grabs Claudette by her waist, bringing her in for a kiss. The bar cheers and whistles at the two of them as if this whole attraction is commonplace here. Breaking the kiss Finn motions for Claudette to return to her seat pulling it out like a gentleman. She steps over the man writhing on the floor returning to her seat. Finn returns his attention to the young man still conscious. Turning the man over Finn grabs him by his jaw. Applying pressure he looks into his eyes with a look of satisfaction.

"I want a simple nod on dis. Understood?"

The man nods as well as he can in Finn's vice like grip.

"Take ya friends. Dey ain't too bad off and ya fuck off. If i see ya for I get to my beaches I will fuck ya up. Understood?"

He nods again.

"Now git." Finn says releasing his grip.

Scurrying to his feet he rushes over to his friends. A few patrons give him a hand in dragging them outside the bar before returning to their drinks. Others are paying up on the bets made against the fight. The waitress breathes deeply a sigh of relief as their bar returns to it's normal clamor. The crowd slowly dispersing as Finn returns to his wooden throne. A confident and smug look across his face. Anna glances back up from the table to the both of them.

"Well done." Anna compliments.

"Tanks Annie. Had to have one last fight ere'. Tradition an all."

"Of course you did. You weren't in on this Claudette were you?"

"No." Claudette says pausing. "Yes."

"I can't believe either of you." Anna says laughing. "It's like you wanted to have a fun night."

"Oh our fun hasn't even started yet. Me and Dette are gonna have a fun night. Ain't that right Dette?"

"Too much information. Don't need to know." Anna says interrupting.

"Oh shove it. All those times I heard you and Tabitha going at it. You wasn't nearly as quiet as you think. Me and Dette are just makin up for time lost. If dat includes makin you a bit squeamish den so be's it."

"That's a name I never thought you'd bring up."

"Eh. If I don't say er' name at least once she'll haunt ma dreams. Need to keep the ritual alive. Usually there's curses involved. Fuck. There. Better."

"Much better. Enjoy the rest of your night. Hopefully you end up home by the end of it. I'll catch the check for us."

"You're not getting out of this easy. You said you had a job?" Claudette asks.

"I'll talk to you about it tomorrow. I'm not sure what it entails yet and I really don't have a plan set up. I'm not so sure you two want in on this one."

"We're family Anna. Of course we want to help. When you're comfortable you can let us know and we'll be there."

"Cause dats what families for."

"Thanks guys."

Standing up from the table Finn and Claudette both wrap Anna in a hug. Anna leans her head into theirs. Breaking the hug Finn begins walking off toward the door to applause from other regulars. Raising one hand in the air as he exits the bar pretending to conduct their praise. Mixed commotion from outside leads to further cheering and chanting. Claudette waits behind allowing Finn to ride out his popularity. She leans her head into Anna's.

"You sure you don't want us doing this job?" Claudette asks.

"I would love nothing more than for the two of you to help me but it's dangerous. Military operations dangerous. You both worked too hard for me to risk your lives on this." Anna says softly.

"Why would you accept that kind of job?"

"Because it puts lives at risk if I don't."

"You always had a great heart. Don't let the wrong kind of people abuse it."

"I have a habit of making bad choices in my life." Anna says sourly.

"I know. You took us on board." Claudette returns, breaking the tension.

"That is the best decision I ever made. When you have very little family you learn to create your own. I would trade you in for nothing." Anna says moving her head slightly, kissing Claudette on the cheek. Anna puts a hand on her shoulder calming her. "The only thing I want you to worry about is what flavor of drink you want on that beach. Not what type of patrol the guards are taking. Enjoy tonight. Take in our home one last time before home changes."

"You always know what to say. Be safe Annie. I'll see you back home later."

"I would say the same to you too but I know you have no intention of being safe tonight."

They share a laugh together and embrace in another hug. Anna pats Claudette on the back as they go their separate ways. Claudette heads toward the commotion in the front shaking her head in disbelief as she watches Finn in his element. Annastasia makes her way to the bar. The waitress pours a few drinks for the waiting customers before noticing the magician waiting politely at the end of the counter.Pulling a small rectangular device from her pocket Anna tosses it in the direction of the waitress as she catches her attention.

"The rest is for you." Anna says smiling.

"Thank you so much." The waitress says appreciatively, pouring over the money chip in her hand. "Have an awesome night."

"Already have. Blessed with amazing friends. Thanks for the wishes."

Anna parts her hair to the side neatly placing the strands back to their places. She walks out from the bar back into Providence's warm lighting. The light envelopes her as she makes her way through the crowd in front of the Bourbon and a Brawl. Again the people clap and cheer for her. This time more inebriated. She blushes at their less than sober thoughts while dodging drunk hands reaching out to congratulate her. Making way out to the cities street the smell of burnt exhaust fills her senses as cars leave the parking lot.

If only Finn were here to say something nostalgic. A smile runs across her face thinking of all of the possible things he would say. Something about a mountain and climbing it both ways. Passing back to the other side of the street she catches another glimpse of the Heart of Providence.

Staring at it's beautiful lights Anna loses herself for a moment before coming to a halt having caught another glimpse out of her peripherals down the same alleyway. Turning suddenly to look back down the pristine alleyway only to see everything still as neatly placed as it had been previously. Straightening up Anna ventures down the alleyway investigating what she seems to have seen both times. Making her way into the center of the alley nothing out of the ordinary seems to catch her eye. Papers lay strewn in a corner of the back road, a trash container overturned. A steady dripping sounds from the corner of a building as water steadily drops from the rooftop. Not a soul in sight. Packing up her investigation Anna walks back down from the alley and out onto the sidewalk keeping her normal pace. The thought nagging the back of her mind. What could it have possibly been. Saw no food. Shouldn't have been an animal.

Catching herself gazing outward at the neon expanse she finds solace from the puzzling shadow she saw. Their lights shimmering throughout the city leading her home safely. Reaching the Eldritch Flame Anna relaxes against the outside wall. Taking in the sight of her home once more before retiring for the night. The stars shining brightly even though the fog of lights. Hovers passing by at a decreased frequency as the night burns strong. The pollution of noise comes in waves and leaves just as quickly leaving a murmur on the city street. One more job. I owe this city that.

Taking keys from her pocket Anna opens the Flame to the sound of silence. The bowls and glasses strewn about her tables neatly placed across the bar, emptied and cleaned. Floors free of debris and chairs pushed back into their assigned spots. Walking through the interior Anna finds a note attached to the stage. Everyone has to earn their keep. Consider this a portion of mine. Anna stands atop the stage looking back out recalling her countless performances. Recalling the feelings, emotions and everything in between. Rubbing the dream like feeling from her eyes Anna returns to her bedroom past the backstage. Opening her door the room is still and empty. Placing the miscellaneous things from her pockets onto the desk Anna changes from her clothes to something more casual. She runs her hands along the belongings on her mantle, smiling as she recalls each memento before slipping into bed.

Chapter Four
See it through

Waking from slumber to the chirping of birds and the slightest gust of wind Anna slowly raises her head from the desk. Eyes blinded by direct sunlight from a nearby window. Wind blows through her hair rustling it from its near perfect positioning. Through squinted eyes Anna peers around the room. Questioning the bright light and air flow. The few glimpses paint the picture of a different room than which she fell asleep to. On the desk lay drawings where military documents were sprawled out. Upon closer inspection the drawings become familiar. Two girls sitting on a rustic porch. The youngest of them has her head half buried on the others shoulder the hint of a smile present. Anna rubs her eyes shaking the cobwebs of her hibernation. Thumbing through the drawings Anna pauses. Each picture becoming more and more familiar. The last picture simply drawn in colored pencils reads Illiyana, Bravest. Below is a picture drawn hastily of a girl in armor holding a sword and shield. "Fear me beasties! I am Illiyana!" scrawled in a text bubble above their head.

Lifting her focus from the pictures Anna scans the room. To her own shock the room is the exact way she remembers it. A pastel drawing of flowers above the door frame. Posters of bands tacked in random spaces covering an old wallpaper. Cats occasionally poking out from behind the boy bands. Opposite the desk she is sitting at is another desk wit outdated computer technology and cords laying in piles beside it. No semblance to the chaos. Beside the desk is a twin size bed. A lump dead center under the sheets. Head hiding under the covers, likely protecting their eyes from the "harmful" sunlight. As Anna turns back around she pulls out the drawer of the current desk. Music paper topples out in heaps. An introductory book for violinists sticks out of the now open drawer. Opening the book, loose paper falls to the ground. Lyrics and notes scribbled across the paper. At the bottom is a signature 'The future grandmaster Annastasia Arlenko'. Anna chuckles as she puts the paper back in its previous space. This is home. Everything is just the way I remember it. I must be dreaming. Let's test, shall we.

Standing from the chair a squeak groans out. Still needs to be oiled. Anna walks to the opposite desk moving the cords and junk computer pieces out of her way. A small diary lay hidden in the center of the cord pile. On its front reads Stay out. Arlenko property. Important documentation inside. Foregoing the warning Anna opens the journal.

Entry number one. I guess I should just date this thing. Would be much more efficient. Also in a world of tech I would much rather be the magician hiding her secrets in the real world. I just finished writing this song for my sister. It's about our family. I titled it Kindred. It's really simple but I made it for her. Anyway journal i'm going to give you a name. You will be called my enigma. Mostly because people will probably question me writing in you. Love Anna, see you soon.

"I haven't read this in so long." Anna says blurting aloud.

Shooting a sideways glance toward the lump in bed Anna receives no reaction to her words. The figure in bed tosses slightly pulling the blanket tighter over their head. Anna sits at the foot of the bed and the room falls silent again. Flipping through more pages of the journal Anna begins to recite lines from its pages.

"I feel like what I do doesn't matter. I'm not Illiyana. I'm no soldier." She quips sarcastically. "Trust me dream me it gets better from here. You're super famous now." Holding the book out and flipping to the last page. "We argued enigma. I hate it when we argue. Can't they just come home now." The words pour out tensely from Anna. "Yeah. That doesn't ever change. You get used to it. It's more like a constant nagging now."

If you could go back and tell yourself one thing what would it be? Another chuckle escapes Anna as she narrates her own life. A pounding at the door cuts the silence grabbing Anna's attention. A sequence of three knocks in repetition followed by a long pause. A foot taps impatiently from the other end. Under the door their shadow can be seen pacing in small circles. The doorknob is given a slight twist as a key is inserted. Swung wildly the door crashes into the wall. Sound echoing out into the long hallway. A blonde teenager storms into the room. Long hair swaying fury dominating her blue eyes, face bent like steel. Dress in a set of white formal exercise gear. Determined she stomps toward the bed paying no attention to Anna as if she did not exist.

Anna watches this unfold as if a home movie. Expressionless and statuesque in demeanor she closes the journal. I know what day this is now. The blonde stares at the sheet covered person. Her arms crossed.

"Get up." Illiyana barks. "We will be late for training."

Groaning projects from the sheets. Her younger self rolls back over in bed pretending her sister isn't in the room burning a hole through the sheets with her glare.

"The lord will be angry with us again if you don't get out of this bed. We cannot be late again."

"It's the weekend Illy. We don't have practice today."

"Warriors never sleep." Illiyana snaps.

"They just take naps and get cranky." The lump retorts. "Kul will not be expecting us on a weekend."

"He expressed this weekend would be good for the both of us. Tandem exercises to build trust."

Illiyana grabs a handful of blanket and rips it from her sister's grasp. Holding it above her head Illiyana watches her sister shield their eyes from the bright lights. Another groan comes from younger Annastasia. She sits up in bed putting a defiant face on slowly opening her eyes to the vision of her sister glaring at her.

Watching from an outside perspective Anna has moved to the corner of the room bumping her head on the slanted wall knocking a picture loose. Looking down as it falls slowly to the ground her name is written in red ink upon the back of the photo. More words appear as she continues to focus on the dropping poster. He's coming. Remember today. Etched underneath her name. Anna's attention is pulled back to the ensuing argument. Briefly looking back the poster is hung back on the wall.

"You need this." Illiyana says.

"You want me to do this. I want a free weekend."

"Anna! You are so infuriating. You tell me you want us to get along. To do things together. I'm giving you the option and you're flat out refusing me!" Illiyana balls her hands into fists.

"I'm refusing to train for something I never want to be. You wouldn't want to learn how to play violin. How about we go watch some vids together. Spend a day in the mall?"

"The mall?" Illiyana repeats. "Do you even realise the way you sound? You sound like a child."

"I am a child."

"No. You're an Arlenko. Arlenko's are the masters of their craft. You're the master of nothing and at this rate you'll never amount to anything.

Complacency is the reason for failure. I want you to strive to be better than this. Stronger than this. At the moment you are no better than complacent. Now get ready we're going to train."

Annastasia stares blankly at her sister. Her eyebrow arched and speechless. Taking this as a sign Illiyana marches toward a dresser and ruffles through its contents until she pulls from it a workout uniform. A matching black shirt and pants. Tossing the clothing behind her back Illiyana hits her mark using her sister as a clothing rack. Pants hanging from atop Annastasia's head as the shirt slinks into her lap. Groaning projects from underneath the pants.

Anna lets a chuckle out as she removes herself from the corner, separating Illiyana from her younger self. She walks right up to her sister waving a hand back and forth. No reaction. She can't see me. What is this? Placing a hand to Illiyana's chest the magician phases through to the other side. Retracting quickly Anna inspects her hand giving it a once over. Before Anna can react Illiyana walks through her toward the bed again. A slight tingling overcomes Anna as her sister passes through her body. The tingling starts in her core and expands outward like an ocean current. Illiyana makes way towards her younger sibling with her hand outstretched.

"I promise it will be fun. We'll be a great team. The Arlenko sisters working together. The world should tremble at our feet." Illiyana smiles genuinely. "You know i've never broken a promise. I won't start today. So chin up. Let's go enjoy today."

"You promise?"

"I do."

"Can we go to the mall afterwards?"

"You bet."

Annastasia grabs her sister's outstretched hand and pulls herself out of bed. With her free hand she tosses the pants back in Illiyana's face. Striking a victory pose Annastasia watches the pants fall to the ground. Illiyana's hair disheveled from the attack. Pursing her lips and making a weird face Illiyana lunges toward her sister tackling her back onto the bed. Frantically tickling, Illiyana pins her to the bed as Anna attempts to squirm out from underneath. Giggling engulfs the room as both parties collapse in laughter.

"I give!" Annastasia screams in false pain.

Illiyana pulls herself back up from the bed. A smile spread across her face. Eyes soft and calm replacing the fury that once claimed them. Annastasia sits up blowing her hair from the front of her face. They share a smile and embrace in a hug. Anna holding tightly unwilling to let go.

"I'm sorry." Illiyana says.

"I accept your apology Illy." Anna says. A bear grip around her sister's waist.

"Promise me you won't tickle the other students into submission."

"No promises sis."

"I can already see your title. Annastasia Arlenko, tickler supreme. Meet me downstairs in ten minutes. I'll have the hover waiting for us."

She loosens her grasp on Illiyana slowly letting her sister go. She parts Anna's hair and straightens it out. With a final touch she bops her on the nose. Anna scrunches at her touch jerking her head back. Laughing Illiyana exits the room closing the door behind her. Anna gets herself in order grabbing the pants from the floor. Changing from pajamas into the new outfit. Looking in the mirror as she does her older self comes to stand behind her. Watching as she places butterfly barrette' in her hair. I was so practical. Rushing from her mirror she grabs her new sneakers. With shoes on out the door goes a young and naive Anna. Leaving her adult self alone in the room.

Anna takes in the sights of her old room. Nostalgia creeping over her once again. Breathing deeply taking in the all too familiar smells for one last time. The light outside begins fading as darkness creeps out of the corners seeping inward towards her. A burning stench replacing the prominent cherry blossom scent. Fresh air soured with sulfur. Shadows begin forming extinguishing the light. Anna closes her eyes forcing them shut. The darkness engulfing her within its grasp. Cold to the touch it weaves around her form growing tighter every passing second. Inaudible words whisper into Anna's ear their tone wispy and ragged. Sending chills down her spine. Eyes clenched tight Anna does not budge. Taking deep regulated breaths and standing stationary. Tendrils crawl across her body pressing tightly forming to Anna, creating a cocoon around her. Anna's senses cut off from within though her position staunch and firm conforming to the darkness rather than fighting for control.

●

As fast as the cocoon formed it begins to dissipate slithering away from Anna's body in retreat. Slowly the silence is replaced with the clashing of weapons though faint at first beings growing in dissonance. Eyes fluttering open to bright sunlight momentarily stunning the retinas. Focusing more on the growing noise Anna is able to pick out a few distinct sounds. The resonance of hovers over head. Their engines a quiet purr as they zip above. The buzz of a shield generator. A soothing constant among the rest. Prying her eyes back open to a familiar scene. A tower stood in the center of a courtyard tall enough to pierce the sky. Vehicles flying to and from its ports on multiple levels.The tower shines. It's silver exterior shimmering in direct sunlight. Anna takes her eyes from the tower and onto the noise. The courtyard is bustling with all walks of life. Businessmen and travelers flood the walkway. A group of students sparring in groups of four. Each in their own respective colored uniforms.

Their master standing staunch inspecting each of his students. His hands clasped in front of him as he watches his students perform. Dressed down for the weekend his attire is casual for his military like stature. His expression is soft and calming. Smiling and clapping as each finish up their individual sets.

They group up around him intently listening to his words. Unable to make out his words Anna moves closer to them. Closing the distance she cuts through a group of dignitaries on their way toward the tower. Phasing through them rather than weaving around. The tingling sensation growing in her chest as she passes through.

"You are all exceptional. Each excel in ways I would never have dreamed you could. I am proud to say you are all under my tutelage. Form ranks. We will begin our next training exercise shortly." Their master proclaims.

As Anna comes upon the group they break their huddle and take place in a line. A hover swoops in from above landing close to the training grounds. The hover bears the seal of the tower. Illiyana and her younger self exit from the back of the hover dressed in their respective outfits. The doors closes and the hover returns to the sky melding into the sea of other drivers. Their master gives a smile in their direction. Annastasia watches herself run playfully toward the group of other children as Illiyana approaches their trainer. Keeping her distance from her younger self she approaches Illiyana's conversation. Casually observing the two of them.

"My Lord Kul." Illiyana says as she curtsies. "Apologies for being late. Where should we fall in?"

"Afternoon Illiyana. You can fill in where needed." He responds. "I see you brought your sister with you today as well. Extracurricular activities are not generally her forte."

"I had to do some persuading."

"The mall?" He chuckles, stroking his chin.

"You would be correct."

"She does have a way to pull at the heartstrings. She gets that from your father."

Illiyana's eyes widen. A moment of grief striking them. Kul places his hand to his forehead. He reaches for Illiyana and embraces her in a hug, patting her on the back. An excited scream pulls the two from their moment. Annastasia runs from the crowd of trainees toward them. A megawatt smile across her face as she splits the two of them apart. Barrelling into Kul with tremendous force. He pretends to be struck off balance. Falling to a knee he quickly picks Anna up from the ground and begins to twirl her in the air.

"KUL!" Anna screams, laughing as she floats in his arms.

"Hello there little flame. You here to brighten my day?" Kul says.

"Of course."

"I'm glad. The day was boring without you here." Kul whispers into her ear.

Anna giggles as she continues to twirl through the air. Kul sets her down gently kneeling down beside her. He kisses her on the cheek. The stubble of his beard tickling her and tugs on her left ear. As he rises Illiyana rolls her eyes visibly to him. He smirks, tugging her right ear. Straightening his form he stands before the rest of his class. Illiyana motions for Anna to follow her to finish out rank. Anna sheepishly follows her sister in line standing beside her.

Taking up position near Kul standing parallel to him. Anna looks out over the heads of the other trainees spotting herself and Illiyana taking up the rear. The kid in front of her younger self turned around to talk to the two of them. The flirter. Always the gentleman Aiden. Kul clears his throat returning all attention to the front. Heads whipping forward at dizzying speeds to see him standing at attention. Following suit every trainee readies themselves with their hands at their sides. Annastasia turns her focus back to Kul tying her hair back in a knot and preparing her stance. Kul begins going through an array of martial arts kata beginning with punches and kicks. Annastasia waits for him to begin then mimics his movements. Each change in technique flawless as he goes through the basics. One. One. Two. Breath in. Breath out. FOCUS. Kul begins at the top picking up speed on his strikes. Anna keeps pace with him. The repetition continues for two more sets until the trainees are worn out. They return to stance and bow to Kul as he reciprocates

"Very good. Some of you have more endurance practice to work on." Kul jokes looking at the young Annastasia catching her breath. "We will be splitting off in pairs. Go ahead and pick your partner."

Anna grabs ahold of Illiyana's hand tugging her towards an open area. Illiyana resists and pulls her hand free from Anna's grasp.

"Not today Anna. I have to square something up." Illiyana says looking into her eyes.

"With who?"

Illiyana smirks at her sister as she points across the way to a teen about her age. The boy among a group of friends. Laughing and trading quips.

"Him?" Anna questions.

"Yes."

"Do you have a crush on him?"

"No. Why would you even suggest that?"

"Because I read when people pick on others that it means they like them."

"Remove that thought from your head. It's a matter of pride. He has made fun of our family. I intend to make sure he never does that again."

"Oooohhh. I got it. Good luck!" Anna says cheerfully.

"I won't need luck." She retorts. "But thank you Tasia."

Illiyana walks away from her younger sister cracking her knuckles as she makes her way toward her 'sparring partner' and his friends. As she approaches the young man's demeanor changes. Moving from her position near Kul toward her sister Anna begins eavesdropping on the conversation. I never knew what they said to each other. Illiyana grabs the young man by the shoulder spinning him around, though he stands taller than Illiyana. They lock eyes for a brief moment. His smirk turns cold as he eyes her up and down.

"What do you want pet?" He asks. Monotone and cold.

"Is that the nickname you've given me this week Trevor? I'll add it to the list. You'll be my sparring partner today." Illiyana retorts in disgust.

"I have my partner already." He gestures to the crowd. "So you'll just have to play with the rejects. Like your sister."

"How dare you. She is the youngest-"

"Of a failed and dead family. Have you yet realised Illiyana no one cares who you are or what your family did. You'll never be one of us. Go back to teaching her how to land a punch."

Illiyana looks down at her own clenched fists, balled in rage. She takes a second to breath. Small calm breaths. Helping regulate her approach. She unclenches her fists and slumps her shoulders.

"Did I finally leave-" Trevor begins saying before being interrupted.

"Never interrupt me again."

●

Aiden approaches Annastasia from behind tapping her on the shoulder. As she turns around Aiden spins around to face her back again. Laughing to himself he taps on her shoulder again this time staying in place. Anna turns quickly finding Aiden posing. His arms at his side and chest out. They both let out an audible laugh.

"Hey again Aiden." She says

"Looks like you require a partner. I would do my best to fill in." Aiden says bowing before her.

"You want to be my partner?"

"I believe I just said that." Aiden says sarcastically.

"Sorry. Illy went off on her own. It threw me off a little."

"No need to apologise. I understand all too well."

Anna and Aiden walk towards the sparring grounds. A smaller circled off area in the courtyard. Passersby watch briefly as they trot along to their destinations. A few travelers stay and watch the bravest new recruits train in the heart of Providence. Aiden has his back turned to the circle chatting Anna up as they continue. They stop shy hearing a commotion just past the way leading to the sparring grounds. The corner of a building blocking their view of the incident. Screaming and taunting filling the air.

"We need to get over there!" She exclaims.

"Hold on Anna." Aiden says placing his hand across her chest. "We don't need to create extra panic over there. It's best we stay put."

"Stay put? What if someone needs our help?"

Anna bolts off moving just out of Aiden's reach. She crosses the threshold of the building to see Illiyana and Trevor in the sparring circle surrounded by all of the other trainees. Illiyana lay on the ground with Trevor circling around her like an animal. Anna pushes her way to the center of the circle placing herself between her sister and Trevor. He continues to circle around them wiping blood from the corner of his mouth. Anna holds her hand out in stopping motion as Trevor continues to stalk them. Taking her attention away from him she kneels down beside Illiyana as she tries to pick herself up from the ground. Trevor takes advantage of the situation and strikes Illiyana in the ribs dropping her back to the ground. Air escaping as she wheezes for oxygen.

"STOP!" Anna screams at Trevor.

"Or what? You'll go get Kul? Give me a break she deserves every bit of this."

"You don't get to decide what she deserves." Anna barks. Her concern turned to anger.

"That is enough." Kul intervenes as he parts the crowd making his way to the center. "Trevor this is the last time-"

"Whatever. You protect them. They're your golden children. Can do no wrong."

"This is not the attitude I expect from a soldier."

"Shove it old man. Someone had to knock her from her pedestal." Trevor says spitting at the ground. "You know it as well as anyone else. Someone was going to lower her a peg or two."

"So you like to fight?" Anna interjects. Her voice less than cheerful. "Then fight me. You want to show us Arlenko's that we aren't anything. Prove it."

"Anna!" Kul erupts in shock.

"You don't get to beat up my sister and walk away."

"I'm not going to beat up a child."

"I challenge you to a bout Trevor."

"You really want to do this pipsqueak?" Trevor begins to chuckle.

"I made the challenge. Do you accept? Say no and you risk losing your pride."

"Are you taunting me into accepting? You Arlenko's are all the same. All talk and nothing to show for it. Sure I accept." His pride getting the better of him.

"Perfect." Anna says smirking. "I will give you a moment for rest."

"I don't need it." Trevor says smugly.

Phasing through the crowd Annie comes upon an all too familiar scene. She makes her way toward Aiden who muscled his way into the front of the circle. This was not your best day sister. Illiyana returns to her feet with the help of Kul. He helps her return to the edge of the circle next to Aiden. Annastasia stands firm on her half of the circle. Eyes focused. Piercing though Trevor. He begins warming up and stretching across from her. His cohort behind him talking him up, inflating his ego. Trevor starts laughing and points at Anna. Her focused gaze never leaves him as he begins walking a semi circle. Kul returns to the ring. Walking first to Anna.

"Anna. This is not in your best interest." Kul says. "Trevor has been training for a few years."

"Illiyana would do this for me. No one gets away with what he just did."

"I'm just making sure this is what you really want. Canceling a duel is not shameful."

"You don't think I can do this?" She responds. Second guessing herself. Her eyes showing her hesitation.

"Of course I believe you can. I will never second guess your spirit. If you have faith you can do just about anything. I will start the bout."

Kul returns to the center of the ring. He relays the normal rules of a bout. Making sure both opponents understand the terms. Anna and Trevor nod in agreement. The two fighters square off in the center as Kul returns to Illiyana's side. Trevor leans in close to Anna as they begin.

"You'll be just as big of a disappointment to your parents as your sister is." Anna's face turns into twisted shock and is replaced with blank anger as Trevor slaps her across the face. A bright red mark left on her cheek. The embarrassment left behind fades quickly as Trevor goes again to slap her. Annastasia blocks the incoming blow and returns with a slap of her own. This one flooring Trevor with the amount of force behind it.

"Never talk about my parents."

Trevor retreats. Rolling backwards and catching himself on his heels. Anna becomes the aggressor using the basic punch and kick combo taught by Kul. She lands a few mid range blows on Trevor as he regains his guard. As she lands the last punch Trevor grabs her arm and pulls her into his knee knocking the breath out of her lungs. Letting go of her arm Anna drops to the ground. Trevor circles behind her and wait for her to return to her feet. Giving Anna ample time to recuperate. She turns around on the ground, looking up at him. Trevor grabs her by her chin and whispers into her ear.

"When your parents died they might as well have taken their legacy with them."

"You talk too much. You'd be a much better fighter if you just shut up."

Trevor pushes Anna backwards by her face sending her tumbling toward the center of the ring. Anna reels back on her heels as Trevor charges in. In a blink of an eye she changes position slightly. Creating a mirror image of herself to Trevor. As Trevor closes in he grabs ahold of her image. To the rest of the audience Trevor grasp at Anna and missed wildly. Anna twirls around behind Trevor and strikes at the back of his knee. He twists around infuriated for missing her and goes to strike her in the stomach coming up short again allowing Anna a few torso shots. Each blow beginning to weaken his endurance. Trevor squares up with Anna adjusting his guard.

"I'll give you one chance to leave with your ego Trevor."

"Just like your sister."

He throws a punch which Anna easily sidesteps, slapping him across the face. Becoming more irritated Trevor's punches become wild. Striking at air each time. With every blow he misses Anna lands two more into his midsection. After a few repetitive hits Trevor drops his guard to his midsection allowing Anna to capitalize elbowing him across the face. The blow dazes him dropping him to the ground. Anna places her foot on his throat. Pressing gently on his windpipe. Trevor's eyes grow wide as he begins gasping for air.

"I'm not my sister Trevor. Give up." Anna says sternly.

Trevor taps on her leg and Anna releases the pressure. Turning her back to him for approval from Kul. As Anna turns around Trevor hops to his feet eyes wild with anger, reaching out for Anna. Illiyana comes rushing out to her sister as Trevor grabs a handful of Anna's hair and turns her around raising his fist. Illiyana reaches them just in time catching Trevor's arm and retaliating with a right hook laying Trevor out in the ring. Anna embraces Illiyana in a hug, holding her close. Illiyana reciprocates gripping her sister tightly.

"Never turn your back on your opponent. No one fights fair Tasia."

"I. I understand." She stammers.

"Never again. Do you understand? This sort of behavior is unbecoming one of my students. I understand you were protecting Illiyana but you could have been hurt." Kul says. His tone harsh yet fatherly.

"Why did you let her do that?" Illiyana questions.

"Anna invoked a rule I have always stood by. I won't show favoritism by denying her the right I have given everyone else. She has a flame inside her. One to match your competitive spirit. That is not something I can simply stop."

"Do you really mean that Kul?" Anna responds.

"Of course I do. Fighting should be your last method to handle a situation. I do not want a repeat of today. Is that understood?"

"Understood." Anna replies.

"Trevor's punishment is much worse than a stern talking. Illiyana from here on out you will be leading this unit in his absence. A few days for an official change of duties. By weeks end I want you prepared for this job." Kul says. "You are all dismissed." Kul says to the crowd of onlookers.

Leaving towards the tower Kul meets with a few men in soldier like attire. Pausing for a moment in conversation Kul heads off into the tower as the soldiers make way towards Trevor. They help him to his feet. His eyes sunk to the ground below as they pass Illiyana and Anna. From there he is directed into the tower with their assistance.

Illiyana lifts Anna's chin up to make eye contact while straightening out her sister's hair again.

"That was brave of you Anna, i'm glad your ok."

"I couldn't let him hurt you anymore. Are you ok?"

"I'm fine. Let's go to the mall shall we? I think training is done for today."

"Really?"

"I promised. I never break a promise."

The crowd begins to dissipate with trainees packing up their gear. Trevor's friends quickly dispersing in different directions heads hung low. Standing off to the side of the ring Anna watches as her younger self and Illiyana head back to toward their hover. Aiden approaches them as he finishes packing his gear.

"Hey! That was awesome!" Aiden says excitedly. "Anna the Trevor slayer."

"Eh. The title could use some work but thanks!" Anna responds her cheery demeanor finding itself returning.

"Anytime. You'll have to teach me how you do that."

"Do what?"

"Bob and weave like that. You were magical. He couldn't touch you."

"It's all instinct really. You'll get there Aiden. I would stay and chat but I have a date with the mall." Anna says backing up slowly heading back to the hover.

"It's all good. I'll catch you around." Aiden responds, his face flush.

●

The magician stands in the center of the ring watching from afar her subsequent dialogue with Aiden. Anna swoops down touching the ground of the ring below. So many hours here. So many good memories. Searching around she spots something out of place from her memory. Another hover landing just down the way from her. A darker shade of black almost void of color. Appearing out of thin air. The door opens lifting up from the hover. A figure appears beside the hover draped in a dark hooded coat which sinks into the ground boots protruding from underneath. The figure stares directly at Anna sending chills down her spine. Motionless it peers at her with its eyeless figure. Unable to break eye contact Annastasia blinks. In that instant the hover disappears into nowhere. The ghostly visage vanishing as well. A heavy breathing rings through Anna's ear freezing her in place. Feeling it's dreadful aura Anna turns to face the faceless getting lost in it's void. Cold dead fingers grab her shoulder as it continues to breath in her face. To her surprise it's breath is warm and odorless.

"Can I help you?' Anna asks raising an eyebrow.

"Wa..ke. Up. Wake..up. Wake UP. WAKE UP. WAKE UP!" It screams in her face.

Chapter Five

Intentions

Anna's eyes snap open and immediately surveys the area. A look of shock and awe struck across her face mixes with the frantic feeling of her search. Looking for any sign of intrusion, beginning to come up empty handed yet again. Removing herself from bed she looks at the clock on her dresser. Six forty-five in the morning. Only slept for a few hours. Anna reaches out to her dresser and begins dressing accordingly for the morning. Tan shorts. A white low cut shirt. While dressing she begins humming a tune and tapping her foot. Trying her hardest to forget the end of her dream.

Going to her tea cabinet she begins rummaging through the different flavors. Mango passionfruit. No caffeine. Yeah not this morning. Digging to the back she removes a box labelled "Oasis nights" written in black marker on a white box. Opening the box Anna finds only three bags left. I guess i'll have to use this cautiously. Pulling one bag from its container Anna begins to boil some water. She places a cup under the machine. Waiting what feels like an eternity for the water to pour.

Walking away from the machine she turns to her desk and the cup left upon it. The string left draped outside left as a reminder of its now chilled contents. Never drink cold tea. Anna removes the cup from her desk. Setting it down beside her tea drawer she returns to the now beeping machine. Taking the cup from its position she steeps her new brew into the steaming water. An aroma of ginger and lemon perforate the air. The mixture does a kindness to the sense of smell. Smiling Anna returns to her desk and sits down, taking in the pleasant perfume.

Taking time to relax and recall the events of her dream from moments ago Anna leans back in her chair, sipping from the cup. Memories continue to flood through her mind. The training yard with the blackened hover. The hooded man screaming in her ear. No mistake it's similar to the man in Bourbon and a Brawl. What are you trying to tell me subconscious? Who's coming? Anna lets out a sudden chuckle as she realizes she cannot answer her own questions. Leaning forward in her chair Anna removes the files from her desk drawer again. This time searching through them meticulously. Pulling a section from its binding she traces a finger down the page Anna stops on a line.

"Bingo." She blurts out. "If you're looking for a ghost where would you start? A handler. Who are you Mind and what is your plan?"

Reading through the small section on the teams dossier again she finds mention of him twice. One of them a longer read than a heading on a dossier. You didn't like Audrey. It's apparent. Claiming she wasn't skilled enough for a spec ops group but my beautiful ex overruled you. Odd. I'll have to find more out about you. Something other than a code name.

Closing the documents Anna shoves them back into the drawer. Anna takes a long drink of her tea before moving onward from her desk towards the entrance. Walking past the mantle as she exits Anna picks out the Arcadian ring and places it on a necklace. She palms the necklace and puts it in her pocket before walking out from her room toward the stage. The dimmed lights leading outward in the early hours of the morning break through the curtain. Anna strolls through the area as she has so many times stopping at the sound of laughter coming from the front of the bar. Sipping casually from her tea she sneaks her way to the curtain. Leaving the slightest gap Anna peers through an opening to find Xylen and his mystery date relaxing around the countertop. The redhead pours a drink out into the sink as they converse. His demeanor relaxed and inviting as his smile seems to brighten up even Anna's mood. The woman at the countertop seems intent on listening to his monologue. Leaning in close, hanging on his words. Her short dark hair beginning to hang low from the night beforehand. Losing its textured look. Her hands propped under her head as she stares enthralled with her dates stories. Her rebellious choice of clothing eye catching. Jeans ripped with a tattered black shirt to match. Her toned physique showing through the tears in her clothing. Anna moves to a better vantage point as to can continue eavesdropping on her friend. Moving to the edge of the curtain by the bar she focuses on listening to their conversation.

"Am I rambling? Tell me i'm not." He says looking into her eyes.

"You aren't. It's actually quite interesting. The whole hand motions and everything. You really are the character you put over on stage." She responds. Curiosity in her tone.

"The best character to be is yourself." Xylen quips. His bright smile beaming. "Speaking of characters. We've been playing parts all night and I don't even know your name mystery girl."

"I could give you any name I want. You'd have to take me at my word. Sometimes being yourself is dangerous."

"Are you dangerous?" Xylen asks. Propping himself up on the countertop.

"The worst kind. I'm a mystery."

"Every mystery can be solved."

"Who even talks like that?" She laughs, brushing her black hair to the side.

"Detectives on vids?"

"Are you using your detective skills on me?"

"Answering my question that I answered with a question. Touche." Xylen arches his eyebrow eliciting another laugh from his mystery date. "After that pause that's when you give in and tell me your name."

"Oh is it?" She says imitating shock.

"It totally should be." Xylen replies running a hand through her hair.

"You're infallibly cute Xylen. I'm Audrey."

"Well Audrey, it's a pleasure to finally meet you. There was this nice girl saying all kinds of pleasant things about you. She seemed to have disappeared. Funny thing is she sat in the exact same stool."

Listening from behind the curtain Anna raises an eyebrow. Audrey. Tabitha said her team died. What is she playing at. Anna keeps to herself behind the curtain. Content to allow their conversation to play out in it's own manner.

"What did she say about me?" Audrey questions.

"Well. For starters she said I was to be so lucky to be out with you tonight. That the green of your eyes pierces even the deepest of hearts and I should watch out because you are dangerous."

Xylen's smile morphs into a half smirk. Confidently he looks deeply into her eyes to gauge the reaction. Audrey's green eyes gleam reflecting his image in them as she quickly creates her own smile. Genuine and innocent. She rests her hand on top of his grabbing ahold timidly, unsure of her own response.

"I am dangerous." She replies. Her voice taking a serious tone. "I shouldn't even be here."

"Then everything that other woman said would have to be true. She didn't mention you leaving so early. I haven't even made breakfast yet. Yes it's pancakes. No I don't have your favorite syrup."

"You're a good talker." Audrey chuckles between her words.

"It's what I got hired for. Bartending is more Finn's domain. With him drinking and all. You should stay."

"Xylen-"

"Audrey."

"Shut up." Audrey says laughingly. "My friend wouldn't be too pleased with me being here all night."

"Are you having a good time?" Xylen says leaning in closer.

"Yes." Audrey quickly replies.

"Shame on your friend then. They should be happy for you."

"Work before pleasure Xylen."

Anna walks through the curtain tea grasped firmly in her hand. Making her way down from the stage she makes her presence known to the both of them. Xylen's eyes light up another smile runs across his face. He motions towards Anna, inviting her behind the bar. Audrey turns toward the magician as she passes by, sipping from her now lukewarm tea. As they make eye contact Audrey looks away averting her gaze and narrowing her eyes. Giving a once over Anna nods to Xylen before crossing the threshold to the back of the bar. She leans up against the countertop setting her tea to the side. Audrey returns her focus back to Xylen, a shy smile plastered across her face. He darts his gaze between them, breaking the silence with the sound of his laughter.

"Morning." Anna says brightly.

"Hey there!" Xylen replies. "How was the night out?"

"It went well." Anna replies laughing. "As to be expected with that duo. Am I interrupting something special?"

"No." Audrey responds quickly. "I was just telling Xylen I had to leave."

"I was trying to tell her to stay for my pancakes. She isn't having any of it."

"I'm really not hungry." Audrey quips.

"He really does make the best pancakes." Anna adds.

"I'm sure he does." Audrey responds retracting her hand from atop Xylen's. "I just have work to get to and all. Nothing crazy, just a day job."

Xylen furls his eyebrow as Audrey begins to rapidly pack a few items left upon the counter. Anna relaxes herself letting her shoulders down and her guard drop. She lets out a small sigh before interrupting Audrey's exit.

"Stay for breakfast miss Kemple. Your employer is upstairs. No need to leave so soon."

The atmosphere changes as the air thickens around the trio. Audrey freezes in shock from the statement, her eyes darting to the ground in panic. Xylen tilts his head questioning both her reaction and Anna's statement. His hands rest upon the counter propping himself up. His eyes marred with confusion. The silent exchange gives Anna more confidence and conflict. The body language radiating from Audrey speaks volumes where her words fall flat. Rubbing the back of her neck Anna raises her head to look at Audrey, taking another sip of tea. Looking at the immobilized girl Anna reaches her hand across the counter offering Audrey a kind gesture.

"I'm Annastasia Arlenko. It's a pleasure to meet you."

Audrey's eyes trace their way up the bar to Anna's open hand. Lost deep in her own thoughts she blinks rapidly, processing the sight before her. A timid handshake is exchanged as Audrey extends her hand toward Anna. Xylen shares a questioning glance with the two ladies, still speechless.

"You are everything she said you would be." Audrey remarks confidently. "Everything."

"Thank you." Anna says with a smile. "Will you stay for breakfast?"

"Of course." Audrey replies.

"What in the nine sectors is going on?" Xylen says, finding his words.

"I-" Audrey begins.

"We'll get to that in time Xylen." Anna says interrupting Audrey. "For now a nice breakfast between new friends is all that's important."

"Right." Xylen replies. His tone lost yet confident. "Strawberry pancakes it is. I'm just going to let you two have this awkward conversation."

Xylen retreats from behind the bar toward a side door. His hands thrown in the air as he mutters under his breath. Sorry Xylen. The door swings shut behind him. Anna returns her attention back to Audrey's mesmerized stare.

"I hope you like strawberries." Anna remarks.

"They're fine by me." Audrey says easing back into her chair. "Your performance was great last night. I've never seen anything quite like it."

"I'm glad you enjoyed. I've been told it's one of a kind. Would you like some juice? Tea?"

"I heard you prefer tea."

"It's not about what I prefer."

"I assume we're not talking about a drink." Audrey retorts.

"All in how you perceive it. You're too tense. Relax." Anna says. Her words soothing.

"I wasn't trained to relax."

"I'm not a hostile." Anna responds. "These short sentences? All it's doing is drawing the conversation out. Xylen is my friend Audrey-"

"I would never hurt him." Audrey snaps.

"Never said you would. Guilt is a hell of a thing. Makes you say what you think I want to hear. You were in my bar on the same night as Tabitha. No coincidence. Why were you here?"

"Reconnaissance."

"You're going to have to be a bit more specific than that."

"On you. I'm supposed to keep an eye on you."

"Xylen doesn't know anything does he?"

"To him i'm a small town girl plucked up and brought to Providence. No real friends and nowhere to be."

"He knows differently now. Our conversation has brought that to light. Do you know anything about him?"

"Only what Tabitha told me. You were all friends at one time. Then you both split. She went military and you became a ghost. He was just an upstart when the team broke up. Computer smart and business savvy."

With a small ruckus the door to the kitchen opens. Xylen walks through propping the door open with his left foot. Warm strawberries and syrup permeate the air. Their rich smells wafting through the Eldritch Flame. The ever present smile brightly shining as he makes way for the counter. Three large plates of pancakes balance in his hands, a mountain of pancake and strawberries on each. Setting them down on the counter he hands out three forks. His attention drawn to Anna as she smiles wide in his direction.

"Ta da! Make sure to tip your waiter after the meal." Xylen bellows comically. "Pancakes the way mom made them."

"This looks amazing!" Audrey exclaims.

"Aren't you glad you stayed?" Xylen replies.

"Yes." She responds with glee.

"I think we owe you an explanation." Anna says returning to the conversation. "I took a job. Just so happens Audrey here is also taking the same job."

Each of them dig into their meal, toppling the strawberry towers. Xylen watches as they begin eating, quickly making way on each dish. He slowly begins working on his own meal, keeping their conversation in mind.

"A job?" Xylen questions between bites. "Aren't we leaving for Syndros tonight?"

"You three will be. I have to work."

"How did you get roped into this Audrey?" He continues. Pointing at her with his fork.

"I told you i'm dangerous." Audrey replies, taking a moment's break from her pancakes. "My employer has employed yours. We need her help."
"With what?" Xylen asks.

"Stopping a government from releasing a plague." Audrey says continuing to eat.

"Well isn't that- Wait. A plague? Anna you can't be serious. Tell them no." His happy demeanor giving way to exasperation.

"I can't Xylen. If what they say is true- I can't let Providence down."

76

"Then go tell Kul. This isn't our business. We've done our service to this planet."

"That's selfish and you know it. Over the last five years we've touched the hearts of this city. They are all apart of our family. I won't let something happen if I can help stop it."

Each plate lay bare on the table after their short conversation. Reaching down underneath the counter Anna grabs the kettle of tea and pours herself another batch. Xylen lets loose a drawn out sigh as he places his hands on his waist. Removing herself from the tabletop Audrey moves around to the side, leaning on its end, staring into Xylen's eyes. As they connect, a door slams shut upstairs echoing throughout the room and down onto the stage floor. Slow and deliberate steps reverberate down the long hallway.

"You make a compelling argument Anna. I know how much you love home. Did you think it over at least?" Xylen questions watching the second floor cautiously.

"I did. They came to me last night before I left with Finn and Claudette. I told them you wouldn't be involved. That I can't risk my team." Anna says, brushing off the echoing noise. "I'll be contacting my- Kul. I'll be contacting Kul and informing him what this paramilitary group has planned. We'll proceed from there."

The haunting noise continues it's repetition growing louder as they enter the staircase. Each step monotonous. Xylen's sight fixated on the position of the staircase. Waiting to see what manner of person this could be. Audrey grabs ahold of his right hand and squeezes down gently, replacing his fear with warmth. He averts his focus to her and smiles tensely. Anna rests herself on the countertop, drinking from her new cup of tea. Each sip growing larger. A voice echoes outward into the open floor, filling the room with disquiet.

"You two look wonderful together." Tabitha's voice rings clearly through the air. "And here you are Annastasia with no one to hold your hand."

"If I were five I would be concerned Tabitha. Good morning." Anna returns.

Their exchange continues as everything slows to a crawl. Xylen's heartbeat and pulse quickens. He stares onward at Tabitha as though she were a ghost of his past and not an able body standing before him. Tabitha saunters out from the shadows, through the traffic of tables and chairs. For every step forward Xylen retreats little by little until his back meets the wall. Shooting a sly grin in his direction Tabitha sits in the chair closest to Anna.

"I-I-" Xylen stammers unable to hide his loss of words.

"Adorable." Tabitha quips.

"You shouldn't be here." Xylen says. "This is your job? This psychopath?"

"I prefer sociopath if you feel like name calling." Tabitha says.

"We are not getting into the semantics of my choice here nor are we recreating our history. I think you should show Audrey a bit more of our fair city Xylen. Get some fresh air while I discuss business." Anna cuts short the argument.

"I don't think Audrey should leave." Tabitha calmly says.

"I don't care what you think." Anna responds in kind.

"Fine. Take her along with you. We really are going to have to work on the terms of this agreement unless you like dancing with two left feet." Tabitha relents.

Xylen finds his way toward Audrey avoiding eye contact with Tabitha. His gaze directed only at Audrey. Without a word he grabs her hand and heads toward the entrance swiftly, held up by Audrey's own hesitation. She looks back at to the counter, finding Anna and Tabitha engaged in their own quarrel. Seeking some sort of approval she waits, not even budging at Xylen's continuous urging. Tabitha turns toward the couple nodding toward Audrey, a twisted smile strung across her face, giving her approval.

"You may go Audrey." Tabitha says. An eerily soothing tone whispered in

Audrey's direction.

Nodding in response Audrey takes her leave from the Eldritch Flame with Xylen in tow. A calm comes over the building. The confusion and anger subsiding as the door slams shut. Tabitha stares deeply into the eyes of her former lover. Her arrogant smirk muted as she peers into the blue, losing herself in their beauty.

"Must you ruin my fun? It's a family reunion." Tabitha questions.

"Generally when the nieces and nephews become uncomfortable, you send them out to play."

"Do you have a book of witty remarks or have you just gotten better at this?"

"I just get better with age."

"I'll have to take your word for it. Unless of course you'd like to prove that to me." Tabitha says leaning in closer to Anna.

"I could. Though this tease is much more exhilarating." Anna says running her finger up Tabitha's chin.

"I take what I want. You of all people know this." Tabitha replies through clenched teeth.

"Then what are you waiting for?"

Fighting her basic urges Tabitha relents, resting back in the chair. Her eyes still left gazing into Anna's, a hint of regret flickers as she blinks the thoughts away. Calm and composed Anna continues taunting Tabitha. Her eyes like mirrors reflecting Tabitha's own stare. A devilish grin appears as Tabitha backs away from an easy temptation. An air of confidence surrounds Anna as she finishes her tea. Turning from Tabitha she sets the cup off to the side, leaving herself purposefully vulnerable.

"You temptress." Tabitha mutters.

"I prefer magician if you're going to resort to name calling." Anna quips.

A moment of silence falls between the two as Anna returns to her previous space. Projecting confidence in her body language toward Tabitha.

Leaning over Anna makes wide eyes in her direction forcing an eye roll followed by a long sigh.

"Magician." Tabitha says dryly.

"You called?" Anna wittily responds.

"Stop. It."

"Not as confident as last night now that we have equal advantage I see."

"I wish I could see you shaken every night."

"You've only seen me shaken once. It wasn't last night."

"I never saw you that night-"

"Why did you leave?" Anna interrupts. Her face growing stern. "I needed you."

"You're so beautiful when you're angry. It brings out the best in you. I have my reasons for leaving and i'm not about to topple your perfect tower again. It was what was best for us." Tabitha coldly replies.

"Best for you." Anna snaps.

"No."

"Abandoning me-"

"Was the best thing I could do. I'm a poison and everything I touch is infected. This problem, I made this. You have become so much more than what we ever were. I don't want to infect you too." Tabitha says softly.

"You have always seen the darker side of yourself. Over these years it's only amplified to an undetermined amount. I know you. The woman you are. You are tough as nails and a master of your craft but you will never be my poison."

"That's touching. I'm sure many years ago that would have won me over. Made me stay but now I know the difference. I'm made for killing. It's my business and I do it well."

"I don't buy that for a second."

"I'm not selling it." Tabitha says dryly.

"You're so hot and cold. Tabitha, I want you here. No need for this wall between us. This mission is important and we'll get to the bottom of this. I promise you, we'll stop them."

Anna's eyes pierce through Tabitha, staring into her open heart. Like an ocean's wave they come crashing through her defenses. A stillness settles in the Eldritch Flame. For a moment Tabitha's burning passion subsides, finding serenity in each other's company. Anna takes this moment to move around the bar to Tabitha's side keeping an arm's length between them, erring on the side of caution.

"I don't know what I want." Tabitha says under her breath, trailing off in thought.

"When you find out i'd like to know. For now, let's keep our head in the game. That file you gave me. I had a few questions."

"Go ahead." Tabitha says snapping back into the conversation.

"Who's Mind?"

"He's who formed our division. The man who backed my personal vision and made it a reality. I never saw his face. Always hid behind a mask. Talked real deep, heavy. Like it was hard to breath. He only ever came in person for the final test. Where he killed my team."

"Except Audrey."

"I had an "Anna" moment. Had a feeling that the last location was too rural for us. We had beyond perfected this disease, no reason to test it on a low populated area. We needed widespread panic and results. I told Audrey to run. I was right."

"She seems nice. I'm glad to rub off on you even if you'll never admit that again."

Anna closes in on Tabitha, wrapping her arm tightly around her shoulder and pulling her closer. Closing her eyes tightly Tabitha lays her head upon Anna's arm resting it in the crux of her elbow. Both parties relaxing in their shared embrace.

"This is acceptable." Tabitha remarks.

"I know."

Taking a deep breath the scent of cherry blossoms fills her senses. Tabitha looks up into Anna's peaceful eyes, exhaling as she finds her own center.

"I don't know how you do it. You always find a way."

"I'm a magician. My secrets will never be shared."

"Every situation could look bleak but here you are with the perfect answer. Your social awareness, an arm around the shoulder, the perfect vantage point, words that cut through all the bravado. You just know."

"It's never easy. I try to be the person I need to be when the situation arises. Let everything flow. Never lean back or give your opponent a second to respond and most importantly your heart must be in it. Everything comes from there. My words, thoughts, movements. Without it i'm a violinist with a stage show."

"I could listen to you speak all day." Tabitha says. An arrogant smirk crossing her face.

"I wish I had the luxury of time."

"The great magician has work to do, people to sway and babies to kiss."

"Two out of three isn't bad."

Lifting her head from it's resting place Tabitha faces forward, returning her hair to its straightened fashion. Letting out a small sigh of frustration she turns towards Anna. They share a glimpse of each other as Anna parts Tabitha's hair, pulling it behind her ears. Smiling and without words Anna turns towards the door leaving Tabitha bewildered and craving more attention. Tabitha begins to say something and stops herself, second guessing her own gesture. Content with letting Anna walk away she rests her elbows upon the counter, leaning back, as she watches the magician exit. I think this is going to work. Anna turns, giving another smile to a satisfied Tabitha.

"I'm going to the Heart. Hopefully I can win them over."

"Work your magic."

"This is a bit of a tougher crowd."

"Do I have to use your name as an adjective?"

"I will certainly not be "Annaing" them" Anna says, chuckling.

"When you put it that way. It could mean a lot of different things to different people."

"I'm not about to find out which version they prefer." Anna says exiting the Eldritch Flame.

The whir of engines and the chaos of packed city streets fill the Eldritch Flame with cacophony. People rushing past, proceeding toward their destinations. Anna melds into the crowd as she closes the door, leaving Tabitha to her own devices.

CHAPTER SIX

ERR IT OUT

Left alone Tabitha takes in this new silence, the last of this city echoes quieting to a murmur. The Eldritch Flame lay bare to her, open for her own wandering. Shaking loose the memories dredged up merely moments ago Tabitha rises from the seat and looks around to the stage neatly packed of all its decorations. The bar floor swept clean, it's tables and chairs neatly pushed together. Strolling past the stage Tabitha passes the curtain to the back area. Everything in place, packed up and ready to go. She begins running her hand down the side of the wall, passing by the familiar markings Anna had earlier.

"Forever and a day." She mutters underneath her breath. "Forever came early."

Continuing until she reaches Anna's bedroom door, her hands tracing the grooves in the wall along the way. As she reaches for the door hesitation sets in, leaving her unable to press forward. Her mind races with old emotions both distressing and pleasant. Each argument and the hurtful words said. Every smile and words left unspoken. Her hand wavers in front of the door completely unsure of her own decision.

A slam emanates from the entryway, rippling it's way through the backstage. Footsteps like lead weights bound through the Eldritch Flame. Their effect felt even behind the padded curtain. Tabitha returns from her thoughts, disgruntled by the distraction. Turning her attention toward the slow moving sound she removes her hand from in front of Anna's door, focusing herself on the steps.

"One set. Slow and deliberate." Said under her breath. "How did he track me?"

The repetition of movement continues. Each step heavier as she focuses intently upon it. Their plodding speed staying consistent, routine. Surveying her surroundings Tabitha recalls a service exit leading back out to the front entrance. Deftly, Tabitha makes for the doorway keeping her ears keen on the continuing sound. Crossing the threshold of the doorway Tabitha continues along the side wall closest to the bar top. Reaching the corner quietly Tabitha draws in silence again, the footsteps having come to a halt. Tabitha draws her sidearm, hid discreetly underneath her leather jacket. Squaring up alongside the wall Tabitha dips her head out.

Back turned in the opposite direction stand a man. His hair short and dark, shoulders raised and back arched. His demeanor is off putting, a general sense of hurry and anger. A rushed search of his character gives little information to her. No visible weaponry and an absent sense of perception.

"They sent an amatuer." Tabitha again mutters.

Keeping her profile low to the ground she weaves between tables expertly, her feet swift and hushed. Reaching the gentleman intruder, Tabitha raises her gun toward the back of his head. Clicking off the safety and racking the chamber Tabitha holds enough distance between her and her would be assailant. His hands go into the air, an instinctual reaction to the sound.

"Good boy." Tabitha mocks. "You know the sound of your future. Move and I shoot you, talk out of turn and i'll turn your head into paste and most importantly if you so much as look at me i'll rearrange your entire anatomy."

"Dat really paints a picture Tabby. Glad ta know ya are still a sadistic bitch. Oh, I talked outta turn. Ya gunna have to threaten me again. Make dis one convincin." A familiar voice quips.

Hearing Finn's voice takes Tabitha aback. The hesitation being all Finn needs to disarm Tabitha of her firearm, quickly spinning and ripping the weapon from her hands. Surprised further at his speed Tabitha takes a few steps back, assessing the situation. Looking down at the weapon Finn ejects the clip and unloads the remaining round in the chamber, setting the emptied gun on the table beside him. Finn glares in Tabitha's direction, a building fury in his eyes.

"If ya gonna hold a weapon, ya best be prepared ta kill with it."

"A couple seconds longer and I wouldn't be having this conversation." Tabitha says leaving her guard up.

"Shame. Hesitations da real killer here." Finn remarks.

"Why are you here?"

"I live here, love. Real question is why in the living fuck are ya here?" Finn says pausing. "Don't waste ya breath, Xylen told me. Ya come to take my Annie away."

"You're a caveman Finn. You wouldn't understand what is even going on, nor have you cared about anyone before this. Don't give me that goddamn crusader speech it doesn't fit your ego."

"Who da fuck are ya ta tell me what I am. Last I know ya was a traitor. Fittin though, you're da kind ta stab ya own lover in da back."

Without thought Tabitha lunges forward striking Finn across the face. Moving with the blow Finn stands statuesque, allowing her to put her full force into it. Reeling back for another attack Tabitha unleashes a flurry of blows directed towards Finn. His combat expertise allows him to sidestep her first few attempts. The last few strikes find their way into Finn's readied hands. He briskly pushes her away from him, holding back his urge to counter her rushed frenzy. His relaxed treatment of Tabitha only serves to drive her further into a rage. Clenching her fist and gritting her teeth Tabitha readies herself. A smile creeps across Finn's face, arrogant and prideful. His left hand outstretched beckoning Tabitha forth.

"Struck a nerve. Let's see how many more I can rattle. Ya never deserved her just like ya don't deserve her kindness now."

Tabitha's face twists, his comments digging deep into her core, enraging her further. Honing her instincts she presses forward, seeing red. A flourish of jabs keeps Finn on his heels as she continues to push him backwards. Every attempt connecting with Finn's quickened hands, as he artfully moves through her advance. Distracted with her lightning quick jabs Finn misjudges her approach allowing Tabitha to close the gap between them landing an elbow in his solar plexus, driving the wind from his lungs.

"You think you have all the answers. That i'm just an easy read. I never asked for your opinion and I honestly don't give a fuck Finn." Tabitha says regaining her composure. "While you're gasping for you're next breath think about what you want to say real carefully. If it wasn't for Anna it would be your last."

"Fuck. You. Cunt." Finn says, his breathing normalizing.

"Inspiring." Tabitha says rolling her eyes. "I'm done with this. If you're not on board then get out of my sight."

Sauntering her way behind the bar Tabitha gives her back to Finn, enticing him to retaliate. Bringing his breathing under control Finn gives chase to Tabitha, watching her closely as she crosses behind the bar. Grabbing two glasses from underneath the countertop Tabitha grabs a bottle of Finn's favorite whiskey, Iron Will, and pours between the two cups. Finishing the drink with a few ice cubes she slides it over to Finn's waiting hand. Looking down at the contents of the cup Finn reaches his way behind the counter, grabbing another bottle of spirits. With one finger he moves the cup away from himself back towards his rival. Finn lays his side to the counter keeping an eye on Tabitha as he uncaps the pourer to drink straight from the bottle.

"Iron Will isn't your favorite anymore?" Tabitha says condescendingly. "Isn't it cultural for the victor to pour the loser a drink on that backwards planet you call a home?"

"Sure." Finn says between drinks. "Ya have ta lose for dat to happen. I ain't lost yet."

"Of course you haven't. Wouldn't want to tarnish that perfect record you have going. If you aren't going to drink it i'll be more than glad to." Tabitha retorts, swiping the drink from the counter.

"Ya are a fuckin piece of work but you know dat. What gives ya the right ta fuck up my retirement?"

"Oh. Just like your boss, right to business. I'm not going to go over the details more than once so listen real close."

Finn swallows his sentence in the bottle of alcohol, drowning out the shrill voice in front of him with a constant stream of liquor. As she continues on with her speech Finn drifts further away from the conversation, caring little for what she actually has to say.

"Dat's all real nice. Ya gunna save Providence from a epidemic or whatever. You seem to have forgotten the last time you ran an op like dis. I member. Let me paint da picture for ya.Seein as ya weren't there ta witness it. It was a dark night, heavy rainfall. Rescue op. Save Natela Leto-"

"I remember-"

"Fuck off I ain't finished. Save Natela. We did dat alright, all the way until our evac never showed up. Ya never came." Finn curtly says taking another swig from his alcohol. "Natela died because ya weren't ta bother showin ya face. What makes this matter any different? Karma is a bitch and ya done finally got yours."

"I'm glad she died."

For a moment time stands still between them, her words echoing off the walls of the Eldritch Flame. For the first time Finn is left speechless. His mouth wired shut as he stares blankly toward Tabitha, taking in her cold emotionless demeanor. She shoots back her drink slamming the glass on the counter.

"I did you a favor. That was one less head to count, one less mouth to feed. A faster retirement for you. You're welcome." Tabitha comments, cutting the still air.

"The fuck ya did. Ya nothin but a self righteous twat." Finn spits out, slamming his bottle onto the counter.

"Didn't your beautiful Claudette join in my place?"

"Don't ya even dare."

"I gave you everything you wanted. If I was still here you would be an afterthought. A toy to be used and discarded at our pleasure. Face it Finn. You owe me your happiness and I can take it away from you whenever I choose."

"Well den, let's finish what we started ya. I'll make an exception to a rule just for ya." Finn states, backing away from the counter.

"I'm quite comfortable back here." Tabitha says pouring another drink from a different type of liquor. "This bar really does have the best selection in town. Remind me to give my compliments to the bartender."

"Take the piss why don't ya? This ain't some game for ya ta play. Play little miss badass all ya want but my foots down, ya not taking her on ya excursion."

"You have no choice. She can make adult decisions all by herself. I'm doubting the fact you're able to though."

Finn snatches the bottle he placed on the counter, whipping it past Tabitha's head into a shelf of neatly placed alcohol. Shattering on impact, shards fall to the floor in a cacophony of broken glass. Without flinching Tabitha rests her hand on her hip, a look of displeasure replacing the growing smugness.

"This little exchange is cute." Tabitha says, sipping from her new drink. "Do you throw a tantrum every time you don't get your way? I'm not backing down, neither is she. See past yourself for once and do the damn job."

"Why would I ever do something for ya? I see not one fuckin reason to trust ya."

"You dolt i'm not asking you to trust me. I'm asking you to trust the same person you've put your faith in for nine years. How hard is it to see this is important?" Tabitha says growing agitated.

"Retirement sounds better-"

"There will be no retirement when they're done!" Tabitha exclaims. "This outbreak will destroy everything. Entire ecosystems will crumble in its wake. That's just day one. I'll spare you the scientific terminology, it will spread to everyone you've ever cared about, slept with, drank with. EVERYONE. In record time it will turn their entire being into excruciating agony and eventually leading to a harrowing death. Thick skull or not you can't punch your way out of this, unless you help her steal this disease."

Tabitha slams the cup onto the counter for emphasis. She stares directly into Finn's eyes as he paces back and forth, acting like a caged and cornered animal. His demeanor holds nothing to the fury in his eyes. Like a burning pyre he stares through her to the alcohol stained shelving. Letting go his breath, Finn stands tall unclenching his fists.

"You ain't lyin…" Finn dejectedly says.

"I've never lied Finn." Tabitha quickly responds.

"What if I just say fuck it and leave with Dette?"

"Then you leave. Simple as that. Enjoy your vacation because if we fail there will be no way of stopping Frostscythe."

"So… This is the way ya sold it to Annie. Survival or death. Nothin in between. I don't have a choice. Do I?"

"Choice is an illusion of convenience. You pick to fight or run. The options are slim and neither guarantee survival. You can choose, but the choice is not up for debate."

Finn relaxes his posturing, coming to terms with the proposition laid before him. Tabitha's smug smile returns as she rolls out two more glasses and another bottle of whiskey, labelled Leighton's Brew. Pouring between the two glasses Tabitha fills both to the brim, sliding one towards Finn gingerly. Hesitantly Finn drinks from the cup, careful not to waste any of its contents. Tabitha responds in kind taking a long sip from her cup. Shaking his head Finn grins devilishly.

"Cheers bitch." Finn says, raising his glass to Tabitha.

"To our continued health." Tabitha says smiling. "I'll let her know you'll be joining us."

"Ya do dat."

A ringing of glassware commemorates their unique toasts. Both parties drink the remaining liquor before returning their cups turned upside down onto the counter. Finn clears his throat and turns away, moving towards exit.

"Pleasure doing business with you mister Leighton."

"It's more like a fuckin then business and don't get me wrong I do enjoy my fair share of dat, but I generally have to like the person for it ta be enjoyable. Ya just leave a bad taste in the mouth." Finn retorts.

Pausing in the doorway Finn turns halfway, raising a middle finger in Tabitha's direction before exiting the Eldritch Flame.

Chapter Seven

City of Dreams

High above the city of Providence Anna looks out to the bustle of traffic and tips of skyscrapers below. A wide smile spreads across her face as she watches her fair city from atop its highest tower. Taking in its grand sights for the first time in what seems like ages. Hovers fly freely in and out of the tower beneath her. A never ending line of traffic streaming from the mouth of Providence. Glancing back she notices dignitaries stepping out from their hovers. Their demeanor rushed as they pass off their belongings to an attendant. They group together making busy talk amongst each other as they make way for the stairway. A husband and wife break off from the group and make their way to the balcony beside Anna. Both wide-eyed and whispering to each other. Their first time here. Making gestures between themselves they burst into genuine laughter. Anna's smile turns to a smirk as she returns to look out at the beautiful scenery. Squinting she looks for her own personal slice of home among the many nondescript buildings below.

"I think that's me." She says aloud.

"Hum?" The excited couple responds inquisitively, turning to face Anna.

"I think I live right down that way past the rail track. My sister says you can see my house from here. I think she cheats and uses a hololens though."

"We're looking for our home as well." Says the wife.

"On the oceanfront. We're from the smaller area of Kaelinds." He chimes in.

"Oh Kaelinds. You want to be on the south side of the tower for a better look."

"Really?" They say in unison.

"Totally. North gives you a beautiful view of the mountain range, east and west amazing to watch at night if only just for the light show and south is a stunning view of your home."

"Thanks!" The lady quickly retorts.

She pulls her husband from his relaxed position on the rail toward an entrance to the south end of the tower. A small laugh escapes Anna as she mouths the words 'you're welcome'. Turning from the railing herself she heads toward the staircase leading inside.

The interior of the tower matches its bright and shining exterior. Exposed metal walls give it a military feel, though the light flowing along the corridors makes it warm and inviting. The main passage is kept free of most visitors at this level keeping the clamor to a minimum. At the entryway stands a younger man dressed formally, his focus drawn to the tablet firmly planted in his hand.

"Welcome to terminal one." He says. His voice almost robotic. "Are you here by appointment? Or by invitation for the assembly of thought?"

"I've come to see Kul Forsworn."

"He is currently meeting with a head of Sector 5. I see no further appointments on his ledger for today. I'm sorry miss…"

"Annastasia." She replies almost chuckling.

"Miss Annastasia. I'm sorry for the confusion. May have been a clerical error in our computer system. I will put in a petition for a meeting with him before he is to head off to the assembly." He says hastily typing away on his tablet.

"No need. I'll just go make a visit. He won't be bothered. Much." Anna says holding in laughter as she walks past the attendant. "Nothing like surprise visit."

"Ma'am." The clerk says courteously. "With all do respect you cannot just walk into his office."

Looking up from his tablet he sees Anna strolling aimlessly down the corridor looking at the art pieces adorning the walls. He scrambles to catch up with her. His clumsy walk leaves him lagging behind slightly.

"Miss. Excuse me." He says, placing a hand on her shoulder gently.

"You're excused." Anna retorts, spinning to be face to face with him.

"You cannot just make a meeting with our lord. It must be arranged and accepted before he will even see you. Again I am sorry for the confusion but we have to follow proper channels."

"Well then-" Anna says playing up the role. "I would suggest you give me someone with the proper authority to approve this matter. I believe I spoke with sector commander Illiyana Arlenko about the matter. Comm her to this location."

"As you wish ma'am." A sly smirk rolls across his face. "I assure you Lady Arlenko is very busy and has requested not to be disturbed. This may not be the best course of action."

"While I understand that, this matter is of utmost urgency. I'm sure she will be keen to resolve this dispute." Anna continues. Her smile almost giving up the deception.

"Very well."

The young man works away on his tablet. His smile widening as he types in the information given to him. Anna stands there curtly tapping her foot as she waits for his response. A moment passes as he awaits a response, though it feels like an eternity of time for him.

"There we go. If you would be kind to wait just a moment. It seems she is on her way." He announces.

Illiyana rounds the corner into the main corridor dressed in formal military attire. Her footsteps heard echoing long before she is seen. The young attendant looks on expectantly as he awaits their impending conversation. Anna turns to face the young attendant, keeping her back to Illiyana.

"Lady Arlenko please meet miss Annastasia." The young man says gleefully.

Illiyana stops short of her sister staring past her at the young attendant. I can't turn around, but I want to see the look on her face. Anna bursts into laughter unable to contain it any further. She turns around and embraces her sister in a hug burying her face into her chest, keeping her chuckling to a dull roar. A look of confusion and disbelief strikes the attendant. His face left agape at the sight before him.

"Hello sister." Illiyana says smiling.

"Hey." Anna exclaims pulling herself away from Illiyana's chest. "Was taking your new greeter for a trip. What happened to Roland?"

"Promotion."

"Wha-" The young clerk begins to question.

"You're dismissed." Illiyana says interrupting his thought.

"Yes ma'am." The attendant exclaims.

Scurrying away the young attendant scrambles to his post. His head shaking as a list of questions runs through his mind. Illiyana continues to trace his steps until he returns to his post, greeting the newly arriving dignitaries. Anna relents her grip and breaks the hug, bringing Illiyana's attention back towards her. Looking to her sister, Illiyana smiles before wrapping one arm around Anna's shoulder whisking them both towards her office.

"To what do I owe the pleasure of seeing my baby sister?" Illiyana says inquisitively.

"You mean I need a reason to visit?" Anna retorts beaming a wide smile. "I missed you."

"And?"

"And a friend needs some help. I needed a few questions answered."

"There it is. Let's talk in private."

"That sounds like a plan."

The main hallway leads into a large decadent chamber. Furnished as a waiting area for noblemen and women. They truly spared no expense. As in the main corridor art lines the walls. Pictures depicting great heroes of the past standing statuesque as if posing for the artist. A red carpet dictates the direct path toward each adjacent room, offsetting the white polished flooring. The foyer is full of waiting dignitaries and house advisors patiently awaiting their appointments, passing the time with idle chatter. As Illiyana crosses into the room with Anna in tow most eyes gravitate towards them. Standing straight, her back arched Anna walks forward behind her sister. I think I could pass for upper class if it wasn't for the jeans. Paying no heed to the onlookers Illiyana quickly passes through the room into her own office. Anna slowly follows, waving to the crowd of onlookers as she walks on by. Her beaming smile returned with their own soft smiles. Stopping mid stride just outside the office door Anna turns to her crowd.

"Thanks guys. I think I made it safely." She quips beaming her infectious smile, motioning towards the onlookers.

Illiyana shakes her head as she listens to her sister's banter. Grabbing Anna by the shoulder, Illiyana drags her inside, slamming the door shut as she stumbles in. Laughing erupts as Anna throws herself into a giggling fit. Illiyana rolls her eyes as she makes her way toward the desk. Anna, finding her way past her laughter, looks about the room. Simple in design. A desk, two chairs and a filing system placed neatly in a corner. The balcony behind the desk looks out over western Providence, giving a stunning view of most of the city itself.

"Look at that. I think you added something to this room. A new photo shaking hands with another commander?" Anna says sarcastically.

"Plain and efficient. Just the way it should be." Illiyana retorts.

"Are we talking about you or the room now?" Anna says glancing to her sister from the corner of her eye as she paces the room.

"You'd know if you bothered to stop by more often."

"Playing that card early."

"If you play dirty, so will I." Illiyana says planting herself in the chair.

"I did miss you. I've just been so busy closing up the last few strands of business. Retirement is not an easy gig." Anna says continuing to pace about the room.

"I missed you too. It's boring up here, I mostly file paperwork and go to meetings. Not exactly what I signed up for."

"That attendant seemed quite afraid of you."

"Occasionally I get to have a fun moment or two. You had a few questions for me? How can I help?"

Anna sits down across from Illiyana. Sliding comfortably into the chair Anna pulls her hair to the side nervously tucking it behind her ear. She glances up towards her sister her brilliant blue eyes giving away her hesitation.

"My intel says a corporation under government jurisdiction is mass producing a chemical weapon that's already gone through its preliminary tests and is ready for release. They have stressed to me that this weapon is going to be used here as its first run. I wanted to come to Kul with this because I think this is a bit further out of my league." Anna says rapidly, pouring out her thoughts.

"Alright."

Illiyana pauses for a moment taking in the information. Her eyes narrowing as her face grows stern. She leans closer to the desk, placing her elbows down to prop herself up.

"I know it's a lot. Hear me out." Anna pleads.

"How do you even know any of this is true? Who's your source? What company? I have a list of questions almost as long as this desk. You can't just make accusations like this without solid proof." Illiyana says grimly.

"I have proof. I have their files at the Flame."

"And how did you get them?"

"Legitimately."

"Then who gave them to you?"

"I'd rather not say." Anna says quickly. Her hand running down the nape of her neck.

"If you want my help you have to be honest. No secrets between us anymore. Last time we did this dance number it almost backfired. If i'm going to give you information, you'll have to trust me with yours."

Looking across the desk to her worried sister Illiyana lifts herself up from the desk and reaches a hand across to her sister, in her own way conveying her sincerity. Welcoming the gesture Anna takes her hand before continuing.

"Tabitha is my contact." Anna says dejectedly, awaiting the verbal barrage. Her shoulders slumping as she flinches internally.

"By your posture I would assume it is exactly who I believe it to be. I asked you if you knew this is true. You still trust her?" Illiyana says inquisitively, gripping her sister's hand tighter.

"She has no reason to lie to me. This isn't about her or trust. This is about Providence. About them." Anna says vehemently, pointing out the window. "If there is some shred of truth to her statement, I would be doing a disservice to the rest of this world if I didn't follow up. I came to you so we can resolve this mess together. So that I can put an end to the heartache that doesn't ever relent."

"What company? We do have a few we use for military purposes." Illiyana responds her tone still and peaceful.

"It's Frostscythe. I didn't have an opportunity to do any research on them. This kind of just sprang up."

"That's an interesting name to bring up. You're sure?"

"Positive. I read the file last night. What makes it so interesting?"

"They're undercutting competitors and pushing to make their contracts more appealing to us. It's a strong business move that i've been overlooking. Thought it may have been a way to solidify our partnership."

"They're trying to moving into the Heart?" Anna says, worry lingering in her tone.

"Affirmative. They've been a helping hand as far as the council is concerned. Supplying us with new and upgraded technology. Portable equipment, lightweight and simple for use on the field. If this is who you believe is behind these 'attacks' there is nothing I can do."

"Why Illi?"

"Hands in too many pockets. Half the people you see outside my office probably have some unwitting connection to them. They are the biggest market in the industry. They provide medical supplies and treatments for our soldiers."

"There has to be some dirt you have on them. Don't brush me off on this." Anna replies clearly irritated. "I know what you're doing but you know that won't work on me. I'm not afraid of this."

A moment goes by in silence. The bond of good faith broken as Illiyana retracts her hand from Anna's grip. Leaning back in her chair Illiyana closes her eyes, sighing deeply. Anna despondently turns away looking towards the door. The air of uncertainty between them becomes palpable.

"Why have you adopted this bold plan?" Illiyana retorts. "Is it because Tabitha needs your help or you just don't want to retire? I know you love this sort of thrill, it's in your blood."

"I've been asking myself that same question." Anna's voice echoes her sullen body language. "I'm doing this because I have no choice. I am as responsible for the safety of this city as you are. I can do the things you can't-"

"Illegally." Illiyana adds.

"To make this city safer for everyone."

"There is no grey divide to the law. Just because you believe it to be right doesn't magically make it true. I'm looking out for you by telling you to lay low on this. You've been a straight arrow for the past few years and i'm proud of you. I don't want you caught up in this."

"So there is something going on." Anna says returning her attention to her sister. "You don't want me caught up in what?"

"I meant the situation with your brilliant ex." Illiyana says dryly. "I don't want you chasing dreams, hoping you can make something happen that won't. She's using you for something. The second Tabitha finds it she'll stab you right in the back again. Only maybe you won't survive the exchange. I know you Anna. You're a romantic. A lover and a fighter."

"And you're family not a roadblock." Anna retorts.

"Stubborn."

"I learned it from you."

The door to the office swings open. Both sisters hush and forward their attention toward the entryway. Kul, dressed in a white formal suit, walks through the door. His greying hair cut short much like his beard. Looking to his two pupils he flashes a quick smile as he closes the door behind himself. Walking up behind Anna he puts a hand on her shoulder. His presence brings her warmth as she looks up to his towering stature from her seated position. Illiyana stands at attention beside her desk saluting him. He chuckles and motions for her to lower the salute with his free hand.

"Hello little flame." His boisterous voice booming through the small office. "I heard you were spending some quality time together. I figured I would make a visit down to say hello."

"Nice to see you." Anna says warmly. "I'm glad you could make the time. How are you doing?"

"I'm well and I hope all is well in your world. It's been some time since you last visited."

"I wish it were on better terms but I have reason for being here. Other than to see both of your beautiful faces." Anna responds determined for answers.

"She came to ask us for a favor father." Illiyana adds.

Kul looks down into Anna's waiting eyes. He shares a smile with her before ruffling her hair around. Anna moves forward to escape his playfulness. Standing up from the chair she positions herself to face both her sister and Kul.

"I needed information that Illiyana doesn't seem keen on leaving with me. Information on Frostscythe." Anna says.

"I see. Illiyana's hesitation-"

"I know they're a valuable company. I know you can't help me personally. I just need a foot in the door." Anna interrupts, her tone becoming serious.

"Why can't we aid you in this endeavour?" Kul says glancing in Illiyana's direction.

"It would be unwise for us to look into this matter while they are currently vying for our contracts. An investigation would mean a stopped shipment of any and all supplies they may provide to us." Illiyana responds.

"I'm glad you have Providence's best interests in mind Illiyana." Kul states.

"Of course." Illiyana responds, nodding in his direction.

"That's bullshit." Anna exclaims. "This isn't some nobleman you can tell to screw off. I know you better than anyone in this building. If you're not willing to help me bring an end to this controversy do me the kindness of being blunt, which Illiyana has had the pleasure of doing already."

"We may be able to facilitate some sort of arrangement for you though. I'm not sure on the matter at hand but anything that has made you this fervent shouldn't be taken lightly. I believe we can all agree on that. Illiyana and myself have made some contacts with this company and I would be willing to set up an appointment for you to speak with them."

"Father." Illiyana begins to retort.

"I will have no squabbling between us." Kul says shutting down her statement. "If her heart is set on this meeting I would rather it be on our terms than theirs. Illiyana I would appreciate you setting the appointment. Anna when would you like this to be?"

"This afternoon would be wonderful." Anna answers.

Kul nods in agreement, his smile fading into into a rigid straightness. Anna, smiling in his direction mouths 'thank you'. Their conversation tapers off as Kul moves toward Anna enveloping her in his arms. His hug firm yet gentle.

"Illiyana, may we have the room?" He says over his shoulder.

"This is my-" Illiyana begins. "Yes sir. I'll arrange the meet right away."

Illiyana composes herself before heading out of the room, straightening her jacket as she storms off. Kul releases the hug and returns to the entryway, closing the door and locking it behind him. Leaning up against the wall he runs his hands through his hair, letting out a frustrated sound. Anna stands her ground feet away from him looking away slightly. I'm sorry dad. Kul wills himself forward leaning over the chair beside Anna. Propping himself up onto the chair he looks directly at her, the look of a concerned parent. Not angry, just ashamed.

"Anna." Kul begins. "I thought this was behind you."

"It was." Anna responds. Her sight still focused away from him.

"Then what changed? This isn't some pirate crew you can outsmart. This is a well funded organization. One who is not afraid to play hard to get their desired outcome. I've been dealing with them for years."

"So you know they're corrupt?"

"I would never do any business with a corrupt entity. However, I would do business to keep something under control. I've had my own eyes on them for some time. It's odd timing that brings you with these questions now, with it being so close to the contract deadline."

"So you believe me?" Anna says looking up into Kul's eyes.

"I would never dream that you would lie to me. If this 'case' is your passion, who am I to stop you?" Kul asks rhetorically. "You have always been special to me and I have always tried guiding your path. I'm proud of you. From here on I allow you to guide yourself."

"Kul-"

"You need not say anything."

He wraps his inviting arm around Anna's shoulder, walking with her to the window overlooking eastern Providence. Opening the sliding glass door, they step out together. His arm still wrapped tightly around her. Taking in the morning view they stare outward into the busy open city as Anna rests her head lazily upon his shoulder.

CHAPTER EIGHT
SECRETS

Anna, hands in her pockets, arrives outside a towering glass structure. The sidewalks bustle with business. Men and women in suits passing by talking loudly into their headsets mostly oblivious to the world surrounding them. Anna looks upon the four story building in awe. It's design sleek and appealing, a glimpse into Providence's new architectural style. Their logo matches the design of the building. Set as a centerpiece to define the rest of the structure.

Weaving through traffic Anna makes her way up a small set of stairs and through a set of double doors into the foyer. Simplistic in style, Frostscythe's interior is bright and inviting. Traces of light flicker through the tinted inner windows leaving a warm radiance throughout the building. Upon arrival Anna is met with nods and greetings from gentleman on either side of the entryway. Anna continues her awkward gaze as she maintains her course, spinning slowly around to take everything in.

Four security guards, two on the doors and two patrolling. Ten cameras in the lobby alone. A very perceptive receptionist and from the looks of it a F1500 Unimax security alarm system. They keep a tight ship.

Anna walks around seemingly aimless, making her way toward the receptionists desk. A man and woman both sharply dressed intersect her path. The man smiles invitingly towards her, reminding her of a used hover salesman. Brushing his black hair to the side he greets Anna, his hands clamped together as if in celebration. He extends a welcoming hand to Anna. The woman follows closely behind him grasping onto a clipboard. Frantically writing notes while balancing the clipboard in one hand and answering calls directed into her headset, working up a sweat as she hurriedly performs her tasks.

"Hello! You must be Annastasia, yes?" He says through a thick accent.

"I am." Anna responds, stopping short of his outstretched hand.

"Perfect! My name is Alphonse Cervantes. I believe we have a meeting together." He comments, directing his confident smile in her direction. "Forgive my boldness. I tend to greet people at the door."

"I'm glad you take your job seriously Mr. Cervantes." Anna says extending her hand to him. "I'm Annastasia Arlenko."

"The pleasure is all mine milady." He replies.

Gently taking her hand Alphonse rests a kiss upon her hand before releasing it. Anna gives him a quizzical look as she retracts her hand.

"Where I come from that is how you greet royalty." He says noticing her reluctance.

"I'm flattered and also taken aback." Anna says genuinely.

"I'm sorry for the inconvenience. It's not everyday you get to see such a person."

"I can assure you i'm no royalty. I'm just lucky to have the family I do."

"Either way welcome to Frostscythe. Our aim is to make you better."

"Spoken like a true salesperson." Anna retorts.

"Ha! Yes! Come we'll have a seat in my office." He says boisterously. "Oh. Where are my manners. This is Monica, my assistant. I hope you do not mind her company."

"Nice to meet you Monica." Anna says directing her attention to the frantically busy woman behind Alphonse. Monica waves quickly to Anna before delving back into her work writing notes on the clipboard.

Alphonse motions for Anna to follow him up a lofty set of glass stairs leading to a crossway just above the first level. Monica follows obediently behind without moving her gaze from the notepad. Anna chuckles to herself as she takes after them up the staircase. As Alphonse passes along the crosswalk he stops and motions toward the citizens busying themselves below. Anna glances through the glass walkway watching the busy work at hand. She smiles to herself, admiring their commitment.

"This my dear Annastasia is the best view in Frostscythe. These people are our customers, our blood, our life. Every advancement we create is with them in mind." Alphonse says sincerely. "Our founders left us with a plan; no one is left behind and to this day we have not left a single person behind us."

"That's admirable." Anna begins.

"That is only the beginning." Alphonse responds. "We have helped over one hundred thousand people return to a functioning life and that's only in the previous ten years."

"You're pitching to me again." Anna says dryly.

"Indeed I am. I get caught up in such things."

"It is refreshing." Anna says smiling. "Shall we continue?"

"Of course!" He replies boisterously

Continuing past the walkway they arrive to a vibrant day room suspended above the lower level. The soft blue of the walls offsets the white countertop of the kitchenette in the corner. A nice seating arrangement circles a small centerpiece table, a few tablets neatly placed on its surface. The area is calm and quiet as outside noise is drown out the further they move in. Anna takes a seat, melting into the comfortable chair. Alphonse takes his seat across from her while Monica stands behind his chair keeping herself busy.

"Would you care for a drink? Some tea perhaps?" Alphonse asks.

"An odd question." Anna says raising an eyebrow. "So precise."

"You look quite parched. Our mutual friend said to have some tea steeped for you." Alphonse retorts, resting his hands on his chest as he leans back in the chair. "Which do you prefer?"

"I'm feeling plain today." Anna says grinning. "With a lemon wedge."

"Plain with a twist." Alphonse adds. "Monica, brew us some tea would you kindly."

'Yes sir." Monica says attentively.

Setting her belongings in the seat beside Anna and Alphonse, Monica walks off towards their kitchen. Anna briefly glances at the clipboard, taking in the quickly scrawled notes before returning her attention to Alphonse. Looks like an address and time. Possibly a meeting.

"So, I was not informed as to what this meeting is about. You'll have to forgive my lack of reconnaissance. How may I assist you today Annastasia?" Alphonse questions. Smile spreading wide across his face.

"I would like a matter cleared up. I have received a most troublesome report linking to your company." Anna says shyly, tucking some hair behind her ear.

"Many people would wish to slander the name of our company. Sorry, continue."

"I was wondering if you had any field tests with your many manufactured products."

"Well of course we do. We cannot get anything approved without the consent of your fath...the lord's council. Many field tests must be done to insure quality and safety."

"Have you tested any experimental airborne substances?"

Alphonse raises an eyebrow before smirking in Anna's direction. His demeanor changing slightly as he leans forward. Anna beams a shy smile back in his direction.

"Such a specific question and an odd one at that. You said you heard a report. May I ask from whom?" Alphonse wittily responds.

"You never answered my question."

"That is fair." He accepts. "We test many airborne products, most are still in their infancy and their knowledge is not publicly known as of yet. I hope you understand I must speak in hushed tones when talking about them."

A whistle of the kettle breaks their conversation, drawing attention to Monica as she takes the teapot from the heat. Returning to the table Monica pours both Anna and Alphonse each a glass, careful not to spill any tea. Alphonse looks to her approvingly before dismissing her with a wave of his hand. Monica nods, picking up her belongings.

"It was a pleasure to meet you Ms Arlenko." Monica says smiling as she exits the room with a rushed walk.

"Thank you." Anna says quickly.

"I hope you understand our predicament. I can assure you every product has had extensive testing done to insure its quality. I understand your worry. You have lived in this city for many years yes?" Alphonse says, taking a sip from his tea.

"I have. It's more than home to me now. I feel like I have the obligation to protect it."

"You just wish what we all do. That the world you live in can be safe. It is admirable"

"You really are good at public speaking." Anna says chuckling.

"That is why they hired me." Alphonse responds cockily.

A moment passes as Anna prepares her tea ritually, making the 'perfect' cup. Alphonse takes in her method, watching as she works the lemon into her tea. Setting his cup down he returns to the kitchen giving her time to prepare.

"So, who gave you this unsettling information?" Alphonse asks, leaning across the kitchen countertop.

"An old informant. Her name is Tabitha Cosgrove." Anna says.

Anna turns from her comfortable spot to face Alphonse, sipping from her tea as she readjusts. He squirms to the mere mention of Tabitha. A look of disgust moves across his face momentarily as he repositions himself, his thoughts betraying his body. Step one, admit you have a problem. Alphonse bites his lower lip, swallowing the forming statement in his mind.

"She came to me worried. She had files implicating this company in military like operations and tests. Tests on the very civilian population you so eloquently call your 'blood'. Such an odd term to use given the plethora of phrases you could use. This file has months of 'product quality assurances'. I asked about an airborne substance and you claim to have many in their infancy, could this be one of those 'products'-"

"I will not stand to be berated. This is a courtesy Ms Arlenko. One that I can end at any time."

"Forgive my boldness."

Alphonse moves from the countertop deceptively quick leaving his tea behind. He comes to stand beside Anna looking directly into her eyes, a piercing confidence projecting outward from his gaze. Anna matches his stare with her own confidence and wide smile. Her calm demeanor subtly grinds against his growing fury.

"I seem to have angered you. You take this job very seriously, as should anyone in your position. Though I should point out, unlike people in your position, you handle yourself poorly. This would be the perfect opportunity to shut out this ludicrous accusation yet here you stand, furious and speechless. While I admit the two happens quite often, it is generally in the opposite order."

A moment feels like eternity as they exchange glances before Anna raises her teacup between the two of them sipping loudly. Her confident smile beams in his direction.

"I apologize Ms Arlenko. I take these matters to the heart." Alphonse says straightening his suit collar, reclaiming his calm presence. "I am worried this Tabitha Cosgrove is slandering our good reputation for her own personal gain. You said she gave you documentation, perhaps it is falsified. I am unsure as to why and what lengths people would go, but this seems outlandish to say the least."

"There is the rebuttal I was looking for." Anna says snidely. "It was a very insightful conversation. I would love to do this again but I keep a busy schedule."

Anna stands up from her relaxed position, placing the tea onto the tabletop. Turning towards him Anna straightens herself matching his rigid stance. Placing her hands upon his jacket collar Anna runs her hands down the seams, straightening out the lapel. As she reaches to pat his shoulder Alphonse grabs her by the arm with an unnatural quickness, taking her off guard as she attempts to pull herself away. His grip cold to the touch.

"Annastasia. You disrespect me." Alphonse mutters.

"Let go of me." Anna responds.

"I have yet to return your kindness."

Alphonse pulls Anna to him using the grip on her hand to drag her inches from his face. With his free hand he caresses the side of her face leading his hand down her cheek, tracing her jawline with his finger. Anna's face grows stern as she lurches from his wandering hand. Alphonse releases his grip allowing her to retract further from him.

"Is this all too personal for you Annastasia? Are you not in as much control as you thought? I'm sure you will go scurrying back to the rat who fed you this information. As far as we are concerned our company has no involvement in this scandal. Thank you for bringing this to our attention. It truly has been enlightening."

"Don't you dare touch me ever again." Anna says in disgust, ignoring his statement.

"Let us not resort to threats. Is it not beneath us?"

"You're right. You are beneath me." Anna says exiting the room.

Heading quickly across the walkway Anna retreats. Shrugging off the absence of noise coming from the lower level she focuses on leaving. I overstayed my welcome. Not far behind Alphonse slowly gives chase as she makes her way to the staircase. With a sort of swagger to his stride he waits atop the crossway leaning over the edge, patiently waiting.

Exiting the staircase into the lobby Anna stops, her dragging feet echoing throughout the empty hall. A stillness comes over her as she perceives a peculiar sight. No soul in sight, outside of the two guards set beside the front entryway. As if everyone disappeared into thin air. A faint set of footsteps echo along the emptied halls, pulsing off the walls. Each step heavier as it crashes onto the floor below. Continuing towards the lobby doors confidence follows in Anna's footsteps.

As she nears the doorway the two statuesque figures converge on her location barring a convenient exit. Each figure bearing a unique mask, with their own embossments. Tribal yet different both masks give an off putting feeling through the air. Their dark eyes burning holes through the slits of the mask.

Pausing feet from the towering guards Anna looks over each carefully. Upon further inspection she notices a faint inscription on their masks, 'body' and 'soul'. If they knew anything about the Arlenko's it's that if we put our mind to it, we can achieve anything. I don't care who you are, I will persevere.

"I must have struck a nerve for you to be so brash as to threaten the departure of the lord's own family. Brilliant is not a word I would use to describe this tactic. Gentlemen if you do not step aside I will be forced to make you." Her tone steady and confident.

Neither of them budge at her demand. A dead stare taking their eyes as they center their attention on her. Anna breathes deeply, cracking her neck and knuckles, warming up. Closing her eyes Anna calms her flooding heart and mind preparing for a small altercation.

The echoing footsteps come to an abrupt halt screeching across the floor above, breaking Anna's concentration. Expecting Alphonse, Anna looks back. To her own shock beside Alphonse is a nightmarish guest. Their long flowing hood drapes over the sides of the railing. Their face obscured by a growing shadow, surrounding it in a wisp of darkness. A shiver runs up the Magician's spine, recalling the words it said and feeling she received from its presence. Anna closes her eyes tightly in disbelief. It's real.

"Annastasssia." The voice hisses shrilly. It's metal covered hand extending outward, beckoning her. "Join me." A grasp upon her shoulder forces her eyes open to a welcome surprise, as quickly as it showed the entity had disappeared leaving only behind only it's echoing voice in her mind.

A rush of noise floods her hearing as the clamoring of business fills the vacant room. Suddenly Anna is surrounded by hurried business associates and customers alike. The hand on her shoulder grips more firmly garnering her attention. Anna brushes the hand off of her shoulder as she moves towards the now unobscured entryway. Looking back through the closing door Anna locates Alphonse on the catwalk above leaning over the railing waving in her direction. A conceited smile left wide across his face.

Quickly making her way down the outside staircase Anna pulls a phone from her pocket. Scrolling through a list of contacts she pauses on one, Westhouse T. Looking over her shoulder Anna checks to make sure she isn't followed from the building before placing the call. It rings for a few seconds before the line connects.

"I need a meeting." Anna says confidently yet shaken. "I have a favor to ask."

Chapter Nine

Precipices

Shadows begin to creep across the sky above Providence blotting out the burning sunlight as nightfall slowly swallows the day. Building lights begin illuminating the city streets, coaxing the nightlife out. Tabitha drifts through busy walkways careful to not make contact with any individuals. Making her way through the flood of people she veers off course into an alleyway, creating as much separation as possible from the public. Their cheers and laughter continue to echo down the length of the alley, seemingly increasing in volume no matter the direction she chooses. Their carefree demeanor grating on her nerves quickly. Taking a deep breath Tabitha continues to the opposite end of the alleyway, making a active effort to sidestep any filth separating her from her goal.

Neon lights dance across the alley walls as she crosses into a sea of inebriants, pausing momentarily before plunging into their depth. A glow of lights catches her eye, scrolling the open air above a stylish building. Lights dance across the screen creating a word in brilliant calligraphy, 'Precipices', before fading and starting from the beginning. Below a line has formed awaiting entry into the upscale establishment. A mix of both men and women wait impatiently for approval from the muscle in front of the door. Tabitha carves a path through the intoxicated toward Precipices, making no qualms about being forceful. Few people even react to her forceful approach, keeping to themselves and their joyful conversations. The few objections are met with dagger like glares as Tabitha proceeds to her destination.

Walking up to the line the stern woman pauses, analyzing the herd of people before sauntering past the lingering line. Running her hand down the rope separating them from the sidewalk Tabitha smirks at the hushed displeasure of the crowd beside her. Approaching the doorman a confident smile widens across her face, stopping inches from him. He pays her no attention, dealing with the growing unrest of the crowd. His hands raise up in a hushing manner and the crowd dies down, keeping their remarks to themselves. He opens the ropes motioning for the first few people to enter.

"What can I do for you?" He asks glancing in Tabitha's direction, before closing the ropes again.

"You can let me in." Tabitha replies dryly.

"I need a name." He remarks, turning his attention toward her.

"Tabitha."

"Cosgrove?" A tone of wonder and surprise catches his voice.

"That would be me."

"You have a space reserved inside." He says, motioning her through.

"Why does she just get to go through?" A woman's voice perks up from the crowd.

"Because-" Security begins to say.

"You're here to find a man to take you somewhere 'romantic', a back alleyway perhaps, and have his way with you. Enjoy your drug induced night. I am sure someone will find you fitting." Tabitha says as she moves into the open doorway. "And while you're face down over some trash can i'll be conducting business. Business always comes first."

114

Crossing the threshold Tabitha follows a straight path towards another set of double doors. The hallway is lit from below and above with a dark blue hue, giving the room a cold and emotionless appearance. As she progresses down the hall a faint boom of bass begins to grow louder. Groups are huddled off to the sides. Some gathering with friends and gossiping amongst themselves before heading into the nightclub itself, others escaping the powerful music to speak on their phones. Tabitha presses forward, opening the second set of double doors. A flood of deafening electronics carries through to the other room as she enters into the main floor.

The main bar sits directly in eyesight, the center attraction for most newly arriving guests. It's circle design acting as a pillar going directly up to the other two levels of the building. The area looks professionally and elegantly decorated. Bottles lining the mirrored walls leading up the pillar. As a spot opens around the bar Tabitha approaches to a warm smile from one of the few bartenders. Leaning with her back to the bar she inspects the establishment, searching.

"Hey there beautiful. What can I get ya?" The bartender asks.

"Something strong and a magician." Said coldly.

"Alright. I'll just whip up something magical." He quips.

Returning to her search Tabitha checks the dancefloor to her left, scanning through the congregation of club goers. Coming up short she notices a few matches for Annastasia's style. Appreciating her view Tabitha watches them mingle with the crowd, taking in the sight.

"You sure are taking your time."

"You said magical." He retorts, spinning a bottle in his hand as he mixes together her drink. "I aim to please."

"Just give me the drink. Skip the pleasantries." Tabitha counters.

"Pleasant." He says as he sets her drink on the countertop. "Drinks ready."

Grabbing her drink Tabitha returns her attention outward. Broadening her search Tabitha fixates on the entryway. People pour in through the bottlenecked hallway, splitting off to their respective cliques. Out of the corner of her eye she catches Anna slink into the building in a form-fitting pair of jeans and low-cut t-shirt. Setting her drink back on the counter Tabitha moves to intercept Anna, briskly moving through the crowd. Coming up behind her, grabbing her by her hips pulling her close.

"Hey there." Tabitha whispers in her ear, her demeanor seemingly chipper.

"Tabitha." Anna says, placing her hands overtop Tabitha's. "I'm not surprised you picked me out of the crowd."

"I didn't have to look hard. A few others share your style of fashion here but no one with the looks to match." Tabitha says moving her arms to envelope Anna's waist. "You seem tense. Are you ok?"

"I'm a bit shaken." Anna says tentatively.

"You should never have went there. They're-"

"They're like you." Anna interjects.

"Yes."

Anna spins around in Tabitha's arms. Their eyes lock showing her overwhelming amount of weakness. Staring into them Tabitha falters pulling Anna in closer, embracing her warmly. Anna reciprocates in kind, placing her head on Tabitha's shoulder.

"I would never let them hurt you." Whispered softly into her ear. "I'm sorry."

"I saw something Tabitha. It was in my dream and again in Frostscythe."

"Was it what you described, the cloaked figure?"

Anna shakes her head softly, burying her head further into Tabitha's shoulder.

"It was Mind. I'm sure of it."

"I don't really want to think about it."

"I understand. Should we go right to business then?"

"Thomas will be a few minutes. He messaged me while I was on the way here. We have some free time."

"What shall we do with it then?" Tabitha asks sincerely.

"Enjoy the night. Like old times." Anna replies, lifting her head from Tabitha's shoulder.

"Lead the way." Her cold demeanor lightening into an uncharacteristic smile.

Breaking their embrace Tabitha extends her hand to Annastasia, a show of surrender. Grabbing ahold of her hand Anna guides her toward the already overflowing dancefloor. Making their way into the center the raven haired beauty cringes as she is pressed into other individuals. Anna expertly weaves through the crowd into her own preferred spot taking Tabitha along for the ride. Music pulses through the area, keeping in time with the rhythm of the crowd. Each person lost in the individuals surrounding them, giving themselves over to the rhythm.

Reaching out Anna pulls her close, clearing the space between them. I forgot what this feels like. The air between them becomes relaxed as Anna takes control of the situation pushing herself into Tabitha, eliciting a small gasp from her counterpart. Standing beside herself Tabitha watches as Anna deftly dances around, teasing every ounce of her being. Anna breathes softly into her ear, jolting her nerves.

"Do you know what you want yet?" The aggressor whispers softly.

Giving no response Tabitha returns the gesture whirling around to be face to face, nuzzling her neck and allowing her hands to roam. Moving up her body Tabitha places a hand along her cheek, carefully caressing her soft skin.

"I know who I want." Her confidence radiating. "I don't think i've earned it."

"You're so serious. Lighten up." Said lightheartedly.

Running a hand through her perfectly straight dark hair then down the swell of her back causes Tabitha to lurch forward before stopping herself, enjoying the attention. Slowly continuing across Tabitha's silhouette elegantly, the temptress traces her outline.

The lights dim as the song changes tempo, changing from blue to purple. Everything slows down, almost as if time itself changed. Tabitha takes in a deep breath before weakly exhaling. Continuing to tempt her grim companion, Anna places a kiss on her cheek.

"I still love you." Anna whispers before backing away, retreating from the dancefloor.

"I am not chasing you." Tabitha says vehemently.

Beckoning her with a finger Anna smiles, disappearing into the crowd. After a moment she yields, giving in to her basic urges. Moving through the crowd Tabitha searches for Anna, finding her climbing the base of a back staircase, racing her way to the second story. Cutting through the crowd swiftly with minimum contact, ruthlessly weaving through the obstacles. Making her way to the staircase Tabitha begins to climb, her stride long taking two stairs at a time, rushing her way to the top. Reaching the second level Tabitha sees Anna in a relaxed position leaning up against the wall, waiting. Blinking slowly she takes in Anna's form, committing it to memory once again. Opening her eyes to a wide smile and alluring blue eyes staring back at her, teasing her further. With her hand outstretched Anna invites Tabitha forward, drawing her in. She obliges.

"What was it you told me this morning?" Anna asks softly, barely audible over the music below.

"I take what I want." said with excitement, biting her lower lip.

"Then what are you waiting for?"

At her limit Tabitha presses forward, pinning her prey to the wall. Staring deeply into Anna's brilliant blue eyes Tabitha melts, losing her cold demeanor building tension between them. Anna leans forward biting on her lower lip, instigating an advance. Wrapping her free hands around her waist they draw each other closer together, closer than they have been in years. Sharing their moment of passion Tabitha returns to Anna's neck, working her way up.

"Infect me." A sound of wanting escapes Anna.

Hearing those words only seem to entice Tabitha. Slowing her approach, enjoying every second of this moment. Tilting her head back, finally giving in to the passion of the moment. I missed you so much. Reaching down she directs Tabitha upward, kissing her passionately before allowing her to work downward again.

"Fuckin eh. Just gettin reacquainted, ya? I'll leave." Finn says unabashedly walking through the open door beside them, drink firmly placed in hand. "I'll be needin another drink. Preferably something with more whiskey." Shouted back through the open door.

Tabitha backs away from them both like a teenager caught for the first time, equal parts embarrassed and frustrated.. Anna winks at Tabitha as she moves towards her, a cheshire grin replacing the innocent smile. Exiting the stairway Finn walks back into the reserved area towards his own lover, his hands raised above his head in an exaggerated manner. Anna comforts Tabitha, placing her arms around her neck, closing the distance for another kiss.

"We'll be back after this brief intermission." Anna teases, breaking the kiss.

Tabitha lets out a audible sigh, clearly not ready to move forward. Anna runs a finger down her lips before turning towards the open entryway. Tabitha takes a moment to collect herself in the stairway, regaining her presence.

Anna moves into the private room, locating her friends at the bar across the way. Unlike the floor below this room glows various shades of red, starting vibrant and darkening in color over time. Claudette, Finn, and Xylen are taking up relaxing positions at the corner of the bar, away from other patrons upstairs.

"So ya. I walked out and there they fuckin was just snoggin. I was like, cuse me you two but do ya mind doin that somewheres else ya. I mean that girl has horrible taste. Her choice in women is underwhelmin to put it nicely."

Walking up behind the meddler, Anna overhears his conversation. Taking the opportunity she snags Finn's drink as he tells his tale. Reaching for his beverage coming up empty.

"Cuse me." Anna says mockingly, drinking from his whiskey. "You mind tellin that story somewhere else, ya?"

"Das it. Ya done for." Finn says playfully.

Setting the whiskey on the counter beside her, she readies herself for the juveniles brand of playful. He fakes grabbing for her to swipe his drink back from the counter. As swiftly as he grabs the drink Finn shoots the glass back, emptying it. Turning the glass upside down he places it back on the counter. Anna gives him a hug which he returns. Turning her attention toward the others, she greets them cheerfully. Claudette places an arm around Anna's shoulder, pulling her in.

"I heard you can't do this without us?" Said wittily. "Don't worry we'll hold off on the beaches for you."

"Ya. Can't be leavin without my conscience. No matter how many bad decisions they be makin these days." Finn adds.

"Could you keep my personal life out of your mind for possibly a second. I know i'm fascinating and all but it would be greatly appreciated." She rolls her eyes. "And thank you Claudette. It means the world to me."

"I know. What's the situation? Finn left some blanks spaces when filling us in."

"This is the information gathering portion. We need schematics, entry points, and some key cards. Thomas had to go through some contacts but i'm pretty sure he found what we needed. If everything goes smoothly we'll be in and out faster than Finn on prom night."

"I was well seasoned by then." Finn retorts.

"More than I needed to know." Xylen says, hiding his face.

Anna bursts into laughter at Xylen's outburst, causing a cascade of chuckling from everyone else. The bartender interrupts their conversation, setting another drink down in front of Finn. The others eye the bartender disapprovingly.

"Keep um comin Jack." Finn says, raising his glass to the bartender.

"So this is serious then. Why don't you just report it to the tower?" Claudette says, refocusing the conversation.

"Without proof Illiyana won't take any action towards them. She made that quite clear. We just need some dirt on their facility and operations. She'll have no choice but to shut them down."

"You sure you don't have ya head in da clouds, high as fuck on cloud Tabitha. That girl does tings to ya. First hand proof tonight. I know ya heart's in the right place, just checkin on that mind a yours."

"You don't need to be concerned about my purpose. I took this job before making any such commitments."

"I's just checkin."

Finding her composure a stern faced Tabitha saunters towards the group with Audrey in tow. Without introductions Tabitha grips Claudette by her pallid right hand holding it palm down, the scratch from the night prior visibly worse than before. Startled, Finn prepares to retaliate on behalf of his companion.

"Where did you get this?" Tabitha says aggressively.

She investigates further pulling up the young woman's long sleeve. Her veins look like a darker shade of red, almost as if she is bleeding from them. More noticeable due to her paling complexion. Everyone's eyes drop to her arm. A look of dismay and horror stricken across their faces as they register the information. She whips Claudette's arm downward in disgust, the sentiment echoing on her face. Putting himself between the new acquaintances, Finn acts as a barrier between them. The rest of the crowd stands in stunned silence, watching this exchange.

"How long have you had this?" Tabitha exclaims.

"Since yesterday." She replied, hesitantly.

"How bout you back the fuck up." Finn says, pushing Tabitha back.

"Your girlfriend is infected you fucking dolt. It's getting worse by the moment. This is what happens when stupid tries to hide their infection. These are the types of moments I could have capitalized on." Her voice growing louder. "Do you feel sore or dizzy? Have a loss of appetite or a general numbness? Any of these things."

"Tabitha." Anna's voice booms. "You're scaring her."

"I'm not going to apologize she could have killed you all. Would you like me to paint a happy picture? You're infected Claudette. They targeted you for a very specific reason. This means they've anticipated my arrival and knew exactly where I would flee. This was intended. You were hunted."

Finn turns towards his lover reaching out to cradle her in his arms. Tears flow freely from her eyes, the realisation beginning to sink in. Audrey crosses the gap between them making her way back toward Xylen, clutching his free hand firmly. Cold eyes stare through the back of Finn's head. Her gaze fixated on the wounded right hand wrapped around his core.

"It's gone be alright Dette. Ain't nothin that can take you from me. Don't pay no attention to her. She's just a twat with a shit attitude." Whispered softly.

"Then fix it." Anna demands, snapping her attention away.

"I can't. I don't have the cure."

"So then we go in there and get the damn cure." Xylen interjects, clearly working himself up. "I'll be the first to volunteer."

"That's cute. Is this your first job Xylen? Don't try and play the hero, you'll only end up hurt in the end." Said condescendingly.

"Don't talk to him like that! You're just as afraid as he is." Audrey warns, cutting in on the conversation. "No more secrets. Tell them about the serum."

"What serum?" Perking Anna's interest.

"I have something to isolate the disease. It contains it for a few hours at a time. By no means does this cure the infected, rather it allows the user to analyze the spread of the pathogen for further research. I can give this to her but I cannot save her. Thank you Audrey."

"What are ya waitin for? A fuckin invitation. We ain't no damn mind readers. Fix it up."

Glaring around the level, Tabitha pushes through the overprotective boyfriend to Claudette. Taking her by the hand she leads her to a unclaimed VIP booth in the back corner. Anna places a hand on Finn's chest, passively asking for him to stay with the rest of the group. Looking down into her eyes she can see the uncertainty in his watering eyes. Sharing with him a look of optimism Anna hopes to calm his rushing thoughts. Sharing more than words they come to an understanding.

"I know." Finn states shakily.

Sitting Claudette down she begins to close the curtains surrounding the small room, closing off visibility from the rest of the floor. Returning her attention to her patient Tabitha kneels down beside her, checking her pulse.

"You need to keep your heart rate down. The more blood you circulate the worse it'll be for you."

"Finn said you were aggressive, psychotic even-"

"That's nice. I'm trying to prolong your life. We're not here to trade stories." Her focus preoccupied.

"This is the only way I can keep calm. He told me you and Anna were inseparable."

"Did he?"

She rips the sleeve off of Dette's right arm. Running her hand along the infected arm she searches for more symptoms. Pulling a small gun like device from her jacket, placing it on the table. Searching her other pockets she pulls out a tube of blue liquid.

"You just have that on hand?" Her tone unsettled.

"You never know when you'll need to have an anti-viral on hand." Tabitha quips coldly.

"You knew."

"I suspected. I don't think you've been properly introduced to me or my employers. If i've thought to do it, you have my guarantee that they will do it. You do not create a plague to cripple humanity without knowing the potential risks involved."

•

Ordering another drink Finn waits beside the bar nervously, his focus directed towards the closed VIP room. Downing his glass in one drink, he motions for the bartender again, mouthing the words two more.

"She'll be ok." Audrey says comfortingly, breaking the increasing tension. "Tabitha knows-"

"Oh she knows alright. She fuckin did this. This is her dream design. Spread the infection, claim the rubble. You seem new to this Audrey, so i'll let you in a little something. This... whatever she is to you is nothing but a twat, hell bent on her own self-serving goals. She dragged all of us into this and put my Dette in the crosshairs. She better be more than ok."

"We don't know the whole story." Anna interjects.

"Don't you start in on it too. She's got you so tightly wound around her finger, she pulls any harder and you'll snap. You can't see it but I sure as hell can and i'm not picking up the pieces this time. She is da cause of all this."

Anna freezes in thought, debating on which terms to talk with her irate companion. Twirling her thumbs end over end, Anna turns back to face him. Here goes nothing.

"I can handle myself, thank you for your concern. I'm not going to argue with you. You're distraught and concerned for Claudette, I get it Finn. She is the best option we have to save her. If you don't have faith in her, at least have some in me. I'm the captain of the ship and i'm not about to let us all drown."

Anna gazes into Finn's raging eyes, past his anger and pain. She places her hand on his shoulder, never breaking eye contact. He looks away, attempting to hiding this fear from his best friend. Xylen rounds beside him, knocking

124

into him with his shoulder.

"We're all here for each other." Xylen adds. "Me and you might not like her but right now she's what we've got. She brought Audrey to us and she's pretty swell."

"We can't let anything divide and conquer us. That was always something Tabitha taught me. We have to be a unit." The newest addition remarks. "I told her about Claudette's condition before she came in here. I saw the symptoms, i've been around it too often not to."

"Why didn't you says somethin?" He snaps like cornered animal.

"What could we have done? Panic?" said confidently. "The best thing we could do is keep Claudette calm. Keeps it's spread minimal. She is such a strong woman to have had it for this long and not show greater symptoms than a fever and outbreak. Most people don't survive the initial contact."

"My Dette's is as tough as they come." Finn exclaims, drinking from his latest beverage.

●

"Bite down on this." Tabitha says handing over the ripped sleeve.

Claudette complies biting down on her own sleeve. Tabitha pulls her head to the side, reaching back for the injector on the table. Grabbing a handful of hair Tabitha grips firmly, tugging her head backwards. A look of fear flickers in her eyes, realising her life is in the hands of a demented woman. Her unease worsens, watching the injector come into contact with her exposed flesh. A quick prick from the cold steel sends shivers down her spine as it administers Tabitha's creation. A cool sensation envelopes her neck and upper chest almost immediately. Quickly replaced with a uncontrollable burning, bringing tears to her eyes. The burning trails from her chest and lungs to her right arm. Screaming into her makeshift gag Claudette pulls away from Tabitha, moving further on the sofa.

"How does it feel?" Asked quizzically.

"Fuck you." Claudette retorts, spitting the gag from her mouth. "You know exactly how it feels."

"Where does it burn?" Tabitha says, rolling her eyes.

"Everywhere. My chest, in my lungs. It's like you poured boiling water in my veins."

"This is important so listen closely as I will not repeat myself. That burning, it's the disease spreading throughout your body. Every time I give you another dose of this the pain will intensify as the disease fights to survive. This will give you a few hours of comfort. I cannot prolong the inevitable, if we can't get to Frostscythe none of this will matter. Would you like to ask me another question about my personal life?"

"I've got plenty to ask now." Claudette quips leaning weakly against the furniture.

"I think you've earned a question for being such a good patient." She snidely replies.

"Why did you come back?"

"Is that honestly the question you want me to answer?"

"It is. I might be a little fuzzy on the details, but you didn't come back for a mission. No, it goes far deeper than that doesn't it Tabitha?"

Tabitha leans in closely, encroaching on her space. Hovering inches from her face Claudette smiles with pleasure, causing a scowl to creep across Tabitha's face.

"I'll tell you the same thing I told your belligerent boyfriend. My reasons are my own. One of them being this mission. You look to be a quick study. A quick tip for you, you will never be able to read me and you certainly do not want inside my head. It will do you no favors."

"Is that your best answer? I should get a second question."

"You take after him. Enjoy it while you can."

Tabitha places the injector back into her jacket, tossing the emptied dispenser behind the sofa. She looks back into Claudette's smug eyes with a glare that could pierce even the toughest exterior.

"I came back for her."

"Clearly."

"None of you matter to me. If I had it my way I would watch you writhe in agony as a personal achievement. You're body won't hold out forever, eventually the disease will destroy you piece by piece. It'll tear that muscle bound idiot apart. I wouldn't even have to lift a finger. But you see Claudette, here's where it gets tricky. You matter to her." Pointing in Anna's general direction. "So i'll play the role i'm given. I'll give you this serum, but i'll be watching as it fails and relishing every moment. So go ahead, give me your best one liner. Tell me my darkest secret, tell me i'm not as maniacal as I let on because i'm sure you have no idea of what I am capable of."

Unable to reply Claudette looks at her assailant, her mouth slightly agape. Pulling open the curtain, Tabitha saunters out from the VIP room. The air shifts around her as she approaches the group again, her calm and confident manner sends chills down a few spines.

"Never push me again." Her eyes like daggers.

"I'll do what I feel. If it comes ta puttin hands on ya, then so be it."

"I do not have time for this bravado. Go tend to your bleeding heart, she'll be needing your comfort. Don't forget the bottle of alcohol, we wouldn't want you being without your both of your loves."

"Fucks dat mean?"

"Exactly what I said."

A tense stare between the matching attitudes is broken apart by Anna, pushing her way in between them. With her back to Finn, she moves her other half away from the situation. Shifting her gaze to Anna, Tabitha cannot help but stare deeply into her calm ocean-like eyes. She lets go her breath, letting the moment fade.

"Enough. We understand you're both driven and wound up. No need to match ego's tonight. That goes for the both of you. We're here as a team and we need to act like one. Finn, please go check on Claudette."

"Aye. Dat sounds like a plan Annie. I don't need any of ya along.

Bartender, a bottle a booze, ya?"

Behind the counter the bartender grabs a sealed bottle of whiskey and hands it over to the approaching Finn. Turning on his heels Finn makes way for the VIP lounge.

"At least take this." Xylen perks up. "It's our only means of communication if we're splitting up."

Xylen holds his hand out halting Finn's departure, a pile of small earbuds clumped in his palm. Finn grabs two before continuing off towards his significant other. Xylen extends his hand towards Anna allowing her to grab a set for her and Tabitha as well.

"Thank you Xylen, what would I do without you?"

"Probably be blind and deaf." He says jokingly.

"Naturally."

"Audrey and I are going to be out on the dance floor. We'll do recon from there. Hopefully we won't need it, but just in case, this keeps us all safe. Have fun with Thomas, tell him hello for me."

"I will. Enjoy your time together."

"We will." Audrey says. A natural smile crossing her face.

"Audrey." Tabitha says, looking towards her pupil. "Keep your wits about you. Don't lose your edge out there. We know what's at stake here. We have no room for complacency."

"I know." Erasing the smile and hanging her head low. "Will always have my eyes and ears open. I'll report my findings."

Xylen slings his arm around Audrey's waist pulling her in close. He runs his free hand through his red mane, an audible groan muffled by the growing pulse of music. They slowly exit back to the dance floor. Xylen looks over his shoulder with an elongated face towards Anna, making her crack a sincere smile. She gives him a cross-eyed look in exchange breaking an increasing tension with funny faces. Returning her attention back to Tabitha, Anna runs a hand through her partners darkened hair twirling it around her finger. Nudging her head into Anna's arm she begins slowly caressing her way upwards, kissing along its length.

"You are insatiable."

"Would you have me any other way?" Continuing her way along her delicate skin.

Digging a buzzing phone from her pocket Anna checks the display. One missed message. Retracting her other hand from Tabitha's hair she opens the phone. Scrolling down to the message it reads, 'im rdy'. Tabitha finishes her journey along Anna's arm ending at her neck, lingering there for a moment before stopping.

"It's time. Could you be cordial to Thomas at least?" Anna questions.

"Promise."

●

"Hey there you." Finn says peeking his head through the velvet curtain of the VIP lounge. "Have a look see what I brought ya. Our favorite bottle of win- whiskey."

Across from the entrance sits Claudette her complexion pallid, made more noticeable by the bright lights reflecting off her skin. Her head hung low with her hands covering her eyes. Drawing her head upward to gaze towards Finn, tears streaming down her cheeks. Wiping the remaining droplets from her eyes she fakes a smile, reassuring him that everything is indeed not alright. He sits down beside her, setting the alcohol on the table before them. Cozying up to her he envelopes Claudette in his arms, cradling her. Tears begin to flow freely again as her mind races. Statuesquely Finn holds her in his arms as she begins to pound on his chest in frustration.

"It's ok darlin, just let it out. I'm ya punchin bag, you know dat."

"Why? We were so close to Retirement. Why us?" She utters between sobs.

"Cause love we can never have it simple. There's always someone to come long and tell us how ta live. Ta fuck it up for da rest a us." He lifts Claudette's chin to his looking directly past her tearful face, into her brilliant green eyes.

"We's stronger than that. We get knocked the fuck down and ya better make sure it's fa'good cause ain't nothin can keep us down."

"You're not one for speeches." She retorts, snickering to herself.

"And ya not normally one for listenin, so there's dat."

"You've got me there." Said with a half smile.

They share a kiss, quick yet passionate. Enough to break Dette from her depressed frame of mind temporarily, finding herself longing for another kiss. With her eyes still closed she smiles, enamored with the man she fell in love with. Finn moves just out of range grabbing glasses from the table pouring two drinks. Returning to Claudette he places one to her mouth, taking her back slightly at its cold touch.

"You do something so sweet-"

"You don't have to say anythin. I poured a glass for both a us this time."

"Exactly." She replied, beaming her smile toward him.

Finn brushes aside her hair, matted from her sweat. He genuinely smiles back, his heart sinking as he stares longingly into her eyes. Shooting her drink back Claudette finishing it in a few gulps, placing it in between them. Finn nods in agreement then follows suit, shooting back his glass of whiskey.

"You remember the first time we went out together?" He questions.

"It's fairly hard to forget with your abrasive personality and all. Didn't we go to McCleary's?"

"Aye we did. Remember what I told ya?" Finn asks while pouring two more drinks, one slightly more full than the other.

"Didn't you say something like. 'Did he just slap ya ass? I'll kill um.'"

"Well yeah I said dat. He deserved it, but dats not what I meant. It was somethin I said only to you."

"I'm only here for two things tonight, drinkin and fuckin, you down?"

"Oh ya, forgot bout that line, ha. Can't believe dat actually worked on ya."

"It didn't. You told me I was the only woman in the world you could see yourself being with forever. That's what you said to me." Claudette quickly says, tears forming in her eyes. "You're going to make me cry. You told me and I quote. 'I has to say dis right now. Dette ya da most beautiful woman I ever laid eyes on. I'm not good at these sorts a things, fuck it. I love you.' End quote."

"And your response was. 'I've never met a man so horribly into himself. So much so dat his ego gets in da way of a good time. Not until today at least, and I couldn't be more intrigued. Let's see where life takes us.' "

"You missed a few lines here or there but i'm not complaining."

"You never complain. I meant what I said there and I mean it even more today. Dette, I love you. I'm not going to let this be the end of us. Fuck, i'm still not dat good at dis."

"You're perfectly imperfect at this. I love you more than you could ever know."

"Cheers ta us." He raises his cup to her. "Ta many more sunny afternoons, sandy beaches and long nights of desire."

"I'll cheers to that."

Entwining their arms together, Finn and Claudette drink from each others cup. Gazing lovingly into each other's eyes as they knock back their glasses of liquor. He caresses the back of her neck with his free arm, comforting her. Finishing their drinks they release each others arms. Finn gathers the drinks placing them back onto the table before turning back to his lover. Dette wraps her arms around his frame holding her head to his chest, clinging to him. He beams a smile she can't see as he combs through her hair with a hand. His other free hand directs her closer into him, pulling her into his supporting embrace. Warm tears bead down onto Finn's shirt.

"Ain't nothin gonna hurt you while ya in ma arms. I'll keep ya warm and safe love." Finn whispers. "Just let it out ya, until the taps run dry."

Finn places the device given to him by Xylen into his ear, switching it on in the process. He takes another look down at Claudette, sadness taking to his eyes as he watches her huddle against him. Pressing his arm against her Finn lifts Dette to eye level. He leans in for another kiss. Tears stream from her eyes onto his face as they meet in a warm embrace.

"Let's take the night shall we? No need to sit here and mourn when nothin happened yet. Dat's just a fucked way to spend a night in a place like dis when we could be havin so much more fun."

"Are you telling me to stop being a bitch?" Claudette chokes out.

"Aye."

"Thank you."

"Anytime darlin."

Finn extends his hand towards her as he raises from his seated position. Happily taking his invitation she rises with him, wiping the tears from her eyes. Finn wipes the last trickling tear from her cheek, smirking as he does so. Together they stride towards the dance floor downstairs, hand in hand.

CHAPTER TEN

A THORN IN THE PLAN

The thrum of music faintly echoes through the back staircase leading up to the third floor of Precipices. It's halls blindingly lit with an off white, offsetting the vivid color display of the previous two levels. The winding staircase leads into a hallway leading to a closed door. It's darkened glass walls give a view to the club floor below. The vibrant colors bouncing off of its reflection. Anna and Tabitha ascend the staircase, looking out over the amassing crowd below. Trailing behind Tabitha watches the patrons partaking in the entertainment below, slowly dragging the tips of her fingers along the railing. Clearly lost in her own thoughts. Coming to a dead stop she surveys her surroundings picking out what appears to be Audrey and Xylen, watching them for a time. Noticing her pause Anna approaches the railing, leaning her head onto Tabitha's shoulder.

"Such a nice view." Anna says gazing outward. "That's not what you're taking in is it?"

"I'm watching your computer wizard corrupt my protege. The things people will do when given the opportunity."

"Corrupt is a relative term isn't it?"

"What would you consider it?"

"Growth of character. We both know we don't need another you in the world. No one could match up to your strict standard of crippling dread. Especially now."

"Is that all you see in me? Dread?" Tabitha turns, looking deeply into Anna's eyes.

"I see you as the girl who showed up on my doorstep, cold and hurt. Who needed someone to let them know it's going to be alright when we both knew it never would change. I see hope and courage when no one else would. I see the face I fell in love with, but I know you've changed. You've become something darker because of something sinister."

"It's always been there. I thought I could change-"

"No need to explain to me. We are who we have become. Good, bad or indifferent. I only see through shades of grey. I'm not judging but you are. Audrey seems like a good one picked out of a terrible crowd. She doesn't need molding. She needs moments like these."

"You're right. You always are." Tabitha says putting her head to the glass wall. "I need her. She believes in me faithfully."

"She's a mirror. You trust me, believe in me, and you are looking for someone to do the same. If she truly does believe in you, she'll follow you to the end of the world. No direction needed. That is what we call friendship."

"I've never heard of that."

"I'm aware."

"Why do you always have to be so spot on?"

"It's frightening isn't it?"

"Unsettling."

Anna looks out onto the dance floor lazily into the tangled mess of dancers. A small smile crosses her face as she spots Xylen and Audrey further into the growing crowd below. Together Tabitha and Anna watch as they enjoy their night alone. A door across the walkway opens quickly as a gentleman steps out into the open hallway. His attire looks as though he were going for a casual business style. He buttons up his cufflinks on both sides before coughing to grab the two ladies attention. Tabitha quickly snaps her head in his direction, glaring at the man who interrupted their conversation. Slowly Anna follows suit her smile only growing wider as she turns to face the businessman. He stands sternly at the door, returning his hand to his side after the interruption.

"Mr. Westhouse is ready to see you now. See yourselves in when you see fit." He says before walking off towards the staircase.

"Thanks." Anna says happily.

Anna watches as the man strolls past her. His hands fidgeting inside his jacket pocket, head hung low as if in shame. She cocks an eyebrow, a question poised in her mind. Odd. Shaky hands, what's making you so nervous?

"Where is the security?" Anna asks, stopping him just before the staircase.

"Excuse me?" His tone cold and straight.

"He always has a man on the door."

"I'm on break, someone will be up to relieve me soon enough. Mr. Westhouse said I could leave once I delivered the message to the both of you."

"Maybe i've just been out of the game for too long. He's lightened up."

"I wouldn't keep him waiting. Not one for patience."

"Of course not. Best for you to go numb those nerves of yours, if you can even lift a cup with how badly you're shaking."

A look of stunned bewilderment spreads across his already emotional face. He grasps for words to say, coming up short. Anna makes her way towards the nervous individual to make their conversation more personal. Stopping her, Tabitha holds her arm out across Anna's chest.

"She does that to people." Tabitha says, entering the conversation. "Best thing you can do for yourself is close your mouth, turn around and retreat because there is not a single thing you could say that she wouldn't throw back into your face."

Taking her advice the gentleman turns to the staircase and makes a hasty escape. Anna shoots a sideways glance in the direction of her companion before relenting. Tabitha slings her arm around Anna's shoulder, pulling her close and dragging her towards the office door.

The two enter into a modestly sized office overlooking the establishment below. Darkened glass makes up the walls just like its walkway. Its decorum is tidy and well kempt. Not a single item looks to be out of order. A long backed chair is turned to face away from the desk and door. The music nearly inaudible within the room, only faintly heard through the open door. The pair stand in the doorway waiting to be greeted. Anna closes the door hoping to receive a reaction from just beyond the desk. A stillness falls over the room as the last remaining ambient noise is extinguished. Replacing the ambiance snickering echoes softly throughout the office, as if trying to keep in laughter. Tabitha charges forward toward the desk slamming her hands down hard onto its surface in another attempt to garner a reaction.

"Thomas, i've had enough games for the night. Can we act like adults and proceed in kind?" Tabitha snarls.

"I've had enough of the games!" A raspy voice mocks. Their voice cracking between words. "But we haven't even gotten started."

The snickering comes to a halt only to be replaced with an innocent giggle. The voice sounding almost feminine. Tabitha stares at the back end of the long chair. A disgruntled look splayed across her face as she impatiently waits whatever act to be over with. Looking around the room Anna attempts to glimpse a reflection off the darkened glass. Squinting her eyes she makes out the shape of what looks to be a white top covered in something dark while the rest of the image is blurred from the distortion on the glass. First the nervous guard and now an odd display. What type of trick is Thomas going for? The chair begins to rock back and forth keeping Tabitha's attention fixated on it. The rocking quickens in pace as their laughter escalates.

"I'm not finding this amusing." Anna declares. "If I wanted a show i'd be performing."

"I'm amusing. I promise." The raspy voice spits out. Their words slurring together. "Who says you're not performing in my show tonight? I would love a performance."

Anna comes to stand beside Tabitha. A look of focus accents her face as though she were attempting to solve a riddle. Unaware of Anna's presence Tabitha flinches as she brushes beside her. Anna quickly turns and flashes an 'im sorry' smile.

"You want a performance?"

"Very. Much. So."

The laughter quits abruptly causing silence to fill the room again. The crackling of static cuts through their earpieces as they turn on nearly deafening the pair. Turning away from the chair Anna readjusts her earpiece, turning its volume down. Returning her attention back Anna notices a cocked eyebrow from Tabitha and a quizzical look plastered on her face. Out of the corner of her eye she observes a head rising over the head of the chair. It's hair matted and wet. As it slowly raises upwards more of its facial features become visible. Their eyes sunken and swollen, beaten and bruised. Echoing of pain. Drying blood clings to the side of their face. Thomas...That couldn't be. Finally his mouth is visible, twisted in pain it lay agape. Underneath the base of his head is a hand where there should be a neck, open palmed, propping up his decapitated head. Their other hand appears from just beyond the chair covered in dried blood.

"Did you wanna say hi Thomas?" A female voice asks, replacing the once raspy voice. "I think they're angry at us. No more games she says. I told her we haven't even begun yet. She's no sport that's for sure. What do you think?" Their tone innocent and childish.

The innocent giggling gives way to a manic cackle, laughing at their own comments. Tabitha withdraws from the desk toward the door. Clearly shaken by the display. Anna stands firm, staring into the lifeless eyes of her former friend. Her eyes begin to tear as she runs through the scenarios and possibilities of Thomas' last moments. Reaching outward towards Anna,

Tabitha grips her on the shoulder tightly to pull her away. Brushing her hand aside Anna defiantly stands in front of the desk, listening to the repetitious cackling. The laughter quits abruptly causing silence to fill the room again.

"Quit being inquisitive Rose! I think we should welcome our guests. Make them feel at home." The female voice says mocking a male tone. Her second free hand playing with his open mouth, giving the appearance of speech. "I thought we were off to a good start. Stupid, stupid, stupid. What do people usually give others... Oh, you're a genius Tommy!" She continues, having her conversation with Thomas' head, being quite animated with their gestures.

Thomas' head falls out of the woman's hand crashing down onto the desk with a wet thud. The sudden slam jars Tabitha causing her to flinch. The head rolls onto the center of the desk, perfectly making eye contact with Annastasia, it's features still frozen in pain. Tabitha steps away from Anna, closing the distance between herself and the exit. Standing unphased beside the desk Anna looks directly into his cold gaze. Clenching her jaw she swallows her fear, reaching outward towards the chair.

"I hope you like my gift. Sorry I didn't have time to wrap him. We didn't ruin the surprise did we? Tommy is such a knucklehead sometimes." She happily adds. "Go ahead, touch it. Get it. A head. Tommy gets it."

Grabbing the corner Anna twists the chair around to reveal a petite woman. Her complexion pallid, offset by the sheer amount of blood covering her and saturating her white dress. Hair stuck in clumps to her face. It's silverish grey tint marred with the bright red of his blood. Her twisted smile, horrifyingly innocent. For a moment Anna stares blankly into her void colored eyes, becoming lost in their emptiness.

"Do I scare you?"

"Not for a second." Anna says confidently, snapping out of her trance.

"That's not what her eyes say." Pointing her dark red finger in Tabitha's direction. Biting down on a fingernail temptingly with her other hand. That twisted smile still beaming in their direction.

"You would be a moron to confuse fear and caution." Said from the back of the room.

"Oh. I'm special. I've always been told that, but i'm not simple. I know fear when I smell it and you reek of that delicious scent. If it makes you feel any better so did Tommy boy." She says smacking the skull with her open palm. "He's in a better place now. Doesn't have to worry about getting caught anymore. What are you so afraid of little miss backstabber?"

"I thought you wanted a performance." Anna perks up, dragging this woman's attention to herself.

"I do, I do, I do." She says clapping loudly onto Thomas' head, as though it were a drum. "We don't have any instruments here though."

"I can make due. You'll have to give me a name to dedicate this to. I love connecting with my fans." Her composure relaxing, as she gives a genuine smile to the monster in front of her.

"I'm Rose!"

"Nice to meet you Rose. I'm-"

"You're the Magician. I know you very well. You make pretty music."

"Thank you. What would you like me to play?"

"You're asking me?!" Said with genuine shock.

"You're the conductor tonight."

"Oh. I. Was. Not. Ready for this. Give me a minute."

"Can I speak with my friend for a moment then?"

"Yep. I'm going to be busy for a moment." She says trailing off into her own thoughts.

Without hesitation Anna gives her back to the murderer in the chair. Tabitha glares bitterly at her lover, disdain written in her look. Pivoting around Anna's frame Tabitha notices Rose braiding her filthy hair as she continues mumbling to herself as she spins back and forth. Anna grabs ahold of Tabitha's face, palming her cheek warmly, bringing her attention back.

"What are we even doing here?" Tabitha whispers.

"We came for information."

"Clearly that was a bust. She has his head splayed on the table."

"Are you nervous?" Anna asks, narrowing her eyes.

"We are sitting in a room with a woman who cut a very skilled thief's head off. Let's just say i'm leary of the situation."

"He must have found something. I'm not letting this death be in vain. I'm in too deep to turn back now. If you want to leave, go ahead. I won't stop you but i'm not going anywhere. I have a plan."

"You have a plan set aside for a severed head?"

"I'm working this as I go. Are you in or out?"

"I'm faithful."

"Remember smoke and mirrors?"

"You think crazy is going to go for a parlor trick?"

"Just work your end and make sure to be quiet."

"Do we have a plan B?"

"This is plan B."

An unexpected clap draws the attention of the couple, interrupting their conversation. Rose twirls herself around again in her chair facing them both. Her warped smile growing wider. Leaving Tabitha's side Anna returns to the desk. Leaning over she gives Rose her undivided attention, staring into her moonless eyes as they flick from side to side in thought.

"Tommy and I had some words and i think we picked out a fan favorite. It's a classic of yours." She says clapping excitedly. "Would you play it for me?"

"I'll have to know what it is first." Anna says smiling. "I may be a magician but despite popular belief I can't read minds."

"HA!" Rose breaks out in laughter. A mixture of the manic cackling and her giggle. "You're funny. Not on purpose funny either. The song is sad. I think you called it 'Light'. Can you play that one for me?"

"You only get one song. Are you sure that's the one?"

"Does Tommy get a song too?" Rose motions towards his lifeless head.

"I believe he has heard his last song already." Anna responds sternly, biting back emotion.

"Then I guess this song is both of our picks." Her grin beaming brighter.

"Are you ready?" Anna asks, avoiding the unsettling scene she has placed herself in.

"Oh hold on!"

Rose scrambles from her chair across to the desk ripping Thomas' head from its spot, lifting it up from the open hole underneath. She wields his head like a bowling ball her fingers jammed into his neck line. Plopping back down into the comfortable cushion she lets out a amused sigh before placing his skull in her lap facing outwards towards the Magician. She pats his matted hair while keeping her attention drawn to Anna. Tabitha, frozen in place, watches as her significant other prepares to perform. Her heart pounding quickly as she contemplates retreat. Closing her eyes she practices her breathing, focusing her mind solely on Anna.

"Rose do you believe in magic?" Anna's voice pierces Tabitha's concentration.

"I believe in yours." Her tone slightly off putting. "I've never personally seen it though. I'm ready to be amazed...wait no, astonished or something like that." She looks down into her lap, staring into the blank expressionless face. "Tommy agrees. He says you're the most wonderful mage ever."

Anna flashes her infectious smile at Rose as she prepares herself to perform. Taking a deep breath she looks down to her own outfit. With a snap of her fingers she changes attire. Changing from her low cut shirt and jeans into a dark blue shirt with matching pants. The saying across the shirt reads 'we each have our own music mines just louder than yours'. She brushes off the shirt as though it had been recently pulled from the closet. Rose sits with her mouth much like Thomas', agape.

"Had to make a few quick changes before I begin. Can't perform without the proper attire."

"You did what? You. How? WOW! Do it again!" Her tone exuberant.

"I usually get too many complaints that I swap outfits too often. Glad to have a change of pace."

Cupping her hands together Anna begins to move them in a circular motion, starting slowly and increasing with each revolution. A light emits from the center of her palms, faint at first but growing suddenly into an small flame. Removing one hand she palms the fire in her right hand.

A gasp of joy escapes Rose's mouth as she watches the Magician work. Taking her free hand Anna places it over top of the flame guiding it upwards, molding it into the shape of a violin. The blazing violin begins to take shape the longer she focuses on the form. She brings it closer to Rose walking around the side of the desk. Surveying behind his desk she notices his cabinets opened, wildly rummaged through. Rose looks up at her, her abyss like eyes reflecting orange blaze back.

"I need help from the audience. I need someone to breathe some life into my violin."

"I'm in the audience. Pick me!" Rose says fervently. "Shut up Tommy. You can't breathe life into nothin. You don't have any left. Don't give me any lip, i'll put you in the corner mister."

"You seem like the perfect person for the job Rose. Go ahead and give it a shot."

Rose happily stands up from the chair, her motions becoming animated and almost comical. Anna holds the flame closer to her, enthralling Rose with it's brilliance. Heat pours from the blaze between her fingertips causing Rose to almost recoil instinctively. Rose purses her lips and blows on the center of the construct causing it to solidify. Like a child her eyes grow wide as the violin begins to take physical shape. Its core morphing into a darkened wood. As she continues to exhale onto the violin Anna spins the newly created instrument in her hands until it forms fully, modeling it for the both of them to see. Tabitha rolls her eyes as she watches the display in front of her. With her hands over on her hips, she waits for the act to continue.

"I created that?"

"I certainly needed your help to create something this grand. I promised you a performance and that includes a show. Shall we take our new violin for its maiden voyage?"

"Are we going on an adventure?" Asked inquisitively.

"To the ends of the universe."

"Oh boy, oh boy, oh boy. I love adventures."

A melody begins to ring throughout the room as though played through speakers above as Anna rests her violin to her collarbone, drawing her bow across the strings. The edges of the room begin to sink into darkness creating a spotlight around the Magician, engulfing her in bright lights as she proceeds to dance around a seemingly unlimited amount of space.

Closing her eyes she gives into the overwhelming emotions allowing them to feed into her playing. The consonance of each note stringing together perfectly to create the sentiment of sadness. Rose watches intently cradling Thomas' head in her arms, her sole focus being on the violinist. Tabitha slowly slinks her way around the back wall of the office careful to not divert attention to herself, each step slower than the next.

Her violin work slows down significantly as it reaches a crescendo. The bright spotlight changes into a darker blue as she continues a slower pace with her violin work. Staring directly upwards Anna opens her eyes directly into the beaming light, breathing in slowly she takes in it's darkened beauty. Swaying back and forth Anna takes to tracing an outline in the ground below. Moving out of the blue circle Anna disappears off into the shadows surrounding the safety of her spotlight leaving only the outline and the phrase 'never forget where you came from' left on the ground within it's blue shimmering light. Her notes begin to fade out barely becoming a faint echo as the circle begins to become engulfed by the surrounding shadows leaving only the inscription behind.

Watching from her chair Rose searches the darkness for a sign of her performer slightly becoming frustrated with their disappearance. Watching from the outside wall of the room Tabitha watches with an unobstructed view of the act, seeing Rose's complete enthrallment in the illusion set before her. She makes her way towards the open desk drawers beside the crazed murder, quietly searching through them for any hidden items Thomas would leave.

"You can never forget where you come from. That place is your home. That is where your light rests. In an instant you can forget who you are. In that moment you are cast into the shadows that no light can penetrate." Anna whispers, her voice carrying throughout the room. "And in the darkest of your hours it is up to you to decide who you will be once you emerge from it's chilled embrace. Will you remember the light that shines only for you?"

The inscription appears to erode from the floor below. It's pieces scattering through the air. Leaving nothing except pure darkness in the room. A sharp draw of the violin pierces the dead air breathing life back into the room. A small ray of light emits from the center of the ceiling, the same dark blue as previously. It's cone widens casting out the shadows from the room until the whole room is left in a blue tint. Anna reappears out of thin air into the room, posed with her violin waiting to start anew. Her bow hand outstretched beckoning Rose forward from her chair.

Lifting herself from the confines of her padded seat she catches herself rushing towards the Magician, Thomas' head tucked firmly under her left arm. Coming inches from Anna's extended hand she stops, watching her with that wicked smile etched onto her face.

"Nice of you to join me." Anna warmly says. Her smile comforting.

"Stage side seats don't cut it when you can be on stage." Rose returns the smile.

Quickly retracting her bow hand Anna renews her playing. Her tempo much quicker, creating an upbeat rhythm. A synthetic beat protrudes from the walls matching her cadence, keeping in time with her playing. Feeling her music Anna starts to sway around Rose, making her the center of attention. Her playing quickens further as she rotates around the captivated woman leading into a gradual climax. Intensifying in pace the rooms hue begins to transform from it's dreary blue into a vibrant orange, matching the rhythm of her music. Ashes rain down from the ceiling piling directly in front of Rose. Making her way towards the gathering of embers Anna skirts around them watching as they fall from above. Rose pulls Thomas' head out from under her arm, opening his mouth wide. She places his head underneath the falling flakes attempting to catch them in his mouth. Shaking her head Anna persists with her own movement moving side to side keeping herself confident, preparing for the songs apex. Stopping abruptly behind Rose she motions in Tabitha's direction with her bow, an obvious hint to proceed. Time for plan C. Let's hope this works out.

"Are you afraid Rose?" Whispered into her ear.

"I hate spiders." She responds naturally. "Who has eight legs? Those creepy little bastards."

Anna chuckles at the remark as she resumes her dance, her song beginning to wind down. Rose turns to face the chuckling Anna, her smile sincere as she holds Thomas' head outward towards Anna.

"Tommy wasn't afraid."

"Thomas has found his own light. Do you know what i'm afraid of?"

"Spiders?"

"Actually. Yes." She chuckles again.

"I knew it! Who likes getting a face full of cobwebs right? What elseeee are you afraid of?"

"I'll show you. Are you ready for an encore?"

"Am I ever!"

Kneeling down beside the now heaping pile of ashes Anna moves the pile to each side revealing another set of words underneath, 'be reborn in the flames or perish to their lingering passion'.

With frantic pace she searches through the remaining torn apart drawers, coming across files and paperwork, nothing resembling their meeting. Tabitha runs her hands through her hair, clearly distraught and cursing to herself.

"It has to be here somewhere." She mutters to herself angrily. "If I knew I was going to be found by a homicidal maniac where would I hide my work? Not in the open that's for sure, but with limited options it would have to be in the desk somewhere. Unless he failed. For her sake I hope he didn't."

Closing the desk drawers Tabitha notices a distinctly shorter container, holding only half the amount of items. Pulling on the container she rips it off of the track, holding it carefully with both hands as to not make a ruckus. Dropping to her knees she searches inside the cubbyhole. Sighing with relief Tabitha spots a small box in the back corner. Reaching back she knocks something above it lose, it drops with a thud onto her hand. Putting her hand around the grip she pulls out the loose item, a gun. Instinctively she checks the clip, then racks a shell. Putting the loaded weapon into her waistband she quickly returns to the box, retrieving it from its hidden home. Opening the top Tabitha lets out a sigh of relief. Two freshly minted badges for the Frostscythe Corporation and a set of passcodes lay in the small box. With a silent cheer she raises up the two badges like a champion holding their trophy. For the second time tonight Tabitha expresses her happiness with a smile.

Anna smiles in Tabitha's direction as she begins to set up for her next song. The dazzling orange rays return to their normal hue bringing closer to reality. Rose waits anxiously in anticipation for her next song, returning the head to its previously location under her left arm. The words left etched in the ground burst into flames, slowly burning away. Anna holds the neck of her violin out handing it to Rose across the smoldering flame.

"A gift. I'm sorry I didn't get a chance to wrap it."

"You want to give me your firewood breath violin?"

"You're an odd one Rose. I would love for you to have something to remember me by."

"Well i'll take it!" Rose excitedly says. Carefully taking the violin from Anna's grip she lets loose Thomas' head carelessly letting it roll away from her, fascinated with her new gift. "I have my own magic violin. You're the best mage. Tommy was right."

"I'm glad to bring a smile to your face. Perhaps you can help me with something."

"The Magician needs my help? I can't play the violin!"

"That wasn't the help I needed. I've been wondering exactly why you're here and who would go through all this trouble for a few access codes. Can you help me solve my puzzle?"

"Oohhh. You want me to tell you things. I hate puzzles but i'd be in so much trouble. Yes I would."

"Are you afraid of them?" Anna redoubles her efforts.

"They're not spiders. Lots of people are afraid of them but not me, they can't hurt me. He makes it so they can't hurt me. Some say i'm not fit for these things, that i'm too stupid to act out our orders. They're wrong. I stopped Tommy. I have you here."

"Are you supposed to keep me here Rose?"

"Those are orders. I don't know if I want you to live in darkness little bird. You're so bright. So fun. We could have fun together. Do you wanna have fun?"

"We were having fun. Would you like to come with me? We can have more fun together." Anna says, placing a hand on her shoulder.

"You wanna be friends? Like real friends. Like skip down the road holding hands best friends?"

"You know friends tell each other secrets. Things that would affect each other."

"You're a smart one little bird."

"I'll tell you a secret first. Hows that sound?"

"Deal."

"I pretend to be fearless when deep down i'm just as afraid as everyone else."

"So you're afraid of me?"

"Not anymore. We're friends."

"Well duh. I turned the fear button off for your performance. My turn I guess. We have something very big planned for you. I can't completely ruin the surprise. It'd be like a birthday with no cake. Si- Mind is on his way here. He wants to 'retrieve you' himself."

"Is that the man in the mask?"

"I'm afraid for you. They won't tell me what they wanna do."

"You've skipped the question."

"Oh! Sorry! We all wear masks. Well except me. They just aren't practical, you know. Your turn."

"I'm afraid you're going to hurt my friends."

"I won't."

"Who will?"

"Are we really best friends?" Rose asks, placing her open hand onto Anna's arm.

"I am many things but a liar is not one of them Rose. You hurt my friend and that hurts me. More so than I think you know. I can also see you're wounded, that you need a friend more than anything in this world. I would be willing to place my trust in you. You would have to do the same."

"Mind tells me we have to move faster because you are involved. We're not supposed to hurt you but I think he's got other plans little bird. I don't want you covered in darkness. We're friends." Rose removes her hand from Annastasia's arm placing it on her cheek. "You're so talented. Your parents would be so proud of you-"

A earsplitting blast fills the room deafening Annastasia. It's reverberations echo through the closed door and down the hallway. In a moment of stillness Anna races to gather her jarred thoughts. Feeling the hand remove itself from her cheek Anna stares into Rose's darkened eyes, watching them fill with fear and panic. The Magician stand in shock as Tabitha rounds the desk corner gun held steadily in hand, aiming again for Rose's exposed back. Sadness fills her eyes as she watches her new friends eyes well with tears and confusion.

"NO!" Anna screams in Tabitha's direction.

Another shot echoes throughout the enclosed space as Tabitha confidently moves in closer, closing the distance between them. Rose turns to meet Tabitha's emotionless stare, her cold eyes meeting their exact mirror. With determination Tabitha fires twice more at close range causing her victim to scream in pain as she falls to the floor, her body becoming still and lifeless.

Anna wrestles the gun away from Tabitha, her face twisted with anger and disgust.

"Why? I connected with her Tabitha!" Anna says bitterly.

"I saw my opportunity and I took it. Call it Plan C. She clearly had you wrapped around her finger and I wasn't about to let her do to you what she did to Thomas. If you need a reminder his head is lying on the floor, discarded like Finn's ex's."

"I had this under control." Her anger balling into a building fury. "She was going to tell me something about their plan. A time table they had to advance and you had to go and-"

"And what? I had to do what you do to all sick dogs. Put them down. Grow up, get over it and let's move on. We have work to do."

Anna watches Rose's lifeless body. Her sinister smile still smugly across her face as lay dead in the center of the room. She leans down over Rose's body, closing her eyes and saying a few words before returning to her feet.

"Next time you use this remember why we're so different."

Annastasia returns the gun to Tabitha, releasing her grip on it hesitantly. Taking the firearm back she quickly tucks it into the side of her waistband, covering it with her jacket. Tabitha grips her lover firmly by the arm pulling her in close, kissing her passionately. Her cold eyes melting upon contact with Anna.

"I was only looking to protect you." Breaking the kiss, biting her lower lip.

"We have company." Audrey says interrupting their moment. Her voice coming through crystal clear over their earpieces.

CHAPTER ELEVEN

ON A MOUNTAIN HIGH

Claudette presses into Finn leaning against his frame weakly. Supporting her body weight they walk towards the circular bar, his hand gripping her tightly around the waist. They share a brief smile before both again become solemn. Around them the crowd remains hyped, their night steadily continuing. People step to the side as Finn bulls his way through, propping Claudette up at the countertop leaning her against its surface. A worried look grows along his face as he traces his hand up her infected arm, watching as her veins slowly grow darker. With her free hand Dette attempts to calm her significant other running her hand through his short hair, twirling it nervously between her fingers.

"*It looks worse.*"

"I'm fine. She said I had a few hours with her serum. It doesn't hurt right now."

"*Ya look paler. Like its not helpin at all. Ya arms burnin up, hows this fine?*" His tone concerned.

"Just because I look like hell doesn't mean I feel like it. I can handle this."

"*Fa how long love?*"

"As long as it takes. Now focus. We have two guards on the bottlenecked front entrance, no way we leave through that exit."

Claudette motions toward the front door, gesturing towards two gentlemen sharply dressed in suits. Their pose stoic in front of the entrance, blocking exiting parties from leaving the club. Eyes shifting from side to side as they scan the building once over. One begins allowing a large group to leave after a brief search of items, motioning them forward with the whisk of his hand.

"Ya and the exit behind the stage is blocked. Stop changin the subject."

Finn directs her attention to the packed dance floor. Men in similar suits walk along the outside edge of the crowd, working the same routine as the guards on the front entrance. Audrey and Xylen stand tenuously in the center of the floor, mingling with the crowd to keep a low profile.

"I'm not changing the subject. If you want me to get better we have to make sure Tabitha leaves Precipice without her escort. So, back storeroom has an exit right?"

"They'd need ta. So much liquor, it has to come through the back."

"So that's our exit. Audrey do you read me?" Claudette asks, turning her earpiece on.

"Loud and clear." Audrey replies through the headset.

"Plan is for the back storeroom. We need to make sure it's clear for them-"

"Dette we should clear da trash yeah?"

The pounding music comes to a halt mid song leaving the audience in bewilderment. They quickly shout in the direction of the jockey, some with profanity others in anger. The blindingly white flood lights snap on, making everything clearly visible. Claudette and Finn cautiously turn their heads, surveying the surroundings. The guards circling the crowd begin to converge towards its center, taking advantage of this unique opportunity. Two more guards approach the front entrance, bolstering their numbers as well.

"I'm thinking it would be decent to thin the herd. They're boxing us in."

"I hope they expectin a fight." Finn cracks his knuckles in excitement.

"Something tells me they are." Claudette says confidently.

"Bartender. A shot and brew ya?"

The bartender pulls his attention away from the ensuing chaos on the dance floor, directing it instead to Finn. Smiling and nodding he begins working on the order. Claudette rolls her eyes in Finn's direction all the while beaming a bright smile. He returns the look to her, raising his shoulders as if to say 'what' sarcastically.

"I'm currently working on solving the problem folks." A booming voice sounds over the loudspeakers. "Show your bartenders some love while I work on the technical difficulties."

The barkeep slings two drinks Finn's direction, motioning for cash in return. Digging into his pocket Finn drops a stack of small bills to the counter.

"Keep um comin tonight and dat's all you."

"You tip me like that all night and i'll feed you as much booze as you want."

"You don't have enough. Cute you tink you could try though. If you see a glass overturned dat's me. Refill me kindly."

"Sure thing." The bartender says, moving on to the new influx of customers, his sentence trailing off in the crowd of voices.

Throwing his shot back Finn downs both alcoholic drinks swiftly, turning them over on the countertop. Claudette watches as he scans the room like a lion hunting for its prey, slowly shifting his gaze through the people on the dance floor. He turns back to her with a look of wanting, his eyes alit with a fiery passion.

"Did you find what you were looking for?"

"A couple a twats harassin the fine people a this establishment. Ya I did. Ere's the play-"

"Blitzkrieg. I'll be the thunder. You're the lightning."

"I prolly should be both Dette. You ain't look all dat hot-" He pauses, thinking on his words. *"Let me get it straight ya definitely hot, just not in health. I'd never hear the*

end a this if you thought, i thought ya beauty was fadin."

"Stop stammering would you."

"'T's just sayin I don't want it crossed ya. It's better for ya if we keep that heart rate down until after tha party's over. Don't need ta be worryin bout you while i'm crackin skulls."

"Finn-"

"I mean it dis time. Just be my eyes and ears. Nothin physical."

"I-" She begins to protest before thinking better of the situation. "I don't need you to remember these moments as arguments."

"There's no argument, just da best damn support." He says feinting a smile.

The passing bartender leaves two more drinks at the counter for Finn awkwardly pointing at him as he passes by to serve another patron. Finn reaches out to grab the beer and shot only to have Claudette scoop up the drinks, pushing his hands aside and holding the beverages hostage. He looks to the rafters of the building, clenching his jaw in slight irritation. Dette responds with a hearty chuckle, deriving pleasure from his impatience.

"You get one before and one after. Which is it?"

"Oh fuck me."

"That was not an option."

"Ha. Ha. Real funny dearest. I'm takin the shot first. Need the sour before I get to my treat."

Claudette carefully hands over the shot glass, placing the beer behind her back. Finn seizes the small glass from her hand. In one swig he downs the shot again placing it upside down on the counter beside Claudette. He gives her one last confident smirk before initiating his hunt.

●

"Here we go ladies and gentleman! We're back up and running with no time to waste. Let's officially get this party started!" The DJ again booms over the loudspeaker.

154

The music returns to an almost ear splitting level as he spins the next track and with it the room returns to near darkness. The glaring white lights slowly return to the usual dim blue of the house lights.

Like drones, those crowded around the central bar migrate back toward the dance floor, keeping within their tight knit groups. Audrey and Xylen begin to file out towards the bar moving against the flow of traffic, effectively hidden within the large crowd. Keeping a low profile Audrey darts through the crowd gripping tightly to Xylen as he moves swiftly on her heels attempting to keep up with her pace. Keeping the bar in her sight she carves a path towards Finn and Claudette, using its tall stature as a compass.

"Come on we have to move. This is our opportunity." Audrey screams overtop of the music in his direction.

"Are they even looking for us?" His tone hesitant.

Audrey doesn't respond to his comment, her focus clearly on the bar almost in their reach. He tugs at her grip, stopping them both just shy of their exit. Turning back Audrey furls her eyebrows, clearly annoyed with the statement.

"Would you like to wait and find out Xylen?" A bite to her tone. "It doesn't matter if they're here for us or Tabitha and Anna. If we don't move they can use us against them. Don't think twice about why were here, that will end up getting you killed."

"You sound like her." Xylen says holding his ground.

"She is my best friend and the only-. The-. She saved me and I owe my life to her. This is no time for this conversation. We're defenseless and unarmed, if they ARE looking for us it's six on two." Said confidently. Her eyes flashing in each direction, staying vigilant on lookout.

"I get your point." Xylen concedes.

"Then let's be on our way. We no doubt look odd standing in the middle of this crowd. Hopefully it hasn't drawn their attention."

Catching the shine of something metal in her peripherals Audrey twists around quickly, clenching her hand into a fist, confronting a woman with a drink tray passing through the crowd. The woman raises a quick eyebrow to Audrey, shocked by the girl's speed. Letting out a relieved sigh she grabs ahold of Xylen's hand. Turning back to him she smiles wide, almost as if in apology. The apology is cut short as a barrel of a weapon digs into Audrey's back. The smile fades transforming into immediate distress, the feeling of a gun jammed into her back all too familiar. Picking up on her change of expression Xylen assess the situation from his vantage point. A tall man in a black suit coat skulking behind her petite frame, looming over her. His eyes almost vacant as he stares lifelessly into the back of her head. Audrey releases Xylen's hand, motioning him away from her, mouthing the word 'go'. Audrey locks herself in place, cautiously evaluating the situation while continuing to ward Xylen off.

"Can I help you?" She asks, gulping down her courage. Slowly lifting her arm up she places her hand outward palm first stopping Xylen from interrupting the conversation. "You're infallibly cute but I don't know you. Why don't you just move along and go find your friends."

Xylen blinks rapidly, processing her cryptic words. He backs away from her, his hands held outward in the same stopping motion. Faking a disgusted look he brushes beside her, slamming into her shoulder. Moving with the blow Audrey uses his momentum to spin herself around to face the suit. Distracted, the man first feels the grip of a hand and then the snap of a wrist as Audrey disarms him of his firearm before using his weight against him, flipping him over her shoulder onto the ground.

Aiding Audrey, Xylen puts his knee into the man's chest, using his body weight to help her hold him. With minimal effort Audrey controls his movement by wrenching on his broken wrist, keeping him stationary. Surveying the area Xylen spots two more of them making their way through the crowd. Made even more noticeable as the crowd diverges at the sound of gunfire echoing from the second floor. People begin to panic spreading out towards the exits, giving Audrey and Xylen protection from the oncoming assailants.

"I didn't want to alarm you Tabitha, but now would be the time to move. We will have the back storeroom exit cleared for you by the time you are down here. I hope you're safe up there." Audrey comms.

Removing her hand from his wrist Audrey slides her hands around his neck, twisting violently. The sudden crunch of bone and cartilage sends shivers down Xylen's spine. His mind wandering in bewilderment he stares directly through Audrey in shock. Looking for her next move Audrey takes ahold of his pistol, checking the magazine and racking a shell.

Everything slows to a crawl in front of Xylen. The sound of their neck snapping playing over in his head repeatedly, blocking out the cries of fear, reverberation of music and clearing of the chamber. He looks down to the man who was attempting to hurt his friend, it's motionless body being ransacked. Audrey places her hand on his shoulder attempts to bring him out of his trance like state.

"Xylen." Her voice echoes through his head. "We have to keep going."

"I-I-I." He stammers.

Shaking him frantically Audrey tries again to wake him from his catatonic state. He continues to stare at the corpse underneath his knee. His hands shaking as he replays the event over in his head.

"Please Xylen. We have to go." She urges "I'm fighting all of my instincts just to stay here. I'm not leaving you."

The suited men begin to close in on their position, weapons drawn as they wade through the sea of people. Intently focusing on the couple overtop one of their own. Each of them has their weapon trained on Audrey, as the remaining five converge on their location. Shouts and random expletives are bandied about at her. She looks into Xylen's drained eyes, raising her hands slowly over her head, dropping the gun.

"Where is she Audrey?" A speaker among them asks.

●

"*Where da hell is she Annie?*" Finn exclaims.

"She'll be on her way. Tabitha is never on time for anything important." Anna retorts. "We just have to keep going. She'll be there."

Working their way up a narrow flight of stairs Anna, Finn and Xylen make way towards the top level of a building with Finn bringing up the rear, a wounded woman cradled in his arms as he bounds up the staircase with ease. The wounded woman is bruised from head to toe, clothes in tatters, hair nappy and matted to her face. As they continue up the steps she groans in pain as Finn juggles her weight with each passing stair. The sound of crashing footsteps echo a few levels lower as others give chase. With each passing floor the crew begins to slow down, their pace becoming sluggish.

"*How fuckin close are we? I don't think she'll last much damn longer.*"

"We're close." Xylen replies. Digging into his satchel for a touch pad. "Just two more floors. I'm already working on the security code clearance. They thought a Verit R Pro500 series was unhackable." He laughs to himself.

"*I don't give a fuck bout a security alarm. Keep ya computer speak to yaself. I'll stick with women.*"

"Always cracking jokes."

"*It's how I keep my stunning youth. You punch in codes. I'll punch in the guys tryin to shoot us. Less you can hack them too.*"

"Enough. Xylen's never been in the field Finn. Could you at least be decent enough to wait until he's saved our asses. You couldn't open an automatic door."

"*Do we have ta bring dat up now? It's embarrassin.*"

Working their way up the final flights of stairs, they burst through the unlocked emergency door. Xylen shoves his touch pad back inside his satchel before exiting into the pouring rain. In the pitch black of night clouds block out the natural moonlight, leaving only the few artificial lights lingering around the rooftop. Finn shields the nearly unconscious woman from the heavy rain, sloshing his way through the downpour. Anna exits last. She begins surveys the surrounding buildings, looking for their means of escape. A jet black hover sit parked on the central landing pad. Noticing the craft Xylen runs towards it with Finn following close behind.

"Anna! I'm going to work on another means of travel."

"I'll keep an eye out for Tabitha." She shouts back nervously.

Working his own form of magic, Xylen begins to tinker with the door unit on the hover. Taking out a small phone like device he attaches cords from the device on the security mechanism, using it to find its unique passcode.

"What ya thinkin princess?"

"I'm thinking Tabitha abandoned us. Didn't you hear the way she was talking about Natela. She's the whole reason we're even in this mess."

"Ya ain't wrong. Girl's got a haze over her eyes when it comes to that one's ways. Can ya get this thing movin?"

"She might be the magician but i'm a technomancer."

"Ya. A technowhatdafuck are you on about? A simple yes or no would be welcomed, fucks sake."

"Yeah. I can get it." Xylen replies snickering under his breath.

Across the building Anna continues to frantically search for her significant other. Drenched in water, her hair clings to her face. She paces about the building, unable to accept the horrible reality. In frustration she pulls off a necklace from beneath her soaked clothing, hurling it from the building top. Balling her hands into fists Anna screams defiantly into into the black skies.

The door opens with a loud popping sound. Xylen turns to Finn with a sense of accomplishment.

"Gold star for ya princess. You'll get another if you get this damn thing flying." Taking a second to collect himself Finn notices an absence. *"Fuck. Where's Annie? Damnit. You take care of her."* Finn demands, his tone irritated. He hoists Natela into the passenger's seat. Her body almost ragdoll esque. *"You keep her safe. If anyone gets close to her you take them out. Got it short stuff?"*

"How?"

"Any means necessary. If me and Annie don't come back soon. You leave. Natela is the mission and i'll be damned if we ever fail a mission you got me." His words coming off intensely. Finn grabs ahold of Xylen's shoulder firmly before disappearing into the downpour.

Xylen hurriedly prys open the control panel on the vehicle exposing its wires and cords. Producing his handheld tool from his pocket he begins to work on overriding the systems and starting its engines. His gadget begins blinking a consistent red light as he works on the control panel A groan emits from his passenger as she comes to. Slumping over in the seat she turns to face Xylen. Her face written in pain as she stares at him deliriously.

"Hi. This is pretty awkward. My names Xylen, I work with Anna and Finn."

"Hi." She groans softly. "Where- where are we?"

"Currently we are in trouble." He chuckles to himself as he continues working. "Don't worry. We're professionals. This sort of thing happens all the time. We'll be fine."

"Xylen." She trails off.

"Yeah?"

"I don't think i'll be making it." Wincing, she lifts her shirt revealing two nasty gashes, bleeding profusely. Looking up from his project he takes a glimpse in her direction. Cringing at her wounds he looks her in the eyes.

"Can you put pressure on them? Let's see what these assholes left in the hover." He says nervously. "I just need something to wrap around your waist."

"He's coming." Her voice trembling, eyes flickering with fear.

"Who?" Xylen asks, searching throughout the cabin for anything to help stop the bleeding.

"The leader." She says with bated breath. "He has plans for us."

Natela attempts to reposition herself. Her muscles give out and she falls back into the seat screaming. Returning his full attention to the wounded woman Xylen looks hesitantly at her and the pain etched across her face.

"I was bait." Her face frozen in fear. "This... this is a trap."

"What?" Said in shock. "Guys come in. You need to get back now! Natela is bleeding out, if we don't leave soon she might not make it. I almost have this thing going. Just a few more wires to cross." He says into his comm unit.

"Workin on findin Annie. These bastards have knives, can you believe that? Fuckin Knives."

"You're not listening to me." Her breathing deepens. "They never once cared about the ransom. This is about something else."

"I am listening, I also have to make sure you take it easy. That will help with the bleeding. Your brother sent us and we're going to get you back home. Keep your hand on the wound." His tone coming off like a worried parent.

"I'm glad he cares." She faints a smile. "And i'm glad you care." She adds, applying pressure to her wound.

"You're in the right hands-"

"Look out!" She screams, wincing as she points behind him.

The driver side door whips open letting in the rain. A suited man grabs ahold of Xylen by his damp hair dragging him outside the hover and onto the ground, landing with a thud onto the pavement below. The rain beats down on him as he tumbles to the ground. Quickly Xylen scrambles to stand upright. A kick strikes him in the solar plexus with a follow up knee directly to his face. Lying face up in the downpour Xylen takes a moment to get his bearings straight. Hearing screaming from the direction of the hover Xylen struggles to his feet, holding his chest. Squinting he makes out a familiar shadow just off in the distance. Coming up behind the shadow Xylen discerns the black jacket and a gun held in his left hand.

Throwing caution into the wind he leaps for the man's back taking him off guard. Surprised the guard falls to a knee, unable to support the hackers weight on him. Taking the opportunity to continue his assault Xylen rains elbows frantically onto the man's back and shoulders attempting to weaken his defenses. Using his superior mass the man flings Xylen from his shoulders, sliding him across the rooftop again.

Returning his attention to Natela, the guard aims in her direction. Xylen rushes to his feet seeking to disarm him before the follow through. They wrestle with the gun firmly still in his enemy's grip. Two shots fire rapidly before Xylen finally drags the weapon away. Worried, he looks back to Natela, curled into a ball in the seat a bullet hole on either side of her. One breaking open the window to the hover and the other directly above her head. The suited man presses the attack tackling him to the ground, taking Xylen by surprise. The gun slides underneath the hover in the ensuing chaos. Once on the ground they wrestle for control. Pushing his opponent off of him Xylen redoubles his efforts, Finn's words echoing through his mind. Landing on top of him Xylen gains the upper hand, throwing punch after punch towards his unprotected face. The man again uses his strength to push Xylen away. Like a feral dog Xylen whips himself around continuing his attack as the man tries to regain his footing, moving around him to his back hastily. Locking a chokehold in Xylen wraps himself around the struggling man. Writhing around he attempts to pull Xylen from his back one more time. Instinctively Xylen pulls away twisting at his opponent's neck. The cracking of bone rings through Xylen's ears over the pouring rain as the man falls limply against his grip. Letting the body fall to the ground Xylen runs his hands through his soaking red hair, heart racing as he attempts to calm himself. The pouring rain beats down heavily, the sound like gunfire cascading through his ears. A voice cuts through the building tension in his mind.

•

"I'm sorry." Audrey says, almost brought to tears. Her voice brings Xylen from his stupor. His attention immediately drawn to the crowd of suits surrounding them, aiming with the intent to kill. Blinking slowly he notices the pistol lying between him and Audrey. For a fleeting moment he thinks to prepare for the ensuing conflict.

"This is the last time i'll ask." One of the suits says, losing patience in the situation.

In the ensuing chaos the music continues on like a revolving jukebox with an absent DJ. Rising to her feet Audrey turns to the vocal member of their unit, her hands still raised in the air.

"What was it you asked? The question seemed so redundant I figured it was rhetorical." She sneers cockily. Brushing her hair from her field of vision she smirks confidently in his direction.

"Listen Audrey. We don't want to have to go about this the hard way. Give her up. You and the red rooster over here can leave. No questions asked."

"While I appreciate the gesture-" She pauses, thinking to herself. "Lackey number one, i'm going to have to decline. See, I worked for the same company and I know with doubt that we aren't leaving here without a fight or in a bodybag. So you'll have to shoot me because i'm not about to betray the woman who saved me."

"Who said I was going to shoot you?" He quips.

Xylen cautiously reaches for the weapon just feet before him while their attention is trained on Audrey. Taking a deep breath he readies himself for combat. The lingering patrons of the club maintain their steady escape from the dance floor, most trying actively to avoid the conflict. Audrey raises an eyebrow at the comment slung her way. Moving towards the team leader she steps slowly, a swagger to her stride. Tenuously the men react to her bravado, their weapons at the ready

"Do your worst." Taunting him with her smirk as they meet face to face.

His confidence dissipates standing face to face with the young woman. Her confident stride swallowing up what little conviction he had in his statements. Keeping up the facade he spins the end of his weapon around, swinging for her face with the butt of his pistol. Audrey steps into his space striking his head with her own as he drops his guard with the attempted attack. Her follow up attacks prove to be just as detrimental, a well placed knee to the groin and another blow to the head. Dropping to his ass, the suit stares at her thunderstruck.

"First thing you learn in training. Never underestimate your opponent. Second lesson I learned was you never leave them alive. Would you like me to show you that lesson? I've seemed to master it." She quips, pointing at the dead agent behind her.

The remaining four look to the downed leader as they hesitate to retaliate backing away guardedly, widening their semi circle. Grimacing he returns to his feet, gun trembling in his hand. Blood flows freely from his now broken nose. His eyes full of malice he stares down Audrey.

"I thought you weren't going to shoot me."

"I won't shoot you." He says, aiming his gun at Xylen. "Now-"

Reactionarily Xylen quick draws his pistol putting two bullets into the man's chest, dropping him to the floor before he can even finish the sentence. His weapon held closely to his chest Xylen returns to his feet, aiming at the remaining men. His trademark smile and poise returning.

The audience and onlookers shriek in fear at the gunshots, furthering themselves as much as they can from the conflict. Most attempting to leave through the front and side exits, bulling over the security stood in front of those doors.

Audrey moves into the fray, reacting to Xylen's surprise attack. Moving past their dying leader she catches the gun as it falls from his hands. In a flurry of movement Audrey fires rapidly towards the four remaining men. Each shot executed perfectly, meeting their intended targets. The two men on the outside edges drop to the ground, her shots finding home embedded in their heads.

In reaction the men return fire towards their aggressors. Firing wildly in the chaos of the moment. Audrey weaves through the close range gunfire, predicting their movements by keeping in time with their aim. Closing the distance between her targets with each shot fired, she uses their aim against each other causing an inadvertent crossfire. While within close range Audrey uses her momentum to swing herself around one of the last two targets, moving underneath his outstretched arm. Placing the firearm to the back of his head she lets off another round. With a thud his body falls to the floor. Standing across from the last remaining agent she aims down the sight of her barrel, as he does the same. Xylen stands guard, his weapon at the ready, as he filters through the frightened crowd searching for more agents to appear out of the woodwork.

"Ere I was trying to get some fun in before we had to leave and ya done went and had all o' it without me. Hurry up Audrey the guards up front are toasted. Just waitin on ya trigger happy little bunch." Finn says over his commlink.

They stand locked in a standstill, both parties waiting for a reaction from either side. His hand trembles as he stares her down the end of his barrel. Audrey shoots first, her weapon malfunctioning. Taking this opportunity the suit shoots back catching her in the right shoulder just below the collarbone. The shot takes Audrey aback, spinning her around as she clutches at her shoulder, cursing under her breath. Wincing, she closes her eyes as another shot is fired. Hearing a loud bang she opens her eyes to the agent lying on the floor, gun still clutched in hand. In her field of vision she notices Tabitha briskly walking towards the downed suit.

Standing overtop of the downed agent, she kicks the gun out of his weak grip. Tabitha places the gun to his head while lifting him up by his shirt collar, his body limp in her grip. Audrey stares on in wonderment, her jaw clenched in pain.

"How dare you!" Tabitha spits out in rage. " You wished to find death, here I am and I welcome you." She screams at him.

Emptying the clip, she lays waste to his head leaving behind a pulped stump. Anna pulls her away roughly from the cooling body, the remainder of his form plops wetly onto the dance floor. Tabitha pushes away from Anna's grip. Blood drenched she walks towards Audrey, pulling her hair to the side and running her hand through its length. Her calm demeanor replaced with a burning anger. Audrey stares up at her while being attended to by Xylen. His hands working along her shoulder, checking the open wound out. Her protege lets out a small smile, acknowledging her presence.

"Get back." She demands.

"Like hell." Xylen retorts.

"I told you to get back." Said while holding the empty weapon towards him. "She doesn't need your help, you soft hearted weakling."

"You don't know what she needs."

"I need stitches." Audrey butts in. "And I can speak for myself. If I didn't want him here I would make it well known."

"They hurt you." Tabitha kneels down before Audrey, checking on the wound. "I never want to see you risking your life carelessly again. Do you understand."

Audrey looks down at her wound, a shot that went clean through. Gulping down a large breath she stares straight into Tabitha's eyes. A ting of hesitation forms in her mind as she stops herself before saying anything.

"Yes." She replies, hanging her head low.

Anna looks around the nearly abandoned club. With most of the clubs patrons having evacuated the building lay barren. Music continues to play, skipping and repeating the last verse of the final song, 'His name that sat on him was death and hades followed with him'.

Drinks and various other items litter the floor throughout the area. Tabitha lowers herself to Audrey's level, practically sitting on the ground. She puts her hand on the other shoulder and rests her head against her proteges. Xylen rolls his eyes at the display as he watches Anna gaze off throughout the bar.

On the far end by the front entrance is four unconscious guards, tied up and left in the doorway. Finn and Claudette approach the arguing group from that direction, with him holding her up as they go. Finn smiles weakly at Anna as they come to stand in front of the group. Looking around at the crew before him, noting Audrey's apparent pain as she clutches her shoulder. He looks to Annastasia, her hair disheveled and demeanor distraught.

"Fucks the hold up? We ain't tuggin on each other in the middle a this place is we? Last I knew we get in and get da fuck out."

166

"Audrey got shot." Anna says, her words short.

"*Somethin we can patch up and go?*"

"Yeah." Audrey chimes in. "I can make it." She stands up, leaving Tabitha kneeling on the ground. Xylen reaches out for her as she begins walking past him, wrapping his arm around her waist and pulling her back to him.

"*Atta girl. I knew she'd be a tough one. Right off the ole block you are.*"

Audrey leans into Xylen, relaxing in his arms. Tabitha stands upright, brushing off the last of her emotions. Her eyes tell the tale of betrayal as she watches Audrey cozy into Xylen's grip. Lips curling in contempt, Tabitha turns away beginning to head for the entrance.

"Tabitha." Anna's voice cuts through her like a cold wind.

"Yes?" She replies, pausing her advance.

"Growth of character."

"Sure."

Tabitha strides up to Finn and Claudette, pulling the same device from her jacket pocket. She loads in another vial of the blue serum and without warning doses Claudette again, picking another spot along her neck for it's injection. A yelp escapes the toughened fighter as the cool liquid invades her system. Finn's face contorts, anger taking shape in his features.

"*The fuck Tabitha?*"

"Growth of character."

"*Das da last straw.*"

"I'm the only thing keeping her alive. Do not attempt to lecture me on how I should handle the situation. There are two badges to Frostscythe and I count six of us. If you do the math right, which we all know you can barely even count, we are four short. So only two of us can go. She won't get her cure in time, so I have to prolong the effects until I can make it back. Anyone else have anything they want to discuss while we waste precious time standing in a crime scene?"

"I do." A raspy voice says, seemingly echoing through the room. "Did I catch you all at a awful time? The conversation seemed very tenuous."

Chills roll through Tabitha and Anna's spine, a familiar voice to the both of them. A darkly dressed man steps into the main hall. An ornate mask adorning his face, wrapped completely around his head. It has markings and words scrawled across it in multiple languages. Trading in his dark cloak for a sleek set of padded clothing. The mask moves with the sound of his voice as he speaks, shifting and contorting into a mouth able to produce sound. He walks with a soft step, progressing toward them.

Finn releases his grip on Claudette, letting her gather her bearings and regain her balance. He turns to face the direction of the voice. Looking upon the darkly dressed man, he looks rather unimpressed. Tabitha retreats in the same fashion as earlier with Rose, as though she has seen a ghost. Anna grabs ahold of her hand as she backs up to comfort Tabitha. This time she allows the gesture and even reciprocates, clutching onto her partners hand.

"You seem to have made a mess here. What a shame. I always liked this establishment. It did serve as great entertainment." The man in the mask states, slowly moving forward. "Nevertheless. Did you appreciate my welcoming present? I wanted you to feel wanted. I know how much that means to the both of you."

"You must be the individual known as Mind." Anna dodges his question.

"My reputation precedes me." He bows before the group. "You have quite the able crew here Annastasia. Have you put any thought into my previous offer?"

"You're offer came to me in an altered state, I can officially mark that as a no."

"That is a shame. We could do so much with this world and the many others just like it. This is a horrid time for my business proposition, I must apologize. I just cannot seem to adhere to this technology you all cling to so fondly. I'm very much a people person."

The air in the room grows stale as he inches his way forward, his hands grasp together firmly behind his back. The looping sound continues in the background, clearly heard in between their pausing conversation. Tabitha grips hard onto Anna's hand drawing blood from the pressure. The group stands still tentatively awaiting the masked man's approach.

"You sent your attack dog after us!" Tabitha starts in. "What did you come here for?"

"Simply to acquire an amazing addition to my team."

"I'm not interested." They say in unison.

"Well that is most definitely a shame to hear. Although I will be honest I did not come here seeking approval. I will state this as simply as possible. I request your presence at my side, any objections will be met with harsh punishment. Tabitha dear, you of all people standing in this room should know exactly what I am capable of. I welcome you home, with open arms." He swings his arms out in front of him openly, gesturing a hug. The mouth on the mask a twisted metallic smile.

"Her home is here. With me." Anna states clearly, gripping tighter onto Tabitha.

"Ah, yes. Let us not be cliche shall we. It insults the present companies intelligence collectively. You are an intriguing sort Annastasia." Her name rolling off his lips in a hiss. "You seem to take on many problems that are not your own. Does that weight ever become encumbering? You need not answer. I've met someone very much like you before. They attempted to put the

weight of a world on their shoulders. Something you seem very keen to do yourself."

He strides past Finn and Claudette, oblivious to their existence. The face on his mask shifts towards them staring directly at Claudette as he continues forward, his conversation with Anna and Tabitha uninterrupted. The face smiles as Claudette takes notice of it, winking at her as it shifts back to its rightful place. Finn runs his hand over his mouth, watching as this ominous man strolls past him casually. Audrey digs herself deeper into Xylen's arms, shielding herself from Mind.

"I'm sorry." Xylen whispers into her ear.

"This is the best second date ever." She faints a smile, looking up into his starry gaze. "Up until now it's been a blast. No need to apologize Red."

Stopping shy of Anna and Tabitha, Mind again holds out his hands in merriment. The mask forms a giant smile, from ear to ear. Tabitha clenches her jaw, balling her right hand into a fist. Anna lets go of Tabitha's clenched hand, stepping in front of her lover.

"I'm happy you found love in this cruel world. I've always told her it's family that brings you together and here you stand before me, proving me right. I have never been standing before such unique specimens in my life. Your energies are unlike anything I have seen before. I will extend my graciousness to one last offer only because I am curious."

"No." Anna says firmly standing her ground. Her confidence shining through her tone.

"And what decision have you made Tabitha? Do you let her speak for you now?"

"I won't go back. Not after what you've done." Tabitha responds grimmly.

The masks smile disappears replaced with a set of stern lips, like a child hearing no for the first time. The eyes darken and narrow, glaring into Anna's waiting eyes. He retracts his open arms, placing them at his side.

"This makes me quite vexed. I despise it when someone crosses me especially when I give them ample opportunity to join our revolution. This is where my decisions diverge into separate paths. I could easily force you into submission, but I feel as though you will just resist only to spite me. While that can be-"

His monologue is cut short as Finn lands a punch connecting with his mask, rattling Mind and taking him off guard. Finn lays two more punches into him as he turns to face his attacker. One landing in the midsection and the last an uppercut, flooring the masked man. Anna grabs ahold of Tabitha pulling her towards Xylen and Audrey hurriedly.

"We have to go now." Anna commands, running into the rest of her team.

"Nah Annie. You go, CreepyMcFuckface and me has a date. I'll be there shortly ya? You need ta get the rest a the team out a here."

"I'm not leaving." Claudette says, finding her balance. "Where will we run to?"

"Just away, I don't know. Ya can't stay here love."

"I'm not leaving you." She stands defiantly.

Audrey moves towards Claudette, breaking free of Xylen's comfort. She rests her hand on Claudette's shoulder, receiving a dirty look as she approaches. A sly smirk crosses her face as she mouths 'don't worry' in Claudette's direction.

"I'm not leaving." Claudette reiterates.

"I'm not going to ask you to. Tabitha had a good point, only two of us can go. The rest of us should hold the retreat. I know this character and he isn't one to stay down for long. You guys go ahead. Xylen can use the extra badge, seeing as Tabitha still has hers active. You three can go."

"Are you sure?" Xylen asks, his tone worried.

"I hate to agree with Xylen, but I echo his sentiment." Tabitha adds.

"I've never been more sure in my life. Get to that building because they will need you for the security protocols. I'm better suited to stay behind."

"It's not like I cleaned his fuckin clock, are ya done with da get together?"

"It's decided then." Anna proclaims. "We need to get this cure for Claudette let's make sure that's our focus. If this gets too rough, you know your way out. Don't try to fight a losing battle. Don't make me worry about you."

"Worryin's your life girly. I'm fraid you'd end up dead if you didn't has somethin to worry bout. I'll keep it real close to the chest don't you worry."

Anna hesitantly looks in Finn's direction his back turned away from her, staring down his next opponent. His hands open, back arched and shoulders rising, calmly taking in breath after breath. *He's in his element. If there was someone i'm not worried about it's you Finn.*

171

Without another word she turns toward the exit with Tabitha in tow. Xylen reluctantly follows suit, gazing one last time into Audrey's eyes before departing. Making haste towards the back storeroom, away from the prying eyes in the front of the building. Audrey blows him a kiss goodbye. His ever present smile widening at her gesture as he disappears out of sight.

Finn returns to the remaining two teammates. He runs his hand through Claudette's hair, pulling back and caressing her face. She grips onto his hand as he lays it across her cheek, holding his warm touch to her chilling skin. Gazing longingly into her brilliant green eyes, Finn begins to tear up. Audrey removes herself from the moment quickly making her way to the bar and returning with the same rapidity, holding two drinks in hand.

"I figured you'd want these." A tongue-in-cheek comment.

"*Whew, thought we'd lost the last a the booze. Every fight need a good drink. You'd make a good bartender if you ever needed a job.*"

"Thanks, i'm also good at breaking the tension and wedding photography."

"Perfect. We'll need those three things in the future." Claudette interjects.

Stirring from his momentary daze, Mind finds his footing once again. Shaking loose the short lived stupor, he turns to face the trio. His mask monotonous and expressionless. Watching the figure stand to his feet, Finn guzzles down one of the drinks given to him, his gaze never averting from the man in black. Looking for a place for his empty mug he shrugs before tossing it onto the ground. Beside him Claudette and Audrey stand attentively.

"What a way to make an introduction Finnius Michael Leighton. I knew you to be a brute but I must admit I did underestimate your loyalty. You don't mind if I call you Finnius do you?"

"*Only if ya mind if I call you fuckface.*"

"Not in the slightest."

"*Well dat backfired.*" Finn chuckles to himself.

"You have an primitive mindset, I could only imagine the limited vocabulary you posses."

"Primitive enough to put you down."

"I do expect you to have some use Finnius." Tilting his head, Mind looks past him to the women standing beside him. The mask reflecting his questioning look. "As for you lovely individuals, what purpose do you have standing between me and my objective?" His tone grave and hopeless. "I can only imagine the tales woven to bring you to this place in your life. Do you even know why it is you are here?"

"I know why i'm here. It's to put a stop to a violent plague." Audrey says commandingly.

"Which you helped me facilitate. At what point did you grow a conscience? Unless of course you simply expected me to forget that you are just as guilty as I am."

"Spin your web however you want. We built a weapon to stop wars, not start them."

"LIsten I could watch you monologue all damn day but to be honest, I could give half a shit bout this plague, you or the end a the world. So unless ya got somethin important to say I suggest you get to da part where I smear the floor wit ya fancy ass mask."

"We were getting to the important part Finnius." He says with emphasis on his name, making Finn cringe with every use of. "If you had been paying attention moments ago I outed Audrey as a conspirator in our little plan. Of course you already know of her apparent connection to Tabitha but I assume they have been less than honest about their own plans."

Looking back to Audrey, a sly grin spreads across Finn's face. He subtly motions for Claudette and Audrey to follow his lead, a small hand gesture to the both of them behind his back. Covering the distance quickly Finn cuts off Mind's monologue with another well placed strike to his unprotected chest.

"Enough fuckin talk"

Finn strikes again quickly, a heavy handed right into the center of his mass. Mind stands unphased after the two vicious strikes, much to the chagrin of Finn. His attention still placed on the individuals behind their protector. Continuing his combination Finn throws a right elbow. Palming his offense

Mind shuts Finn down, catching his attempted blow mid swing. Without a second thought Mind lands a blow of his own into the ribcage. With a cracking sound two of Finn's ribs break under the extreme pressure of the quick hit. A gasp of air leaves his mouth as he tries to refrain from shouting in pain. Taking the advantage given to him lowers his grasp on Finn from the elbow to his wrist, controlling the arm. Twisting violently he drags Finn to the ground onto one knee. From that position knees rain onto Finn's unprotected face. One after another Mind repeatedly smashes in his face, in the blink of an eye. Letting loose the wrist Finn lands with a harsh thud to the ground, struggling to breath.

Jumping into the fray with a renewed energy Claudette swings brashly for his face, the strike missing wildly. Audrey follows suit, leading in with a kick to the sternum using her momentum to create a gap between him and them, causing his attempt to grab for Claudette to miss. Pressing the attack Audrey lands a low kick to his knee while Claudette pushes in past his defense striking at his neckline with precision. Retaliating, Mind creates his own offense in lack of his defense. Moving deftly through the two women's dynamic attacks he positions himself beside Audrey, moving out of their impending next flurry of offense. A short jab to the gut reels Audrey over, cutting Claudette off from himself momentarily. Pulling back on Audrey's hair he wraps his left arm underneath her chin squeezing tightly, cutting off her oxygen.

"We can be alone now Claudette Samantha Coltier." He says, applying more pressure to her windpipe. Audrey struggles against his grip, using her two arms to aggressively pull at his arm. Claudette struggles to keep her composure, worry written across her expressions. She tenses her body, preparing for his next sentence.

"I see you've expressed worry for this one's life. You do not have to be frightened. Death is an experience for all of us. For some it comes swift, like wind through your hair. For others it is slow and torturous, like oxygen deprivation. Audrey here is suffering Claudette. I asked a question earlier and if you have the correct answer I may let her free."

Audrey's face begins to pale as she continues her frantic effort to free herself from his clutches.

Heavily breathing, Claudette looks on at the display, taking a second to remember his previous statements. Her eyes light up brightly as she recalls his question. Finn slowly makes his way to his feet, blood flowing freely from his forehead.

"You asked what I was doing here. I was finding a cure." She hides her shakes underneath her arrogant tone.

"Did you find what you were looking for?" His mask contorting into a jester like smile.

"You said."

"Answer the question!" His voice becoming stern.

"Alright, alright. We found where the cure is yes."

Audrey's fighting spirit wanes as her grip around his arm weakens. Her face showing signs of fear, gasping desperately for air. Her wide eyes begin to shudder as her body slowly shuts down. A glass mug shatters overtop of Mind's head as Finn begins anew, wrenching Audrey free from the madman's arms. Audrey drops limply to the ground, her body reacting to the sudden rush of air. Claudette rushes over to her fallen friend in a bid to help.

"Xylen would kill me if something happened to you." Claudette stutters in her panic.

Mind rotates slowly towards Finn, his mask mimicking anger and disappointment. Wiping blood from his eyes Finn stares intently at his opponent.

"*Ey, fuckface. I ain't done wit you yet.*"

"Eloquent. I admire the tenacity though you lack the wherewithal to complete your designated task. If you wish to match brute force, I will be required to dispatch of you Finnius."

"*Only me da can call me Finnius.*"

In a clash of the titans they begin trading blows. One hard bone crunching shot for another. For each hit Finn receives he churns out two more, using his unique style of boxing and martial arts. The slender masked man slower on the attack makes each hit count using his full strength to cripple the indomitable fighter. Pushing back the monster before him with his own fiendish strength Finn gains the upper hand for a moment, learning the rhythm of Mind's strikes. Attacking inside of his strike range he is able to counter a majority of the opponent's assault. Quickly adapting, Mind changes his style mid swing, aiming high and hitting low, again taking control of the fight. With a mighty blow to the chest he sends Finn tumbling backwards. Reeling from the blow Finn awkwardly returns to his feet clutching his chest.

"*Is dat da best you can do? My grans dead and she could hit harder ya weak bitch.*"

"That bravado is in full effect tonight."

Holding on to Audrey, Claudette begins to drag the unconscious young girl from the center stage, off towards a corner VIP booth. Her body begins to give out as she exerts herself further bringing a friend to safety. A hacking cough brings blood up from her lungs.

"Fuck" She coughs out, spitting blood onto the ground.

Safely bringing Audrey out of the direct confrontation Claudette slumps over beside her catching her breath, watching the ensuing struggle with bated breath.

Finn returns to his fighting posture. Breathing heavily he marches back into the fray, broken ribs having begun to imped his breathing. Awaiting the return to combat Mind holds his hands to the side taunting Finn, goading him into an attack of opportunity. He looks away to Claudette, noting her labored breathing.

"Death is a beautiful thing Finnius. You have caused your fair share of it over the years. The red in your ledger has been running over for years. In all of your experience have you ever lost?"

"*I'm done dancin.*" A ting of anger to his words.

"You most certainly are not."

Anticipating Finn's next attack Mind simply side steps his punch, grabbing him by the hair and tossing him to the ground. Crashing to the ground Finn screams in frustration pulling himself to his feet only to be swept back down onto the ground. Mind reaches down pulling Finn in the direction of Claudette by his hair, stopping just shy of the two women.

"Are you prepared to lose her?" Mind asks dryly, motioning to her with his free hand. "By my estimations she isn't long for this world. This looks to be the work of TC-750. That would be the technical term for it. We refer to it as the Cosgrove Scourge."

Finn remains quiet looking into Claudette's paling face as she stares back at him weakly, her eyes like half moons. Mind pulls back on his hair, eliciting a sharp breath from Finn.

"Like music to my ears. I'll continue if you have nothing to contribute. Were you aware the cure for this disease is non-existent? Your lover seems to think they will find one."

"Tabitha said-" Finn stops himself mid sentence. *"She said there was a cure."* He attempts to convince himself.

"She has said a great many things hasn't she? Far too many to recall i'm certain. Between just us three there is no cure. It was a fabrication, a device to make you all obedient."

"She fuckin wouldn't." Muttered under his breath.

"Isn't it odd that she returns to your life exactly when everything fell to ruins? Tell me, was she aware of the origin of infection?"

"Aye." He says, admitting defeat.

"Again I will say death is a beautiful thing Finnius. For you, for her, for us all, but it doesn't have to be that way. What would you do to keep your bed warm at night? There may be no cure, but there is certainty that I could save your beloved."

"I'd say shove your sales pitch up Tabitha's arse."

"Brazen until the last breath. I wonder how long your defiance will last in the wake of her screams. I assure you before this is over you will have heard the many screams she has to offer."

Mind drags Finn to his knees, holding tightly to his hair. The mask smiles eerily at Finn as they share one last lingering stare. Defiantly Finn spits blood onto his body armor, laughing grimly as he leans back raising his middle fingers in the air. Releasing his grip Finn falls to the floor unable to balance himself on his heels. The cold surface comforts his bloodied face as he wrestles with his body to stand again. As he rises from the floor his muscles give out from exertion collapsing back to the polished floor below.

Finn's vision begins to blur, his sight set on Dette. He watches as Mind moves towards Claudette, his steps unhurried. Reaching down he grabs her by the throat, his gloved hand cool to the touch against her burning neck. Lifting her from the ground he slumps her over his shoulder heading leisurely for the exit. Reaching out feebly Finn attempts one last time to return to his feet, failing he crumples back to the floor as his vision of them dims. 'His name that sat on him was death and hades followed with him' the final words echoing through his head as he loses consciousness.

CHAPTER TWELVE

HOPE FLOATS

Anna, Tabitha and Xylen soar high above the streets of Providence, their hover on route toward the Frostscythe corporation. Passing by civilian traffic Tabitha weaves through the slower vehicles in their lane. The air in the cabin is still, all three quiet and tense. Looking into the backseat Anna quickly flashes Xylen a smile, noting the concern across his face.

"She'll be alright Xylen." Anna assures him. "She is in the best of hands."

"No one had to stay." He returns dejectedly.

"He would have followed us. As it is we may already be too late. Mind is the smartest individual I know, if he even thought for a minute I would return here he would have countermeasures placed." Tabitha bellows, keeping her focus forward on the traffic ahead. "I agree with you Xylen she didn't have to stay. If she didn't have any connection to you she would not have. Remember that if anything is to happen to her."

"Let's not place blame on each other. We are a team and we have to act like one. This blame game only does what he wants it to do."

"Here comes mother again with another inspirational speech about unity." Tabitha rolls her eyes.

"This is your crusade, your mission but don't forget who leads this team. I call the shots."

"Then you're going to have to deal with me breaking some rules. This is unlike any op you've even ran. Your whole 'I don't kill people' that doesn't work here. I saw bodies littered on the ground and not even so much as a peep from you. I killed a person with a severed head-"

"A what?" Xylen arches his eyebrow.

"A severed head. You heard me right."

"It wasn't your call."

"What was the call then? Sit down and play tea time for three and a head?" Tabitha spits out. "I can't live in the moment like you. I saw a threat and I ended it. You could have done any number of things. What if she realised what we were doing? I won't sit back and risk someone hurting you. Ever."

The hum of the engine takes over the cabin as it falls back into silence. Anna stares out the passenger window watching the brilliant lights flickering below. The stream of hovers passing below them steady and relaxing. The bustle of people in the streets hurried as usual. A smile creeps across her face, recalling the many great moments spent in the depth of the city. She turns her attention to the Heart of Providence, its height towering over the city it keeps. Hovers pass through and around its towering frame lighting up its surface in a rainbow of colors. A stray light flashes into Anna's eyes momentarily blinding her. Spots dot her vision as she continues staring along the rooftops and streets below. In the corner of her eye she catches a wisp of fabric flowing in the wind. Focusing on its location she makes out a humanoid shape standing in the midst of the fabric. It stands tall in the enveloping cloak of shadow, watching vigilantly. Blinking, Anna shakes the image out of her mind. Within her blink the figure disappears from sight. *I'm definitely going crazy. Yep. That's what's happening here. First, a woman with clear psychosis, then a masked man. Now hooded figures again. This is what crazy feels like.*

A hand runs through her hair softly playfully twirling its length around their finger, pulling her away from her thoughts.

"You always grow quiet when you've nothing left to add. Allow me to carry the burden of those I kill and understand it must be done. You cannot solve the problems of the world with words, they only tend to plunge the knife deeper."

"I guess i'll never understand." Anna retorts, clutching Tabitha's hand.

"Not until they threaten someone you care about."

"I can always find another way."

"Someday you won't. I don't need you to understand it today, I need you to accept it."

"I'll never be able to accept death as a means to an end. There will always be a way to solve the puzzles placed before us. I accept that you kill Tabitha, if only to bring closure to the topic." Anna says despondently.

Tabitha removes her hand from Anna's hair, focusing her attention back to the lanes between them and Frostscythe. The building comes into frame over the dashboard. Its intricate logo shining like a beacon welcoming them in. The structure is well lit from the inside. Even during the night people pour in and out of the facility, finishing up their busy work. Tabitha attempts to land just beyond the building, maneuvering her way into a parking space along the sidewalk. The trio sits in stillness in front of their destination, the ambient light reflecting from the glass.

"Are we just going to take in the beautiful lights?" Xylen says breaking the silence filling the cabin. "I was thinking it sure is a beautiful night to break into a medical facility and steal a plague."

"Retirement." Anna chuckles.

"Retirement." He repeats.

Taking a nervous gasp of air Anna exits the hover, heading towards the front entrance. Tabitha follows closely behind, her stride confidant. Xylen brings up the rear, hustling out of the hover to quickly take his place beside the two women. Ascending the flight of stairs the trio make for the door leading in. Tabitha hands over a fresh badge to both Anna and Xylen.

"Um. Do I look like an Amber to you?" Xylen quips, looking over his badge. "It's the red hair isn't it?"

His badge reads *Amber Lockheed* in small print below the corporation logo with a picture matching Tabitha's stock company image. Anna freezes, a grin spreading widely across her face. She looks over her own badge. On it is written *Mia HighGarden* with a bubbly picture of her underneath, her smile bright and contagious. Shrugging her shoulders at her own badge she turns to Xylen.

"Hi Amber, i'm Mia." Anna extends her hand outward to him.

"Pleasure to meet you. I swear I look nothing like my picture, i'm much more pleasant in person."

Anna snags the id from his hands, looking over the picture. She keeps a laugh to herself, trying to not cause a scene just outside the building. Tabitha stands off to the side, her eyes narrowed in their direction.

"Are we done children?" Tabitha impatiently remarks.

"Just about." Anna says, smile beaming towards her lover. "You look so angry in this picture."

"They told me to smile." Tabitha retorts, a grin slowly creeping into being. "So I did."

"That's a grimace if i've ever seen one. I'm going to call this vintage Tabitha." Anna waves the badge in her face. "Can I frame this when were done?"

"Please put it on your mantle next to the missing weapons."

"I have a special place for this."

"I do not need to know where that's going." Xylen snatches back the id badge hurriedly, holding it close to his chest. "Poor Amber. She doesn't deserve this."

"Are you getting attached to your cover already?" Anna laughing says.

"Let's get on with it." Tabitha interrupts.

Tabitha leads the others into the foyer. Guards stand to either side of the team as they walk in, dressed in dark tan uniforms. One guard approaches the group, his hand held out in a stopping motion. He smiles at the sight of Tabitha, a friendly gesture.

"Hello Miss Cosgrove, late night? You know we'll need to see your badges and have you sign in." He says politely.

"Hello Jacob. Of course, I only work late nights. I never thought that procedure has changed." Tabitha removes a badge from her left coat pocket, smiling back at the guard. "How's the family?"

"Growing. We have another one on the way."

Holding a handheld scanner in his hand he takes the identification from her, holding it underneath the device. Taking a few second it reads the barcode attached to the badge. The red light on the underside of the device turns a bright green, accepting her identification. Xylen exchanges glances with Annastasia, looking rather confused as he motions to Tabitha. Anna watches Tabitha exchange words with the young gentleman.

"What'll that make three now?" She says continuing the small talk, her posture relaxed as she carries on the conversation.

"Yeah." He proudly responds.

"I'm glad for you. Please give Emily my best would you." Said genuinely.

"I will. She'll want me to invite you over for dinner again. We're having her mother's special."

"I'd love to have dinner. Can we hold out for a couple days though, i'm slightly overbooked as of right now."

Raising her eyebrow Anna looks on at the conversation pleasantly impressed with Tabitha's demeanor towards the guard.

"Sure. Let me know a date. Are these two with you?"

"Yes. They're just assisting me with a project."

"I know, I know. Super secret." He chuckles to himself. "Identification please."

He reaches his hand out to the both of them. One by one he goes through the same process with each of them, accepting both of their identifications.

"Mia?" He asks holding the badge outward.

"That'd be me." She responds, a little pep in her response.

A bewildered look spreads across Jacobs face as he stares at Xylen's identification. He does a quick double take, looking to the badge and back up at him. He pauses on his words carefully before blurting them out.

"Amber?" He asks hesitantly.

"I'm going through a serious phase right now." Xylen quips, holding back laughter.

He holds the id beside Xylen's face getting a good look between the two before handing back the card, the same look of unclear confusion written across his face.

"Not my business." He responds. "Tabitha, you have a great night."

"Likewise."

Tabitha leads the trio past the front desk her step relaxed as she strolls through a familiar stomping ground, running her hand over the desk as she passes by. Reaching the staircase Anna freezes briefly, recalling her moment from before. Mind standing above her on the bridge leading across to the suspended second floor. Xylen brushes past her, looking down at the badge in his hands, his face showing the same bewilderment as the guard. Snapping out of her thought Anna pushes forward, returning to the group. Laying her head on Xylen's shoulder she smiles, looking at him mulling over the card in his hand. As he rotates it the picture changes from Tabitha's 'smile' to a picture of Xylen with longer darker red hair.

"Oh you're good." Xylen says unsurprised.

"Just a simple parlor trick. Tabitha's friend was a bit distracted." She replies, staring in Tabitha's direction.

"Get on with it." Tabitha exclaims, keeping up her stride.

"What?" Anna says bashfully.

Rounding the corner a row of elevators becomes visible. Tabitha swiftly moves to the middle elevator like clockwork, her hands tapping on her sides. Taking her head from Xylen's shoulder Anna strolls past him towards Tabitha. Wrapping her arm around Tabitha she leans into her as they wait for the elevator to descend.

"Yes. I did make pleasant conversation with the guard."

"We saw." Anna chuckles.

"I spent six years of my life here. Day in and out he greeted me with the same hello. Told me about his kids, his wife. It was sickening." She takes a deep breath. "At first."

"You're telling me Tabitha grew a conscience?" Xylen adds, making his way into the conversation.

"You don't listen to someone prattle on without hearing them speak on occasion."

"He invited you to dinner." Anna adds.

"His wife is a chef in a bistro downtown. She makes quite the delicious plate of food."

"You don't have to sell me on the idea. It's just surprising."

"There are some things worth going the extra mile for and in return you always receive some boon. Life is give and take. People like Jacob are what reminded me of you in this hellish space. I'll take my memories when I can get them."

"Tabitha-"

"It's not my normal. I know that, but it's his. He knows Tabitha the engineer, the work horse. Not who I am. You know me better than anyone. I'd rather keep the two worlds separate."

"I'm glad to be able to witness this side of you. It's refreshing."

"We have work to do."

The elevator doors open slowly. Workers pour from the opening doors like scurrying rats, moving around the group. The three walk onto the now emptied elevator, it's walls plain and unoriginal. Tabitha reaches for the controls, selecting the fourth floor before closing the doors behind them. Anna leans against the railing, her megawatt smile shining in Tabitha's direction.

"Would you stop staring at me." Tabitha says slightly irritated.

"No." Her smile brighter yet.

Tabitha looks around the small corridor, attempting to clear her mind of the intoxicating beauty staring in her direction. Grinning she licks her lips before sighing deeply. Xylen backs into the far corner pulling from his pocket a personal phone, waiting for the elevator to open. He begins fooling around with his device, clicking away at the screen. Tabitha moves across the platform towards her significant other, placing an arm on the railing on either side of Anna. She peers deep into Anna's ocean like eyes, innocent and beautiful.

"When this is over. I'll let you meet that Tabitha."

"I'll be waiting for the moment she arrives."

Anna stares back into Tabitha's dark eyes. Their exchange lasting for what feels like eternity in the cramped space. Tabitha leans in close to Anna taking in a deep breath, breathing in her scent.

"You still smell like cherry blossoms."

"Is this the time for that? During this time I deactivated the alarm system for the top floor, found out where your lab was located and ordered a pizza. Which should be here in roughly fifteen minutes." Xylen pulls his attention from the phone to the duo on the opposite end of the elevator. Tabitha glares over her shoulder at him. Her stare frigid like winter. "I didn't really do all of that. I messaged Audrey, found your office and made sure we weren't walking into a trap."

"Xylen's right. Game time." Anna says, sliding out from between Tabitha's arms. "We came here for a mission let's not get distracted."

"This has been rather uneventful. Maybe Finn did his job." Tabitha adds.

"Trust but verify right?"

"Exactly. There'll be time to play later."

The elevator door cracks open to a vacant hallway. The moonlight shines through the darkened glass of the fourth floor. Leaning out from the elevator Tabitha looks side to side, searching for any remaining workers wandering the floor. Seeing no one she leaves the elevator moving towards the left, to her laboratory. Xylen pulls his computer from his pocket again, checking the screen.

"I put the camera's on loop. Last thing they saw was us in the lobby." Xylen says, motioning to his device.

"I'm glad I don't have to ask you to work your magic. Have any idea what this floor is?" Anna inquisitively asks.

"All I could get from their connection is that its research and development. It's a pretty secure line, i'll have to access if from this floor if we want any other information."

"I want everything they have on Tabitha's project and why they were developing it."

"Got it. I'll dig up what I can. I'll try to find traces to that character we ran into as well."

Stepping out of the elevator they continue the conversation, keeping to a hushed tone. Following Tabitha left the two move through row upon row of cubicle office space, each desk neat and orderly. The room falls to darkness, the moonlight being the only light to guide their way through. A somber ambiance comes over the room, only the faint movement of air resonating through the floor and their footsteps. Anna searches through the cubicles as they pass by, keeping a mental note of their tidiness.

"I'm getting a weird vibe from this place." Xylen blurts out.

"They are a medical company focusing on plaguing a world. If you didn't get even the slightest of chills, I would be concerned. I want you to focus on the task at hand. Not the horror vid lighting in a office."

"The nerdy one always dies first. You know the rules."

"You didn't hear about the new rule? Computer geeks are in now, they make it through to the end."

"You didn't say we lived."

"Better odds." Anna smiles coyly at him.

Passing through the remaining desks Xylen and Anna come to a round set of doors, brightly lit in comparison to the rest of the floor. Tabitha stands just underneath the main light leaning against the metal door. She motions to security system attached to the wall beside it, holding out her badge.

"They changed the codes." She says dryly.

"Are you saying you need-"

"Just open the door." She interrupts.

Xylen walks to the doors, analyzing the security system attached to the wall beside it. Reaching into his pocket he pulls out his computer. He moves close to the system before beginning to click away at the screen, his focus completely on the small screen before him. Tabitha backs away from the door, moving closer to them both. Looking around Anna scans the room of shadows for anything out of place. She notices the cameras throughout the hall and leading into the laboratory entrance, each of them pointed in their direction. Nudging Tabitha, Anna points in the direction of the recording devices.

"They're always like that." Tabitha comments. "No one cares what goes on outside of this lab."

"They watch you that closely?"

"I'm not the only scientist here. Many of them were working on projects they had no clue were in relation to ours. 'Our aim is to make you better' or some bullshit like that. Bunch of award winning blowhards here to save the world one person at a time."

"I take it you didn't get along with them."

"Never much cared to hear about how they cured a disease or found a new biotic limb implant. In the end it never really mattered, they were all going to die."

In the background Xylen works diligently on the access codes, muttering under his breath as he plugs along at the systems interface. The access panel lights up and the doors roll open. The pressurized air system releases, the oxygen hissing back into the room. He slides the gadget back into his pocket before turning back to Anna and Tabitha, smug confidence radiating through his grin.

"After you ladies." Said motioning them forward.

"Took you long enough Amber."

"Amber forgot where she learned how to hack. I had to subroute-"

"I've already lost interest in this conversation."

"Too technical for you?"

Tabitha moves through the sealed door with the others in tow, brushing aside the question. The laboratories are separated into four different blocks. Each area with their own individual equipment unique to their area of expertise. Walking through the threshold feels like moving between night and day. The lights overhead shine vividly against the marbled tiles below creating a glare against their eyes. Each room is in pristine order, spotless and clean. Tabitha heads for the furthest back laboratory, her stride confident. Anna takes a moment to look over the area, looking at the designation on the individual labs. 'Animal Research' and 'Biotic Enhancement' are the first two divisions she passes by followed quickly by 'OSR' written in bold letters. The 'OSR' lab glass is frosted over, making it unique to the other departments.

Anna pulls lightly at the door handle with no give in return. *Of course the door is locked.* She moves forward, following closely behind Xylen.

"Getting spooked yet?" Xylen says looking over his shoulder, his voice echoing down the hallway.

"In that eerie, this has gone too smoothly kind of way."

Moving with purpose Tabitha strolls into the furthest back laboratory, using her key to unlock the glass door. The sign on the door reads 'Outbreak Prevention and Control. Ph.D Tabitha Cosgrove'. Before passing the door she runs her hand across the lettering of her name, smiling to herself as she passes. Laying eyes on her workshop for the first time in months Tabitha's smile widens. A sprawling work space outfitted with the latest of technologies. Various surgical instruments and medical equipment left in the exact order in which she last left them. She runs her hand along the edge of an examination table, her fingers moving through the grooves and indents along the left side. Making her way to a side wall Tabitha stops, staring along its length. Closing her eyes she pauses here for a moment.

Anna and Xylen make their way into Tabitha's workspace, eyes wide in wonder at the sight before them. Xylen makes his way towards the back end of the laboratory, spotting a computer along the back wall. Anna stops just inside the entryway, taking in the overwhelming amount of information. She moves towards Tabitha running her hand along the same grooves in the examination table, the marks feel coarse and jagged to the touch.

"Such a lovely place you call home." Anna says, moving up behind Tabitha. Her words startling.

"I- This isn't home." Tabitha opens her eyes slowly, taking in the sight of her personal workstation again. "This room has seen much death with no one but me to witness it. Everyone who walked this floor has died. No one can ever know just how truly enlightening it was. How each person that expired gave me a sense of accomplishment. My legacy is in this room. It should terrify me, but it doesn't."

"Then what is this place to you?"

"It's a milestone."

Anna lowers her head, lost in thought. Her voice lost as she tries to find the words to say to her lover. Tabitha turns to face Anna, reaching out to grab ahold of her hand. She lowers herself down to make eye contact with her clearly distraught significant other.

"You're quiet. You disapprove."

"This event shouldn't be the landmark of your life. It's a scar that you'll never forget but not a milestone."

"I am proud of my accomplishments. Everyone wants to change the world. I made it possible. Now I have to destroy what I created because it threatens the one thing I care more about." She grips Anna's hand tightly. "I have never been a decent human. I am what the world created for me to be."

"You can be so much more than that."

"You always have so much faith in me."

"I'll never quit believing."

"Bad habits die hard."

Letting go of Anna's hand Tabitha moves towards a locked chest beside the examination table, leaving Anna to stare at the sterilized countertop. Tabitha bends down, leaning over the locked cabinet. Placing her left hand on the case it begins to read her handprint. It opens to her touch immediately, letting out a wisp of cool air. The contents of the chest lay bare, a note placed on the center rack addressed to Tabitha replacing what was formerly there. She quickly snatches it, placing it in her jacket pocket. Her face solemn as she returns to her feet.

"We have a problem." Tabitha sternly says. "There is nothing in my cabinet."

"Is that-"

"Yes. That is where all of my research and test results are. It's been cleared out. Clearly someone wishes to continue my work without my consent."

"Can you make something here?" Anna's tone grows worried. "You can recreate the cure right?"

"If given the right amount of time I could replicate it. We don't have that time. I do have one more backup plan."

"Which is?"

"I have more of the anti-viral in a hidden compartment here. That could severely slow down the rate of infection but…"

"She'll still die."

"Without the proper time and equipment I cannot duplicate my cure. Not on a whim."

"Damnit!" Anna's tone becomes aggravated, balling her hands in anger. Her eyes well with tears as the realisation sets in. "There has to be something you can do."

"I'm afraid not." Tabitha speaks softly.

Tabitha deftly moves back to Annastasia's side, wrapping her in a warm embrace. Anna places her head on Tabitha's shoulder. Tears stream from her cheeks onto Tabitha's leather jacket, forming a small pool of teardrops.

"I love you." Tabitha whispers into her ear.

"Guys!" Xylen shouts, interrupting their moment. "You need to see this."

Making their way to Xylen, Anna and Tabitha crowd around the computer. Displayed on the screen is a list of documents, each listed with coded names. '0145-D, 0034-E and 112-C' are the files highlighted by the cursor. Each with a locked tag next to the file name.

"So you asked me to look up information on Tabitha's..work. I was able to access the mainframe from the computer fairly easily as it already was connected." He looks around at the duo. "Ok. Boring technical talk aside. I hacked in and was able to find Tabitha's backup notes and research."

"I'll need a copy of that."

"Already downloading now. Should be done soon. That's not what I called you over here for. These three files have planned sites for use of the neurotoxin/disease. Two of them are already completed. The first being-"

"Braxtleridge. The second site was Dourhaven." Tabitha interjects.

"Yeah, both tested well according to the paperwork."

"I wrote the paperwork Xylen. There was never a third test site."

"Not yet. We're the third test site."

Xylen clicks on the folder marked '112-C'. A mess of documents and photographs open from the subfolder for each of them to see. Pictures of building surrounding the tower and interior designs of the tower become visible with a few clicks on Xylen's behalf. Points of weakness, Entry points and escape routes are marked out on the towers schematics, each given a different color code.

"They're striking the tower." Anna says trailing off. "When?"

"I had to read through a lot of bullshit jargon, to get the jist of it. They're looking to strike while the diplomats are in town. People from all different solar sectors. They're target isn't the city. It's the dignitaries. It looks like they've moved the schedule up to the morning conference tomorrow."

"Genius." Tabitha mutters to herself.

"No." Anna's eyes flicker back and forth, the motor in her mind running overtime. "We have to warn them. They'll be sitting ducks for an attack during the conference tomorrow morning."

"You have far greater things to worry about than that." A familiar voice sounds throughout the still laboratory.

The computer screen goes blank before emitting a brilliant white light. As the light fades the face of Alphonse Cervantes is made visible. The backdrop of the night sky prominent in the background of his picture. His businessman like smile as notable as before.

"Hello my dears. It's good to see you in one place." His condescending tone ever present.

"Cervantes." Tabitha forces out.

"Our- My employer would like to extend his greatest sympathies for not having been able to be present for this conversation himself. He is quite pressed at the moment for time. Though he would have been impressed at how well you passed through security."

"I always told him our security was lackluster."

"We figured you would come here looking for hope Annastasia. There is a flaw in being a hero and we are generously taking advantage of your 'love'. When posed with a problem you have fewer options left at your disposal. You must solve the problem before it becomes too large to handle."

"We've become a problem to you. Thank you for the compliment." Anna wittily quips

"For my master to believe you a threat it is quite the compliment."

"From employer to master, that was a quick transition."

"Your wit is as sharp as it was during our first encounter. Are you going to berate me again? Continue, you are the one losing precious time."

Xylen begins to type away at the keyboard, trying to pull any information from the connection he can. Tabitha stands behind him, leaning over the chair, intently watching Alphonse and the surrounding area. The loud clicking of the keyboard continues as Xylen desperately attempts to disconnect from their servers with his own device. Anna stands stoically beside the desk her attention grabbed by the smug smirk across Alphonse's face.

"You look tired." Alphonse continues.

"Forgive my lack of exuberance. It's been a long night." Anna replies shortly.

"I wouldn't wish to bore you my dear. I will speak frankly for the others in the room. Our plan cannot be disturbed, therefore we cannot allow you to leave this building. There is a device in this facility, one Tabitha knows extremely well."

Anna and Tabitha exchange glances as Xylen continues his work, disconnecting his device from the main drive of the computer and pushing it back into his pocket discreetly. Tabitha turns her attention from Alphonse to Annastasia. Her eyes hesitant to make contact. Anna stares at the screen, watching Alphonse intently as his laugh echoes from the speakers. Slowly she turns away from the screen to face Tabitha, a quizzical look strewn across her face.

"Go ahead Tabitha. Tell her about your master plan. The devices you hid throughout the building. I would hate to ruin the surprise."

"We need to leave." Tabitha spits out, an underlying tone of anger in her voice.

"Why would that be dear?" Alphonse questions.

"This place will be contaminated in less than twenty minutes." She says through clenched teeth.

"Good thing all essential personnel are already evacuated. Though I do believe there are over three hundred and twenty one people still in this facility. Casualties for a better tomorrow I suppose."

Tabitha moves out of view of the camera, towards a chest of things beside her desk. Digging through the contents she pulls an intricate gas masks from the bottom of the box, throwing it to the ground. Looking further she unearths another set of small vials, the blue hue gleaming off the bright lights above.

"How dare you. All this talk and speech about making a better tomorrow, a better you. You're willing to commit genocide to follow someone's ideal of a brighter future. A future he will not share with you." Anna says.

"You speak as if you know him" He coyly replies.

"I don't need to know him. I know his style. He threatens the peace my family has fought and is continuing to fight for. That is enough for me. I'll be damned if I don't follow in their footsteps to see a better future for Providence." Anna visibly frustrated slams her hands onto the desk.

"Beautiful speech. Such a big heart, it's a shame we couldn't have come to some agreement. You have six minutes until Miss Cosgrove's curse is administered throughout the entire building. Choose to save yourself, or be the hero Miss Arlenko. Good luck."

The screen goes black as Alphonse terminates the connection. Xylen pushes himself away from the desk hastily standing to his feet. Disgruntled,

Anna retracts from the desk, her hands clenched into fists. Tabitha returns to the others, the small box of vials and masks in hand. She looks to the two as they pace about.

"Xylen can you find the signal and jam the receivers?" Anna asks hurriedly, her mind flooding with thoughts and questions.

"I might be able to but if I fail we won't have enough time to get out of here. I'd have to find the signal source first, then broadcast another frequency over it that wouldn't disrupt the original. I'd need more than six minutes." He runs a hand through the length of his hair.

"Forget saving people. I set up the dispensers to auto disperse at the slightest of tampering. This building is lost. We need to save ourselves. Elevators are too slow, can be manipulated. We'll need to go down the stairs."

She grabs Anna by the arm pulling her away from the desk. Anna hesitantly moves along with her, her mind continuing to process all the information. Xylen leads the rear, his hands fidgeting in distress. Dragging her along, Tabitha heads down the brightly lit path back into the moonlit office space.

We can't just leave them to die.

"We have to help these people." Anna stutters.

"That's what they want you to do Anna. They want you to risk your life for people you'll never be able to save, because that's what an Arlenko does. If you die here, more than three hundred innocent people will die today. Don't let them control you, this city dies with you."

Tabitha increases her pace, tightening the grip on Anna's hand. Weaving through the cubicles they pass through the same way they came, retracing their steps. The darkness of the main room seems darker yet in comparison to the beaming fixtures in the laboratory. Xylen follows closely behind Anna, keeping the rear guarded as they pass through unhindered. The trio rapidly approaches the hall leading toward the elevator, taking a sharp left Tabitha swoops into a side room containing an emergency exit.

Taking no time Tabitha begins heading down the flight of stairs towards the main floor with the others in tow. A cascade of footsteps reverberate through the staircase as they stampede down the stairs swiftly making way for their destination. At the third floor landing Anna stops, ripping herself free from Tabitha's grip momentarily. She runs to the door, slamming into it with thunderous bang. The locked door doesn't budget to her weight. Through the pane of glass Anna can see a few workers down the hall staring toward the door, bewildered at the sudden jarring thud. Xylen catches Anna as she moves backwards, pulling her along with him down the staircase.

"We have to go Anna." He says into her ear, his voice echoing off the walls.

Xylen escorts Anna past the second story landing down, directing her focus downward to the main lobby. She tenses as they pass by the second floor door, tempted to check the floor for civilians. Noticing her reluctance Xylen forces her down the staircase, into the lobby entrance.

Ahead of the group Tabitha bursts into the lobby, waiting for an eventual ambush from their pursuers. The lobby area lay bare, apart from the guards on each exit and the receptionist at the front desk. The warmth of the lights feel almost dulled in her frantic state of mind. She quickly surveys the area for any signs of Mind or Alphonse, expecting the worst of the night. Xylen places his hand on her shoulder as they approach from behind, warning Tabitha of their arrival.

With no time to rest on their laurels the group dashes towards the front entrance. Breaking into a full sprint they burst through the front doorway into the safety of the outside city, with little time to spare. Tabitha stares through the glass windows into the open foyer, watching for her creation to fill the facility.

"Where is he?" Tabitha asks herself out loud, searching the main floor.

Pulling herself together Anna stares at Xylen as she catches her breath. Her eyes begin to well with tears, knowing the outcome in a matter of moments. Xylen closes the distance between them wrapping his arms around her, holding tightly.

"It's not your fault." He whispers into her ear.

I know.

Tabitha returns to the front entrance, placing her hand on the cool glass. She watches as a dark gas cloud begins to fill the lobby, pouring in through the ventilation shafts. Creeping across the once warmly lit room the toxic cloud crawls across the building, slowly engulfing it in a light haze. A cacophony of screams and shrieks fill the air as panicked figures become apparent in the fog. Tabitha presses her head to the door, it's chill pleasantly welcomed. She closes her eyes as she takes in the screams of her latest victims.

Anna turns her head to watch the four story building fill with a dirty yellow haze. It's reach covering every corner of the building. On the upper floors shadows move through the fog, some pounding on the windows. Their shadows twisting in pain and fear as they struggle helplessly against the window pane. Anna buries her head into Xylen's chest, attempting to erase the horrible memory from her mind.

A thud against the door causes Tabitha's eyes to shoot open. She holds her ground against the glass door, keeping her weight firmly against it. With her forehead still pressed against the window Tabitha peers in at the figure attempting to exit. Her eyes soften as she recognizes the face. Jacob stands on the other side of the door, using his remaining strength to attempt an exit.

"Jacob." Tabitha says calmly through the door.

"Miss Cosgrove? The doors seems lodged. I can't get out." He says, choking on the thick gas.

"I know Jacob. I know." Her voice soft as she watches him struggle further.

"Help me." He frantically coughs out, blood spraying from his mouth onto the door.

"I am. The faster it goes through your system the quicker it will be." Her composure calm.

Tabitha stares into Jacob's frightened eyes as she watches the symptoms overtake him, his veins turning a darker blue. Blood runs down the front window in streaks, blocking her view partially. Jacob continues his struggle to survive, pushing back on the glass door futily .

"Just think of Emily, your children. A warm dinner. Your favorite moments with them Jacob. Cherish those, it'll be over soon."

The resistance on the door lessens as Tabitha watches Jacob's hand slide down the glass, leaving a trail of fresh blood. She closes her eyes as the last remaining gasps leave Jacob's body, shutting out the sound of the fading screams. Tabitha drifts from the door somberly, the small box of vials held tightly in her grip. She brushes past Anna on her way by, nudging her with the case. Anna pulls her head away from the comfort of Xylen's embrace to gaze once more into the desecrated building. The yellowish hue lingers, contained inside the facility. A hush falls over the city streets, the surrounding area echoes the loss of life. Anna stares blankly at the scene before them, her face a mess of tears. Xylen places his arm on her shoulder, his best attempt at comforting her. They stare together into the abyss.

CHAPTER THIRTEEN

TRUTH

Waking from unconsciousness Finn winces in pain, his ribs throbbing in agony. Squinting, he slowly opens his eyes revealing a poorly lit room. The corners of the room covered in shadow, the only light dangling overhead in the center of the room. Glancing at his surroundings he spots Audrey tied to a chair opposite him, her head slumped over. He attempts to rise from his seated position, unable to feel his own restraints due to the numbness of his upper body. Finn relaxes himself, drawing in the view of the rest of the small room surrounding him, focusing on the corners, looking for windows and doors. The only door to and from the room sits directly behind Audrey.

"Gotta love wakin up strapped to a chair in the middle of a basement." He mutters to himself. *"No continental breakfast? Shit service."*

Dried blood clings to his face, a present left by his captor as a reminder of defeat. He licks his chapped lips, the taste metallic yet stale. Finn slows his breathing making every breath more shallow, to lessen the ache of his ribs. Checking the bindings on his wrists, Finn tugs on either side, searching for a weakness in the knot tied. He looks down towards his lap to the cords tied across his chest and legs keeping him in place.

"Dette?" He asks, clearing his thoughts. *"Where is ya?"*

Finn scans the room again, hastily this time. The room sit empty besides Audrey and himself. Footsteps echo off the walls of the room, slow and deliberate. The sound grows quiet as the individual moves further from the room, until only silence remains.

"Dette?" He calls out again, his voice unsettled.

He struggles against his bonds with renewed strength. Twisting and turning he pulls at the cord binding his hands together with disregard for his own physical condition. Finn screams out in pain and anger as he struggles against his fractured bones. Slumping over Finn relents, staring down his blood stained shirt.

"FUCK!"

His scream startles Audrey awake. She lets out a groggy moan as she comes back to consciousness. Lifting her head from its resting spot she flings her hair to the side, focusing on the aggravated voice. Looking across the way to each other Finn notices her neck is blackened, a solid bruise runs across her throat.

"Finn." Hope present in her tone. "You're awake."

"Aye. How are ya darlin?"

"I'm alive, so at least I can look on the bright side but I have a throbbing headache."

"I think he gave each of us somethin to remember him by, ya?"

"He's faster and stronger than I thought." Audrey admits.

"*For a paper pushin twat, he's not half bad.*" Finn spits out. "*Wasn't expectin to be hit by a brick wall. I'm not worried bout him though. Where's my Dette.*"

Audrey shifts her head to each side, her eyes wide and startled. Finishing her search Audrey stares directly into Finn's bothered gaze. Her eyes fill with sadness as she turns away from Finn.

"We were brought in together." Her voice trembling. "I don't remember much else before passing out."

"*It's ok love.*"

"It's not ok." She snaps. "I failed."

"*Nothin you coulda done. Stop thinkin you did somethin wrong. Tabitha put dat 'failure isn't an option' shit in ya head. Fuck her.*"

"She never put that notion in my head. She's my friend Finn."

"*You don't have to protect her no more. A cunts a cunt no matter what you call it.*"

"If it wasn't for her i'd be dead long ago- fuck this. I don't need to explain anything to you. You have a grudge against her and I understand why, but that doesn't give you the right to spout off at the mouth about her."

"*The fuck it doesn't. She's got ya wrapped up nice and tight, she could never do no wrong. News flash kid, she created a plague to fuck the world and if not this one, one just like it. Innocent people get caught in dis shit and die. They pay da real price fa her 'genius'.*"

"You mean civilians like Claudette?"

"*Ya.*" He replies, waiting on her next words.

"She's not going to die Finn." Audrey says matter-of-factly. "We won't let that happen."

"*Who's we, love? It sure ain't her.*"

Finn leans slightly back in his chair, as far back as the cords will allow. Audrey returns her sight to him, catching his blank stare in her direction. He continues to move his hands about behind his back relentlessly pushing against the restraints, attempting to loosen their hold. Audrey gazes into Finn's emotionless eyes returning his stare back to him, with wide eyed sadness.

"You're worried bout her, just the same as I am. We both know she ain't making it out alive, ain't that right?"

"What are you saying?" Audrey wearily asks.

"There no cure for this disease, ya? No need to bullshit me."

He watches Audrey's eyes dip from view. Out of sight Audrey balls her fists, gripping the restraints tightly. She exhales deeply, as if preparing her nerves for a confrontation. With pursed lips Finn nods his head, accepting her silence as an answer.

"I don't know." She says, cutting through the quiet like a knife.

"You don't know?"

"No."

"So when she told me there was a cure, that was a flat out lie?"

"I don't know." She repeats.

"Don't fuck me around. Dis ain't no interrogation. I just want honesty."

"There is no cure." She solemnly says. "She lied, alright."

"Das what I figured. Why da fuck didn't ya speak up?"

"I wasn't sure."

"So ya cover for her, until she can make it worse."

"I had hope-"

"Don't we all?"

He begins to tap his foot against the basement floor, his mind partially lost to thought. Worry replaces the bitter emotionless stare along his face. Feeling his constant stare Audrey keeps her sight to the darkened corners of the room, ignoring Finn's piercing gaze. She chokes down another breath.

"It was never meant to be like this." Audrey says swallowing hard. "I'm sorry Finn."

"No apologies. Why'd she infect my Claudette?" His tone sharp.

"What?" Said with genuine shock. "Why would you think that?"

"Come on Audrey. Ya expectin me to believe it's all coincidence. Open ya fuckin eyes, da bitch strung us along. Really expect her to keep us around once shes done?"

"You act as though she's a monster."

"I stared into da eyes of a monster earlier and i'm still hesitating to know which one I trust less."

"Trust me."

"You say it like it'll make everythin better darlin. I'm not listenin to the sales pitch. You'll have ta prove ya trust like everything else."

"We did not poison Claudette. I couldn't look you in the eyes if I was going to take something you love away from you. You may consider her a monster, but you know i'm not. You know i'm not lying to you!"

"Do I?"

Steps resonate down the hallway leading into the room. Audrey and Finn hush their conversation, listening to the quickening of the footsteps. Behind the quickened set of feet another can be heard, slow and deliberate in their approach. Finn takes in a deep breath, awaiting whatever may be behind the door.

"I'm sorry." Audrey repeats, her tone hushed.

"I know ya are. You wouldn't a stayed behind-"

"That's what teammates do."

"Dat's what friends do. I know ya trust Tabitha and she might have saved ya from the worst of fates, but don't think that makes you beholden ta her. You have far exceeded the amount ya owe her. Now's where you make ya own decision. You get to choose which life be worth livin darlin'."

"We have to make it out of here first."

"I suppose ya'd be right. First we crack some fuckin skulls." A smile escapes Finn's cracked lips.

The same smile crosses Audrey's face as she lets out a long held sigh of relief. They both work towards freeing themselves from their constraints, struggling against the tight bonds.

The door knob to the room rattles as the first set of steps approach. Audrey and Finn freeze in place, ceasing their progress towards escape. The knob twists halfway and suddenly stops. A jingle of keys rings softly through the small cell like room. Another quick twist and the door opens half way, giving Finn a clear look at the woman entering the room. Her smile devilish as she eyes him from across the room. Her silverish hair parted to either side in ponytails, the tips a dark red. Eyes an inky black. A voice cuts through the air, sending chills down Audrey's spine.

"STOP." Mind calls out.

Before turning to meet the voice, the woman winks in Finn's direction, blowing him a kiss as she closes the door. Finn cocks an eye in Audrey's direction, quizzically looking at the door behind her.

•

Rose greets Mind with a exaggerated wave and hearty smile. Changing from her blood soaked dress Rose presents herself in another new white dress. The bullet holes in her chest and back hidden underneath the fabric. Mind approaches, returning to his cloaked attire, unmoved by her display of happiness. Her devilish and bright smile distorts into a sneer as he turns away from her briefly. Walking past Rose he locks the door behind her. Rose sticks her tounge out toward him as he passes.

"What do you think your doing Spirit?" Mind says, turning back toward her.

"How dare you call me by that name!" She howls back, her face contorted in anger. "I'm not some nickname, I remember who I am."

"What are you doing here Rose?" He rephrases, his irritation growing.

"I'm here to finish the job Si-"

"You would do well to remember to call me Mind. The job is already well underway and close to completion. You are not needed for the final stages. I suggest you find whatever hole you crawled from and return there until you are further needed."

"Some of us don't fear what we used to be."

"I believe the term is 'who you used to be'. I have no need to cling to the pleasures of being mortal Rose. Temptations are distractions. Something you become rather quickly."

"No, no, no. You let the little bird get away. I remember the plan, that wasn't a part of it. You don't get to blame this on me. Nope. You promised us, you promised him the little bird."

"All in due time." He confidently replies. "The little bird will be yours."

Rose pulls at the edges of her dress, playing with the loose ends of the fabric. Her hands trailing the hem of her dress. Mind brushes beside her, the face on his mask turns as he passes by, staring into Rose's abyss like eyes.

"What if she stops you?" She blurts out.

"How can she Rose?" Mind pauses his advance. "I have thought of numerous possibilities and built contingencies around them. Your simple mind can't look past the fact that she outsmarted you. Let alone fathom the amount of work i've put into my project."

"She's an Arlenko. She can do anything she puts her mind to." Rose says coldly, her blank eyes staring through him.

"Do not. That name holds no merit with me." He furiously retorts, emotion seeping through his words.

"What'd that sting mister genius? For all your big brains you really can't see anything." She teases. "She has their spirit, their passion and here you are underestimating her. She really is something special and you refuse to see it. I should be rooting for her." Rose says tauntingly.

"All these years and I thought you would become a diamond in the rough. Turns out all you are is the coal I should have discarded years ago."

"You sweep me off my feet with words like that. They make my heart all a flutter." Rose fans herself. "You can say what you want about me but I haven't failed him. You pushed up your timeline because 'YOU' failed to keep the backstabbing witch under control. Look where she is now. Can you say uh oh?"

"I am working on separating them."

"Yeah, cause clearly that worked before. All it did was drive tabby cakes crazy. She shot me. Four times! Do I have to remind you what a bullet feels like 'Mind'? Let's get a play by play provided by your very own Rose. Oh Anna you're such a great magician. Oh thanks Rose. BANG BANG BANG BANG. Then I flopped to the floor like a fish. All really embarrassing."

"You were careless."

"It was fun. I was remembering."

"Memories are fleeting, insignificant things."

Rose steps back from Mind, keeping his face in view. Reeling back she pushes her hand through a solid brick wall beside him. She stares at him through his mask, her innocent smile twisting into one of hatred. Without even a flicker of emotion Mind returns her gaze stoically. She lets loose a scream of frustration in his face.

"Are you done child?"

"I told the Outrider you failed." She remarks childishly, narrowing her eyes. "That you couldn't handle the responsibilities he gifted you."

Her innocent smile returns as she utters those words. Her scream turning into a slow building cackle as she glares through him, in her own show of defiance. The mask's expression becomes almost animated, a wide beaming smile from ear to ear.

"How kind of you to care, Spirit. I will await his arrival and show him the fruits of my labor when he does indeed make himself known."

"Be sure that you do Simon."

Rose's smile grows wider. With a flick of her hair she twirls around skipping back down the hallway she entered from, humming a low tune as she gleefully walks away. Mind impassively stands by watching as she leaves up the staircase before following, slowly making his way down the long hallway in Rose's shadow.

Chapter Fourteen
Consequences

Claudette wakes herself with a violent cough, her lips peppered red with trails of blood. She begins gasping for air, her lungs partially filling with liquid. Her eyes wide with fear as she sucks in equal parts air and blood. Her face pale and drained of color, veins running along her face darkening to a deep red. Turning to the side she coughs again, spitting the liquid onto the observation table she lay on. With a groan she attempts to lift herself to an upright position on the table, unable to budge against her bonds. Looking to her side she stares at the leather restraints attached to her visible right hand. Her vision blurs as she stares at the binding. She lay back against the cold steel, it's surface uneven and jagged, making her arch her back in slight pain. She closes her eyes and slows her breathing, keeping herself calm.

"Where am I?" Her words coming out gravelly. "Focus Claudette. Where are you?"

Claudette struggles against the cold leather bonds, beginning to work her right hand through its loop. Simultaneously she runs her left hand along the observation table, searching for some possibility of releasing the shackle with less effort. Her right hand reaches midway through the shackle before becoming caught by the leather bond. Her hands begin to tremble as she forces out another hacking cough.

"Come on." She hoarsely says, willing herself forward.

With her head spinning in circles Claudette looks about the darkened room, her vision blurring in and out. A blue light glares off the metal walls of what looks to be a laboratory giving her a vague outline the rooms contents. Another cough breaks the slight humming of a computer tower, followed by the sound of liquid hitting the medical table. Clenching her fists Claudette grits her teeth, blocking out the burning pain associated with her affliction.

She lay on the table for a moment in complete stillness, the humming of the computer breezing through her ears, her body burning in agony. A single tear runs down from her eye, tracing down the side of her face and mixing with the blood underneath. Thoughts of her friends and family running through her mind as she lay helpless on the cold slab of metal.

Footsteps echo into the room from the end of the hallway breaking Claudettes train of thought, each step sounding her impending doom.

She struggles again with her trembling right hand, pulling at her restraint with more fervor. The bond has no give, stopping her hand once again. Claudette lets out a sound of frustration, clenching her jaw. The steps continue, slow and unnerving, pushing her to renew her efforts. Her sunken eyes light up, entertaining an idea. Lifting her head from the table she begins coughing purposefully, projecting the blood towards her right hand and restraint. A way to loosen the grip around her hand.

With one final effort she wrenches her hand free from its confinement with a small popping sound as she frees herself from one constraint. With no time for celebration she quickens her resolve and begins to unlatch her left hand, bracing herself for a confrontation. The second restraint falls away with a loud thudding sound as it rattles into the observation table.

Lifting herself from the table once again she easily undoes both binds around her feet in a hastily manner, releasing herself from the table. A sigh of relief escapes her lips as she calms herself down, her hands continuing to tremble. Draping her legs over the table top she vaults down onto the floor, her legs giving out underneath her. With a thud she falls to her knees onto the tiled floor, again gritting her teeth, eliciting a small whimper. Claudette puts her back to the table, hiding underneath it's frame. The faint markings of a conversation can be heard over the footsteps outside the door as they close the distance to the room. Claudette scans around the room, her vision giving rough silhouettes of the objects visible, barely being able to make out a medical tray a few feet in front of her. Scrambling to one knee Claudette reaches for the tray, bringing it closer to herself. Pulling the tray down she pours over the items on it, skipping over the forceps, clamps and retractors in favor of a set of scalpels. She quickly arms herself with the small blades as the door to the room opens wide, letting in a warmer light.

"Dammit. Where's the girl?!" One of the two figures yells aloud.

"Breaker one, we have a tango loose in the building."

Looking along the side of the table Claudette gets a fuzzy image of two men standing in the doorway, dressed in odd military attires. She squints into the bright lights, searching their silhouette for any weaponry before ducking back behind the table. The guards cautiously walk towards the observation table, looking over her recent escape.

"She couldn't have gone far." The first remarks. "Look at all this blood, surprised she isn't dead already."

"Looks like she struggled against the restraints. Blood on the cuff. So she's injured as well. Breaker one we're in pursuit. We'll find the girl and bring her to the tower as requested."

Claudette's hands shake furiously as she listens to the conversation. She winces in pain as she suppresses another cough, silencing her cry of suffering with her arm. Raising up to meet the edge of the table she prepares the scalpels, forcing her hands to quit their trembling as she grips the instruments firmly. Peering around the edge of the table Claudette watches as they spread out, diligently searching the room for her whereabouts

"This is my best chance." She whispers to herself, her breathing staggered. "Fuck it, it's me or dem." She says smiling, readying herself.

Cautiously Claudette steps out from behind the table, keeping herself low to the ground, blurred vision making it harder to keep track of her targets. With weapons in hand she rounds the corner confidently, squinting to keep her vision intact. The two men begin to spread out from the table searching for her in the small laboratory. With their backs turned to her, Claudette makes the first move. Opting for a stealthy approach Claudette moves in close, wrapping her arms around his neck in a rear naked chokehold. The man struggles against her firm grip, placing his hands over her arm and wrenching at her hold. The look of shock apparent in his eyes as she closes off his oxygen. Prying at her arms he fights to gain control, letting loose a small groan. His aloof partner continues his search just outside of reach. Claudette struggles to keep herself on her feet, the guard giving her far more trouble then she is accustomed to. In a last ditch effort the guard leans forward lifting Claudette off of her feet and slamming himself backwards onto the ground, knocking the wind out of both fighters and garnering the attention of his partner. Claudette rolls out from underneath the nearly unconscious man, making it to her hands and knees before violently coughing up more blood. Her vision flickers as she maintains consciousness. The guards partner grabs the back of Claudette's neck lifting her off of her knees, onto the tips of her toes. Instinctively she spins the scalpel around in her hand, thrusting it into center of his shoulder. In a grunt of pain the man lets her loose. Weakly she lands on her feet before quickly turning to face the second guardsman. With haste she capitalises on her offense, adrenaline coursing through her ailing body, burying the second scalpel into his neck. His eyes jolt open as she pulls the blade away from his throat. Their eyes meet, each filled with the same fear of death. He covers his throat, as blood begins to pour freely from the open wound. In his attempt to grab for Claudette he falls to the ground on one knee, blinking rapidly as he processes his own demise.

Wiping her hair from her eyes Claudette scans the room for her other target, keeping her focus on survival. She spots the man laying on the ground still struggling to regain his composure. She ambles towards him, saving her energy. He looks up toward her as she approaches with a look of disgust.

"What's at the tower?" Her breathing labored.

The man stares at her silently in defiance, slowly rising back to his feet. The sound of his companion gasping for air breaks the silence between them. She peers in his direction, watching his movements closely. From a pouch he pulls out a short bladed knife, holding it out for her to see. Claudette lunges forward, thrusting the short scalpel into his abdomen. With her free hand she disarms him of his blade, knocking it off to the side of the room.

"I'm not going to ask again" She fakes a confident tone.

"The slow inevitable death of this world." He replies, a smirk creeping across his face.

She plunges the instrument deeper into his stomach as he laughs at her attempt to question him. The man pulls back on her hair, pulling her away from him, allowing himself to wrap his other free hand around her throat in an attempt to choke her. Claudette wearily blocks his attempted offense, stabbing the scalpel through the opposite arm in retaliation. Pulling the scalpel from its hole, she strikes just underneath the jaw, driving the blade through the roof of his mouth. His arms go limp beside her as he falls backwards onto the observation table, his smile eerily present as he drops to the ground.

Claudette collapses onto one knee clutching at her chest. The burning sensation throughout her body intensifying, the pain mind numbing. As she looks around the small lab her vision begins to spin. She closes her eyes tightly, fighting back the urge to scream.

"Just a bit longer. Please." She prays aloud.

Taking in a deep breath she opens her eyes focusing their haze into manageable sight, making out the silhouettes of the defeated soldiers. Finding the will to stand Claudette exhales sharply as she makes an attempt to return to her feet, knees almost buckling as she stands straight. Straightening herself out Claudette takes her first shakey step forward toward the exit, a success. Letting out a sigh of relief she continues forward through the entryway out into a long, brightly lit hallway.

Stumbling back into the room Claudette searches out the knife knocked from her aggressors hand, finding it beside the far wall. Moving between the dead she snags the knife from the floor.

Limping back towards the door Claudette stops beside one of the fallen guards, leaning over and examining his earpiece. Her murky eyes grow wide as she touches her ear, her hand brushing over the device Xylen left for them. Static startles her as she turns the device on, her shoulders tensing up out of instinct. As the noise fades she hears the faint murmuring of a familiar voice. A faint smile spreads across her face as she listens to her conversation, giving her a glimmer of hope. Using the wall as a crutch she slides along its length, a trail of smeared blood following her as she continues forward into the hallway. Reaching the exit she slumps over, taking the time to catch her breath before continuing on. Cautiously she opens the door, peeking out into the next empty hallway. A scan of the small corridor leaves her with three choices of travel.

"Audrey?" She coughs out.

"Claudette?" Audrey responds quizzically.

"I'm in some laboratory can't figure out which way to go from here." Her breathing becoming ragged.

"Are you ok? We're worried about you."

"Just tell him i'm alright."

Faintly over the earpiece Finn can be heard in the background, his loud voice booming even in an echo. Claudette snickers, his voice soothing her racing mind.

"Did you hear any of that?" Audrey asks.

"I don't need to make out the words to know exactly what he said. There was swearing."

"A lot of swearing."

"We have to be in close proximity, our earbuds are working. I have three hallways ahead of me and I don't have much time to randomly pick one. I need you guys to make some noise so that I can find you."

"Finn, she needs noise."

Finn's obnoxious voice drowns out Audrey over her own headset. Claudette turns her device off, in order to better hear his muffled yelling. Even in her deteriorating state she hears the dampened voice of her partner coming from the far right hallway. Pressing forward Claudette staggers off in the direction of Finn's call. Turning the earpiece on again she clearly hears Finn's voice reflected back to her.

"You twats gunna let me out or what? I gotta take a roarin piss!"

"I would expect nothing less."

"I think he got a guards attention."

"That's even better for me. Less to have to worry about."

Claudette continues down the passageway, peering into rooms along the way. Her footsteps and Finn's ruckus the only sounds breaching the silent corridor. She picks up her pace, moving from one hallway to the next seeking out Finn's roaring, keeping one foot in front of the other.

"How are you really?" Audrey asks, her tone tentative.

"I feel like kindling. One ember and i'll burst into flame."

"No one has ever made it this long."

"I'm breaking records."

Claudette twists and turns through the hallways following the sound of Finn's obnoxious voice, passing by lab rooms similar to her own. Her movement slows as she tries to push herself forward, her legs giving out underneath her. Falling downward she lands on her knees, holding onto a railing for support. A cry of pain escapes her mouth as she lowers herself to the ground gently.

"What happened?" Audrey snaps.

"My legs are done." Claudette montonely says.

"You-"

"Audrey I need you to promise me something."

"No. We are not doing this over an earpiece."

"Doin what?" Finn's voice echoing through her speaker.

"I need you to promise me you'll take good care of him." She continues. "Finn's a good man. Hard headed at times but worth his weight in gold. I wouldn't trade him in for anything. When i'm gone he'll need someone. Someone stubborn enough to put up with all his boasting and bragging. His innuendos, bravado and shitty jokes."

"Finn, just keep distracting the guard, she's on her way." Audrey says, distracting Finn.

Claudette drops her head to her chest, hair falling perfectly around her face. Holding back tears as she converses with Audrey, Claudette closes her eyes tightly. Her arms burn like lava as she runs her hands up them.

"Someone he can share this pain with. He'll need someone other than Anna. She won't be able to mend his broken heart this time even though she'll try her hardest. I know how much they mean to each other, but I know you'll be a great addition to the team in my place."

"Are you making me your replacement?" Audrey says, using a low tone.

"You're part of the Annatourage now. You have been since Xylen laid eyes on you. It's just official."

Laying her head on the cool wall Claudette sit stationary, her breathing slowing. Her heart pulsing, attempting to break free from her chest. Running through her memories of Finn a smile breaches her sullen lips. Tears flowing freely down her cheeks she prepares herself for what's to come.

"Dette. Darlin' I know you can hear me. I need you." Finn's voice rings through her ears, distress apparent in his words.

Swallowing hard Dette opens her eyes, her murky vision worse yet. Reaching for the railing Claudette forces herself to a standing position. Using the wall she guides herself towards the sound of Finn's echoing voice. She drags herself along the length of the corridor, reaching a staircase going further down.

"I'm coming." She chokes out.

Each step another second of agony on her trembling legs, the coursing adrenaline barely keeping her standing. As she works her way down the staircase Finn's voice becomes clearer, drawing her forward.

"So what? Don't cha have urges and needs man? You should know when a man's gotta piss, he gotta go. Whats da big deal? Either ya lettin me to da bathroom or ya cleanin up me piss, what'll it be? Janitor or Jailer?" His voice resonating with Claudette, warming her broken spirit.

"That's my man." She proudly says, her smile wide.

The staircase leads into another narrow corridor. Claudette peers with the remainder of her vision to the end of the hall, spotting a guard just inside the entryway to a room, Finn's voice coming from just the other side of the man. Choking back her fear Claudette attempts to be silent in her approach, painfully lowering herself from his peripheral vision. She ambles forward keeping her frame low to the ground, cursing under her breath as she presses onward.

"Would you just shut up." The guard remarks. "You're lucky to be alive, let alone worrying about your rights. You'll go to the bathroom when I say you can."

"Be sure ta pass on the word dat ya a loyal pissant. Pun intended."

Claudette reaches striking range on the guardsman, holding the knife shakily in her left hand. His attire similar to the two she disposed of moments ago. She steadies herself behind him, ready to strike. On instinct she lunges forward plunging the blade into his throat, attempting to end the fight quickly. Pushing down with all her weight Claudette drives the blade deeper into the surprised guards neck line, causing him to scream in pain. Twisting the blade Claudette rips the knife from its temporary home as quickly as it entered. The guard turns around slowly, blood pouring freely from the gaping wound. She strikes again using the surprise to her advantage, driving the blade into his stomach. He grabs ahold of her hand in an attempt to halt her offense.

Claudette stares through him, her gaze cold and determined. Droping to his knees, his grip tight around her hand still. His eyes like the guardsman before him flicker with fear as he stares into her dead eyes, the thought of death terrifying. Using the last ounce of her strength Claudette pulls her hand free from his grasp, the blade carving a path through his clenched hands. She moves past the dying guard, stumbling into the room with an unnatural haste before falling to a knee before reaching Finn.

"Dat's ma girl."

Through squinted eyes Claudette makes out her partners form. She scrambles towards him on hands and knees, dragging herself toward the chair. Finn looks on, watching his lover clamber towards him, unable to come to her aid. The misery written across her face enough to send him into a building fury. Audrey's attention preoccupied with the gutteral sounds of the guard as he struggles himself to return to his feet. Wiggling in the chair Audrey begins to slide it closer to the groggy guardsman, his attention firmly on Claudette. Dette approaches Finn, running her hand along the side of the chair, feeling for his restraints. Moving to Finn's back she feels the rope adjoining his hands.

"Darlin-" Finn attempts to look over his shoulder, groaning in pain as the restraints dig into his chest.

"Not now." She replies, beginning to cut loose the bindings. "I have to focus."

"Alright." He says through gritted teeth.

Staggered, the guard returns to one knee. He appears unphased by the loss of blood pouring from his open wounds. Claudette slowly cuts away the rope around Finn's arms and hands freeing him to begin working on the knots around his legs and feet. Resting an arm on the chair she sits behind him, catching her breath.

Making it to his feet the guard pushes himself forward, heading for Finn and Claudette. With one last push Audrey slides herself into the guardsman, knocking him off balance, giving Finn more time to undo his constraints. The momentum of the chair sliding bends its leg sending Audrey to the floor with a heavy thud, leaving her laying face down on the concrete. The commotion is enough to draw Finn's attention to the nearly dead man continuing to press on towards them.

"*Dette?*" Finn's tone coming off concerned.

"I'm. Fine." She says, her breathing ragged still.

"*Sure as shit ain't. You made friends love. Keep distance ya?*"

Finn works his hands against the knots around his legs, finishing the set tying his feet. Stumbling over his own feet the man slowly approaches. Blood drips from his soaked uniform creating a pool underneath each step, leaving enough behind to have killed any normal person. His eyes shifting from Finn to Claudette and back, fear now far removed from them. Reaching into a back pocket the guard pulls a knife from its sheath, brandishing it in front of Finn. He inches closer as Finn begins working on his last knot, his adrenaline kicking in. The guard turns to move behind Finn, setting his sights onto the defenseless Claudette. In her haze she stares blankly at her opponent as he draws in on her. Finn pulls away at the last knot with haste, his composure beginning to wear down. The man grabs Claudette by the hair dragging her to a kneeling position, her body hanging limply in the air. He holds the knife in front of her paling face, brashly taunting her. Claudette swings wildly with her own knife, digging the blade into his outstretched arm. Instinctively the man lurches back, letting go of her hair. She lands back onto her hands and knees, a silent scream leaving her body upon impact. Finn pulls apart the last knot keeping him seated. Flying from his seated position Finn flows like water, putting himself between Claudette and her assailant. Within a blink of an eye Finn reaches out for the guardsman, twisting around his body to be positioned behind the man. A sickening snap ends the momentary conflict.

"*Get fucked.*" Finn roars, letting the man fall limply to the floor, his neck twisted and broken.

Finn rushes to Claudette's side, kneeling down to meet her at eye level. Comforting her, he places a hand along her back. Looking into her eyes he stares for what feels like an eternity, his sight running along the darkening veins crossing her face. He places the other free hand along her cheek, running his thumb along her soft skin. Claudette smiles at him, sadness lingering in the corners of her lips.

"Hi there you." She says weakly.

"Hey." He returns her smile. *"You saved da day."*

"I didn't need you bragging about how you did everything all by yourself." She says, pulling herself together.

"Aye. I'mma have to let you tell the story now. No embelishin it, ya hear?"

"I fought off a horde of guards with one hand. Then rescued my damsel in distress. Slayed the dragon and off to a happy ever after." She quips.

"Maybe just a little embelishin."

Claudette leans over into Finn's open arms, moving out of her kneeling position to sit beside him. Leaning heavily onto him, she rests her head on his shoulder. He places both arms tightly around her waist, sharing his warmth.

"I heard you, you know."

"I didn't do it I swear."

"You said you needed me. I was ready then, i'm not ready now."

"I don't think any of us is ever ready Dette. I'm sure as shit not. I'm glad you came, but I still need you." Finn says, his eyes beginning to water.

"I remember the first time we were together, not the night at the bar. Not any operation we ran. When you and I were finally together. I remember how you held me in your arms. I found out who you really were that night, and I knew I had found my soulmate." She runs her hand across his chin playfully.

"You're my everything Dette."

"And you're mine, Finn."

Finn lays his head down onto Claudette's, tears streaming freely from his eyes. Gripping tighter he pulls her further into him, cradling her in his arms. Claudette nuzzles his chest with her chin, her own tears falling onto his shirt.

"I'm tired Finn."

"Then rest your eyes darlin. You've done more than your fair share."

"They say you see a white light. You know what I see? A beach and free drinks."

"Sounds like my sort of place. What else is there?"

"A great big ocean. Plenty of cabana boys, but something's missing."

"Don't you worry Dette, I know what's missin. I won't be too far behind. You just rest now. I love you."

"I love you more."

Claudette's breathing grows shallow, her words still lingering in his ears. Her hand falls softly from Finn's face, hanging limply on the ground. Finn buries his head into her chest, tears continuing to trickle down his cheeks. The beating of her heart faintly pulses against his face, slowly begining to dissipate with time. Her skin grows colder as the heat begins to leave her body.

Slowly pulling his head away from her chest he lets out a scream that fills the room, letting out his raw frustration and anger. The scream startles Audrey as she struggles against her bonds, pulling her restraints over the bent chair leg in an attempt to free herself.

Finn looks down onto Claudette, her face peaceful and calm, a small smile with a hint of sadness. Finn gently places her on the ground, planting a kiss on her forehead before saying a small prayer.

"They do call me there. They bid me take my place among them in the hallowed halls, where the brave shall live forever."

Running a hand over her face, he closes her eyes. Finn stands straight, running his tongue over his teeth, contemplating. He walks over to the struggling Audrey, helping free her from the bonds. Pulling the last knot loose Audrey pulls herself off of the downed chair, scurrying to her feet and wrapping her arms around Finn. Audrey weeps into Finn's ear, sniffling and sobbing loudly. He embraces her warmly.

"Aye, it's ok darlin. You just let it out ya?"

"She's-"

"*Ya. She's waitin for me now. Can't go disappointin her, but I need to get ya outta here safely.*"

Finn breaks their hug, returning to Claudette. With the gentlest of grip Finn lifts her into his arms, holding her closely to him. Audrey looks on, her face a mess of tears and sadness.

"*Let's go home.*" Finn says, nudging Audrey as he exits the room.

CHAPTER FIFTEEN
HOME

Silence falls over the street just before the Eldritch Flame. It's lingering quiet seemingly following Anna from Frostscythe, hunting her. She departs from the hover leaving Tabitha and Xylen behind. The wind whips through her hair as she moves towards the Eldritch Flame with purpose. The streets lay barren just before daybreak, leaving her alone with her own thoughts.

How is something like this even possible? How can you murder so many people?

Head hung dejectedly she walks along the sidewalk checking her phone for any messages from Finn and Claudette. 'No new messages' scrolls from right to left across the screen. Letting loose a sigh she jams the device back into her pocket, trading it for her keys. Approaching the door Anna fumbles with the keys. Hands trembling Anna matches up the right key opening the door to her home, it's dark interior slightly unnerving to her as she searches the room for possible intruders. She closes her weary eyes, preventing tears from running down her face. *I'm home. The only thing you have in the darkness is home.* Returning her focus to the darkened room she reaches out sweeping her hand across a light switch, banishing the darkness to the corners of the area. Walking down the familiar rows of tables Anna traces her hands along their surfaces, calming her nerves with a familiar touch. She lingers at the stage, her mind flooding with thoughts, questions and accusations.

Xylen and Tabitha enter minutes after Annastasia, closing and locking the door behind them.

Xylen leans against the locked door, his eyes bloodshot and exhausted. Running a hand through his red mane he breathes deeply before exhaling loudly. He slides down the length of the door into a seated position.

"Never seen so much death." He finally musters out, moving his hands down the length of his thighs nervously.

Tabitha weaves her way through the isle of tables, ignoring Xylen's statement. Approaching her lover warmly, Tabitha places a hand along her cheek. Anna recoils from her touch, taking two steps back. Her sorrow filled eyes filling with anguish and disgust.

"Was that enlightening?" Anna snaps in her direction.

"You want me to say no but you know my answer already. Yes, it was." Tabitha retorts calmly.

"How can you-" Anna reins in her own emotions, stopping herself from screaming at Tabitha. "How can you stand here so calmly? Hundreds of innocent people died and it's a high school science experiment to you. I'll never be able to forget those screams. All of the pain and suffering that you helped cause."

"This was never going to be easy. I am so calm because I have to be, for you. I should never have had you come along, a fact I am now regretting."

"Why? You didn't want me to see just what you are capable of."

"Is it real to you now?" Tabitha snaps, breaking her calm demeanor. "These people lied to me and I was looking for revenge. Is that what you want to hear? I will not apologize for what I accomplished tonight. You want me to be this person I was seven years ago, they died the day you thought I abandoned you."

Anna stares blankly into Tabitha's cold eyes. A look of shock and betrayal spread across her face, easily read. Taking a minute to gather her thoughts and emotions before returning to the argument, Anna turns from her companion.

"You screamed into the rain that night. Threw the only gift I ever could afford for you away. You stopped believing and so did I. I'm not going to regale you with tall tales and stories. Mind told me he would kill you if I didn't put my given talents to a better use and I did. I created my own natural selection for him to use, and then I plotted how I would get my revenge. One thing stayed constant, I never gave up on you. You're my anchor, the only thing keeping me here. I don't want to argue."

"You saw me?" Keeping her back to Tabitha.

"He kept me on a rooftop across from the building. I felt every tear you shed that night."

Tabitha closes the distance between Anna and herself, turning her back around. Brushing the stray hair from her face with her left hand as she twines her right hand through its length, playfully running back and forth through its silky touch. Frozen in place Anna accepts Tabitha's advances.

"Just as I feel them today."

Brushing her face across Anna's cheek Tabitha bites down gently on her earlobe, pulling slightly on her handful of hair. She breathes heavily into Anna's ear before continuing down the neckline slowly. Anna pulls herself away from Tabitha's persuasive touch, pulling back to the edge of the stage.

No. Tabitha retracts her hand back to her side, her lips pursing.

"I can't afford this distraction Tabitha. Not when there are so many lives at stake if we fail."

"This isn't about failing. This is about survival now Annastasia. If you couldn't save the people in one building what makes you so keen to try and do so again?"

"If you have to ask that question then you really don't know me."

"Are we going to have the same conversation we had seven years ago?"

"I remember it well. I will always place myself in front of danger Tabitha." Anna's stern eyes gaze back defiantly into her lovers. "I would rather die knowing I tried saving, then sleep well listening to those echoing screams. We both know which choice you would make. I'm going to contact my family and alert them if at all possible, is there anything else you wish of me?"

"Take a shower and get some sleep. You should die well rested."

"Noted."

Tabitha crosses her arms as she watches her significant other retreat, her stare piercing. Anna moves around the edge of the front stage, her eyes welling with tears as she leaves the conversation. Rounding the corner of the stage Anna heads into the silent and sparsely lit back room, its contents untouched since her last visit home. She digs back into her pocket, retrieving her phone. Propping herself up against the closest wall she waits in the darkness for Tabitha to follow her, scrolling through her list of contacts. A single tear falls from her eye, running its way slowly down her cheek onto her phone. Wiping away the droplet she puts the phone to her ear. *Now is not the time to be busy sis.* The connection rings through into a voicemail. "This is Illiyana Arlenko, leave a message and I will return a call at my earliest convenience." Anna mouths as the recording plays out.

"Hey Illy. This is important, I found out what Frostscythe is up to and you need to evacuate the tower immediately. I'll have Xylen wire over the files to you incase you think this isn't worth looking into. You're the soldier, i'm the violinist. Call me back."

Ending the call Anna scrolls again through her list of contacts, stopping on Kul. She hesitates for a moment before clicking on the name and placing the call. The dull tone of the ringing phone distracts her from the hushed silence of the room. *They must be preparing for the gala today. Just as Mind would want it.*

"You have reached the office of Kul Forsworn. Please leave your name, number and a brief message. We will make sure a representative will contact you in regards to your inquiry." A younger female voice says over the recording.

Sighing, Anna ends the second call without leaving a message. Stuffing the device back into her pocket she walks towards her office. Opening the door she flicks a light on, brightening up her room. Everything left perfectly in order. Anna lowers her head as she passes through the threshold into her shelter. She walks unhurried to the foot of her bed, attempting to erase the horrible thoughts from her head. She stumbles past her desk, kicking a leg of the table and sending coins cascading to the ground. The sound of the metal hitting the ground makes her shiver to the core. Frustrated, she balls her hand into a fist before bending over to collect the coins scattered across the ground. Stacking them neatly on her desk Anna continues forward, muttering under her breath as she moves past her bed to the door leading into her bathroom.

●

Xylen lifts himself up from in front of the entrance to the Flame. Casually he strolls over toward the bar. Reaching into the refrigerator beneath the counter, Xylen pulls two old fashion whiskey glasses from within. Grabbing a bottle of liquor, the label marked over in tape with 'the good stuff' penned in Finn's handwriting, he begins pouring its contents into the ice cold glasses.

"Oof. Rough night." Xylen says, catching Tabitha's attention.

Tabitha turns from her position in front of the stage, where she seemed to have been frozen in place. Her face a mixture of anger and frustration. She glares in Xylen's direction, his sarcastic tone grating on her nerves.

"Something to add?" She shoots back at him.

"Salt?" He says motioning to the drinks.

He smiles in her direction, leaning nonchalantly against the counter top nursing his own drink. Tabitha drifts through the tables between her and the bar, her gaze never leaving Xylen's chipper disposition. Coming up to the bar Tabitha leans down to Xylen's eye level, squaring up with him.

"Does it look like I am in the mood for idle prattle?"

"I don't quite care what your in the mood for. Hopefully you're in a decent enough mood for drinking." Xylen replies, sliding a cup in her direction. "Or else I poured this for no reason at all."

Tabitha looks over the liquor, holding the chilled glass in the center of her hand. She brings the glass to her nose, taking in its fresh aroma.

"I didn't poison it. Thought about it, but wasn't worth the trouble. That's more your thing."

"If you have something to say, why don't you just come out and say it?" Tabitha retorts, knocking back a fair amount of the drink.

"You claim to love her, but you're willing to throw in the towel when things get rough. Sounds like Anna about covered it, you don't know her. What did you expect? Her to crumble under the pressure?"

"I prefer to stay living."

"Then why didn't you run away from the start? You needed in that building for something. What was it Tabitha?" Xylen questions, sipping from his glass.

"I don't answer to you."

"No. You don't, but I did manage to pull just about everything off your computer and my hardware answers to me. Do I tell her she was always secondary to your goal? Or am I mistaken?" Smug arrogance permeates from his smile as he awaits an answer.

"For a spineless worm, you have your moments."

Xylen rolls his eyes at her. Motioning with his full hand towards his pants pocket, gesturing to his portable device. He winks at her, spreading the sly smile wider. Tabitha clenches her jaw before continuing.

"Annastasia never comes second to anything." She admits in defeat. "I don't think you want the truth, just a version of it Xylen."

"I think after the past few hours we've had you could tell me you planned on killing her step-father and I wouldn't bat an eyelash. Men in shapeshifting masks, airborne plagues and a corrupt company willing to destroy the planet. What else could possibly be worse."

"There was never a cure for Claudette."

"I retract my statement." His smile fades into solemn disbelief. "And you led us to believe there would be one."

"It astounds me what exactly people do when they 'listen'. If you would listen to more than the basic context I never once said there is a cure for Claudette. She was too far along with no hope of saving. The serum was the only thing I could give her. Your basic understanding of my words is no fault of my own. Everyone believed what they wanted to hear. I am no savior."

"Gross understatement." Xylen slams back the rest of his drink, leaving the cup overturned on the counter. "What were you aiming to retrieve?"

"And here I thought you would focus on the topic of your dying friend. Maybe you have changed."

"Answer the question."

Tabitha pulls herself off from the countertop, standing up rigidly. Her devilish smile poking through the sides of her lips, a devious and unnerving look. She pulls back her hair, letting it fall slowly out from her fingertips. Taking her time as Xylen waits impatiently for her response, Tabitha sits gingerly upon a stool, lowering herself back to Xylen's eye level.

"What I set out for last night. I accomplished." She coos. "Research Xylen. Research."

"You were going to detonate the canisters yourself."

"It most certainly was my plan." Her smile grows wider. "There was never going to be a third testing site. Frostscythe was my last target, I set up the charges in the middle of the night, for months. Hence why Jacob always saw me working late. It never had anything to do with helping them. They figured out my plan I suppose, killed my team before I could get back to the lab to set off the devices."

•

Steam billows from within the stand up shower of Anna's bathroom. The hot water clashing against her form as she attempts to wash away the filth of last evening. Taking in the relaxing tone of water on skin she beings to come down from her heightened tension. She takes extra care around her face and hair, closing her eyes as the water rinses away the restlessness. Her mind flickers between the echoing of screams, the expressions of pain and torture and Rose's last painful smile. Leaning against the furthest shower wall Anna slides down into a seated position, landing firmly on floor below. She buries her head in her hands, letting down her own barriers.

Dear Enigma, today I failed. I failed my family, my friends and myself. I made a promise never to let that happen again but promises are meant to be broken. I've been close to death before in my life, nothing like this. Nothing that leaves a void in the air around it. How could I be so careless, so blindly faithful and trusting? I couldn't even tell you where my best friends are right now, and that worries me. Today I broke a promise to everyone I care about. Finn, Claudette, Xylen, Illy and Kul. I let you down.

She begins to sob silently, digging her palms into her eyes to stop the flow of tears. The cascade of water washes over her head finding its way downward, mixing with her escaping tears. Pulling her hands from her eyes Anna looks into the falling water, letting it pour past her.

But today I make a new promise, one that would be voted most likely to fail in high school. I promise to make it up to all of you. In some way, I will fix what I let break in the first place. The weight of the world doesn't rest on my shoulders, just the conscience of Providence. Of its people and my family. As my father would say, if there is time for tears there's time to fix it.

Love Anna.

Pulling herself up from the bottom of the stall, she nods her head in agreement to her internal conversation. For another moment she allows the water to cover her, taking solace in its warmth.

Reaching out Anna pulls herself from the ground, exiting the shower. With the water running still she makes her way towards a steamed mirror, looking into its dulled reflection. The water hammers down upon the back wall leaving an ambient drumming in the background. Wiping clear the condensation, Anna looks through the remaining droplets to her distorted image. Her eyes fiery and determined, fierce enough to shatter the glass if she chose. Her hands clings to the edges of the vanity tightly.

"You are not your father. Nor your mother. You are your own person Annastasia. Be who you choose to be. Then be better than what you choose to be. Define yourself by what you are and who you will become." She monologues.

Releasing her grip Anna pulls away from the mirror, leaving her reflection behind. Turning off the pressure to the shower the room goes dull, leaving only the sporadic splashing of water droplets. She grabs a towel from its place, taking time and care to clean herself up.

Wrapping herself in the large towel Anna steps out from the bathroom, the change in temperature sends a small chill up her spine. Briskly moving the length of her room Anna heads towards her tea cabinet. *Tea ahead of all things, even freezing.* She quickly turns on the warmer before heading to her own cabinet, ruffling through her massive wardrobe. Quickly finding an odd matching ensemble she lets free the towel, replacing it with the feeling of new clothes.

Like a small child huggin me, or at least that's what Finn would say.

The image of Finn being embraced awkwardly by a small child brings on a smile to Anna, replacing the sadness that recently took up residence. The kettle chimes it's all too familiar tune, widening her smile yet. Roaming back to her tea, she rummages around through her various brands of tea.

"No Oasis Nights, you are in fact going to the back of the cupboard again." She blurts out, tossing the white container to the back of the pile. "I'll forget exactly where you are in a couple of days and have to go looking for you again. Ooo, chamomile sounds nice right about now."

Pulling out another bag, she places it in the bottom of the cup careful to leave the string draped over the edge of the cup. Pouring the boiling liquid over her waiting tea bag Anna fills the cup and air with the an earthy aroma. Breathing in deeply through her nose, Anna takes in the fresh pine like smell.

Sitting herself down at the age of her bed she sits cross legged, tea firmly sat between her legs, both for warmth and caution. Staring blankly at the other side of her room she looks at her belongings. Every trophy and coin. Her eye catches on a dangling medallion on the wall across from her, separate from the others. Rising from her bed, tea in hand, she walks over and palms the small silver circle. Her fingers roaming over the words 'Knight-General' etched across the middle of the pendant. *I wish you were here dad. You'd have already handled this.*

Anna carefully places the medallion back into its spot, easing it back into place on the wall. She drags her hand along the mantle, making her way back across the room. She pauses a moment, her hand running over a blank space towards the front of the shelf. A spot labelled 'Arcadia' lay bare. Her eyes move left to right, looking cautiously about the room. Moving to her desk she riffles through a few miscellaneous things finding the Arcadian ring exactly where she left it, attached to a necklace she discarded on the table earlier. *Stop giving yourself a heart attack.*

Breathing a sigh of relief, Anna returns the ring to its right spot on the mantle. Taking a long drink Anna returns her attention to the mantle, finishing her rounds before making her way back into bed. Setting the tea down on the nightstand Anna pulls herself under her sheets. She grabs for the clock at her nightstand, setting the alarm for an hour.

"Might as well die well rested." She says half-heartedly, laying her head down onto the pillow, slowly drifting off to sleep.

●

Opening the doors to the balcony, Kul trades the noise of a busy

Providence morning for fresh air. Hovers whiz past his balcony, a cacophony of motors running just past daybreak. Leaning against the railing he breathes deeply, taking in the morning air with a smile. Looking out into his city he takes in the sights just as any tourist would, wide eyed and amazed.

"Do you see this?" He ask the young lady standing just inside his study.

She raises her attention from the blazing fire of his well tended fireplace. The young bright eyed Annastasia looks back over her shoulder into the equal bright daylight, catching a glimpse of the hovers passing by. Hurrying to her feet she races to stand beside the Lord of Providence, her sight reaching eye level with the railing.

"I see marble." She responds dejectedly, her shoulders slumping.

"Do you need to sit on my shoulders little flame?" Kul says laughing.

"I just need to grow, about-" Anna begins measuring with her fingers, her tongue peeking out as she counts. "About two inches taller."

"You know that by measuring your fingers?"

"Well yeah. You ever measure your finger with a ruler?"

"Not in some time." Said with a chuckle.

Reaching down Kul lifts Anna up onto his shoulders, her bright eyes widening even further. Anna points out at the sea of hovers passing by, counting the different colored vehicles. Beyond the mass of metal machines the sun begins its ascent past the mountains, casting away shadows from the city below. It's shimmering rays reflecting from the glass of the tallest skyscrapers.

Anna looks on in unbridled happiness. Her hands playing with Kul's sandy brown hair as he steadies her on his back. For a moment they share the dawn together in all of it's beautiful glory.

"It's amazing."

"Yeah." She replies softly.

"Have you never seen the sunset from this view before?"

"No." Her focus bouncing between all the new sights. "Providence is beautiful."

"It sure is."

"Can we stay out here forever?"

"I would like nothing more than that."

Smiling, Kul turns his head to make eye contact with the young girl. She returns the same sincere smile before returning her attention to the bustling city life, seeing it all through a new lens.

"How can you protect a city so big all alone?" She asks innocently.

"What do you mean?"

"You're the lord of the land. You see over everything?"

"I do, but I would be lying if I said I didn't have plenty of aid. Every soldier, doctor, nurse- everyone regardless of job, they are the reason Providence runs. Those workers are the heart and soul of this planet and key to the survival of our galaxy. Without them I would just be a man showing his very wonderful niece a sunrise."

"But you're important too." Anna says wiggling around atop Kul's shoulders, attempting to slide down his back.

"I am?" He asks, leaning down to help Annastasia reach the ground easily.

With a small thud Anna slides back onto the balcony floor with a giggle followed by a few chuckles. She moves around to meet Kul, her hands dug into her hips. He opens his eyes wide before letting out a hearty laugh.

"You are important." She says matter of factly.

"Okay. Okay." Beaming in her direction. "What makes me so important to you?"

"You're my uncle!"

"I see. So am I more popular because i'm the lord or the greatest violinist in the world's uncle?"

"Polls not back yet."

They let out a shared laugh, exchanging smiles with each other. An older gentleman, dressed dapperly, approaches the duo as they continue their laughing fit. His face aged with wrinkles, of which he wears well. Looking back Annastasia shares a smile with him before approaching him arms wide for a hug.

"ROLAND!" She bellows.

"My dear Annastasia. How are you doing today?" His tone sincere and soft.

"I'm swell Ro. How are you?"

"I feel mighty fine this morning darling."

"No aches or pain?"

"Just the lord as usual-" He says grinning from ear to ear. "Sir, I have the box you requested."

"Thank you Roland." Kul replies, taking the box from his assistants hand.

"Tea is on the table beside the desk. Miss Arlenko's favorite, chamomile."

"You're the best Ro." Anna beams a bright smile in his direction. A smile which he returns happily.

"A compliment I gladly accept."

Breaking the hug Roland turns on his heels, making for a quick exit from the study. Reaching the door he half turns toward Anna, winking at her before taking his leave. She winks back, her smile widening into a grin.

Kul makes his way in from the balcony, setting the box on his desk carefully. Anna trots in after him, following like an animal looking for a treat. She peeks around the corner of the desk, eyeing the box wantingly. Hiking up his dress pants, Kul lowers himself into a chair by the fireplace. The warmth of the fireplace presses against his face as he pours two cups of tea, one cup considerably shorter than the other. Anna walks around the desk, running her fingers along the trim, her focus never leaving the box in the center of the table.

"What's in the box?" She asks inquisitively.

"A medallion." He answers shortly.

"Who are we celebrating?"

"Quite astute of you. We're celebrating a coronation."

"Oooo. Of what?" Anna asks, continuing her circles around the desk.

"I lost a friend and natural leader in your father. I need someone new to protect this tower in case I am to ever fail. Someone to take my place when I can no longer do the job required of me."

"Dad was going to replace you?"

"In some time yes he would grow to replace me. Lordship is a title given to select few in our galaxy. I wished to pass it along to your father, he was indeed worthy of its inheritance."

Anna ends her pacing, coming to sit beside Kul. She reaches out for his larger glass of tea, sending Kul into a fit of laughter. Taking her time she balances the contents, carefully bringing it to her mouth.

"You wanted my dad to be the lord?" She asks, loudly sipping from the cup.

"I did. He showed promise in the way he held himself and more importantly in the regard he held this city in. He was-"

"He is." Anna interrupts.

"He is my best friend."

"Mine too."

Letting silence into the room Kul takes a sip from the smaller glass, his attention focused on the young girl. She raises the larger glass again to her face taking another large slurp of the tea. She gazes into his eyes, trying to hold back her own exposed emotion.

"I promised him the day he left that I would take care of you both until he returned home. I intend to fulfill that promise I made to him Annastasia. You and your sister are the two most important things in my life now."

"You think he's gone?"

"I think if he is alive little flame, that he is struggling to return to tuck you in at night. Just to see you smile one more time. In the meantime we shall keep his memory alive by keeping him in our hearts. Can you bring me the box Anna?"

Quickly setting the large cup on the table Anna makes it to her feet hastily racing a few feet away to the desk. Reaching up she grabs the box with her fingertips, dragging it towards the edge of the table. Smiling she returns to Kul with his request. Returning her smile Kul opens the plain box, angling it so the young woman can see the contents. Inside the box lay a plain silver medallion with the words 'Knight-General' engraved in its center.

"This is the medallion I give to my successor. Every lord has their own unique symbol to mark their second in command. Your father returned this to me the day he left for Veldesdal, said that he was passing on the title to another."

"Did he tell you who?" She awaits the ending to his story with bated breath.

"He left for me to decide who was worth enough to take his place. Today I found-"

"You picked!"

"I picked." He says proudly.

Lifting from his seated position he kneels beside the fire, the box in his hands outstretched towards Annastasia. She looks from the box towards him and back to the silver medallion, her eyebrows arched in confusion.

"He told me it had to be someone who could be his equal Annastasia. I have made my choice. You will be my successor when the time is right. I would have it no other way. This pendant is yours to keep until you feel you are ready to claim your right as the Lady of Providence."

"I'm not old enough. I can't run a city or- or a planet." She stutters, not knowing how to respond.

"I'm not going anywhere anytime soon little flame. You have plenty of time to rest easy."

"I don't know if I can accept this. This is a huge responsibility. Are you sure you don't want Illy?" Her tone weary.

"Never been more sure of anything in my life Anna. You have a bright future ahead of you, and I will give you the building blocks to connect

236

everything. I see the way you care about the city and its people. You love to listen, laugh make others feel the same way. You know more people here than even myself. This city is your family and you'll be its heartbeat."

They embrace in a hug, tears streaming down Anna's face. She buries her head into his shoulder, wiping the tears off onto his jacket. He holds onto her firmly, lifting her up into the air effortlessly. Anna looks up into Kul's eyes as hey begin twirling around the room, dancing to invisible music. Her frown morphing into a smile as he begins to hum a gentle tune, one she wrote for her violin.

"Tell the city the Magician is on the job."

CHAPTER SIXTEEN
IN FLAMES

Xylen plants himself at a seat across from Tabitha within the Eldritch Flame, setting a pitcher of water down between the two of them. A tablet lay in the center of the table detailing the access points and weakness of the Tower of Providence. Areas marked in red leading to vents and structural weak points. Blue marking the entry and exits throughout the building. Xylen circles two areas in yellow, the entire top level and a mid-access level.

Spinning the tablet around Xylen gives Tabitha a better look at the layout.

"Are you sure this plan will work?" Tabitha questions.

"I'm sure of it. You set up the same preparations in the Frostscythe building correct?" Xylen gestures towards schematics of the Tower laid out on his tablet. "They drew off your design. I don't have a schematic of the dispensers, but I would hazard a guess that they didn't deviate too far from your plan. I think you were had a long time before now. No way they could come up with a plan this fast. This sort of design takes years of planning to achieve."

"I'm sure they never suspected me." She retorts confidently. "Those are the key areas you circled correct?"

"Yeah. Top level is reserved for the higher ups. Kul and Illiyana would likely be up there if not at the reception. The mid-access area is where the reception is taking place. It's likely the highest concentration of your amazing creation is stocked in these areas. First levels are probably going to be safest, no one on the ground floor is important enough for them to have wasted time on."

"I would have put a canister on each level."

"They aren't you."

"They are that efficient."

Xylen leans back in the chair, resting both hands behind his head. Squinting, Xylen attempts to read Tabitha's subtle cues as she continues to pour over the documents he has accrued. Looking for anything to work from he watches her study the maps. Tabitha pauses on a specific file marked 'AA'.

"Did you look over everything on the drive pertaining to me and the project?"

"Not everything. Did you find something?"

"Nothing important yet. Just some old files and case studies. You could be right, their goal is the dignitaries and council heads. Would be inefficient use of the my neurotoxin, especially if they can't recreate it yet."

"What makes you think they can't recreate it?"

"Despite what you may think, they never had me at a disadvantage. Never once did I write the correct formula to achieve replication. I always altered it slightly after every new test, until it was a complete deviation from the finished product. It will take them quite some time to fix the mistakes and replicate my 'cure'. Even then it's only spread by open air contact." Tabitha says smugly.

"Where would you begin?" Xylen asks, snagging the tablet back from the table.

Tabitha moves from her seat moving to overlook Xylen's. She lowers herself down, hovering over his shoulder. She points to a bottom tiered entry point and the entry from the hover docking above. Xylen peers back towards Tabitha, watching her eyes process the information. She lets out a smile. Brushing a hand over his other shoulder Tabitha runs her finger across an entry point just above the reception hall, one not marked on the map.

"Those two points are where they are going to infiltrate. Chances are they'll have someone on the inside to work the dispensers remotely. If it were me, once the canisters are ignited I would let the chaos consume them before advancing, whoever escapes would likely head either upstairs or try to flee to the ground floor. Easy to contain people in a staircase."

"You've thought this through."

"Once or twice." She lets her smirk grow wider. "There is something good to come out of this though. There is a service door one floor up from the reception hall, leads straight down into the basement from there. It's separated from the main flow of traffic and well hidden, you wouldn't even know it unless you've been through there. Luckily Anna and I have had a few moments to share in that stairwell."

"Thoroughly do not want to hear about this." Xylen shudders at the thought.

"What, Amber? Is my personal life a little too much for you?" She says beaming a bright smile behind Xylen.

"Changing the subject-"

An attempted entry into the front door interrupts the conversation, the doorknob rattling under heavy pressure from the other side. Tabitha and Xylen look to each other, their pride slightly deflated. The knob shakes violently one more time before a thunderous knock rings throughout the establishment and echoing back. Tabitha reaches down for the weapon at her waistband, hesitating to draw it.

Standing up from his seat Xylen inches towards the door cautiously, his hands mildly trembling. Reaching out he unlocks the door. As quick as he reaches out Xylen retracts his hand instinctively. The door whips open revealing Audrey and Finn with Claudette in his arms. Forging ahead Finn moves to the bar, placing Claudette along its flat surface. Audrey sullenly drifts into the Flame, her eyes wandering about the building. Tabitha takes her hand away from the pistol grip, tucking her shirt back over top the weapon. With raised eyebrows she watches Finn gently place Claudette's still body along his workspace, her mind already running with possibilities.

"You're okay." Xylen says, wrapping his arms around Audrey before she moves past him.

"I'm not okay." Her voice monotone and distant.

Holding Audrey close to him, Xylen pans his head to the left looking past Finn at the lifeless body of Claudette. His mouth hangs agape as he stares in disbelief. Audrey clutches onto his hands firmly with her own, reaffirming the nightmare.

The room falls into a momentary hush with no one wishing to speak out. Finn stands watch over top of Dette, as if to ward away evil spirits. Xylen breaks from Audrey, coming to stand beside his friend. Placing a hand on his shoulder Xylen shoots him an apologetic look, a look he knows means absolutely nothing at the moment.

"I-" He begins.

"Ya." Finn interjects, muttering quietly. "*Fuck words, dey mean nothin right now.*"

"My deepest condolences." Tabitha says breaking the silence like a rock through glass.

"*Fuck. You. Ya don't get to give out sympathies, ya cunt. Best if ya just fucked off.*" He says without turning to face her, attempting to keep his cool.

"We're a-" She attempts to respond.

"*I said fuck off. Only offerin' the chance once. Limited time deal. You'd do well to heed my fucking words.*"

"Or what you blowhard? You'll threaten me some more." Her words seeking to cut. "I'm tired of the song and dance Finn. We have more to worry about then something fate destined to happen. You should be thinking forward, to our next objective. We have a city to save."

Finn turns to face her, seething in his posture. A grin slowly forms across her face, only driving him further into the red. With clenched fists he makes for Tabitha, his focus solely on her. Audrey steps between the two opposing forces, placing a hand onto Finn's chest in a bid to stop his stride. Finn pauses his advance, wincing slightly in pain. His eyes burning holes through her as he looks onward to Tabitha, the grin creeping further across her face.

"*Keep runnin ya damn mouth. My Dette died a better woman den you'll ever be. You couldn't even hold a candle to her. For all ya boastin an braggin you're just an insecure twat with daddy issues.*"

Audrey swallows hard, keeping her hand pressed to Finn's chest. Tabitha grits her teeth, Finn's speech cutting a bit closer than she would like to admit. Raising his hands in retreat Finn backs away from Audrey, swagger returning to his step alongside his prideful smile.

"I see." Tabitha finally responds, calculating her next approach. "'You're' Claudette is dead and i'm still here. Leads me to believe i'm the better woman."

"*You fuckin-*" His voice echoing through the Flame.

"Would you fucking stop! What the fuck Tabitha?" Audrey bellows to Tabitha's surprise. "What would make you think this is the time for that bullshit?"

Audrey turns to face her best friend, a confused look drawn across her face. Tabitha's shocked expression fades quickly, leaving her stare emotionless once again. They trade glances, betrayal written across each of their faces.

"Audrey!" Her tone dominant, yet lost. "How dare-"

"How dare I? How could you? He just lost the one person who means the most to him in his life and you're going to sit here and play the cold and emotionless killer role. I know you, if this were Anna-."

"It's not." She cuts in, biting back her anger.

"You're right, because you would do anything to prevent that from happening."

"What are you insinuating?"

Tension escalates within the Eldritch Flame as quiet falls between the two. Tabitha advances on Audrey, coming directly face to face with her pupil. Finn and Xylen watch on from a distance, Finn biding his time until the situation worsens. Xylen attempts to intervene, heading in their direction. Finn grabs him by the shirt collar, pulling him back towards the bar. Shaking his head, Finn plants Xylen in a nearby seat.

"You never meant to cure Claudette. You used her sickness to drive your cause forward." Audrey stares defiantly into her teachers eyes.

"And? Just because you grew attached doesn't mean what I said earlier ever changed. You made a mistake. I warned you that personal attachment would always lead to this decision you're making right here. Emotions are trivial and pointless and those driven by them will always fail. You will be no exception."

"Then I guess i'll fail standing beside people who care. I would hate to tarnish your perfect image of success."

"You had so much promise Audrey. This experiment wasn't completely a failure though." Tabitha says, running a hand through Audrey's black hair. The younger woman shudders at her touch, though not in fear. "You taught me a valuable lesson. Several in fact. When faced with challenge people will

242

always self preserve. No matter the growth of character, self interest at the end of the day will ultimately be the deciding factor when it comes to 'family'. You've chosen your family."

"I shouldn't have to choose."

Audrey pulls herself away from Tabitha's reach, disgusted and discontent. Biting her lower lip she refrains from adding any more to the conversation. With a sneers Tabitha cements her feelings, her own way of further disapproving Audrey's childish view of the situation.

"I never made you make a choice. This conversation, the way you feel, it's about a corpse. You feel as though that husk has given you purpose, a cause to champion. We both know I gave you real purpose that you've since decided to throw away. Good luck with the band of thieves and thugs. I have real work to do."

Tabitha crosses her arms watching Audrey fumble over words in her head, attempting to form a rebuttal. Tabitha's sneer morphs wickedly back into her signature cocky grin. Turning her back to Audrey, Tabitha scoops up the small data pad on the table sliding it into an empty jacket pocket.

She saunters past a silent Audrey, towards the bar. Finn and Xylen trace her movements as she makes her way behind the bar grabbing for an open bottle of liquor, setting out three glasses to pour between. Her eyes stray towards Claudette's still body sprawled out across the countertop. Her features pale yet elegant even in death, brown hair framing her face perfectly. She scoffs at her beauty. Finishing the drinks Tabitha looks between Finn and Xylen, setting the bottle between the three poured shots.

"Winner pours the loser a drink. I poured one for Audrey, her friend and I." She says mockingly, gesturing towards Claudette. "You can have hers Finn."

Gripping the glass Finn swirls the alcohol around, watching its ebb and flow. Looking up from the glass he locks eyes with her. He drinks the contents in one large gulp, furling his brow to her as he downs the whiskey. Finishing his drink he twirls the cup in his open palm. Tabitha grabs her glass, pushing the last towards a hesitant Audrey. Xylen spins around in his chair, snatching the drink from the counter. Tabitha tilts her head, a confused smile lingering along her lips. Audrey watches Xylen, her hands wrapped anxiously around her waist with a feeling of unease.

"Going to take the drink for her? Might as well right? Hopefully I didn't pick a bitter spirit."

Tabitha and Xylen tilt back their drinks together, downing them rather quickly. As Tabitha goes to slam her cup down Finn whips his glass in her direction, narrowly missing her. Glass cascades from the wall behind her in a shattering crescendo. She sidesteps the hurled object, leaving an opening in her guard. Finn reaches out, grabbing Tabitha by the neck of her shirt with both hands pulling her up and over the countertop onto the hard floor below. Air forced out from her lungs, landing flat onto her back.

"*Never waste good whiskey.*" His tone grim and hallow.

Reorienting herself Tabitha blinks rapidly, attempting to regain her bearings. Feeling herself lifted from the ground with a firm hand around her throat she attempts to strike back at her attacker, a well placed elbow into his shoulder. Without flinching he drags Tabitha to her feet, setting her upright. Staring into her hazy eyes, Finn clenches his left hand into a fist and tightens his grip around her throat. She smiles at him, her eyes finally readjusting from the disorientation.

"Do it." She taunts.

"*Believe me I fuckin want to.*" His tone direct. "*Usually you just kick the belligerents outta da bar though. Dey do more harm to demselves than anyone else.*"

Finn loosens the grip around her neck, sliding his hand around the collar of her leather jacket, straightening it out. Tabitha bats his hand away, clearly irritated with his show of force. In a rush she attempts to storm away, leaving embarrassed but on her own terms. Finn grabs her by the back of her neck as she passes, dragging her towards the door.

"*I don't fuckin think so.*"

Pulling Tabitha by the scruff of her neck Finn pushes her through the row of tables before finally reaching the door, applying pressure onto the neck each time she resists. Xylen and Audrey watch on from their view at the counter as Finn manhandles Tabitha. Continuing to struggle against his grip Tabitha throws a stray elbow to his ribcage, sending waves of agony throughout his nervous system. Gritting his teeth he presses forward, slamming Tabitha violently into the wall beside the door. She lets out a short gasp of relief as Finn releases his grasp, her face snarling in rage as they lock eyes again. Taking a step back, Finn runs his hand across his mouth.

"Dis. Dis is for Claudette."

"Do it!" She eggs him on, her eyes filled with a piercing rage, body building a growing fury.

Finn reciprocates her emotion, hatred burning in his eyes as they share their united hatred for what seems an eternity. Finally committing himself to the act Finn reels back, lining up his strike. Tabitha closes her eyes in the brief moment before the strike lands, readying herself for his worst. A crash beside her head, startles her eyes open. Finn's arm rests beside her, buried into the steel wall behind her.

"Go." Finn says face to face, his breath heavy upon her skin.

With a grimace Tabitha reaches out for the door, holding back her pride for another day of her choosing. The cool breeze of the morning air blows across both their faces as the door cracks open, the sun casting its light into the Flame. Finn backs away from Tabitha, taking his hand from the wall. With a quick gesture he motions for her to exit. Tabitha draws her eyes to Audrey, looking to her with veiled contempt. Without another word Tabitha slinks through the open door, slamming it shut on her exit.

"Good fuckin riddance." His tone still covered in anger.

Finn twists the lock shut on the door behind Tabitha's exit. Looking to Audrey and Xylen he motions the red head to pour him another drink. His eyes narrow and jaw clenches as he walks back to the bar, his gaze fixated on Claudette. Xylen turns the corner to the bar, walking across broken glass.

Reaching under the cupboard he grabs Finn's homemade whiskey, 'Leighton's Brew' scrawled across the label in marker. Setting the bottle down he grabs two new glasses from the refrigerator, placing them besides the bottle. He runs a nervous hand through his vibrant hair, a way to ease his tension.

Audrey approaches Finn before he returns to the bar, wrapping her hands around him tightly. He returns the embrace, wrapping one arm around her in a 'Finn' hug. He winces in pain as she applies pressure to his upper torso, causing him to shut his eyes momentarily.

"Thank you." She whispers. "For everything."

"No problem darlin'. Just doin my best to better da community. Sometimes you have ta do some prunin' to find the beauty hidden underneath. I should be thankin' ya. You didn't have to stand up ta her."

"I did. You were right, and I was too afraid to admit it. I got caught up in being important to someone. I blinded myself to the horrible things we did, because we were making a cure for the world. Something to bring about a revolution." Her voice shakes as she continues. "Until I met him. I know how you feel about Claudette, that's what Xylen is to me. He woke me up, him and his dumb pancakes."

"Blueberry or strawberry?"

"Strawberry."

"Get's um every time."

Audrey bursts into laughter as she breaks the hug, a smile returning to her face. Finn smiles past her to Xylen, winking at him. Audrey steals a seat in front of Xylen, grabbing a hold of his hand. She looks into his eyes, her smile causing him to smirk in return.

"I'll be back shortly you two."

Finn swipes one of the two ready made shots off the counter, downing it hastily before turning the cup over on the table. He returns to Claudette's side, lifting her back into his arms. Weaving through the tables Finn heads towards the backstage area, to the curtain. Carefully he lifts himself onto the stage, cradling her in his arms.

246

"You can bring her into my room." Anna's voice rings from behind the curtain, solemn and low.

"*Annie-*"

"I know."

Anna pulls back the curtain, her eyes holding back tears. Finn enters into the dark and silent backstage. The two share a moment of silence and understanding in the dark, before heading into her room. The break in darkness nearly enough to blind them as she opens the door to her office.

Roaming through a closet door Anna pulls out a set of blankets, laying them along the floor. Finn lay Claudette down onto the area, hesitantly releasing her from his arms. Gulping hard Finn looks down to his feet, his mind racing with questions and curses. Running his hand across his mouth he attempts to speak, stopping himself short. Anna watches as he begins to pace in circles around the small area.

"*She's gone Annie.*" He says, continuing to pace. "*She's gone I dunno what ta do.*"

"I do. We fight back Finn. Then we sort out the rest when the dust falls."

Anna grabs ahold of Finn by the shoulder, spinning him around. She rests a hand along his cheek, attempting to calm the caged beast. Sending a weak smile his way Anna leans into him, wrapping her other arm around his waist. Resting her head on his chest she listens to his rapidly beating heart.

"She's never gone Finn. She lives on in all of us. What Claudette means to us will never be forgotten."

"*Does it ever get easier Annie?*"

"Never. You learn to move past it, to accept the world with a void in your heart. You never get over what she'll mean to you. To us. You're not supposed to."

"*We're s'pposed to be-*" He pauses. "*To be together. They took her from me and there wasn't a damn thing I could fuckin do about it. I had to sit and watch her die in me arms. I never-*"

"You'll never have to go through that alone again."

"Audrey was there, but it wasn't da same. I never knew how much I needed you Annie."

"I could say the same for you, Finn."

"You mean dat?"

"Always.

Finn wraps his arm around her, careful to mind his injuries. Together they stand enjoying the accompanying silence, neither willing to break their embrace. Anna looks up to Finn's half smiling face, watching a tear fall from his cheek onto her shoulder. Finn knocks away the second drop with his free hand.

"I'm sorry."

"You got nothin to be sorry for, you's just doin ya job."

"I brought you into this."

"We brought each other into dis. Now we just have ta crawl our way back out."

"Aye."

"Aye."

Loosening her grip Anna pulls away from Finn, nervously shoving her hands into her jean pockets. She looks away from Finn to Claudette, biting her lip to ensure she isn't dreaming. From outside the door they hear laughter coming from the young couple, Xylen's attempt to ease their tensions. Finn does a once over around the office, staring at the blank plaque.

"We could really use her help right about now. She still owe you a favor?" He says motioning to the shelf.

"We cleared up what she owed me a long time ago. I would ask what happened with Tabitha, but I can already assume the worst. I didn't-"

"She's the worst kind a trouble. Kicked her to da curb."

"She clouded my judgement, whether or not it was intended. I have to own up to the mistake I made. You did the right thing sending her away."

"I understand. Girl means a lot to you. She's just fucked in the head. Nothin you can

do ta fix dat, cept maybe a bullet."

"You're putting it lightly. Sugar coating, I believe is the term."

"Well if ya gunna put it like dat. Bitch should get what she gives out, nothin but hell. Never had kind words for her and even less after today. She put you in danger, Annie. Dat is unforgivable."

"She created death, Finn. Crawling and screaming, I watched hundreds of lives get snuffed out last night. I had to listen to their plea's. It's haunting."

"War leaves the kind of scars you'll never want to remember. Memories dat scratch at da back a ya mind. They dig deep in ta ya flesh and never let go. Sorry you had to see it first hand, love. Just remember when you think fondly of Tabitha dat she created dis horrible memory and everything associated wit it."

Anna moves back to her mantle, running a hand across its length in remembrance. She lingers along the rifle, staring at it with great care. Finn tilts his head, a puzzled look creeps onto his face as he watches Anna run a finger along side the weapons barrel. With a smile she removes the weapon from it's stand, holding it at her side.

"Tabitha knew eventually I would see her for what she is and what she's done. That what we both envision is just a lie we told ourselves to make it through till tomorrow. She hid it from me because she was afraid I would reject her."

"Ya always gunna love her. We all make mistakes. In the end she'll always be the cause, but Annie you're the effect. Whatever she's done to you has made you stronger for it. For dat reason alone, I will always be by your side."

"I don't feel stronger."

"It's not a thing you can feel. It's just a truth you have to live with. You are the strongest person I know. Nothing can ever keep you down. Hell I don't even think death could do it. Dis isn't a inspirational speech, i'm shit at those. This is one scrapper to another. You're one tough son of a bitch Annie."

"I've had some amazing help along the way."

"Dat right there. Dat modest bullshit is what makes you, you. Never lose it."

"'Not being inspirational.' Says the most inspiring things i've heard in the last two days."

"*Shove it you.*"

Finn bulls his way over to Anna grabbing her playfully by the head, putting her into a headlock. He begins to ruffle her hair as she squirms around in his grip, unable to free herself. She lets out a frustrated laugh as she continues her attempt at freedom. Letting go Finn backs away quickly, as to get a better look at the frustrated expression on her face. Anna jolts upright, shooting a sideways glance at Finn through her disheveled hair. Anna blows the hair out of her face, a frazzled smile hidden under her long mane.

"Just had to go and be a dick?" Anna asks, pulling her hair back into perfection.

"*Can't go ruinin my reputation, even if it's just da two a us.*"

"Would hate for your ego to bruise."

"*Would be a shame. I heard we had a city to go and save.*"

"Aye." She smirks in his direction.

"*As me da once said, 'What da fuck are you waitin for? An invitation?'. Granted he was askin me ta mow da damn lawn.*"

"I see the similarity." Said sarcastically.

"*Let's get the fuckin lead out. You takin dat cannon wit ya?*"

"It's a present."

"*Hopefully it doesn't have ta be wrapped.*"

Before exiting the office Finn returns to Claudette, covering her with the blanket. He closes his eyes, repeating the prayer from earlier. Anna leans against the door, awaiting Finn's return. They exit together, leaving back into the backstage area. Xylen and Audrey's echoing voices can be heard just through the curtains, a conversation about Providence and the Tower. Anna runs her hand along the side wall for one last reminder of the past, feeling the writing on the walls before returning to the main bar.

"*Exactly da way I left you two.*" Finn boastfully says, approaching the bar.

"I suggested we hide, she shut me down."

"Wouldn't have wanted you to have to look so hard." Audrey says with a wicked smile.

"*I just can't catch a fuckin break. Damn.*"

"Just means they love you." Anna cuts in.

Audrey's eyebrows raise as Anna talks, she spins around in her chair to face her. Anna presents the rifle to her, holding it gingerly before her. Audrey's eyes roam over the gun slowly, her mouth agape.

"Can I?"

"Yes, you can touch it." Anna laughs. "It's yours."

"This is an Incisor. One of a kind. Three round burst rifle with a hell of a kick. Could punch a hole through any material. This is the weapon of an Archangel. Where did you-"

"It's a gift from one angel to another. Welcome to the team Audrey. You deserve it."

"How did you know?"

"I'm the magician, it's my job to know."

"She was right about you. You are amazing."

Xylen leans over the countertop, a smile beaming from ear to ear. His gaze drawn to their conversation. Audrey accepts the gift, laying it across the counter. She runs over the weapons specifications from memory, checking all of the modifications made to the rifle. Xylen watches her like a clerk watching a kid in a candy store. Anna moves over to Finn, ramming into him with her hip playfully.

"*At least she told da truth about somethin'.*"

"You're giving me this? Anna. Thank you." She says confidently, her eyes darting between Anna and the weapon.

"As long as you don't mind being my archangel."

"I won't let you down."

"What'd I win?" Xylen interrupts. "I've always wanted a pony."

"Congratulations Amber. You've won a once in a lifetime chance to tell me what our plan is." Anna leans against the countertop, smirking happily towards Xylen.

"Here we go with the name calling again. It's my hair isn't it?"

"*Amber eh? Ya, I can see it.*"

"Now i'll never hear the end of it." Xylen says, flailing his arms into the air. "Great. Might as well just start calling me Ruby. Or how about red."

"*I'll just call ya late.*"

"Did Finn just make a joke I didn't understand?" Xylen cocks an eyebrow quizzically.

"Naturally." Audrey chimes in.

Xylen begins typing away at a laptop behind the bar, his tongue smacking against the the edge of his lips as he works. Setting the laptop on the counter he spins it in their direction, giving his teammates a good view of the schematics and layout of the Tower. His notes present on the side of the screen.

"We worked out a lot of things, me and Tabitha. She's actually good help when she isn't threatening you or berating you." He looks up from the laptop, making a nervous face. "Then she went and took my tablet. Me being the smart technician I am backed up our- my work. So without further ado here's the plan." He says in his most serious of voices.

CHAPTER SEVENTEEN

CULMINATION

The Heart of Providence shimmers in the morning sun, the bright blue sky offsetting its golden orange hue. Everyday bustle around the tower has crawled to a minimum. Soldiers patrol the grounds below while hovers are redirected around the sprawling base of the building. A small, steady flow of traffic flows into the upper port, their hovers bearing the marks of a slew of foreign dignitaries.

Anna watches her hovers reflection off the windows as she cruises by, attempting to make a landing to the port along the base of the tower. Finn impatiently waits in the passenger seat, his fingers running along the arm rest to relax his mind. Obnoxious clicking echoes through the cab as Xylen taps away at his phone, messaging the absent Audrey.

"You sure you like dis plan a yours Annie?"

"Until we get in the building we won't really have a plan. Xylen had a good base to start from, but our 'friend' Mind will undoubtedly have backups in place. Until we press him to show his hand this is the best we can do. Just make sure you protect the innocents, and dignitaries." She says with confidence.

"Aye cause all a them ain't innocent."

"And Audrey?" Xylen hesitantly asks.

"She knows her part. Smoke and Mirrors Xylen, she'll be fine. I promise." Anna says looking back with a bright smile. "Everyone have your earpieces in?"

"Aye."

"Yep." Xylen replies, continuing to tap away at his phone.

"Copy that." Audrey's voice booms coming through the recievers.

"Good. Audrey find that spot I mentioned to you. Let me know when you can see us." Anna replies, bringing the hover close to the ground.

Anna gently drops the hover along the specified landing zone, setting it down softly just outside the front entrance. Two soldiers in formal dress approach the hover from the drivers side, a quizzical about their faces. Cutting the engine Anna emerges from the cab, approaching the guardsmen.

"Hello gentlemen." She beams a smile in their direction.

"Hello miss. What brings you into the Heart of Providence?" The senior of the two guards questions.

"I'm here for the assembly of thought and gala. Quite the turn out this time I hear."

Finn pulls himself out from the hover, yawning and stretching wildly. The two guards give Anna and Finn a quick once over glance, looking at their casual appearance before returning their wandering eyes to meet hers.

"We'll need a name to cross check with our security ma'am."

"Annastasia Arlenko."

"Ma'am?" The senior guard hesitates. "As in-"

"Yes, Illiyana is my sister. No she won't have you punished for holding me up at the front door, after all it is your job and I wouldn't have it any other way."

"We'll have to cross check your name to make sure, can you hold on a few seconds?"

"Of course."

The older guardsman takes a few steps away from the conversation to have privacy while speaking into his earpiece. Finn leans across the hood of the hover, his impatience growing further. Xylen finally makes his way from the backseat to the younger guards surprise. The younger man grabs for his sidearm before hesitantly pulling his hand away, the tension of the gala today getting to his nerves.

"Sorry." Xylen says, his focus buried into his phone still.

"Put dat ting down. She's gunna be fine. Dun need you to hold her hand and send her messages every five seconds."

"It's getting to be a little much." Audrey chimes in over their headsets. "I'm fine. Cold, but fine."

"Alright, alright." Xylen retorts, shoving his phone back into his pocket.

"You'd think da boy has a girlfriend da way he's typin." Finn directs the comment towards the young guard.

"Not any of my business, sir." The guard lets out with a chuckle.

The higher ranking officer strides back to the group, a slight grin rolling across his face.

"Everything checks out, Miss Arlenko. Roland wants me to tell you 'Welcome home'." He says returning to his partners side. "As for your companions?"

"Where are my manners. This is Xylen Crestmont and Finn Leighton. They go where I do."

"Of course. Will you be needing an escort to the assembly?"

"That won't be necessary. Thank you for your service."

"You're welcome." They respond in unison, arching their backs to proper posture.

The guards begin returning to their post, marching in time with each other. Anna turns back to Finn and Xylen, sticking her tounge out playfully at them while crossing her eyes. She begins walking to the entrance with her companions in tow. Passing by the main courtyard, Anna stops for a moment to watch the training exercise between a group of young cadets. Their sparring reminding her of her formative years.

"By the way, I can see you perfectly Anna." Audrey says.

"Fantastic." Anna says, taking in a deep breath. "My father always told me no matter the cost you see what you've put your mind to through. You never give up on the things that matter. There's no turning back after we enter the building. "

"In for a penny, in for a pound, love."

"I'm all in." Xylen responds.

"We don't stop until it's over." A resounding confidence in her tone.

"Aye."

Anna presses forward through the courtyard, entering the main foyer of the tower, with Finn and Xylen following along closely. The reception hall is stunningly simple, artist renditions of famous events line the walls of the circular base. Each painting fading into the next in a mural like exhibit. In the center of the room is a massive row of public elevators wrapped around a circle pillar leading to the upper floors. Groups of people converge towards the sets of elevators, assumingly heading to the assembly themselves. Anna walks past the receptionist desk, noticing the young man from yesterday behind the counter working away at his tablet studiously. She gives him a nod and wink as she passes by. Approaching the elevators the trio stops just before entering the amassing groups of people. Finn and Anna scout the surrounding area, looking for familiar or out of place faces. During their search Xylen pulls free his tablet from a small bag. Tapping away, he begins to prep his hardware to sync with the security systems inside the Heart of Providence.

"I dun see a damn thing. Not that I know exactly who or what i'm lookin fa."

"We're not supposed to. Chances are they're not on the ground floor, this gives Xylen some time to set up before we head upstairs."

"We're synced in. Ready to go." Xylen says, heading toward an open elevator.

Anna and Finn follow, weaving through the traffic to make it into the opening elevator. Another group pours in with them making it a tight fit. Anna stands at the front of the door as it closes. Watching back out through the crowd she catches a glimpse of a dark figure off in the distance, staring directly towards her. The door closes with a sudden slam startling her, breaking her concentration. She stares at the dull metal door for the duration of the trip upwards to the twenty third floor. Dull voices echo through her ears, as the group of people continue their conversation. Finn works his way through them to stand behind her, keeping his family close.

A bell dings as the doors open to the fifteenth floor. The group behind Anna and Finn exit swiftly around them, leaving just the three of them alone.

"I'm in the system Anna. Can't get to any main protocols I don't have the equipment on hand at the moment, but I do have alerts on doors, elevators and security cameras. Any alert or threat will go through these channels. I'll keep a close eye on them to monitor the situation." Xylen remarks as the elevator begins to ascend again.

"Remind me to get you some clearance next time were here." She jokingly replies.

"Will do boss. I would love to find all the dirty little secrets around Providence."

"*Ey. You won't need ta dig hard to find Annie's dirty little secrets.*"

"If i'm easy Finn, you're an open book."

"*Nothin ta hide. I gots no secrets cept one.*"

"You have to sleep with a teddy bear. Not much of a secret." Anna retorts.

"*Oh who's got da jokes now? I'll have you know me ma gave me dat bear, still soft and cuddly.*"

"He has a giant tear in his throat. All of his stuffing is falling out."

"*He's wounded. Dat's all.*"

"Wounded." She says, laughing.

The bell dings again as the doors open to the twenty third level. Anna diverts her attention from Finn as he prattles on about his stuffed animal. She gazes out into a sea of diplomats and dignitaries, each individual distinguished by their cultures dress and markings. Anna moves out from the elevator slowly, scanning her surroundings. Taking in the room she looks to the stage set in the back, watching as they finalize the preparations for assembly. Unlike the majority of the tower the walls here are a dark red, keeping in tone with the darker lighting throughout the room. *I forgot how massive this floor is. It'll be harder than I thought to pick anyone out of this crowd. I have to make it to Illiyana and Kul quickly before they begin. Guess it's time to venture to the second level.*

The echoes of conversation drown out her thoughts as she wades through people like water, losing her entourage at the door. Attempting to make her way to the front stage Anna passes familiar faces, both younger and older alike. A hand reaches out for her shoulder, grabbing her gently. Anna turns quickly, removing the hand from her shoulder swiftly. She turns quickly, bringing herself to a defensive stance. Finn pulls his hands back in a retreating motion before letting out a slight chuckle. Calming her nerves Anna places her hands back to her side, continuing on towards the stage area. Finn rolls his eyes as he continues to weave through the mass of people to follow her. Along the winding path through the crowd Finn grabs a glass of wine and an hors d'oeuvre from a passing waiter.

Anna stops just along the skirt of the stage, allowing Finn to catch up with her as he finishes off the appetizer. She peers back at him, making sure he kept up the pace. Noticing him finish off his food brings a smile to her face as she shakes her head in disbelief.

"*A man's gotta eat.*" He brings the cup up in a toast. "*I can go get you some if you want.*"

"We're going upstairs." Anna says into her earpiece, ignoring his attempt to derail her focus.

"*Hopefully there's more food and drink ya. I'm starvin.*"

Anna leads Finn along the edge of the stage towards the staircase. Grabbing ahold of his hand she drags him up the flight of stairs, passing swiftly by the slower dignitaries making their way up. Finn does his best to balance the drink in his hand as she pulls him along, only losing a few drops along the way. At the top of the staircase Anna lets free his hand as she surveys the area along the balcony, looking for the biggest gathering of people.

"Annastasia." A stern yet familiar feminine voice calls out behind her. "How was your meeting with Alphonse?"

"Illiyana." Anna lets out excitedly. "We have a major problem."

Anna turns to face her sister, as Finn makes his way up the last few steps drink in hand. To her surprise Illiyana has traded in her formal attire for a modest white dress, her hair pinned up in its usual military fashion. Taking a second to look over her sisters dress decision Anna stands stunned.

"Jeans to a formal occasion such as this. Little sister you know better." Her eyes lingering at Anna's choice of dress.

"Mark it down as a faux pas." She snaps.

"*I told her she needed to listen to the king of fashion.*" He pauses momentarily. "*Das me.*" Pointing to himself.

"Hello Finn. Please keep the crude remarks to a minimum here."

"*Aye. I can fuc- I can do dat.*" Said with sly grin.

"Illy! I need to find Kul." Anna spits out. "The tower-"

"Father will be back momentarily. He's off on business not far from here."

"Are his guards with him?" She hurriedly asks.

"Of course. I would never let him out of my sight if that were the case. Why do you ask? What has you so rushed Annastasia?"

"We need to be somewhere private. This matter is not for the general public to gossip about."

"Fine. Walk with me then." Illiyana says arching her eyebrow, motioning for her sister to follow.

Illiyana leads Anna and Finn away from the party, people making way for her as she passes through the socializing crowd. Bringing up the rear Finn waves happily at all the guests, his smile turned into a devilish grin. People pay no attention to his blatant gesture as all eyes are trained on the two Arlenko sisters. Whispers spread through the upper level, gossip overtaking the smaller crowds. Anna flashes her brilliant white smile, arching her back as she continue to follow her sister through a guarded corridor. Illiyana waves her hand at the guard dismissing him momentarily from his post. Illiyana politely opens the door for her baby sister.

"Guard the door would you Finn?" Anna asks, turning towards him before entering.

"*As long as dey got more a dem drinks and snacks, i'll sure as shi- i'll guard dis door for ya.*"

"Thank you."

Anna steps into room, the brightness of the lights almost blinding. A small couch and a few chairs are set in the center of the room, a table sits between the opposing furniture. The walls do away with the red pattern, leaving only the exposed metal. Illiyana leans up against the wall just beside the door, eyes trailing a pattern in thought. Folding her arms Anna moves inside the room, giving herself enough space away from her sister.

"You wanted privacy, Annastasia. Speak your mind."

"The Heart of Providence is going to be targeted during the assembly today. Frostscythe is behind it. I have a plan for evacuation but-"

"You go to a meeting at their headquarters-"

"Don't interrupt me. They murdered their own people by the hundreds this morning in an attempt to kill us. They have a neurotoxic that spreads at an epidemic level. It can kill in minutes Illy, i've witnessed it with my own eyes." Tears begin to form along the crest of her eye. "I shouldn't have jumped the gun. You're right, but if I hadn't I don't know what would happen to you today. They killed Claudette with the chemical. They infected her right in front of me."

"I believe you." Illiyana replies, closing the distance in between them. Her hard features softening as she wraps her arms around her younger sister. "This is why I wanted you to lay low sis."

"You knew? You knew and didn't tell me."

"I did tell you, but you're the crusader who won't have it any other way Knight-General. I told you to back off but you went over my head. Father and I have been skirting their transactions and limiting their connection to the tower for months. You went and stabbed at the heart of the matter. Tell me what you found."

"A monster named Mind." Anna's voice sunken, her pride fading away. "He's unorthodox. A chess player who manipulates with magic."

"Impossible, there are so few bloodlines left with magic in these sectors."

"He's been in my head Illy. I know the touch of an illusion."

"That narrows down who it could be then. I'll have the department run a search through the known magic bloodlines. Have you been infected?"

"No."

"Some good news at least. I'm sorry about Claudette. She was a good friend to you."

"To us." Anna says, finally returning the hug. "I missed this. I wish it were on better terms. I have a plan to stop them here at the assembly. You're not going to like it."

"When do I like your plans?" Illiyana chuckles at the thought.

"Afterwards."

"Truer words have never been spoken between the two of us. Let's hear your plan." Illiyana breaks the hug. She returns to form, standing rigidly with her hands behind her back.

"They are going to dispense this chemical into the airstream through an automated machine. Xylen's working on finding the wireless connection as we speak. Finn and him are going to direct traffic upstairs to the hidden maintenance hatch on the other side of the room."

"Where you and Tabitha used to sneak to?" Said with disdain.

"That one. It's a separate part of the tower, cut off from the toxins. You can get people safely to the basement from there. I assume you'll be leading the evacuation?"

"Leading by example. As the Sector Commander should."

"Meanwhile. He's the part you won't like. Dad will have to go up on the elevator to his office, its basic protocol."

Illiyana's eyes flicker with a look of distrust, her eyebrows arched in a questioning manner. Anna raises her hands in rebuttal, stopping her sister from speaking. Illiyana chokes down her words, allowing Anna to continue.

"It's crazy. Everyone escapes but i'm sending him into danger. I get it. Only i'm not." Anna's hand motion over exaggerating her speech.

"I'm waiting for something dazzling to stop me from screaming at you."

"Basic protocol during an attack would see the Lord return to his office, accompanied by guards. If they have been infiltrating for months if not years

262

they would know this protocol front and back. What they probably don't know is which elevators will take you to the top of the Heart. If Mind is the player I think he is, he'll be waiting at the top himself. No way to sneak enough of that agent onto the top floors. He'll be there to kill father."

"And?" Illiyana's voice rises, her patience fading.

"And I'll be on the elevator."

"That's it? That's your plan?"

"Yeah." Anna sends a questioning glance and chuckle to her sister.

Finn barges into the room, startling both sisters. In unison they turn and glare at him, a stare that could send a chill down anyone's spine.

"Ya gunna wanna see this Annie." Flashing a smug grin in their direction.

Waving the sisters along he motions for them to exit the conference room. Finn snags ahold of Anna's hand as she approaches the door slowly, dragging her back out into the open second level. Illiyana follows behind, her duty to the Heart pushing her to accompany them. Dignitaries and patrons of the assembly flock to the railings, attempting to get a decent view of the speaker.

The speakers ring out along the hall with a obnoxiously loud tapping noise. The room falls to a faint murmur as the speaker grabs their attention.

"Are you seeing what i'm seeing?" Xylen redundantly asks.

"Aye. I fuckin am." Finn says laughingly.

Approaching the banister Anna's eyes widen, fixated on the speaker, a leather clad Tabitha standing at the podium. Small studded spikes adorn the shoulders and sleeves of her jacket. Tabitha leans against the podium, her eyes focused on the crowd gathering around her. Solemn lips replace the once arrogant grin as she stares through the murmuring groups. Anna turns to run down the stairs, her instincts and gut telling her Tabitha means nothing but trouble for the assembly. Illiyana snags her little sister by the arm roughly, dragging her back to the balcony.

"Tell me she is part of your plan." Illiyana quietly says, her voice trailing into the crowd.

"She's not. Bitch got in here all on her own."

263

"Fantastic. Guards will be showing up shortly." Illiyana confidently remarks.

"They're dead." Anna chimes in, tension building deep in her core. "We both know she wouldn't leave anyone to stand in her way. You have to let me stop her."

Anna attempts to pull away from her sister, pulling back quickly. The crowd around the two begin to watch the growing confrontation, peeling their eyes off of Tabitha's spectacle.

"You're staying right here." Illiyana says, firmly gripping Anna's arm. "I'm not about to let my baby sister run into the mouth of a lion. You have a plan Annastasia, stick to it."

"Then you need to find father. I'll stay put if you find him." Anna says, breaking her arm away from Illiyana's. Their eyes meeting in defiance.

"You had better not break your promise. I will relay the message to him, we will meet you at the elevators. Be safe."

"Always."

Illiyana breaks away from the group. With her head down she weaves through the crowds along the balcony making her way back to the staircase. Silently in her mind she is cursing the thought of wearing a dress even to a party such as this. Anna intently watches Tabitha, her mind racing with thoughts. *What are you getting at by being here? Why Tabitha?*

Tabitha moves from her comfortable leaning position, snatching the microphone from its cradle. She begins pacing about the stage, taking two steps along each side before returning to the podium. The crowd grows silent, anticipation growing throughout the assembly.

"Hello ladies and gentlemen." Her voice cutting through the silence like a scream in the night. "My name is Tabitha Cosgrove. You should remember my name, by the end of today it will be infamous."

The audience keeps to a hush. From the balcony Anna watches as Tabitha strides back to the podium, a hand fidgeting with a bag hidden underneath. Looking back to the crowd Tabitha smiles dishonestly, mocking a familiar sincere smile. From the bag Tabitha pulls out a glass canister, the contents a neon green. With force she slams it down onto the stand for all to see.

"Today marks a special day for me, for all of us. You get to share with me a moment that will go down in history. Toast to yourselves you pioneers of industry, leaders of men. Today, you all will learn the meaning of fear."

Tabitha takes the canister from the podium, raising it above her head like a trophy. The audience stares on in confusion like deer in headlights, frozen in place as tabitha continues on.

Hushed conversations spread throughout the second floor as Anna watches her lover spin a web for the guests. Watching her speak sends chills down Anna's spine followed by a feeling of despair.

"I know what fear is now. Fear is looking into your loved ones eyes for the last time, knowing you're never going to see them again. You all have that look, or you soon will. I will be the last face ingrained into your memory as you wither and die. Remember me because I am the cure to your disease, the solution to your problem."

Tabitha hurls the canister toward the huddled crowd of people on the bottom level. Like scared cattle they spread away from the glass container, letting it shatter across the floor. Anna's mouth hangs agape in horror as she watches the gas escape from its prison, filling the surrounding air.

"NO!" Anna screams from her safe place atop the second floor.

Tabitha's head jerks toward the sound of Anna's voice, searching the area for a sign of her lover. Anna stands frozen along the balcony making her an easy target to spot. People begin to panic, running towards exits and higher ground in an attempt to evade the invading mist. Those closest to the epicenter begin to violently cough almost upon contact with the mist as it weaves its way into their systems.

Tabitha stands back, her view shifting from Anna to the ensuing chaos as she reveling in the panic and hysteria her creation is causing. Her solemn look replaced with a prideful smirk. Carnage ensues along the floor as the screaming kicks in. People shrieking in fear of the prevailing toxin as it inches closer to them. Racing to the elevators dignified people begin to claw and argue in an attempt to escape the gas.

"Xylen's down there." Anna looks to Finn, her face filled with sorrow and remorse. Anna leaves her place at the balcony, heading towards the staircase.

"Annie no. I'm not losin you too." His head hung, hesitant, as he reaches for Anna's shoulder.

"Finn. I'm not letting them all die down there. Not again." Her confident tone masking her anger.

"What's da plan boss?"

"Same as it was before. Get those people to safety, second floor safe passage. Spread the word."

"Got it."

Finn takes off around the second floor, his boisterous voice bellowing for all it's worth.

"Come on ya fuckin lot, exits dis way if ya wanna clear house before ya fucked." He screams as he runs across the balcony towards the hidden exit gate.

Anna makes her way through the stampeding crowd attempting to reach the second level. Anna stands just out of range of the growing toxin. Tabitha watches as Anna linger along the edge of the cloud.

"You're making the wrong choice. Don't you see what i'm doing? Just like at Frostscythe you were going to make the wrong choice." Her voice booms through the speakers.

Anna locks eyes with Tabitha as she skirts the invasive cloud, her gaze like daggers staring through her. Tabitha shakes her head as to ward Anna off. *I can't believe you. I can't believe you would do something like this. Shake it off Magician you have people to save.*

"Xylen?" Anna asks into her earpiece. "Where are you?"

"Never mind me Anna. I'm opening the air vents, I have enough time to clear the place out. You need to get out of there."

"I'm not leaving without you." She sternly replies.

"It got me. At least i'm pretty sure it did." His voice shaky, scared. "I'm doing my job, so that you can do yours."

Anna bites her lower lip in frustration. She closes her eyes for a moment, exhaling sharply before walking into the thick cloud. Tabitha's voice rings dully through her ears, like background noise easily blocked out. Her lungs fill quickly with the saturated gas, causing her to cough profusely. Opening her eyes, Anna keeps her mind calm as she passes through the mist heading toward the stage. Echoes of Frostscythe run through her mind as she listens to the passing screams of dignitaries and nobility. Keeping a deliberate pace she approaches the stage her eyes filled with an an unseen rage as she brushes away the memories for the time being. She lifts herself onto the stage quickly to come face to face with Tabitha, their eyes meeting briefly. Tabitha smiles at Anna, the microphone still tightly gripped in her hand. With her free hand she wipes the stray hair from her face, placing it behind her ear. Anna knocks Tabitha's hand away, her emotions reaching a boiling point.

"Don't touch me." Her voice filled with a building fury.

"You still don't see it do you? Did I fall in love with a magician or a fool?" She retorts, prodding her significant other.

"There are so many things I want to say to you except I don't care to ask them anymore."

"Then-"

As Tabitha begins her statement Anna connects with a right hook across the face, taking Tabitha off guard. Continuing her assault, Anna takes her to the ground with a leg sweep. Keeping up the pressure she drives a knee into the solar plexus, sending waves of pain throughout her body and pushing the air from Tabitha's lungs. Tabitha lay stunned on the ground, her hands holding onto Anna's knee.

"You killed all of these people!" Anna points to the panicked masses, screaming into Tabitha's face. "You did it. You made the wrong choice!"

"Did I though?" She responds between gasps of breath, her smirk still present. "I told them exactly what I was doing. Were you listening or staring?"

"Fear." The word rolls off of Anna's tongue as she whispers it.

Tabitha begins to chuckle as Anna draws all of the pieces together in her mind. Tilting her head back Tabitha lets out a relaxed sigh, letting loose her grip on the microphone. Digging her knee deeper into Tabitha's sternum she pulls herself back to a standing position. From the stage she can see the chaos Tabitha's experiment continues to cause. Anna grabs the microphone as it begins to roll away from her.

"Self preservation." Tabitha remarks from her prone position. "I don't have to kill people, they'll do it themselves."

"Enough!" Anna shouts loud enough it echoes over the speaker system, garnering the attention of the growing crowds.

"I'm not some simple witted moron Annastasia. Watch these people squirm and you'll be able to see who they truly are. Each individual person here has an agenda to be met and a past they're afraid of. No soul is pure anymore, no history clean."

"Spare me the lecture." Her features contorted, clinging to her anger. "Everyone listen up. My name is Annastasia Arlenko. Your best method of escape is on the second floor. There will be guards and staff advising you where to retreat to. I implore you to make for the exit upstairs."

Anna drops the microphone with a loud thud beside Tabitha, it's reverberation echoing through the assembly. She glances back at Tabitha, a look of disdain in her eyes, before returning her attention outward. Tabitha returns to her feet in a kneeling position, regaining her bearings.

"You didn't tell them." Tabitha says, her tone marred in confusion.

"Would it matter if I did?"

●

Finn pushes his way through the ranks of guests towards the newly opened panel, motioning them through the hidden exit door. The passageway leads back into a polished metallic hallway with a staircase at the end. With haste people squeeze their way through the door frame, frantically trying to escape. Hundreds more flock to the back of the second level, led by guards and soldiers.

"All right you lot, lets fuckin get movin. Ya lives fuckin depend on doin whatcha do best. Dodgin bullets." Finn says inspirationally. *"Stop fuckin off and make ya way down here."*

A scream rings through Finn's ears overtop the chaotic commotion. He searches through the crowd, attempting to discern the direction of the scream. In the distance he spots Illiyana storming toward the crowd of dignitaries, her father in tow. Again the scream splits his attention. Narrowing down his search Finn watches as a small group of guards gather towards what he assumes to be a woman down in the center of the fleeing mass. His eyes follow Illiyana and Kul as they march towards the open hatch, greeting them with a waving motion. In his peripherals Finn watches the guards raise up a woman with a distinct dark red tipped ponytail leading into a silverish base. With the guards help she limps in between Illiyana and Kul, splitting them apart.

"Fuck." His basic reaction to any scenario. *"Illiyana! Trap!"*

The guards continue to escort her to the balcony, as she leads them to intercept Kul's path. With their focus on moving her out of harm's way she easily pulls up from her sleeves a pair of knives, cradling them carefully in her hands without notice. She stumbles just before they intersect with Kul, shaking free of their grip. Kul watches helplessly as Rose plunges her knives into the throats of the two aloof guards, ripping the blades across their throats in one fell swoop. With a twisted smile across her face she rises to meet Kul, wiping the blades off on her new white dress.

"Rose." He musters out. "How?"

"For me to know and you to find out old man." She giggles at him.

She strikes out like lightning, dragging the blade across his arm as he parries the attack. Rose spins to her left swinging her second blade, aiming for a kill shot. Kul reactively puts his arm up to shield the blow. He winces in pain as the dagger rips through the flesh and muscle of his right arm. Pushing forward Kul steps into her defense coming down with a thunderous blow of his own, breaking her grip on the dagger buried into his arm. People shriek in fear as the fighting breaks out, clearing themselves away from the two combatants. Rose slinks back in an effort to recuperate.

"Bet that hurt huh? Did you teach that to the girls I wonder." She taunts.

"I've been through worse." Kul volleys back.

He grips the butt of the dagger firmly before removing it quickly from its resting place. Looking towards the balcony he tosses the blade down to the first floor. Returning his attention forward he spots Illiyana charging in behind Rose, each step filled with more determination than the last.

"So've I."

"I can only imagine." His voice hums a tune of sorrow.

Illiyana leaps through the air as Rose prepares to strike again, spearing her mid swing, sending them both tumbling to the ground. Illiyana expertly rolls to her feet, standing between Kul and his attacker.

"Go father." Illiyana hurriedly shouts. "Get to the elevators, Anna will be there waiting for you."

"Father?" Rose tilts her head.

Kul backs away slowly from Illiyana with hesitation in his step. Reaching back blindly Illiyana shoves him by the chest, creating separation. Rose lunges from her crouched position striking wildly at her. Illiyana pushes the blade aside, receiving a knee to the midsection for her troubles. Illy doubles over, the strength behind the blow enough to take her by surprise. Rose presses past her moving again towards the fleeing lord. Grabbing a fistful of Rose's ponytail, Illiyana yanks down hard on the handful of hair, bouncing her head off the solid floor.

"You're wasting my time. Yes you are." Rose mutters to herself as she rolls backwards onto her feet. "What are you afraid of?"

Illiyana cocks an eyebrow to the odd remark, her mind focused on keeping Kul out of harm until her sister can enact a plan. Rose readies herself for another attack, calculating Illiyana's flaws. Within a blink of an eye she stands inches from Illy, a speed that startles the sector commander, her blade aimed in between the ribcage. A hand forcefully grabs ahold of her wrist, wrestling the blade from her grasp seconds before the strike connects.

"Looks like ya dropped somethin love. Shame ya so fuckin clumsy." Finn's ego boasts.

He drives an elbow into her back, keeping his grip latched onto her wrist. Following up his ambush, Finn wraps his free arm around her neck attempting to lock down her speed. Rose struggles against his grip, the surprise of another combatant only serving to increase her strength.

"Who are you?" Illiyana interrogates, her voice shaky.

"Wouldn't you like to know." She retorts, drawing Illiyana closer to her in frustration.

"Do you work for Frostscythe?"

"I work for the Outrider silly. When i'm done with you two here, i'm going to do to him what he did to us." Rose lashes out against Finn's grasp, pulling with all her strength. "Don't worry your pretty little face sunshine, I promise it'll be fast."

"You won't make it past-"

Illiyana moves within range of Rose, reaching out to grab her. Swift on her feet, Rose uses the sector commander as a launching pad to vault backwards over Finn. Landing on her feet Rose put her foot into the back of Finn's knee, driving it into the ground. Spinning around the front of Finn she drives the sole of her boot into his face, causing him to fall prone. Illiyana takes the opportunity to land a kick in the center of Rose's chest taking her off balance. With fierce determination she presses the attack, making each blow count, pushing Rose to the edge of the balcony. Learning her rhythm, Rose breaks through Illy's offense landing a solid punch to the chest, the weight behind the strike enough to cave in her ribcage. Illiyana winces in pain, leaving her guard open as she deals with the pain. Pulling himself back to his feet Finn begins the fight anew. He pushes himself in between Illiyana and Rose, taking the next strike meant for her. He fights back the urge to scream as his broken ribs take another beating.

"Dat pencil pushin twat has a better punch den you lass. Time ta go back to da drawin board wit dat shit." He says, swallowing down the pain.

The calmness in her dead eyes turn to anger, her face shifting to frame the wrath in her eyes. Finn allows her to strike at him again with all of her strength, leaving himself wide open. As she commits to the attack Finn braces himself for her worst, taking in a deep breath. On instinct he dodges her wild right, moving into her guard and striking with a hook of his own. Rose lets out a gasp of surprise as she attempts to correct her miscalculation.

"Fell for da oldest trick in da book. I had to dust dat one off."

Finn lifts Rose easily off of her feet with his second punch, putting emphasis on his strength, giving her all he has left in the tank. She doubles over, his arm acting as a prop to hold her up. Finn retracts his arm letting her fall to her knees beside him, gasping for air. He returns to Illiyana's side, resting his arm on her shoulder.

"You good?"

"I'll be fine." She responds, still short of breath.

Rose reaches out for the dagger discarded beside the balcony as she staggers back to her feet. Gripping the handle firmly she deftly moves towards Finn, itching to place the blade in his back. The movement catches Illiyana's peripherals. As Rose raises the dagger up preparing to strike Illiyana pulls Finn past her, reaching up to catch the blade between her palms. Rose struggles with Illy as they wrestle for control of the blade, inching closer to the balcony. Illiyana moves the blade to the side, slamming Rose's hand into the hard steel of the railing. Feeling Rose's weight shifting Illiyana frees her hands from the dagger, swatting away the incoming strike to her kidney's. The dagger gleams in the faint light as she lifts it once again, bearing down on Illiyana's shoulder. Steel meets flesh as Rose buries the dagger hilt deep in Illiyana's shoulder blade, in a moment of desperation. Illiyana grits her teeth, fighting through the pain. Grabbing Rose's retracting arm Illiyana digs her hip into Rose. Using the momentum Illy lifts her up, tossing her over the balcony to the floor below.

-
-

Tabitha returns to her feet, wrapping her arm around Annastasia's shoulder. Anna shrugs off her advance, moving closer to the end of the stage. She peers out through the lingering smokescreen, watching as the remaining dignitaries file into elevators and down the staircases. Screams still echoing along the halls, the sounds of a scuffle above them. The assembly that had turned into pure anarchy has begun to die down, only a remaining few still finding their way to escape.

"This was not the plan." Anna spits out, her back to Tabitha. "Those people taking the staircase. They'll die to your chemical Tabitha."

"Not if I disabled the canisters."

"If."

"You know I did."

Anna moves her piercing gaze to the balcony railing, searching for any signs of her family and friends. She spots Kul moving at a quickened pace towards the staircase leading to the elevators. Anna leaps down from the stage, her sights set on meeting Kul at the bottom of the stairs. Running through the mist Anna makes her way to the staircase quickly, her path uninhibited. A loud thud sounds behind her as something crashes to the ground from above, the sound reverberating through her ears. Watching from the stage Tabitha gawks in awe as Rose plummets to the ground with a sickening thud.

"Father!" Anna screams up the staircase as she rounds the corner.

"What are you doing here?" His worried tone apparent in his words.

"My job. We have to get you to the elevator, did Illy fill you in?"

"Something about her sisters harebrained scheme. She wasn't all too forthcoming with information."

"I need you to take a normal elevator to another floor besides your own. I'll be taking yours to the top. That's where i'll end this. Do you trust me?"

"With my life."

Wrapping his uninjured arm around her warmly they press on towards the elevator, having to pass back through the green cloud. A sound of giggling rings throughout the thick fog, causing pause in Anna's step. From her vantage point at the top of the stage Tabitha watches as the assassin crawls back to her feet, the fall merely an aid to get closer to her target. Crouched low to the ground, Rose slinks quietly though the mist in their general direction. Tabitha without hesitation gives chase, moving to intercept Rose. Kul urges Anna forward, tugging at her shoulder.

"I know that laugh." Anna says, her eyebrows furling.

"We both do. Lingering here will do us no good."

At his request Anna continues towards the elevators. Looking back over her shoulder into the nothingness of the fog, she spots a figure emerging from it's center tablet held in hand. Xylen pulls himself through its thickened visibility, looking as pale as a ghost. Putting his hands on his knees, Xylen takes a moment for his labored breathing to catch up.

"The ventilation in here sucks." He remarks. "You should probably get that fixed your lordship."

"First thing i'll do when we get out of here Xylen. First thing."

Anna pulls Xylen in for a hug, her arms wrapping around him in a bearhug like vise, her smile having returned to her. Kul waits for the elevator to respond, impatiently waiting for the doors to retract.

"Anna, you'll need this." Kul says, retrieving a key from his pocket.

"Thanks dad." Anna turns to him, releasing her clutch on Xylen. "Xy, you need to get out of here yourself-"

"Come here little bird. I just wanna talk." Rose's voice booms through the emptying room. "After I finish my work maybe you could teach me another violin trick. I'd love to see your show continue."

Rose walks slowly out from the fog twirling about her ponytail, a twisted smile ingrained on her face. Xylen backs away toward the elevator door, giving himself enough space between them. Anna stands in shock as she watches her appear from the mist, her eyes narrowing in disbelief.

274

"I watched you die."

"I've died a lot little bird. None quite as painful as the first." Her tone switching to a serious note as she spots her mark. "Step aside, I don't want to hurt you. You're my friend."

"Remember what I said about you hurting my friends?"

"This one isn't a choice birdie. Outrider wants his head. I've never disappointed the Outrider."

"Then you'll have to kill me to get to him." She retorts, standing between Kul and Rose.

"No, no, no. No I won't. Not if I kill him first." She says pointing to Xylen. "You can't stop me this time mage. No matter how much I care about our friendship, I will finish my work."

A gunshot resounds through the assembly, coming from behind Rose. Her eyes light up, opening widely as she spins to face her attacker. Turning her back to Anna, a hole in her new dress slowly becomes saturated with blood, working it's way down her back. Rose screams into the haziness a sound of frustration and anger. The barrel of Tabitha's gun emerges from its hiding space.

"Didn't I kill you once already?" Tabitha quips.

"You!' Rose screams. "Murderer!"

"Scientist."

Rose splits her attention between Tabitha and Kul, torn between her duty and revenge. Tabitha fires off another shot, blasting her in the torso with precision. The both sets of elevator doors open, allowing Anna and Kul their escape. Kul grabs Xylen, heading for their respective elevator.

With haste Rose rushes to stop Kul from entering the elevator, another two shots finding their way into her back causing her to stumble forward and lose balance. Entering the threshold of the doorway Xylen lashes out at Rose, smacking her across the face with his tablet. The strike sends her reeling backwards, long enough for the elevator doors to slam in her face. Letting out a primal scream, her hands curled in rage, Rose returns her attention to

Tabitha. With a devilish smile Tabitha aims down the sight of her gun, firing off two more shots directed to disable the wild woman. Charging forward Rose throws caution to the wind, the agony of the bullets entering her body driving her further into insanity. Tackling Tabitha to the ground she lets out another scream as she drives the scientist to the ground hard, her head bouncing off the unforgiving floor below. Grasping Tabitha's neck with both hands, she attempts to strangle the life from her eyes.

"YOU RUIN EVERYTHING." Her voice giving way to a deeper anger.

Tabitha desperately struggles against the small girls immense strength, feeling her windpipe beginning to give under the pressure. In her daze Tabitha searches for her gun laying just out of reach. Each second wasted, the longer she goes without oxygen. Rose cackles in her face as she applies even greater pressure. Tabitha flails her arm out brushing against a sharp metal edge. Reaching further she grips the pommel of a dagger driving it as deep as possible into Rose's forearm, causing her to loosen the grip around her throat. Tabitha wiggles out from underneath the psychopath, crawling to her gun. Rose lets out another shriek as she pulls the blade from her arm. She rises from her kneeling position, stalking Tabitha as she crawls away.

"Where are you going?" Her playful tone making a return. "There's no one to save you now. Cat and mouse is over now. Time for the mouse to lay down and die."

Tabitha struggles forward pulling herself along in a daze, moving with only her instincts of survival. She reaches out for the weapon, her fingertips brushing along the grip. Rose grabs at her ankle, pulling Tabitha back to her. Spinning Tabitha around she creeps along her form, straddling her waist.

"My little bird deserved better."

Rose plays with her prey, dragging the blade along Tabitha's side, her smile the size of a cheshire cat. Her dead black eyes stare into Tabitha's cold gaze. Tabitha's expression blank, daring Rose to proceed. Taking her taunt in ernest Rose lifts the dagger from her side, holding it firmly in her hand, drawing out the anticipation. Blood spatters across Tabitha's face as she unloads a barrage of bullets into Rose's chest, knocking her off the prone scientist. Tabitha stumbles to regain a footing, her head still slightly spinning. Before her lay Rose in an all too familiar position, sprawled across the ground still clutching onto the dagger. Her eyes like dark mirrors watch as Tabitha draws closer, smoking gun at the ready. A raspy gasp escapes Rose as she chokes up blood, the smile still etched into her expression. Tabitha disarms Rose of her knife, denying her any further weapons.

"Experiment over."

Rose lifts her head to the hovering gun, butting it up to her forehead. Tabitha puts a foot down on her chest, making sure in no uncertain fashion the assassin doesn't try to escape. With one last thunderous pull of the trigger Rose's head falls limply to the ground.

CHAPTER EIGHTEEN
THE FINAL PERFORMANCE

The doors to the elevator close behind Annastasia, leaving behind the chaos of the assembly. She presses her head to the chilled metal, a brief respite from her overwhelming surroundings. A loud guttural scream reverberates through the small compartment, echoing from the lower levels as the tracks begin to move. Taking small deep breaths, Anna refocuses her mind, keeping herself sharp for the battle to come.

You can do this. Just keep one move ahead at all times and you'll take his king. He's comfortable, in his own mind unbeatable. Use that to your advantage. Remember that even a pawn can become a queen.

"Xylen? Are you safe?" She says breaking the silence.

"Copy that captain. My tablets fried but that's the least of my worries."

"You're not sick."

"Repeat that?"

"Tabitha didn't drop the bomb, it was a dummy canister full of placebos."

"You're sure Anna? Last time we trusted her-" He pauses "She got Claudette killed."

"I'm well aware of that. She's also well aware of what would have happened to her if she did that to the rest of you."

"I don't think she cares anymore."

"Annie? Are you two done wit da chit chat?" Finn interrupts. *"Got mostly everyone out da maintenance hatch. Just watchin ova ya sis as she's gettin patched up. Bitch put a dagger in her shoulder. She's a tough lass though, she'll pull through."*

"I'm relieved. Thank you Finn for the update. You two need to make it out of there just in case Mind has a failsafe. Same with you Xylen, get Kul out of there."

"Annie."

"Please."

"Ya." His voice tapers off. *"Can do. You promise you'll drag your ass out the tower?"*

"I promise." She says confidently. "Xylen?"

"We're already to the lobby. It's like a flood of scared and injured people down here. We'll work on getting everyone out safely. You just worry about you ok?"

"I'm supposed to worry about you, not the other way around." She chuckles out.

"We're family, it don't work dat way."

"That's my line. I'll keep in contact, be safe."

"You too."

The elevator reduces its speed as it reaches the top of the tower. Anna closes her eyes, repeating the same line over in her head. The track jolts as the elevator comes to a halt at the top level, shaking the cabin. *You can do this.* The elevator doors open with the scraping sound of metal on metal. Taking one final deep breath Anna takes her first step from the safety of the cabin. She opens her eyes to a darkened hall, full of encroaching shadows. Where there once was warmth it has been replaced with a vacancy, the darkness leaving a sinister feeling in the pit of her stomach. The hall lay barren, cold and uninviting. Expecting resistance Anna moves cautiously through the familiar territory, her heart racing with adrenaline. The sound of her footsteps fill the room, each step seamingly louder than the last. Slinking off into the shadow Anna watches for any sign of movement. *It seems the king doesn't believe he needs his pawns.* Moving along the exterior wall Anna continues to search the length of the room.

"Hello." A voice rings in her head. "I can feel the beating of your heart magician. It's like an echoing symphony in my mind. If you're that afraid of me you should just give in. No shame in admitting defeat when there is no other option."

"Shut up!" Her scream bouncing off the walls. "We stopped your operation. We beat you already. This is checkmate."

"Checkmate? My dear we've only begun playing the board. Did you think I would honestly employ only one strategy?"

Anna continues down the hall, a fierce resolve overtaking her beating heart. Her eyes dart to the corners of the room as she makes her way toward Illiyana and Kul's chambers. The shadows seem to drag alongside her as she moves faster. Shaking free the images from her mind, Anna attempts to block out his influence.

"Queen up the center. A bold move Annastasia." The voice coldly resounding in her head. "Are you prepared for my next move?"

"You're buying time, distracting me. Something important must have your attention. You must be seeking something Mind if you think a few words will make me crumble."

"Perhaps a change of scenery will help, if my words are not enough."

The floor of the tower melts away, giving way to darkness below. The darkness slowly envelopes her feets, working its way up her lower legs. The walls begin to drift away around her, shutting out the ambient light to the room. Anna struggles against the darkness seeping its way up her legs. Her grunts and gasps echo into the infinite void surrounding her.

"You live in a land of light, surrounded by warmth. If you take all of that light, that love away, what remains of the shell? Hollow screams and despair. Tell me, is that what you feel as you struggle?"

It's an illusion, deconstruct it.

Working its way up her torso the liquid slides under her clothing forming to the shape of her body. Anna struggles harder against the ooze redoubling her efforts to escape as the intruder pushes against her body. Starting at her feet the darkness begins to solidify, stiffening the more resistance she puts forth. With a mind of its own the darkness ascends to her neck, wrapping around gently before crawling along her shoulders. She grimaces at its touch, its intrusion unwanted.

"The light gives birth, but darkness always reclaims what it rightfully owns."

The liquid freezes in place at her fingertips, slowly starting to peel backwards. Anna's eyes narrow as she focuses on the magic, unwinding it at its essence. Lurching in fear the darkness begins to retract fervently from her skin, returning to the ground it grew from.

"Darkness never owned my body. It will never claim my mind."

With a swipe of her hand the walls begin to return to their cold, dull color. Looking to the floor Anna snaps her fingers causing the darkness to retreat from the floor below, back to it's corners. With a sharp exhale Anna steps forward, her confidence soaring. With an added urgency she makes for the lord's chambers, keeping herself focused on the path ahead. The shadows again follow loosely behind her, climbing along the walls. Anna turns to face the shadows creeping along the wall. They scurry at her sight, fearfully leaving her aura. Anna glances at the door to her left, Illiyana's corridors. The door bears markings and claw marks, the words 'bled an Arlenko, died an Arlenko', scratched across the center of the metal.

"Once an Arlenko, always an Arlenko." The voice spitefully says. "Perhaps when I dispose of you, your sister would be a more willing candidate for the future."

"Looking to the future when you haven't gotten past the present"

"You are an enigma, that is an obvious truth. Every enigma has a key. I'll just require the time to find it. Possibly it lies in one of these."

A shadowy figure stands before her, molding its shape from the shadows. Anna stops just before the figure, her eyes widen as if seeing a ghost. As the shape takes form it replicates a mirror image of Claudette before her very eyes. Its eyes stare lifelessly into Anna's breaking facade. Holding back tears Anna looks away, unable to stare her friend in the eyes.

"You're dead." Anna whispers.

"You let me die." The shadowy voice whisps. "You promised, but you failed."

"I never failed you. The real Claudette knows I did everything I could to save her. You're just a figment. Like the floors and walls, you're not real."

Anna proves her point by walking through the darkened figure. It parts like smoke around her, giving way to her physical properties. The shadow skips forward two steps, reappearing as if nothing had happened.

"What about our retirement? We had a plan."

"Tragedy happened shadow. My friend died and we have to press forward without her. You take her image and desecrate her memory."

Another gesture from her hand and the shadows disperse back into the walls with a screeching noise, like nails on a chalkboard. Anna walks through the lingering wisps of darkness, twisting the essence of magic around her hand before extinguishing it.

"Bravo. You sure are a resolute soul Magician. I have seen many wills broken with the ease of magic. I will devour your soul still, if only to see the broken look upon your face."

"You talk too much."

The metal floor creaks underneath each step Anna takes forward. Shadows cling to their corners watching her from afar as she proceeds toward Kul's study, hesitant to lash out again. A cold draft blows down the main corridor sending a chill along her spine as she ignores the blatant attempts to derail her focus. She reaches a hand out for the door, gripping the handle tightly. A deep and familiar voice appears in absence of the groaning under foot, causing her to tense up at his brief statement.

"You are your mother's light." The voice resounds through her mind, like an echo in a cave.

"But you are my life." Anna whispers the end of his sentence. "Father?"

Anna turns with a longing look sparkling in her eyes. The man standing before her resembles her father from memories past. Young and vibrant. A smirk without end crossing his face. She investigates every aspect down to his mid length wavy hair. Every angle a perfect image of her father plucked seemingly from her mind.

"I missed you Annastasia."

"I miss you." She finds herself replying to it. "But you're not really here. You're an illusion all the same. If this is your play Mind, you'll soon find you have nothing left on the board."

"You remind me so much of your mother. That same biting tone, the all or nothing attitude." His smile widens. "You would do her proud."

"I have."

"I know."

Anna takes a step towards the image, her gaze wandering around the base of its legs. Her father reciprocates, moving a step forward. Anna takes a deep breath, waiting for its next comment.

"I spent a long time waiting to come here and see you, you know. You've matured into a beautiful woman. Just as I always knew you would."

"I would have loved for you to witness it."

"I have."

"Because you're a figment of my imagination. You have seen anything he wants you to."

"You'll believe what you want. That, you took from my family." He gazes into her eyes.

"An Arlenko's pride is only matched by it's stubbornness." She retorts, meeting his gaze. "At least this time i'll be able to say goodbye. I should be going now, fate of the world and all."

"Until we meet again little light."

"I love you dad."

Anna turns her back to the illusion, grasping again for the handle. Hesitating, she spins back around hoping her assumption to be untrue. The corridor lay bare behind her, a puff of black smoke remains drifting through the air. Hanging her head dejectedly Anna holds back her sadness, the final illusion finally breaking through her toughened exterior. The shadows hiss in laughter as she opens the parlor doors into the chaos of Kul's study, a single tear streaming down her cheek. Books strewn across the ground, ripped from their homes along the shelves. His desk torn apart drawer by drawer. Mind paces about the room, an old bound tome in his hand. He looks up lethargically in her direction, as he roams through the books discarded along the floor.

"How was the family reunion?" His words filled with a sense of hatred. "Everything you would have hoped for my dear?"

"My father died years ago. Whatever I talked to was not my father." Anna responds, surveying the room.

"I'm sure that would have broken his heart if he could hear you. You are after all, his life." He continues to pace about, his focus turned back to the book.

"You want to know something else my father taught me?"

"You leave me with bated breath Arlenko. Indulge me."

"He taught me to see it through. No matter the outcome, you never give in or give up."

"And where did that get him for his troubles?" His mask contorting into a smile for her to see.

Anna clenches her jaw, swallowing her words. *He's just trying to antagonize you.* She carefully moves her way into the room, stepping over the abandoned books. Mind continues his dance along the edge of the bookshelves, stepping in time with the metronome in his head.

"My father made history. The only thing you'll ever be is a footnote in my history."

The book slams itself shut, dropping to the floor. In the blink of an eye Mind appears before Anna, his uncanny speed giving him the upper hand. He lashes out with a vicious strike, his palm making contact with her face. The hit almost takes Anna off of her feet. Blinking rapidly she shakes the pain from her mind as another incoming open palmed slap sends her reeling backwards. Mind's mask shifts as his grin grows wider, content with his display of power. He moves into her space, attempting to bring Anna to her knees with a kick to the midsection. In the instant before his blow connects she sidesteps artfully. Retaliating with a strike of her own, Anna connects with a direct hit to his mask before returning to a defensive posture. A wicked smile beaming from the Magician, her form reminiscent of Kul's training.

Anticipating Mind's next strike Anna uses her own evasive magic to her advantage, expertly sidestepping his attacks with her mirror images. Each strike finds itself coming up surprisingly short as Mind pushes the boundaries of her abilities. Stepping through her own images Anna counterattacks every missed swing, breaking down Mind's impressive resilience with a barrage of body blows. Growing frustrated Mind lashes out with a wave of dark energy, pushing the Magician away to the furthest wall.

"I've had enough games." His voice growing tired.

"Perhaps you shouldn't have been playing the board."

"You're a nothing, Magician."

"Add it to my list of titles."

Anna paces herself, readying for another attack, magical or otherwise. With his lightning fast reflexes Mind again dashes to Anna, his fist running through her illusion to the bookshelf behind her. The illusion mocks him, wagging a finger in front of his face. Retracting his fist from the shelf Mind searches the room for her physical form. Sending a pulse of magic forward he forces her to appear, breaking her illusion instantly. Moving with great care Anna moves herself into the center of the room, keeping the desk to her back. Retreating from the bookcase Mind stalks his vulnerable prey, drifting through the clutter littered along the ground. His mask morphing from its sadistic smile into a cold and unforgiving stare as he approaches her.

Anna attempts a quick left jab without the aid of her magic. The strike finds its way into the waiting hands of her enemy. A jolt of pain runs through her body as he dislocates her shoulder with ease. She muffles the cries of pain as Mind grabs for a handful of her hair, pulling her head back to gaze into her narrowed eyes.

"I told you Magician that I would break you for the enjoyment of it. You are nothing to me. You never stood a chance."

He drives a knee into her open midsection causing another muffled cry of agony as he holds her in place. Anna lashes out futilely with her right arm, attempting to regain some offense. Another hard strike to the midsection sends her to her knees, her hair floating down in front of her face. Gazing up from her seated position Anna watches Mind intently, her eyes focusing on the balcony behind him. A weak smile replaces the anguished look across her face.

"You really need to work on your chess game. Checkmate."

The sound of shattering glass reverberates through the room as high powered rounds rip through the balcony door, sending the room into further disarray. Chunks of steel and glass scatter throughout the study. Anna lay flat across the ground, her hand covering her head as the chaos continues. Caught in the middle of the carnage Mind turns to face the volley. The rounds tear through his armor, ripping cleanly through his body.

"An archangel." He mutters. "Impossible."

The bombardment continues, round after round continuing to tear holes through Kul's study. The metal of the tower melting like butter to the power of the Incisor. Rounds buzz over Anna's head as she keeps her profile low.

Mind closes the distance between him and the closest shelving unit, giving himself additional protection from her sight. Changing the direction of her fire Audrey focuses on his location, riddling the area with the remaining rounds.

The chaos abates, leaving behind only the sound of crashing debris. Anna lifts herself from the ground, surveying the damage dealt to the tower. The doors to the balcony rattle in the wind, hanging halfway off of their hinges. The far back bookshelves beside the fireplace see the most damage, holes tore into their surface. She glances over to Mind slumped over beside the nearest wall, riddled with wounds. His body twitches in pain as she slowly approaches him. Lifting his head he meets her gaze with his own, his torn mask revealing the left side of his face. A fearless jet black iris stares a hole through her person as she kneels down beside him.

"What you underestimate in me is what makes me better than you. I am not one person Mind. I will always be my family. Try as hard as you might to break us apart we will only grow stronger, we will only fight harder. In the end you played a game, while we played to survive."

"You are clever." His voice soft without the use of his mask. "A brilliant strategist. It's a shame you've wasted all of your talents parading around as an entertainer. You could have been so much more."

The crunching of glass turns Anna's attention to the open study doors as Tabitha enters the room, her jacket smeared with blood. She flashes a wide smirk Anna's way as she takes in the scene before her. Mind's gaze drifts to Tabitha as she approaches Anna.

"Love what you've done with the place." She mocks. "Feels more- Open."

Tabitha watches Anna, studying her lover intently. Taking a moment she takes in her lover in rare form, the traces of sweat beading down her brow, the focused look of her eyes.

With Anna's back to Mind he lunges forward, grabbing her by the waist as he returns to his feet. He wraps his arm around her neck for more control over his situation. Eyes wide, Anna pulls against his stone like vice to no avail. Tabitha pulls the gun from her waistband on instinct, her sights trained on him.

"Anna!" Surprise catching Tabitha's words.

"It looks as though you were the perfect distraction once again Tabitha." Simon drones. "Drop your weapon, we both know you won't be using it."

"I came here to kill you. What makes you think I won't?"

"All of those hours you spent yearning to return to your loved ones side, you'll throw away her life to take your revenge? Seems unlikely."

"All of us in this room know the meaning of sacrifice. Some are willing to sacrifice more than others."

"Then why haven't you shot yet? I'll give you some incentive."

Mind procures a syringe from a concealed pocket, well protected within his armor. The green liquid gleams in the light beaming through the opening in the wall behind them. Tabitha's expression grows cold, her skin draining of color. Her haunted expression causes Anna to struggle against his grip, his vice like arm tightening along her throat.

"There is the frightened girl i scooped off a building seven years ago." His voice peaking with interest. "Welcome back you fragile little thing."

"You wouldn't." Her voice trembling.

"Wouldn't you?"

"I-"

"What would you do to keep your precious love alive Tabitha? Are you willing to let me walk out of here?"

The remaining portion of his mask grins widely at Tabitha, taunting her. Anna closes her eyes, dropping her hands to her side, placing her faith in Tabitha. Tabitha's hands tremble. Her mind floods with scenarios, playing them all out within the blink of an eye.

"I know that my choice is an illusion. You've already made up your mind." Determination replacing the worry in her tone.

With certainty Tabitha opens fire, giving Mind little time to react to her decision. She closes the distance between them, aiming for the syringe with her first few rounds. Mind uses Anna as a shield, keeping her open fire at bay. In Tabitha's moment of hesitation Mind plunges the needle into Anna's open arm, letting loose the viral chemical into her bloodstream. The liquid rushes through her veins, igniting like a flashfire throughout her body. Anna lets out a hoarse scream, her voice being choked out by Mind's hold. Keeping the Magician between him and Tabitha, he empties the contents of the syringe before discarding Anna to the floor.

Even without his impressive speed Mind dashes quickly to the study doors, fleeing from Tabitha's rage. She gives chase, rushing to the open doors with her gun at the ready. Using the shadows to his advantage, he sinks into the darkened hallway. Blindly Tabitha unleashes her wrath, shot after shot disappearing into the darkness.

Letting loose a scream into the black hallway Tabitha turns her attention back to Anna. The Magician stumbles back to her feet attempting to give chase to their opponent, tears pouring from her eyes. Gripping her arm she makes eye contact with Tabitha, showing her first signs of fear.

"Get him." Anna attempts to scream, her voice cutting out.

"No. He was right."

"We have to stop him."

Anna moves past Tabitha, heading into the open corridor. Tabitha grabs her by the shoulder spinning her back into an open embrace, locking her arms around Anna tightly.

"While I admire your tenacity, I admire your life more. Sit. Now."

Anna complies with Tabitha's demand, taking a seat on the desk beside the fireplace. Tabitha reaches into her jacket pocket pulling another syringe from within its depths, the contents a shimmering purple. She grabs Annastasia firmly by the face, distracting her from the burning pain. With a forceful passion Tabitha kisses Anna before plunging the needle into her neck causing a gasp to escape Anna's lips. Tabitha breaks from her display of affection, her eyes wandering down her form. Anna moves forward, instinctively wanting more.

"I love you Annastasia."

"I love you too Tabitha." She replies in a whisper.

Anna's vision begins to blur as the cure begins to take effect. She lifts herself off of the desk, reaching out for Tabitha. Her feet weakly give out underneath her as she clutches for the desktop to bring herself down to a seated position slowly. Squinting Anna makes out Tabitha's smile coming into view.

"You are the only important person in my life. I couldn't live with myself knowing something I created could destroy the only thing I care about. My cure was only ever made for you, because you are the only one deserving of it. You showed me love and all i've ever done in return is give you heartache. The effects of the cure will wear off in several hours, everything you're experiencing right now is just an effect to quicken its progress." Tabitha places a kiss on the Magician's forehead, lingering there for a moment. "When you need me, i'll be there. Just like when I needed you."

"Don't leave." Anna struggles to say.

"I've only ever brought destruction with me wherever I go, and I know now that I can't lead you down the same path that I have to walk. When you wake up, i'll be gone."

Tabitha pulls the loose strands of Anna's hair out of her face as she watches the magician slowly begin to fade off into a slumber. She reaches out to Tabitha, fighting the urge to close her eyes. Tabitha rubs her face against Anna's hand, kissing her open palm. She watches as the Magician's arm slowly begins to fall to her side, losing the battle against slumber. Taking in a deep breath Tabitha moves away quietly from her sleeping lover, looking over her perfect form one last time.

CHAPTER NINETEEN

FIRST DAY OF RETIREMENT

A loud thudding sound stirs Anna from her slumber, the noise pounding through her head. Lifting herself from the comfort of her own bed Anna takes a moment, looking around her home in confusion. The sound of hammering strikes grows louder against her door, more impatient with every passing second. Anna winces in pain as she attempts to prop herself up on her elbows, as a reminder her shoulder is still healing.

"Come in." She coughs out, still processing the situation.

Slowly the door creaks open, bringing the cold stage air through her bedroom. Illiyana stands statuesque in the doorway, dressed 'casually' in slacks and a button down shirt. Shoulders relaxed the sector commander enters her sisters room with an awkwardly approving smile. Taking a chair from beside the desk Illiyana rolls it across the ground, stopping at the foot of her bed. Anna blinks away the sleep from her eyes, watching as her sister slides to her bed.

"Time to wake up." Illiyana says, her arms crossed. "I'm surprised you didn't tell me you need five more minutes."

"I need five more minutes." Said dryly.

"That's more like the sister I knew."

"How's your shoulder?" Anna asks, a sudden worry added to her sleepy tone.

"Stabbed. Yours?"

"Separated. How did I get home?"

"You don't remember?" Illiyana raises an eyebrow. "We brought you back from the hospital. You've been in and out of it for two days."

"Last thing I remember was Tabitha's face. She was smiling at me. What happened?"

"You turned Kul's office into a observation deck. He's thrilled by the way."

"Sorry."

"We're just glad you're alright sis. You realise you could have been killed by any of those bullets, right? Where did you even acquire an archangel weapon? The list of stupid questions goes on."

"My plan worked didn't it?" She retorts, smiling wide. "As the Archangels are concerned, they owed me a favor."

"You almost died. I wouldn't call that successful. An acting Knight-General shouldn't be basing their achievements off of half cocked plans."

Anna eyes Illy wearily, as if waiting for the follow up to her sentence.

"Yes it worked." She caves to her sisters stare.

Anna struggles to lift herself from bed, her muscles straining with every movement. Illiyana moves over to her side, wrapping her arm around her upper back for support. With her sisters help she rises to her feet. Weakly she takes her first few steps, allowing her muscles to adjust to the changes.

"I don't need the kid wheels Illy."

Anna pulls herself free from Illy, using the bedpost for support. Illiyana retracts her arm, her features narrowing in slight anger. Anna flashes her blue eyes at her sister, attempting to ease the tension between them

"I didn't mean it like that. You always taught me to never let them catch you slipping. They're still out there Illy. I didn't do enough to stop him."

"An Arlenko's pride knows no bounds, a true statement even for my little sister. I would be doing the same thing if I were in your shoes right now. You did stop him, father is alive because you were there. Just because you didn't take him off at the head doesn't mean he wasn't wounded. He won't forget that."

"That's what i'm afraid of."

"You'll just have to half ass a plan again next time."

"I'll quarter ass it next time."

"I'll go up the elevator alone. Worst plan ever."

Laughter fills the room, an even harmony between the two. Illiyana ruffles her sisters hair about causing Anna to scrunch her nose. Sticking her tongue out Anna crosses her eyes causing more laughter to erupt from the pair.

"I miss days like this. Why did my sister have to grow up to run the military?"

"I ask myself a similar question, why did my sister have to grow up to be a violinist?"

"Rebellion I suppose."

"I don't think we'd be nearly as close if you never gave me problems."

"You call them problems. I call them quirks. You'll never get rid of me now."

Pulling Anna to her Illiyana squeezes hard, her embrace like a bear hug instead. With one eye closed Anna winces in silent pain, her shoulder throbbing. Anna returns Illy's affection, laying her head on their shoulder.

"The rebels are meeting for a funeral today." Illiyana whispers. "I was hoping you'd be awake enough to attend."

"Today?" Anna's eyes flick about the room nervously.

"They couldn't wait, family was getting anxious."

"I don't even have-"

"Do you think I didn't come prepared? I have a dress for you. It's white, your favorite color."

"My favorite color is green."

"I knew that." A sly grin catches the corners of her mouth. "I'll be right back. I left it upstairs."

Illiyana releases her vice like grip, her grin catching the Magician's attention. Anna takes in a deep breath, breathing out in a sigh of relief. Rolling her eyes Illiyana hastily makes for the door, heading towards the second floor. With regained strength and balance Anna makes her way toward a body mirror, her muscles still tensing with every step she takes. Raising her shirt above her head Anna abandons the article of clothing into a corner of the room, her shoulder disagreeing with her choice in movement. Clasping a cold hand over the sore points gives temporary relief to her aches and pains. Taking a moment Anna takes in her own reflection, her eyes drawn to the distasteful bruising across her left shoulder. Taking a step closer to the mirror she begins straightening her hair out, tucking the excess strands behind her ears. Gazing at her reflection, their blue eyes reflecting her own whimsical sorrow. *You did it. You survived.*

"I don't know what your worried about. You'll look beautiful." Illiyana says.

Entering the room with dress in hand, Illy glides back to her sisters side. The white of the dress shimmers under the lights. Holding it to her waist, Illiyana models the dress for her younger sister, quickly twirling around with the fabric as if along a runway.

"I think you found your calling." Anna says dryly. "Watch out Providence, military has never looked this good."

"Try it on."

Illiyana forces the dress into her sister's hands, a genuine smile spreading from ear to ear. Anna hangs the dress over her mirror, pulling at the comfortable sweats she was placed in. Removing them, Anna tosses the discarded pants behind her back with the rest of her laundry 'pile'. With another long winded sigh the Magician pulls loose the dress from its perch.

Casually she slips into the outfit, the fabric hugging nicely to her curves. Modelling it off in the mirror Anna glimpses a letter misplaced on her desk, the letters 'Payment' written boldly across the front with a dark marker. Turning her attention back to the mirror Anna watches as her sister's smile grows further, clearly a good sign from her usually stoic other half.

"You like it." Anna states.

"It fits you well. Modest yet appealing."

"Are you describing me or the dress?" Said with a chuckle.

"The dress obviously, who would find you modest?"

"You need to work on your sarcasm."

Anna's eyes drift back to the note on her desk, her mind wandering with questions. Snapping her shortening attention back to her sister Anna takes a final look at the dress in the mirror, her gaze fixated on the glaringly apparent bruise.

"It's still noticeable."

"Wear your scars proudly. You earned those marks. The Magician I know wouldn't give a damn about what others thought of her as long as she stays true to who she is."

"Would you stop being right?"

"Would it kill you to be wrong?"

A silent break in the conversation leaves an air of awkwardness between the siblings. Anna looks down and away from Illiyana, the question cutting closer than she would like. Clenching her jaw the older sister swallows her pride, placing a hand on her uninjured shoulder.

"Stop doubting yourself, you saved millions. Your friends need you at that funeral. Are you going to let a bruise stop you from attending?"

"No."

"Then stop pretending like you will. Be the Magician, not a disappearing act."

Dragging her gaze from the floor to Illiyana's waiting eyes Anna begins to tear up, her internal struggle becoming more evident. Collecting her composure Anna lets out her pent up breath, wiping away the building tears.

"I needed that."

"All soldiers need a rally."

"Thanks sis. I mean it."

"You're never alone, remember that. When you find what's troubling you, you know where my office is."

"It's the smaller one right?"

"Exactly. I'll expect you later this week Tae."

"I'll have the counselors fee up front."

"Always keep your wit handy." A small chuckle escapes her stone facade, the corners of her mouth curling happily.

Anna bites her upper lip to keep her smile from escaping. Grabbing ahold of her sisters arm the Magician pulls her in for another hug. They share a few seconds in silence before Illiyana heads for the doorway, lingering momentarily to wave goodbye. The door closes softly behind Illy, leaving Anna to her own solitude.

In her curiosity Anna moves to the desk, her eyes fixated on the letter strewn blatantly along her table. Lifting the paper from the desk a thin metal object lands onto the table, slithering free from the center of the letter. Flipping open the note Anna reads it aloud.

"I thought you may want to keep this close to your heart. A memory is better than nothing at all. We never agreed on terms of payment so consider this payment for services rendered. Forever and a day. T."

Her eyes wander to the metal ball of a necklace laying on the tabletop, a smile escaping her lips. *You found it.* Anna grabs the chain, bringing it in for a closer viewing. Caressing the necklace between her forefinger and thumb Anna recalls the rainy night, the twisted feeling of anger and betrayal. Memories flood through her mind as though they had been on constant repeat for the last seven years. Surrendering to them Anna closes her eyes, allowing them to take her back to her weakest moment.

"Thank you." She whispers.

Chapter Twenty
New Beginnings

The screeching of a sliding metal echoes down the abandoned corridors. A pale green light emanates from beyond the door, filling the empty hall with a sickly light. Tabitha crosses the threshold of the door into the expansive room, her face covered with the discarded mask from Frostscythe, hands full with equipment. The mask comes to eye level, protecting her nose and mouth from hazardous chemicals yet leaving her eyes unprotected. The filters protrude from along the sides, each adorned with a set of spikes.

She looks about the room, placing the instruments along the first steel examination table, its surface shimmering in the paling light. Removing the mask from her face Tabitha takes in a breath of musty air, smiling as she does so. The spikes of the mask gleam in the light as Tabitha admires its adorning features, tailored to her choosing.

Walking deeper into the chamber the lights begin to flicker on as she passes by them, her focus on a terminal just out of range. As she walks by the examination tables Tabitha runs her hands over the cool metal, tapping a tune as she goes along. The terminal flashes to life as she approaches. Using the keyboard below Tabitha scrolls through a list of menus and folders. Tabitha opens the document labelled Subject Zero, its font bolded. A list of medical procedures and checklists appear on screen, followed by times and dates.

"Today we begin to administer your first treatment." She says aloud to the empty room, entering data into the terminal. "The last few days of preliminary testing have yielded quite a remarkable amount of data. I have determined that you are suitable for the next phase in the program."

Tabitha reaches down to a drawer beside the terminal, pulling forth a syringe fitted with a muted yellow liquid. Putting the syringe between her lips she finishes typing her thoughts onto the document before closing out of the computer entirely.

"I do apologize about the conditions. Usually my working spaces are far greater than this, but considering the circumstances I hope you will find my accommodations pleasant enough." She continues, taking the syringe from her mouth.

With her slow stride Tabitha walks briskly towards the back of the long room, every step resounding along the confined area. The lights continue to flicker on as she passes along another set of observation tables, coming to the back wall. With a smile she turns to the last table, hidden behind the lip of a wall. The form of a female lay on the table unmoving, their face covered with a dark bag tied at the opening. Her clothes stripped away and tossed in a pile just beyond the edge of the table. The color of her skin faded, black veins appearing more prominently along her arms and torso. Standing back for a moment Tabitha watches as the subjects chest heaves with heavy breaths.

With an outstretched finger Tabitha traces her way down the subjects arm from her shoulder, causing the person to jerk instinctively. In a circular motion Tabitha lingers along the crux of her elbow, the needle held firmly in her opposite hand. A muffled cry makes its way from within the bag, a plea for help stirring from the subject.

"Hush now. We both know this is for the better." Tabitha says rolling her eye.

Lifting her hand from the patient's arm Tabitha's hands slowly wander their way to the victims head, releasing the bag from its binds. The body struggles partially in fear but mostly in desperation for air. Tabitha slowly removes the hood from overtop of her head, revealing the sunken features of Alphonse's assistant. Blinking rapidly the woman reacts at first to the pallid lights before focusing her eyes on her captor. She struggles to breathe, taking in small gasps of breath.

"A normal person, Monica, would have died of suffocation approximately three hours ago. Which leaves me with the question, why are you still alive? Don't worry that's a rhetorical statement."

With blurry vision Monica focuses on Tabitha's grimacing face.

"I'm glad we get to have this time together, just the two of us."

"Fuck. You." The assistant struggles to say.

Tabitha rakes her elbow across Monica's face. The force of the blow enough to rattle her head off the steel table. Grabbing the patient by the hair she pulls harshly, eliciting a gasp of anger and pain.

"You interrupted me. Be mindful not to do that again." Tabitha demands, staring a hole through the subdued woman. "I trust you'll be an amazing assistant as always. This time we'll be making history."

Removing her hand from Monica's hair, Tabitha shifts her view back to the crux of her arm. Monica watches as she traces her way back down the vein, screaming internally. The cold touch of the needle against flesh alarms the assistant. With surgical precision Tabitha inserts the needle directly into the vein, plunging the contents of the syringe through her bloodstream.

"There may be some minor side effects, Monica. Bleeding through the eyes, ears and nose. Internal bleeding. A yearning to commit suicide. None are fatal to you though of course. Care to explain why that may be?"

"The Outrider comes for us all."

"Second verse same as the first. You've already told me that line. I'll be back to check on you in a few hours. Feel free to scream when the pain becomes intolerable or when you feel like talking."

Tabitha pulls the needle from her skin, discarding it into a nearby bin. Straightening out the collar of her jacket she withdraws from the patient, lights flickering out behind her as she makes her way back to the entrance. Little by little the room grows darker, the pallid green fading as Tabitha continues along her path. Monica screams into the dark corridor, her voice shrill and broken. The sound of her struggles linger in the air as she resists against her bindings, her body crashing back onto the table below.

Crossing the front entryway Tabitha doubles back to the first examination table, grabbing her gas mask before exiting. The door slides shut with emphasis, leaving the room again in total darkness.

"He will claim her too." Monica howls into the blackness, her voice echoing down the halls.

CHAPTER TWENTY ONE

SPIRIT

Dressed in brilliant white, Anna walks along the hilltop overlooking the cemetery below. She skirts the rows of tombstones, clutching tightly to her vibrant bouquet of flowers. The funeral procession marches on just ahead of her, carrying the coffin to its final resting place. Finn and Xylen despondently lead the pallbearers forward, tears hidden in their eyes.

The sun, peeking through the clouds above, beams brightly across the grounds. Anna glances back toward the light, sending a smile its way as a thank you. The gusting wind catches her hair, ruffling it in the breeze. Rolling her eyes she continues forward, trying to push away a feeling of coincidence.

In the distance Anna makes out the form of Audrey, walking towards her, her elegant black dress flowing in the gentle breeze. Scars mark her exposed arms, most looking faded from over the years. She attempts to cover them from prying eyes with a shawl, her insecurities getting the better of her.

Audrey runs her hands up her arms nervously as she approaches, meeting with her just beyond the gathering. Anna wraps her arms around the younger woman, greeting her with a warm hug.

"It's so good to see you." Anna says, her tone somber.

"You too. Glad you could make it."

"I wouldn't miss this." Anna says, breaking the embrace. "Thanks Audrey. For everything."

"You're welcome. You look stunning by the way."

"So do you. Come, i'm pretty sure Finn wants to talk your ear off after the week he's been having."

Audrey grabs Anna's arm, quickly pulling her towards the gathering of family and friends. She guides the Magician through the tombstones, weaving her way towards Finn and Xylen. Looking back a smile grabs the corners of her mouth, a fitting look for the troubled youth.

"He's had her family over since after the attack on the tower." Audrey laughs heartily. "It's only slightly been a disaster."

"I could only imagine him as a host. 'Ya loves, beers in da fridge and loo's over there. Other den dat if you don't need nothin i'll be fuckin off.'" Anna mocks, her impression spot on.

"Scarily accurate."

"Sometimes I amaze even myself."

Anna cocks an eyebrow as they approach a dapperly dressed Finn, his hair slicked back. A grin replaces her usual smile as the two sneak up on the unaware gentleman, his attention pulled away to Claudette's immediate family.

"*Right so there we was, Me and Dette. We had just gotten back to da Flame ya? So naturally Dette turns to me and she says 'bet I can drink ya dumbass under da table'. To which I replied 'like fuckin hell'. We each grabbed a fifth of me favorite drink at da time, Iron Will. I says to her 'alright love, you beat me chuggin dis drink and i'll dress up like a pretty princess ya, but if I beat you, ya have ta spend a week at da Flame in a bikini a my choosin.'*" Finn waves his hands about in grossly exaggerated motions, a smile carved into his face. "*So i'm chuggin along and here comes my girl just poundin back my favorite drink like its fuckin water. My ass was left wearin a damn princess dress behind da bar for a week.*"

"We actually called it princess retreat weekend at the bar." Anna adds. "Where everyone can feel pretty in pink."

"*Sure as fuck did.*" Finn retorts, turning to greet Anna. "*Annie!*"

She buries herself into Finn's chest, wrapping her arms around his frame. He reciprocates, tossing an arm around her shoulder, pulling her closer to him. His smile brightens as they enjoy each others company. Finn lowers his head to hers, planting a kiss on her forehead.

"*Everyone, Annie. Annie, everyone.*" He says, motion to and from the crowd of people. "*Feels like it's been forever. I meant ta visit and all, just got caught up in all dis.*"

"Where do you think i'd rather have you be?"

"*Fair nuff. Gang's all ere' now. You look stunnin' by the way.*"

"This is the first time i've ever seen you in a suit. I have to admit, it's a fitting look."

"If you need me i'll be going to find Amber." Audrey interrupts. "Seems like you two need to have a few moments alone."

Audrey scurries off through the throng of people, her head down as she tunnels her way through the masses. Finn lessens his hold around Anna's shoulder, dragging her away from Claudette's waiting family to a more secluded area around the yard. Pulling her head away from his chest, Anna looks up at him with waiting eyes.

"*Look at all these people Annie. They're all here for her, I don't even know the lot of um.*"

"Family is a powerful thing isn't it Finn?"

"*Aye.*" Finn looks over his shoulder, his eyes casting doubt over his next words. "*She never told me bout her family. Never thought it necessary I guess.*"

"Maybe she was saving you for a rainy day."

"*Rainy day, like today?*"

"Where's that Leighton spirit? You know deep down that if meeting her family was important to you, you would be catching up with them at the closest bar complaining about flying vehicles on the regular. What moment

304

you met her family doesn't change how deeply she loved you. Stop doubting and start embracing would you?"

"*Do ya really think I look good in dis suit?*" A quick change of subject.

"You are the king of fashion. I am merely your servant."

"*Shove it you. I was bein serious!*"

Finn attempts to pull Anna down into a headlock. With a quick wit Anna evades his attempts, countering his playful advance by rustling his hair from its perfect pose. Finn retracts from her, holding onto his hair.

"*It took me two hours to get dis right!*"

"The Magician strikes again!" She playfully taunts, raising one finger into the air.

Anna hastily makes back towards the group of people, her dress managing to impede her escape from an ensuing Finn. In pursuit, his pace quickens as he draws closer. Looking over her shoulder Anna watches as Finn swoops in behind her, wrapping an arm around her waist.

"*I'll get ya back soon enough.*" He whispers into her ear, escorting her back to the procession.

Finn directs Anna back towards the rest of the group, where Xylen and Audrey await their return. The two move in beside the others, sharing a comforting smile with their friends.

Xylen turns to Anna, his cheshire like smile beaming in her direction.

"Hey boss, glad to see you up and walking. Even if it is with that horrible limp."

"I told you not to talk about that." Audrey says, elbowing Xylen in the side.

"I only separated my shoulder, nice try though. How's the tablet doing?"

"Giorgio's in electronic heaven now."

"*Most people name they favorite cars and crafts. Not im' though, no, too conventional dat is.*"

An older man walks up before the casket, his attire a deeper shade of blue.

In respect the team hushes their conversation. Bending down he says a few words in confidence before turning to the growing crowd, greeting them with a solemn smile.

"Good afternoon to those in attendance. Most of you may not know me, so i'll keep my speech short and simple. Claudette was my only daughter- my only child and she will be greatly missed by all of her family. I'm glad so many of you could be here today to mourn with us and i'm sure many of you have great stories to share. We, as a family, look forward to hearing her brightest memories and fondest stories. Thank you."

Fighting back tears Claudette's father returns to his family's side. Looking around, Anna approaches the coffin, confidence to her stride. She takes a moment, looking over the calm yet surreal image of Claudette presented before her. She looks off into the distance, waiting for the flood of emotions to pass. Gulping down her nerves the Magician turns to face friends and family, blinking rapidly in thought.

"Claudette came into my life at a tumultuous time. Now I, like most of the people standing before me, feel lost with a hole to fill in my heart. She always had a spark to make the world a better place than in which she found it. After seeing her friends and family gathered here today, I would say she accomplished her goal. I would always ask her why she stuck around me, to which she would reply 'A, your heart's in the right place'." Anna pauses, taking in a deep breath. "And I always responded with 'i need someone to make sure it stays so'. We've been through the best and worst together and there is no one I would rather have been there with. Never will there come a day where her inspiration won't make its way to me. I'm lucky to say i've known her and glad that she would call me a friend."

Anna lingers in front of the crowd for a moment, rubbing together her hands nervously. She turns back to Claudette for one last glance at her fallen friend, her lips trembling as she says her final goodbyes. *It's not goodbye, just until we meet again.* The air around her grows silent, the sound of sobbing whispers its way into her ears. Spinning back to face the crowd Anna takes her leave, returning to her family. Finn smiles weakly as he takes her place before the listeners. Looking around the crowd Finn shakes his head approvingly, running a hand along his face as he prepares his speech.

"Oi. Me names Finn and I have a hard time talkin ya, so bare wit me. Dis day is surreal fa me. Never did I think there'd be a damn day in my life where I wouldn't wake up side' her. People say lots a bullshit about love, but in her case it was all true. Taday I stand before ya all and we all know why, cause my lady is one a da bravest damn bastards I eva met. I'm proud a her. I'm not here ta mourn, i've done dat. I'm here to honor her, cause we all need to remember the stars dat shine da brightest in our lives."

Taking in a breath of fresh air Finn pauses, again looking to the crowd of gathered friends and family. Their sorrow filled eyes locked with his own, taking in his every word. Finn looks to Anna, her bright smile urging him to continue. Breaking eye contact he looks down to his feet, hands shoved into his pockets.

"Me da once said 'Never fall in love. It's what gets ya married.' I always thought he was knockin me around when he said dat cause a course das what gets ya married, ya don't marry someone ya hate. I get it now. Ya never have ta be in 'love' to be together, but ta share ya life with someone forever requires dat somethin special. Rest well in those hallowed halls, love."

He takes a step back from the casket, nodding in approval to the caretakers to lower the lid. Moving forward Anna clutches onto Finn's hand, lending him her strength. He squeezes down on her hand as they begin to lower Claudette into the ground below. Finn sharply inhales through his nose, fighting back the tears forming in his eyes. Anna looks up at the brawler, wiping away a stray tear from his eye.

Other friends and family regail the precession with their fondest moments of Claudette. Each sharing their unique view on the young woman's life, shedding some light on her upbringing and youth. Together the crew watches as one of their own is lowered to rest, the caretakers waiting until the crowd begins to dissipate before proceeding.

The Annatourage waits patiently as the caretakers finish lowering the casket before making their way to the open hole. Bending down, they each grab a handful of soil. Leading the pack Anna outstretches her arm, her hand hovering over top the opening. Finn follows suit, with Xylen and Audrey falling in line beside them, each with their hands outstretched.

"We see it through. Good, bad or indifferent we finish what we started."

"*Hear, hear.*"

In unison they let loose the earth from their hands, a final farewell between friends.

Made in the USA
Monee, IL
10 June 2022

97816316R10184